Sachi – Drawing Pictures on Water

A NOVEL

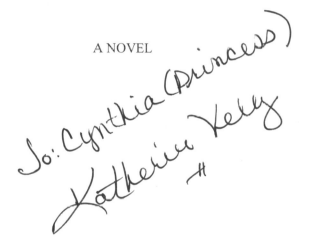

To: Cynthia (Princess)
Katherine Kelly

Katherine Kemp Velez

Sachi-Drawing Pictures on Water is a work of fiction. All of the characters, organizations, and events portrayed in this novel are either products of the author's imagination or are used fictitiously.

Original publication 2017

Published in the United States

ISBN 10: 0-692-81232-6

ISBN 13: 978-0-692-81232-7

e-book ISBN 978-1-48359-166-7

Printed in the United States of America

To all the quiet warriors, especially David, DJ, and Rachel

The Beginning

Tanchoichi, Japan - 1906

The pain ripped through her in agonizing waves, matching the roar and intensity of the ocean and the storm just outside. Her screams competed to be heard over the howling wind striking the tiny house, threatening to knock it flat, as the pain had knocked her to her knees days before.

The village sanba, shrunken and stooped from a lifetime of bowing to new life, conducted herself with the manner of a busy ticket taker in a train station ushering people from one destination to another. The sanba knelt over her, encouraging her to breathe, demanding she push as if it were something she needed to be told. Everything in her wanted nothing more than to push this pain from her body. She no longer thought of the baby, the reward for this agony. She had seen the sanba's face shift from a look of confidence to uncertainty and then alarm at so much birthing, so much blood. She felt her life slipping gradually from her body as her child fought fiercely to stay in the womb. She was weak and drained, past fear of death or hope of prayer.

She squatted again, her back against the wall, grasping the old woman as if she were a tree stump, rooted to the ground, holding her to this place and to this life. Their eyes locked and their muscles tensed working in unison to force life from the single womb. Her legs trembled violently, threatening to collapse beneath her. The blood pounded in her ears. A single thought pierced the fog in her mind. She could not do this. Death would take her and she felt nothing. She could easily move from this life to the next as if passing through rice paper.

She looked into the black, primeval depths of the sanba's penetrating eyes and realized someone was calling to her. It was not the light, melodic strains of *devas,* angels from the heavens, but rumbling, resounding tones sounding as if they came from deep inside the earth. The ancient voices, strangely familiar, urged her on, demanding she sacrifice her last breath, her last tiny bit of *ki,* of life. She recognized these voices as those of her ancestors and, instinctively, she followed their commands as she had when they lived, knowing this was the last that was required of her. She gave a final push mustering strength from reserves that appear only in life and death struggles. All that existed was this eternal moment of pushing and pain and the voices resonating inside her.

As the intensity of the pain faded and the tension released she realized the sanba held a blood-soaked infant. The pounding in her ears slowed and she heard the voice of her ancestors now only in the cries of her baby, robust and loud. An intense cold shook her body and one thought filled her. It is over. She crawled to the futon a few feet away to die.

Her husband entered the room at the sound of crying. The pungent, musky smell assaulted his nose. It was not a familiar smell, the smell of birthing. He hoped to come to know it well. The sanba wrapped the baby in a soft piece of cloth.

"It is a girl," she said in a voice tempered with disappointment.

He accepted the bundle and peeked inside as if to confirm what the sanba reported. Yes, it was a girl and he could not help but smile at her. She was wet and sticky from her long journey of such a short distance. Her dark eyes seemed to gaze into his. Strands of damp, black hair matted to her little cone-shaped head, a temporary war wound from battling through the birth canal. He removed the cloth and examined his new daughter. Few things truly belonged to him in this life, his small fishing boat, his two-room house, his nets, his wife, and now this baby. His large, sea-weathered hands explored her small, tender body. He counted ten toes and ten fingers. He turned her over and immediately cried out, "Something is wrong with her."

The sanba hurried over and he pointed to the child's low back. It was covered in multiple blue bruises.

"She is hurt," he said.

The sanba shook her head and said, "She was reluctant to be born. More so than most babies, but she is fine. Good and healthy."

The sanba had helped deliver almost every baby in the village for over forty years and she remembered each one. She had helped bring him into the world almost that many years ago. She said, "It was much the same at your arrival. These marks are given by the spirit who slaps the infant to life. The more marks, the more slaps required by the spirit in the womb. I knew this one would have many marks as you did. They will go away as they went from you."

3

He covered his daughter in the cloth, relieved she was healthy. Having a girl was a disappointment, but having a girl with deformities would be a curse. He looked at his wife. She leaned back against pillows, drenched in sweat, soaked in blood, still cringing in pain. He assumed all women looked the same after giving birth. The sanba pushed on his wife's stomach. She groaned, but did not move.

"This helps dispel all that was needed to grow life, but is needed no longer," said the sanba as she pressed hard.

He admired his wife, wondering at her experience. Giving birth to a healthy child was no small task and many women did not survive. He silently thanked his ancestors for their blessings. He wanted to assure his wife he was satisfied with her hard work and said to her, "A girl is good. A girl will help you with all the other babies to come."

As if in reaction to the thought of any other babies, his wife screamed in pain. Her face reddened and she grunted as if still in labor. The pain had returned. The sanba checked between her legs.

"Oh no," the sanba whispered.

"What is it?" he asked.

"There is another," she said and ushered him out of the room.

He stepped into the living area. His daughter was already sucking, trying to find a breast that was not there. Instinctively he positioned his finger at her mouth and she tried to suckle, but grew frustrated. She began to whimper. He heard his wife screaming again in pain.

Terror shot through him, but he was a man used to being at the mercy of the elements and nature. He was a fisherman and so many unexpected events, things outside his control, influenced his day and his life. The sanba had said there was another. Amidst his fear was a small space holding hope, hope that a second baby would be a son. He could even say he was first born. Who would argue? The sanba certainly knew the importance of a first-born son. And then there would be more, many more. He would have enough sons to help him with the fishing and they would be good and strong. He would teach them what he knew about the tides and the weather, catching and drying abalone, jigging and casting and netting. They would learn where to find the best fish - *maguro* and *marusouda* and *buri* and *madara*. When he became old, his sons would continue his work and he could rest.

His thoughts turned to what was happening behind the closed screen. He heard the wind and rain buffet the small house as if in protest, but there was silence from the other room. He slid the screen open and what he saw almost caused him to drop the bundle he carried. The sanba knelt in front of his wife, pressing some kind of wet cloth compresses into her. Blood flooded the floor. In all his years of catching and gutting fish, he had never seen as much blood as was in this room. He felt his stomach lurch. Next to the two women, on the floor, lay the body of another baby. His wife lay unconscious on the pillows.

The sanba, sweating and working feverishly, said, "I think she will live. She has lost much blood, but I don't think…there will be no others."

"No others?" he repeated as if he did not understand.

"She will be lucky to live through this," the sanba said impatiently, not taking her eyes from her work. "She may not still."

He walked toward them, ignoring the viscous sound of his wife's blood under his feet.

"This other baby?" he asked.

"Dead," she said shortly. "Born dead. Something happened in the womb."

"What happened?" he asked.

"Only the spirits know," she said. Then she looked up and added, indicating the baby in his arms, "And her."

He walked toward the dead baby sprawled like a broken doll. The baby was ashen with its dark eyes open. He let out a hard, quick breath as if someone had punched him in the stomach.

He whispered, "A boy."

His ancestors had not blessed him on this night. They had played a cruel deception. They taunted him, allowing him to see the son he would never have. His wife would survive, though he did not know it at the moment. She would remember this as the night of her greatest pain and greatest joy, her daughter Sachi. He would remember only death, an ending to sons and dreams and, in many ways, his own life. He never again asked for his ancestor's blessings. He looked down at the baby in his arms.

"All of this," he said, "for a girl."

CHAPTER ONE

JAPAN – 1915

"I am going to learn it all," Sachi squealed, spinning in a circle, her hands above her head as her mother tried to dress her. "I will learn reading and …"

Her mother grabbed her shoulders to stop her motion and said, "You aren't going anywhere unless you stand still and let me finish."

Sachi stopped and smiled up at her mother whose face hovered only an inch above her own. She could smell the ginger on her mother's breath and watched her arched eyebrows frowning as she concentrated on fixing Sachi's light green kimono.

Sachi asked, "I want to wear the red one. Can I?"

Her mother picked up a hair brush and said, "You know you cannot."

Sachi knew the seasons dictated the color of Japanese clothing. Red was for winter. She would wear green today – spring.

"But Amaya wears her red kimono every day," Sachi insisted.

Her mother smiled. "Yes, but Amaya only has one kimono."

"What will it be like?" asked Sachi, her head bobbing slightly as her mother brushed her long dark hair.

Her mother, working through the tangles, said absently, "If you get any taller you will have to start brushing my hair."

"But mother," Sachi repeated. "What will it be like?"

It was a question Sachi had asked every day for seven days. Since the moment she found out she was going to school. It was a question for which her mother did not have the answer. Her mother had never attended school so she responded in the manner generations of Japanese mothers responded to their daughters on questions from cooking to marriage, "It does not matter. You will do your duty. Do you understand?"

Sachi understood. At eight years old she struggled to learn the duties of a good Japanese daughter and her attention often wavered from the lesson at hand. When her mother taught her the art of making tea, Sachi focused on the rising steam from the kettle, wondering out loud why it rose and where it went rather than how to properly set out the tea cups. Her mother instructed her in sewing, but Sachi found the varied textures and shades of cloth and threads far more interesting than the repetitive pulling of the needle through material. While gardening, she chased the Monarch butterflies fluttering, scooped up gelatinous earthworms from their burrows, and followed noisy, yellow bees from flower to flower.

"I will be good," said Sachi confidently, determined to do what was expected of her and not become distracted by the color and motion of life. She bent over, intending to pick up the doll she had dropped while spinning.

Her mother said, "Sachi, leave Amaya and stand straight."

The doll looked up at her, always smiling. When her mother finished tying back her hair, Sachi lifted Amaya from the floor. Amaya had been her mother's doll. She had been well-used through the years. Her round face was topped with straight, black hair left only

8

in clusters about the top of her head. Her perfect little painted nose sat above a slit of a red mouth and four white dots painted on the upper lip indicating a row of tiny teeth set in a smile.

Sachi and her mother entered the living area where Father sat on the floor at the low table repairing a fish net. His massive hands, scarred and dry, moved quickly over the ropes to mend a large hole caused by the escape attempt of a small shark that had become entangled. The sea had weathered Father as it weathered all things. His back hunched as he concentrated on the work at hand. He tugged hard at the worn net and looked up as his family entered. He glared, whether at the stubbornness of the rope or the presence of his wife and daughter, Sachi wasn't sure. There was no greeting as he returned to the task.

Sachi's mother set about preparing breakfast and Sachi looked out the room's only window. The sun had just begun to crest over the jagged snow-topped mountains to the east.

Father grumbled, "The first day and here I sit waiting for breakfast."

"It is ready. Sachi, come pour the tea for your father," her mother said. Sachi knew Father did not like to be kept waiting.

Sachi left the window and knelt beside Father as he tossed the net by the door. Her legs and feet pressed together, bent under her as she sat on her heels. Sachi leaned over the table, picked up the kettle her mother had prepared, and lifted it just inches above Father's cup. The amber liquid streamed slowly from the kettle and into his cup. Sachi's hand shook a bit, but she steadied it. Father's eyes, shadowed by his furrowed brow, never left his cup. She filled it to just below the rim and then tilted the kettle upright. She set it on the table and moved to fill her mother's cup and then her own. When she finished she set the kettle down and sat at her place at the table. She smiled at her accomplishment. Maybe this time he would approve.

"I did it," Sachi said proudly. "Not one drop spilled."

Her mother smiled and said, "It's because you practice. The more you do something the easier it becomes."

Sachi looked at Father searching for praise, but his eyes remained on his cup. He mumbled, "One time is not cause for celebration."

The smile faded from Sachi's face. Her mother, seated at the table with her head bowed, looked up at Sachi with her eyes and smiled approvingly. Her mother understood, Sachi thought, because her mother appreciated how difficult it could be doing things for Father.

Father grunted and said to her mother, "It is a waste of time, this school, when she could be helping you here at home."

Her mother spoke quietly, "I do what needs to be done here. I need no help."

She cast a glance at her husband from the corner of her eye, and continued, "Many of the children attend missionary school now. The Emperor wants his people educated especially in Western ways. It is time."

Her mother taught Sachi that timing, though intangible, was the secret to all things: the making of rice, the brewing of tea, harvesting vegetables, and, as Sachi was just beginning to understand, the art of marital persuasion.

"Do not tell me what the Emperor wants. I know very well. It is the only reason I have agreed she may go," he bellowed, pulling at the ropes in his hands. "This will cause her to daydream even more. She will think she is better than even her parents."

Her mother placed the rice and seasoned seaweed in bowls and then on the table. She said, "She will learn the history of our people. She will learn to read and write. She will even learn English…"

Father threw his net to the ground and cawed, "English! A useless language for a repulsive people. She is to marry and give her husband sons. That is her job."

Sachi saw her mother close her eyes for a second more than it took time to blink and a shadow move across her mother's face, like a cloud blocking out the sun. She noticed her mother's lips tighten as if being restrained, holding back words wanting to escape.

Father continued, "How will an education help to do that?"

"A better husband," Sachi's mother said, gazing hard at her husband, and then quickly added, "A higher dowry and more honor to her family, her father."

Father picked up his *hashi,* his chopsticks, and said, "Giving her husband sons is the only way for her to bring honor to her family."

11

They ate quickly and in silence as usual, but today Sachi was hoping he would speak to her. Today of all days she needed him to say something. Sachi hardly tasted her breakfast. Father finished eating in silence, picked up his net, and sat down on the little bench by the front door and began putting on his boots.

Her mother spoke to Father in an encouraging voice, "Today is a special day for your child."

He rose from the bench and put on his jacket.

Her mother's tone changed to one that sounded almost pleading, desperate in some measure. She said, "Won't you give her your blessing as she begins school?"

Father threw a loathsome glance in Sachi's direction. He looked at her mother and said, "Ask your ancestors. Maybe they can give blessings to her. I have none to give."

He picked up the fishing net he repaired and walked out. Her mother stood in place staring at the closed door and Sachi wondered if she would run after him and beg for the important blessing. Instead her mother let out a deep breath as if she were holding air in her lungs all morning. Her body seemed to relax and Sachi relaxed with her, suddenly realizing her own muscles were tense.

Her mother turned and smiled at her. She said, "No matter. You are blessed, Sachi. You have the blessings of all our ancestors from the very night you were born."

Sachi smiled at the warmth of her mother's words. She had always known her mother loved her as sure as she had always known Father did not. Sachi cleaned the dishes and then picked up Amaya, holding her tight, and whispered to her, "I will be gone a long time today. I know you are not used to me being away for so long and you might be frightened, but I will come home and tell you all about school. It will be fine."

"Come Sachi. Let's not be late for your first day," her mother said.

Sachi, excited to be off on the first day of school and determined not to make her mother wait, quickly rose, absently leaving Amaya on the floor to wait for her return.

CHAPTER TWO

"This is the beginning," her mother told her as they walked to school the first day. "There are so many lessons to be learned."

The dirt path was well worn and the Japanese cedars and evergreen trees stood like well-wishers along the path, waving slightly in the soft breeze. The large mountains rose up silently on the right, rugged sentries standing watch. The ocean, to the left, was unseen, blocked by the trees, but it made its eternal presence known by filling the air with the sound of crashing waves on the rocky shore.

Sachi and her mother walked hand-in-hand, matching steps, as if they were one body moving in one direction. Her mother stopped short of the schoolhouse. It was veiled in a light morning mist with only a small stream of sunlight softly illuminating it. Her mother looked at the building for a moment, gently pushed Sachi forward, then turned quickly and disappeared down the road into the mist. Sachi stood still, staring longingly at the space her mother had just occupied, feeling uncertain and very alone. The anticipation and excitement vanished, replaced by waves of fear. It was Father's face she saw before her in this moment of doubt. Maybe this was not the path for her and she was not blessed. She knelt quickly, feeling the cold earth on her knees, penetrating her thin kimono. She prayed her ancestors would send her a sign, directing her to move forward on the path or go back toward her mother. Sachi stayed in the position for several minutes, eyes open, waiting for something she wasn't even sure she would recognize.

Just as she stood to run after her mother, she heard it. It was the clear, high-pitched invitation of a bell coming from the direction of the school house. She brushed the leaves and earth from her kimono and, with a quick prayer of thanks to her ancestors and a glimpse back to where her mother had been, Sachi turned, and ran toward the sound of the bell.

After school Sachi's mother walked her home. On that first day, as on many to come, Sachi spoke excitedly, without seeming to need to breathe, sustained by her experiences of the day. She described everything for her mother; the other children, her teacher Miss Adams and her funny English accent, the schoolroom and its leaky roof. She was so caught up in reliving her day that she failed to notice the sadness drifting like shadows on her mother's face. Sachi's mother pulled her to a standstill.

"Let's stop a minute and sit here," her mother said, pointing to an old cedar tree that had fallen years earlier. The air smelled of new rain and camphor from the trees surrounding them. The bamboo trees were thick as screens behind them and sprigs appeared around the log with evergreens and cypress.

Her mother hesitated and then, drawing in a deep breath, continued. "I have some bad news for you about Amaya. Your father accidentally stepped on her today."

Sachi's eyes grew wide and all thoughts of school vanished. "Is she…is she broken?" Sachi asked, her small, dark eyes threatening tears.

Her mother cast her eyes downward and said quietly, "You left her on the floor."

Sachi jumped up, grabbed her mother's hand, and started running in the direction of home.

Amaya was broken beyond repair. Her beautiful porcelain face was cracked, cutting her smile in two, and her neck was broken. Sachi's eyes filled with tears. She looked up from the fractured face of her doll to see Father storming about the room as if Sachi had broken something he cherished rather than the other way around.

"You have been told not to leave things laying about the house," Father bellowed. "Of course that doll was going to get stepped on. You have always been careless with it."

Sachi said nothing, but held the damaged doll protectively close to her chest. Her mother interceded and whispered, "No one did this on purpose. It was an accident."

Father's anger intensified and his face grew even redder. He stood over Sachi, his hard eyes boring into her.

"If that blasted doll was so important, then why did you leave it on the floor?" he roared.

Father expected an answer. Sachi fumbled for words thinking this morning seemed so far away. She mumbled through her tears, "I guess…I guess I was in a hurry."

"Yes, you were in a hurry to get to this school," he scoffed. He turned to her mother and said, "You see, it brings bad luck already. If she is old enough for this school, then she is too old for dolls."

Sachi sniffled and wiped her tears on her kimono sleeve.

"Perhaps we can say some prayers," her mother offered.

Sachi took comfort in her mother's words. Yes, prayers. Sachi asked, "Can we take her to the temple and have the priest say prayers over her? Like when you go to the *hari-kuyo*."

Her mother looked at Father who had moved and was standing in the doorway. She waited a moment, but he remained quiet. Her mother said, "You are right. Our energy, yours and mine, is a part of Amaya, just as it is in all the things we use in our lives, and we must show gratitude for her life of service to us."

Father closed the screen and turned to face them. He grumbled low and said, "Gratitude for a life of service. I wish my daughter would think more about showing gratitude to her father than to some doll in some bastard ceremony."

Father continued, "These prayers said over things like shoes, tools, dolls, needles…for crying out loud. A son would not waste his parent's time in such matters."

Sachi's mother smiled at Sachi, ignoring Father's comment, and said, "I think it would help us to be able to say good-bye to Amaya. In fact, we can go the day after tomorrow."

Father frowned and shook his head. He walked over to the cabinet on the other side of the room. He wrapped his large hand around a bottle of sake. Sachi and her mother exchanged quick glances. Mother's eyes then fell to the ground, but Sachi watched as he poured a small cup and walked back to the table, carrying the cup and the bottle.

"No," he announced as he sat down on a pillow and crossed his legs. For a large man he was agile when it came to doing those things in which he had much interest, sitting down to eat or drink sake.

The room was quiet. No one moved except Father who picked up the cup and drank.

"No," he repeated louder.

Sachi's mother said, "We can go and be back before dinner. You won't even miss us."

"I do not want you gone. The trip to temple will take many hours and then the prayers these Shinto priests insist on doing over a doll, they are long and drawn out. You say you will be home for dinner, but you will not."

"Then we will go to the Buddhist temple."

"Bah, the Buddhist priests are just as long winded. No."

Sachi's mother stood and walked over to the counter. She began preparing dinner, cutting the cabbage on a wooden block. With each chop she uttered a word, carefully and clearly. She said, "Amaya was given to me by my father. I am taking her and Sachi to the temple the day after tomorrow. Your dinner will be ready when you get home."

Sachi's eyes grew large. Never had she known her mother to speak in direct contradiction to Father's wishes. Her mother continued chopping as if she had said nothing more than to comment on the weather. Father's eyes glazed over with anger and he looked down at the table. He hunched over his cup. His hands, shoulders, and jaw tightened and Sachi thought he looked like one giant, clenched fist ready to explode in

19

anger. He loosened one hand, wrapped it around his drink, and drained the cup. Then he stared at Sachi and Amaya with such fury that Sachi felt he wished he had broken them both. He slammed the empty cup on the table.

"This is what happens when there are more women than men. They think they rule the household."

Her mother answered with silence and continued chopping, which seemed to infuriate him further. He poured more sake and drank it down, his eyes wandering the room as if waiting for the words to come to him.

"If I had a son," he said. "He would agree with me. He would not be asking to go to some stupid…"

Her mother stopped chopping and turned to face him. She fixed her eyes on his, as if setting her sights, and in a voice as low as a whisper she said, "The child is of the father, not the mother. *Hara wa karimono* (The womb is a borrowed thing)."

Father's eyes grew wide and his face reddened. He stood, but too fast, and steadied himself on the table. His voice sent a quiver through Sachi - through everything - seeming to shake even the foundation of the house. "You say that to me? It is not my fault we have no sons when it is all I ever wanted."

He poured another cup of the dark liquid and downed it quickly, as if to extinguish the fire burning inside him. His words quieted and his manner became subdued. He walked slowly past Sachi, into the other room, and closed the screen behind him.

Her mother turned back to the counter and finished chopping the cabbage for dinner.

CHAPTER THREE

The next day Sachi returned home from school just as her mother stepped outside. The sun was bright and large, white clouds floated casually in the sky. Even with the sun, there was a chill in the air from a soft, cool wind and her mother pulled her wrap tighter around her shoulders.

"I am going to the village to get some things for dinner. Come with me and tell me about school today. What is that in your hands?"

"It is a book about Pandas," Sachi answered, "Miss Adams let me borrow it."

Sachi was anxious to sit down and look at it. She glanced back at the house and asked, "Where is Father?"

"He is inside sitting by the fire."

They started on the path toward the village and Sachi began to cough. After a few moments, as Sachi fought to catch her breath, her mother said, "Go home and sit by the fire. I will be home shortly and make you some tea. I don't want you sick for our trip to the temple tomorrow."

Sachi turned and headed for home, though she dawdled, not wanting to spend more time alone with Father than necessary. She entered the house and could feel the warmth of the fire, its shadow and light playing against the walls of the room. Father sat on a pillow in front of the fire, a cup in his hand. He startled when Sachi entered.

"What are you doing here? I thought you would go with your mother."

"Umph."

Sachi sat on her futon and began to look through the panda book, but she couldn't concentrate. She was too excited about taking Amaya to temple. She set down her book and lifted Amaya's blanket. Amaya was not there. Sachi felt her heart quicken, immediately wondering what she had done with the doll. She looked under her futon, in the cupboards by her bed, in her parent's room, and even outside on the bench. She entered the house and, in desperation, stood by Father and asked, "Father, have you seen Amaya?"

His eyes did not leave the fire. "Umph," he grunted again, his body momentarily tightening and then relaxing. "Have you lost her again?"

"No," Sachi said. "She was..." Sachi's voice trailed off as she looked from Father to the fire. In the flames Sachi saw the face of her beloved friend staring back at her.

Involuntarily Sachi cried out, "Amaya,"

She looked over at Father who was sitting on a pillow by the fire without emotion, staring face to face with Amaya. He turned to Sachi and asked, "I do not see her."

"There," Sachi insisted, pointing to Amaya's face, thinking he just needed direction. "...in the fire."

Amaya's dark, glass eyes bore through the red and gold flames. Her tufts of black hair were gone, but the fire had yet to reach her perfect nose and painted mouth. Father did not look in the fire as Sachi expected. Instead he stared hard at Sachi. He took another drink from his cup and said, "You are wrong. Say it. Say you are wrong. You have lost that doll. "

Sachi was confused. Father was commanding her to speak against the very thing she knew was true. Amaya was in the fire, still smiling, as her clothes curled into ash.

"But…" Sachi began, still trying to make sense out of her Father's commands.

Father leaned toward her, menacingly, as the fire cast shadows and light upon his harsh features. He said in a voice as deep and soft as down, "Say you are wrong. Say you lost her."

Usually as he shouted and blustered about the small house Sachi retreated into herself, somewhat afraid, but always assured her mother was close. Sachi had often thought Father loud and gruff, but not cruel until now. It was different now. She knew, even though he had never laid a hand on her, he would not hesitate to hurt her if she defied him.

She whispered, against herself and her best friend, "I am wrong. I have lost her."

"Good," he said. Father's face relaxed and he leaned back on the pillow. "You lost her and I'm sure your mother will understand. There is no sense going to the temple tomorrow."

Sachi looked back into the fire, tears brimming in her eyes. She *had* lost her. Amaya was gone except in the ashes and smoke and Sachi's memory. She had always known the feeling of Father's indifference, but for the first time she felt his hatred as hot and destructive as the fire before her.

When her mother arrived home, Father reported Sachi had lost the doll and Sachi remained silent, her eyes to the ground, now complicit in the lie. She felt nauseous as if she had been forced to swallow a poison eating away at her insides. She would not share this poison with her mother.

Her mother looked everywhere in the little house, convinced Amaya would turn up. Father did not stop her, as if searching were her penance for going against him. Instead he sat by the fire watching her, his lips pursed in quiet smile. He didn't speak to Sachi the rest of the afternoon. Finally, at bedtime, to Sachi's relief, her mother declared the search over. Her parents went into their room and Sachi lay on her futon, staring into the dying embers of the fire. She could still picture Amaya's face in the flames. In the dark, she could cry and mourn the loss of her doll and any good feeling she had ever had about Father.

CHAPTER FOUR

Eight Years Later - 1923

It was a warm summer day as Sachi walked to the village. The *baiu,* the month long rainy season that usually lasted all of June, was over and everything was green and alive and warm. The walk to the village was short and Sachi always found herself lost in thought on the familiar path, dreaming of her future, placing herself in the role of heroine from the novels she read.

Tanchoichi was a small village. It had begun centuries earlier as a few seaside homes, people living together in community, and as the needs of the community grew so did their village.

The Yamios, with their seven children, ran Tanchoichi's only store. They sold spices, teas, tools for gardening and fishing, pickled vegetables and fresh fish, and cheaper cloth goods. They could place special orders to Nagasaki for things like music boxes or specialty silks, but in the years the Yamios lived in Tanchoichi they had never received a request for a special order. It appeared the things needed for daily life in the village were enough for the residents of Tanchoichi. The small post office sat next to it, opened or closed, depending on the daily inclination of the postmaster, Mr. Yakusho.

Mr. Tammaka owned a blacksmith shop for the wagons needing repair and horses needing shoes. There was a small bank run by Mr. Yamamoto, but it seemed to Sachi he always sat, playing with numbers, instead of helping customers, most of whom had little money anyway.

A few homes were scattered about, including Mr. Samura's. He squatted on the stoop outside his home each day repairing fishing nets while talking to people coming to town, simply to see what was happening in the world or their little part of it. Mr. Samura was almost like one of the buildings or trees in the village, a permanent fixture.

Sachi noticed several women standing in a half circle outside of the Yamios' store. They chattered loudly, like chickens at feeding time, and in the center of the half circle was Yoshida Watanabe. Yoshida was in her early 60's, but, to Sachi, she looked older. Her gray hair was unruly, refusing to stay in the bun on top of her head. Her face looked as if it were being dragged down by the weight of her double chin, sagging skin under her eyes and neck. Sachi wondered if she had ever seen Yoshida smile. Standing next to Yoshida was a large wooden table and on it were household items; needles, pans, incense burners, decorative chopsticks, and linens.

As Sachi neared the women she heard a tone in Yoshida's voice as she spoke. It sounded like pride. Yoshida said, "Takeo has forbidden me to take these with us to America. He said it is time for me to join him and his father. The worst is he is making me learn English. I am too old for such things; new language, new country. But he is my son so I go. He says we have many fine things in California and there is no reason to bring these. So I am selling them."

Life in the village of Tanchoichi was measured not by a calendar, but by the slow progression of the natural seasons of fall, winter, spring, and summer and the human seasons, of birth, marriage, and death. The sounds of the ocean waves served as the eternal metronome. But since Japan had opened itself to foreigners there was another event that marked time and change for the villagers: moving. Most residents of Tanchoichi arrived at birth and departed in death or marriage. Now, with open borders and new opportunities, some villagers were leaving not only Tanchoichi, but Japan.

Sachi stood listening, when the postmaster, Mr. Yakusho, approached her. He handed her a telegraph and said, "Sachi, will you make sure your mother gets this? It is from Kanto, her sister is ill."

Sachi's mother had two sisters in Kanto whom Sachi had never met. They did not visit and only occasionally exchanged correspondence. Sachi pushed the telegram into her pocket and continued to watch the group of women. She and the postmaster stood for a minute listening to Yoshida lament having to leave the home of her ancestors to join her husband and son in America. At that moment Yoshida's son, Takeo Watanabe, exited the Yamio's store and approached the group of chattering women. They fell silent.

Mr. Yakusho, in a voice only Sachi could hear, said, "Takeo has written to her for three years now. You remember when Takeo and his father left here to work in America? He has been trying to get her to go over ever since and she has resisted. But now she will go because he has come for her and will take her back to their farm."

Sachi nodded. She did not question the postmaster's information. It was common for him to have to read letters, especially to the older people of the village who could not see as well or had never learned to read. Sometimes the writers, such as Takeo, relied on the postmaster to translate what they wrote.

"But she is scared," he continued. "Change is not frightening for the young because they think they can do anything, but it can be terrifying for the old who know better."

Sachi thought back to her mother's comments that Yoshida Watanabe was gossipy and cantankerous and should have gone with her husband years ago when he first left for America.

"A wife," her mother said, "must be with her husband, otherwise she is not a wife, but simply married."

The postmaster suddenly stopped mid-sentence and walked back to the post office. Sachi looked around and realized Takeo Watanabe was headed toward her. The group of women continued to talk and Sachi noticed Yoshida staring at her, her face as dark and her look intense.

Takeo stopped in front of Sachi. She had known him as a little girl before he left with his father. He was a kind, round man with thick black hair and stood only as tall as Sachi. Even though he was 25, eight years older than Sachi, he was reserved, almost shy as he spoke to her.

After the initial courtesies were exchanged he asked, "Have you finished your studies at the missionary school?"

Sachi nodded. He asked, "And what will you do now? I mean…have you plans to…to…well, what will you do now?"

Sachi shrugged slightly and smiled at his awkwardness. He was even sweating slightly. It was a humid day and he was a heavy man, but she wondered if the weather and his weight were all that accounted for the sweat on his upper lip.

"I am not sure."

"I remember when you were younger, you always wanted to go to America. Is that still true?"

"Yes," Sachi nodded with more enthusiasm than she intended. She then asked, "What is it really like over there? Is everything as large as I imagine? Are the people…are they…?"

She stopped, thinking she sounded much too familiar and curious than she should. She always struggled with blurting out what was on her mind no matter how many times Father chastised her. She stood still, looking downward.

In a low voice barely above a whisper, Takeo asked, "Would you like to see for yourself?"

Something lurked in his voice and told her this was not an idle question. This was a question with a promise behind it. She looked up, holding his gaze, unsure what he might ask. Did he want a caretaker for his parents, someone to work in his home in America?

Takeo let out a breath and, as if emboldened by her eye contact, continued, "I know this is not how things are done. I know I should speak to the *baishakunin*, the matchmaker, and your father, but I have little time and in America things are done differently. If we are to be Americans, we must do as Americans. If you will…I want to make arrangements at home and then I will send money for you. You will come. I will meet you in America and we will be…we will be husband and wife."

He looked away quickly and Sachi sensed he was uncertain of her answer and fearful, perhaps, of his own vulnerability. Sachi had never considered marriage with Takeo Watanabe. And in this moment she realized he was offering her something much more than marriage. He was offering her a chance to see America and this excited her more than the prospect of marriage. She was not thinking of a wedding kimono or marriage ceremony. Images from schoolbooks about America quickly flooded her mind – horses running on large, wind-swept plains, big cities lit up at night, and funny-looking people from all over the world. Her heart beat fast from the promise of adventure, not passion, and she realized she was unafraid.

Sachi was not physically attracted to Takeo, but marriage was a practical arrangement and romance could come in time. The western books she had read sometimes talked about romance before marriage. Americans fell hopelessly in love as if under a spell, unable to control themselves, and they married for love. Sachi often wondered at feeling such strong, uncontrollable passion. It certainly never seemed to be a sound reason for marriage. Marriage was a contract between a man and a woman to raise children and work together. Maybe, once married, she would find that feeling she had read about in books although she had certainly never seen a hint of it between Father and her mother.

Her thoughts flew to her mother - the only thing holding her here. She smiled at Takeo, turned her head shyly, but with her eyes remaining locked on his. His comments were uncharacteristically feral and familiar, but they did not scare her.

She said, "You do me a great honor. Would it be possible? My mother…she is dear to me as yours is to you. Could she come with me?"

Takeo shook his head slightly, "Three women in the same house? That would be trouble."

Yoshida would be her mother-in-law. The thought hit her swiftly and she realized she would need her mother with her more than ever. She would start small and ask only for this one thing.

She said, "Maybe she could come for a visit. Just to see me married and see where we live. That would be alright, wouldn't it?"

Takeo thought for a moment and then nodded, "Yes. Your mother is welcome to visit. What about your father?"

Sachi shook her head. "He will not come, but mother and I will as soon as you write for me."

Sachi believed she could even endure life with Yoshida Watanabe if it meant going to America with her mother. That evening as Father slept, Sachi confided in her mother the conversation with Takeo and her request that her mother accompany her. Her mother knelt in front of the fire, sewing a pair of pants for Father. Her hands stopped and she sat for a moment without speaking, looking as if someone had taken her breath.

"America," she said, contemplating. "Takeo Watanabe. I hear he is a hard worker and a good man with much earth in him. He is solid and stable."

Sachi laughed and said, "But you always say I have too much water in me and earth absorbs water."

Her mother gave her daughter a small smile as she resumed her sewing and answered, "Sometimes. And sometimes water flows smoothly over the earth. Do you think you can be a good wife to him? "

Sachi nodded and smiled, "I've had a very good teacher."

Her mother looked up from her sewing, her fingers still working, and returned the smile. She looked back down and the smile dropped. She said, "You will need your father's approval."

Sachi lowered her head, thinking how often she felt Father wished she had never been born. She said, "I am sure Father will approve. Then you and I will leave for America."

Her mother did not look up from her work and said, "I could not go with you."

Sachi's heart stopped. She could not imagine leaving her mother. The very thought filled her with fear and dread. Her mother was where she found her courage and to go without her, to separate from her mother and leave her behind, would be too painful.

"Then I will not go," Sachi declared, waiting for her mother to insist or to give in and agree to accompany her, but her mother said nothing.

Sachi listened to the rhythm of the ocean outside their front door. She thought of the many conversations they shared in the evenings when Father slept and realized school is where she'd learned about the world, but it was at her mother's knee she learned about herself.

Laying back on her futon, breaking the impasse with words, she insisted, "I have to go and you have to go with me."

"I cannot leave my home, Sachi."

The light was dim, but her mother worked swiftly as if the light were not even needed, her stitches neat and small. Sachi stared at this woman as familiar to her as her own face or hands. She could not leave her mother.

She sighed deeply and said resignedly, "I wonder if he intends to send for me at all."

"I think if he asked you, then he intends to send for you. However, Yoshida....well she may try and urge him to change his mind."

Sachi responded confidently. "He did promise."

Her mother looked up from her sewing, thoughtful for a moment, and then said, "I know. But you will find that sometimes men make promises they simply cannot keep."

Sachi ignored her mother's comment. She was saying that because the man she married had turned out to be a disappointment. Sachi was sure of that. She said, "You must go with me. I…I cannot go without you."

Her mother looked deep into Sachi's eyes and said, "This is an important time for you, my daughter. I want you to consider what will bring you and your family honor. We will get your father's approval. We will talk about it in the morning."

As if to put a halt to the conversation, she added, "When Takeo sends a telegram for you, we will talk more."

"Oh," Sachi jumped up as if a shock were sent through her. "Your telegram. Mr. Yakusho gave me a telegram for you today."

She retrieved it from the pocket in her skirt and handed it to her mother. Her mother read it quickly by the firelight, a frown coming to her face.

"My sister is ill," she said. "I must go and see her."

"All the way to Kanto?" Sachi asked.

"Yes," her mother responded. "She is dying."

"But you have not seen her for so long."

Mother folded the paper and placed it on the table in front of her. She looked off out the front window as if she were already somewhere else and said, "We are sisters. It may be the last time I will see her in this life. I want to see her. I want to say good-bye."

CHAPTER FIVE

The next morning Father raged. He did not take the news of Takeo's offer or her mother's departure well.

"You will not go to America to join a man who would approach a young girl without getting her father's permission first. That man is trying to get out of paying a wedding dowry and I will not allow it."

He also refused to give his blessing to Sachi's mother for her trip to Kanto, but her mother was insistent, assuring Father that Sachi was old enough to handle the house. She was only going for a week. No time at all.

When Sachi said she wanted to go to the city as well, Father interrupted her and chided, "You should want to stay home and do your duty as a daughter just as your mother should want to stay and do her duty as a wife."

Father tried to bully and guilt her mother, but this time it was to no avail. Her mother was going to Kanto and, even though Sachi begged to go with her, not wanting to stay at home alone with Father, her mother did not waiver.

"You must stay. I need you here to take care of your father. If we both go, it will be that much harder when we return," she explained to Sachi.

On the morning her mother left the house, Father sat staring into the fire, refusing to acknowledge her leaving. Sachi hugged her mother and said goodbye. She stood at the door watching her walk down the dirt path, already wishing she was returning. Suddenly Father stood up and walked over to the door, pushing Sachi out of his way. He yelled angrily at her mother, "This trip is not blessed by your husband. You will have nothing, but sorrow until you return home."

Sachi realized it was all he could do with his anger. There were no dolls to burn. He walked back to the fire, ignoring Sachi, who watched to see if her mother had heard the cruel words. Suddenly, her mother turned and gazed at Sachi still standing at the door. She waved at her daughter and smiled.

Time without her mother dragged, like waiting for spring to come after a long, cold winter. Sachi did her best to avoid Father when possible and Father spoke little to her other than to tell her what he wanted to eat. She felt like they sat on opposite sides of a teeter totter with her mother in the middle for balance. With her mother gone, the balance was lost and Sachi felt abruptly tossed in the air.

One afternoon Sachi was sitting in the corner of the house, reading. Her thoughts kept drifting to the fact that her mother was several days overdue. Every little sound caused her to jump and look out the window, hoping to see her mother coming down the path. She heard Father's loud breathing and grunting even before his footsteps. She quickly slid her book under the pillow, jumped up, and began dinner preparations. Father walked in looking dazed, still wearing his boots, which he always removed before entering. Something was wrong.

Sachi immediately thought he was sick or perhaps more drunk than she'd ever seen him before. She asked, "Father, are you ill?"

He didn't respond or even look at her, but walked to the bedroom and lay on the futon. Sachi continued making dinner hoping food would help him feel better. When it was ready, she walked to where Father was prone on the mat, her heart aching as she noticed mother's empty space beside him.

"Father, dinner is ready," Sachi announced. "Can you come to the table?"

He did not move. She continued, "When mother comes home…"

He rolled over and interrupted her, mumbling, "She's not coming home."

"Of course, she's coming home," Sachi said reassuringly.

His voice was low and steady like thunder in the distance. He said, "No. She is dead."

"But Father…"

Father sat up quickly and looked at his daughter. He reached into his pocket and pulled out a wadded up piece of paper. He threw it at her.

"Here," he said, "This is what that jackal at the post office read to me to tell me of my wife's death. Take it and go."

Sachi smoothed out the paper and took it to the window to read by the light of the remaining sun. It was from her aunt, one she'd never met, a stranger informing them of the earthquake. She had attached a newspaper clipping to the letter.

Sachi read the newspaper account first. It was entitled Great Earthquake Shakes Kanto. There was a picture with people crying and running into the streets with fallen buildings burning all around them. The clipping said the earthquake was devastating.

37

Factory and chimney stacks, towers, and elevated tanks twisted and fell. Homes, temples, and businesses were shaken off their foundations and collapsed around the spirits which occupied and created them. Windows shattered. Monuments destroyed. Sand and mud spewed from massive cracks in the ground. At least 100,000 people were thought to be dead and many more were missing in the greatest natural disaster in Japan's history.

Sachi then turned her attention to the letter from her aunt. The letter said her mother was in one of the markets at noon when the earthquake hit. She had gone there to stock up her sister's home. Her sister was getting better and mother was anxious to come home. She died in the market during the earthquake and subsequent fire.

Lies could exist in all things, even these black lines and dots on this white piece of paper, Sachi thought. She searched the room looking desperately for something true to tell her this was not real. Her eyes landed on Father. She had long ago learned not to trust what Father said and thought herself immune to his deceptions. The only evidence she had was this paper, her Father's words, and her mother's absence.

Visions of what her mother experienced in the last moments of her life flashed through Sachi's mind. She pictured her sweet mother, so gentle, crushed by the rubble of a falling building, terrified and alone. Images raced through Sachi's mind of fire raging, coming toward her mother as she lay trapped, unable to escape. Burning, perhaps even broken, like Sachi's doll in the fire. Sachi was emptied of all breath and filled with only incredible pain, the kind of pain that comes when the soul sustains a loss it simply cannot bear. She thought of Father's last words to her mother. He cursed her, perhaps causing her death. Sachi struggled to breath and her chest hurt. Pain was all she felt. That is when the numbness suddenly overwhelmed her like a curtain falling, quickly and without warning. Her brain simply stopped, refusing to process any more sensory information. As if in the ultimate protective effort, Sachi's mind disconnected from her spirit and the pain was gone. All vision of her mother's suffering disappeared as if it simply had not happened.

Sachi stepped toward the fireplace and threw the stranger's words into the fire. They burned quickly and were gone. She then moved toward the window to look to the path leading to their home. Sachi did not cry or scream out because her mother was not dead. Nothing had changed. She would wait. Her mother would come home.

For the next few days, refusing to believe what she couldn't see, Sachi sat by the window, her eyes never leaving the path on which she had last seen her mother wave goodbye. Father yelled at her to fix him food or to move away from the window, but she would not, could not.

And then on the third day of her watch, toward dusk, Sachi saw her. There was her mother walking the path back home. She was smiling and waving and walking quickly toward her. Sachi's heart was light again and she jumped up from the window with a cry of joy.

Her mother was quickly approaching and she was carrying a basket with a blue linen cover on top. She walked in the door. Sachi cried, "Mother" and collapsed into unconsciousness.

She awoke on her parent's futon. It was dark with the exception of a solitary candle giving off just enough light for Sachi to make out the figure of a woman kneeling beside her.

"Mother?" Sachi called out.

Mrs. Yamio gently wiped Sachi's head with a cloth.

"You're awake, poor child," she said, more to herself than Sachi. "Let me get you some soup."

Sachi sat up on her elbows and looked around the room. "Where is my mother?" she asked.

Mrs. Yamio said, "Don't think of that now. Here. Have some of this."

She held a small cup to Sachi's lips. It was good, but did little more than remind her of her mother feeding her soup when she was ill.

She demanded, "Where is my mother?"

Mrs. Yamio started to rise, but Sachi grabbed her arm, desperate. Her eyes fell on the blue line covered basket.

"There," she said. "My mother's basket."

Mrs. Yamio patted Sachi's hands and then gently pushed her shoulders to lie back.

She said, "Dear, that is my basket. You must rest now. Your father asked me to come this afternoon. He didn't know what to do with you. He said you were looking for your mother. He is in the living area, sleeping. We are having the ceremony tomorrow. You must get your rest."

"Tomorrow?" asked Sachi.

Mrs. Yamio shrugged and said, "Your father thought it best to do this sooner rather than later."

Sachi lay back as Mrs. Yamio directed. Everyone believed the slip of paper. Sachi began to imagine and dream that perhaps her mother, tired of life with a man as harsh as Father, had decided to run away. Perhaps she was still out there somewhere, waiting for the right time to come and take Sachi with her. But then a thought came to her. She realized her mother would never knowingly cause her such pain. Her mother, if alive, would always come home. She knew then that her mother was dead.

Thoughts flooded her brain and she couldn't stop them. If only she had gone with her mother, things would be different. They would have survived or, at least, died together. Why did her sister have to get sick and write to her? She hadn't seen her sister in years. Why did she have to leave? Sachi and Father had wanted her to stay, but she left anyway. Suddenly she felt a sudden rush of feeling, a hot anger deep within her chest, momentarily blocking out the pain and sorrow.

"I hate her," Sachi screamed. "I hate her."

Mrs. Yamio rushed back to her side and knelt before her. Sachi sat up, her face red with rage and her fists clenched. There was something satisfying in the sudden release of strong emotion and Sachi gave herself over to it. She began to beat Mrs. Yamio on the chest until Mrs. Yamio grabbed her shoulders and pushed her back on the bed, holding her down as she flailed about.

"Sachi," Mrs. Yamio yelled, frightened by Sachi's erratic behavior. "Stop this. You don't know what you are saying. You don't hate your mother."

Sachi screamed, "I hate her sister. Her stupid sister. She took my mother from me. Because of her...because of her..."

Sachi could not speak the words. She knew her mother was dead, but to say it would make it too real, draw it too close to her.

"Shhhh," whispered Mrs. Yamio, brushing Sachi's black hair back from her face, annoying Sachi rather than comforting her. She would never again feel her mother's gentle hand. This woman's hand felt calloused and smelled of strong tea while her mother's hand had always felt soft and smelled of ginger and azaleas.

Just as suddenly the anger disappeared as if her body and mind could not sustain it for very long. It took too much energy. With the anger gone, the pain in her heart throbbed as if hit by a hammer. She was so filled with grief she could only draw in short, shallow breaths. Sachi turned away from Mrs. Yamio. She lie where her mother had lain just a few days earlier, her head on the same pillow. It smelled of her mother and she buried her face into it, drawing in her mother's essence, until she tumbled into an empty, black sleep.

Sachi awoke the next morning. For a split second, in that space between sleep and consciousness, she forgot. There was just that moment with the sun shining in the window and the constant sound of the ocean. Everything was the same. Then her mind betrayed her by remembering. Oddly, everything was indeed the same except her mother was dead. Sachi felt like she had received the news for the first time. The pain returned and she prayed for that space between sleep and awake, but she could not return. There was no reason to rise she thought and she buried her face into the pillow again.

Mrs. Yamio slid open the door and entered with a cup of tea and some *okayu* (rice porridge) on a small tray. She slid the door closed and placed the tray on the floor next to Sachi.

"It is time," Mrs. Yamio said. "The guests are arriving. I have laid out your clothes. You must dress and go see them."

Sachi turned toward Mrs. Yamio, finding it hard to speak as if her throat were clogged with the pain of her loss. She spoke as if she were a child again, in little more than a whisper, almost pleading, and said, "I...I don't want to."

Mrs. Yamio knelt beside her and bent over, her lips close to Sachi's ear, whispering in return. She said, "You are no longer a child. It is your place now. Your mother would want you in there greeting her guests."

Their eyes met and Sachi, even through her own agony, realized there was a lingering sadness in Mrs. Yamio's face as she spoke the words, as if she too was familiar with this moment of losing all one held dear in childhood. Without a mother, Sachi was no longer a child.

Sachi remembered the many times her mother had shared with her the night of her birth. Her mother talked of the pain and long struggle to bring her daughter into this life.

She would not dishonor her mother. She would endure the pain and struggle to see her mother out of this life and into the next.

With all the will she could muster, Sachi rose from her mother's place on the futon. Mrs. Yamio patted her shoulder and left the room. Sachi brushed her hair and washed her teeth and face in the bowl of water on the dresser. Then she dressed in the white clothes that lay next to the bowl of water. She picked up the untouched tray Mrs. Yamio had brought to her and entered the living area.

Several women from the village were in the kitchen area along with Mrs. Yamio. Everyone was dressed in white, the color for funerals. Father sat at the table, crossed legged with his back straight, looking almost happy. The table was spread with homemade specialties of fish and seaweed, mochi and fresh vegetables, soups and teas, and, neatly in front of him, were stacked black and silver envelopes. Sachi knew these envelopes contained condolence money. Guests brought money to the head of the household to show their condolences for the family's loss. Sachi wondered if that explained the urgency of the ceremony and his good humor.

There was a shrine, *kamidana-fuji,* a small table covered in white paper, set up near the fireplace with an incense burner and candles. It kept out impure spirits of the dead. The smell of fresh flowers wrestled with the camphor smell of the incense creating a heavy perfumed air in the small home. Sachi stood next to the shrine, watching the flames and breathing it in. It made her light headed and she almost wished she would faint so she could return to sleep, but that would not bring honor to her mother and so she

44

moved away from the shrine into the kitchen area with the other women. Mrs. Yamio handed her a cup of tea and insisted she drink it.

Mrs. Samura approached Sachi. Mrs. Samura was a tiny woman with a deep voice that belied her stature. They bowed to one another. Mrs. Samura offered her condolences and said, "In many ways you are fortunate, Sachi. At least, you know what happened to your mother. There are some people who are missing relatives and still haven't found them under all that mess. It's just terrible."

Sachi wanted to slap the woman across the face, but she held on tightly to the cup of tea in her hand as well as her tongue. "Yes, Mrs. Samura," Sachi agreed. "I am fortunate."

Sachi turned quickly to Mrs. Yamio anxious to step out of conversation with a woman who would proclaim her good fortune at knowing her mother was dead.

"Where is the tombstone to be?" Sachi asked Mrs. Yamio.

Mrs. Yamio didn't look up from her work and said, "Your father decided not to have one."

"What?" Sachi asked in disbelief.

Mrs. Yamio said, "Your father said any kind of permanent memorial or tombstone would just be too painful for him to see every day."

Sachi approached Father and knelt beside him. She bowed low. He bowed his head slightly, acknowledging Sachi.

"Can I bring you anything?" Sachi asked him. It was a question to fill the distance between them as some of the women obviously had already brought Father several plates of food that sat before him.

Father shook his head and asked, "Are you better?

"Yes, Father," Sachi lied.

"Good," he said. "

"Father," Sachi asked, "Where is the memorial?"

Sachi could tell he was immediately annoyed at her question. His brows furrowed and his voice was low, but sharp. "There will be none. There is nothing to place in the ground. No marker is needed for us to remember your mother. The priest will arrive soon along with the other guests to say prayers over your mother's spirit and memory. That is enough."

Everything in Sachi wanted to argue with him and tell him that she desperately needed a tombstone or marker. There was no body. There were no ashes. There was nothing tangible to bear witness to her mother's death, except all of these guests and her mother's very absence. When the guests departed, Sachi would be left only with the pain and memories...and Father.

Sachi tried to focus on what was happening around her rather than the pain inside. She watched the women move about Father, clucking over him. She knelt by the window because her body needed a place to be. She felt distant as if she were not really part of this gathering like a ghost invited to the wrong funeral ceremony. Sachi did not want to participate in this conspiracy that her mother was dead.

She tried to look at Father the way some of these women looked at him, a bachelor now. Several of the women lived with their sons and daughters-in-law. They were still young enough to want a home and a husband of their own and here was one readily available. Sachi didn't care. She wanted to sit and be invisible. No one was speaking of her mother. They talked of the weather, the food, and what Father would do now.

Mr. Tammaka approached Father, bowed, and said, "At least, you have Sachi. She will help you through this."

They both looked at Sachi kneeling at the window. Father nodded. His eyes were cold and his words were painful to Sachi's ears. He responded "Yes, at least, I have Sachi."

CHAPTER SIX

In the four months since her mother's death, Sachi cried every day. Each night she lie awake in bed and the tears came like an indistinguishable force delivered the way Mother Nature brings snow or rain or earthquakes. Each day was like the one before it. Without her mother time blurred into a dull smear of life. For Sachi, life was like looking at the night sky with no moon or stars, black, cold, and distant. Time did not stop the tears nor did it take the pain.

She worked hard each day in the house and the garden, driven by a desire not to remember, wanting distraction from the reality of loss. She found she could not concentrate to read or find a reason to sing as if those abilities had suddenly been removed from her. At night she floated back to memories of her mother, but she could not stay long. The memories only fueled an unquenchable yearning that threatened to consume Sachi.

The days were measured by time when Father was working and time when he was at home. In her mother's absence, Sachi was no longer cushioned from Father's harsh ways, which had grown in intensity each day since her mother's death, until it seemed to be all there was.

One night he sat in front of the dinner table, waiting for Sachi to serve him dinner, pondering aloud his responsibilities and hardships. He often complained of the weather, the catch, his health, the loss of his wife, but, mainly, he complained about Sachi.

"Your mother did you no favor by allowing you to go to missionary school. You are not only tall for a woman, but you are educated in western ways," he sneered, sipping sake from the cup he had poured himself. "Those bastard missionaries elevate our women and then leave them for us to find husbands. What man wants such a wife?"

Sachi remained silent as she knelt by Father and served his meal. Her eyes remained on the table and she waited to see if he required anything more.

"But," Father announced as he picked up his chopsticks, "I am talking to several prospective husbands for you and we will see."

"Husbands?" Sachi asked, her heart beating faster.

He nodded and picked up his bowl of rice and fish. He shoveled the food into his mouth quickly.

"But Takeo Watanabe…" Sachi began, unable to stop herself.

He shook his head and several grains of rice fell from his mouth to the table. He took no notice. It was not his job to clean them up. "No," he said firmly. "What benefit is it to me?"

Sachi knew what that meant. Father, as his ancestors before him, looked to marriage to bring honor to the family name, elevate Father's prestige within the village, and bear something of a financial benefit. Sachi knew he pondered all of this, particularly the money, as he considered marriage for Sachi. Takeo Watanabe offered none of that.

Her parent's marriage had been arranged and Sachi thought her own marriage might come about in the same way, but she had counted on the influence of her mother to

50

ensure integrity and kindness in the search for an appropriate husband. Sachi had always thought she would have a voice in her marriage, through her mother. With her mother gone, everything had changed.

She faced that stark reality one afternoon as she walked slowly down the path leading from the village to the sea cliffs by her home. The sky was overcast and gray. The wind blew lightly, but Sachi could see storm clouds approaching and she felt heaviness in the air. Rain was coming. As she looked down the narrow path in the distance she noticed a small horse and wagon coming toward her. She guessed Father had a visitor, though it was unusual. Perhaps it was a fishing companion or maybe one of the ladies from the temple or church trying to coax him out for supper. If only those ladies with their teas and fancy dishes knew Father and his penchant for drinking more and working less, Sachi thought, they might realize it is sometimes better to have no man in one's life.

She tossed back her hair to shake these thoughts from her head and kept walking. The horse and wagon stopped and she noticed a small man at the reins. His face was not weather-beaten like Father's, but he looked old and disagreeable. Sachi did not immediately notice his thin, black moustache and receding hairline, but she did see his scowl and she immediately disliked him. She quickly examined his hands and judged them to be the hands of a merchant or someone without work, not those of a fisherman. They were too smooth and clean. He wore a long black coat of fine cloth. She examined him with a quick glance, then bowed her head and stepped out of the way so his wagon could pass. To her surprise, he continued to sit in the path and stare down at her.

It seemed minutes before she finally looked up to determine why he did not move and their eyes locked. She felt an immediate repugnance toward him. There was a coldness lurking deep in his dark eyes.

He glared down at her and commanded, "Step over here. Closer to me."

She hesitated and he barked the order again. She stepped toward the wagon.

"Hum. You smell like fish. Like this entire village," he said sweeping his arm in the air, his voice pinched and tight.

"Well, sir," she said, casting her eyes downward. "It is a fishing village. I am the daughter of a fisherman. We are near the ocean. It is…"

"Silence. Do not insult me with the obvious."

Sachi replied in the sweetest of tones, "I meant no insult, sir. I thought you seemed confused at the smell of fish by the ocean."

"Not confused. Disgusted," he sneered. "I will not have a wife of mine smelling like fish. And I will not have her speak back to me in such a manner."

Sachi, unsure of his meaning, assumed he was new to the village and perhaps his wife, to his dismay, was beginning to smell like her surroundings. She remained silent, wishing he would go on his way. Instead he remained and asked, "Have you nothing impudent to say to that?"

Sachi replied, "I do not know your wife, sir, so I cannot comment."

He replied smugly, "Stupid girl. I'm talking about you. You are to be my wife. I am Koji Takahashi. Remember that name. I will return tomorrow to work out the details with your father."

She looked up at him, aghast at his words. He looked down at her and smiled, as if victorious. It was the kind of smile a demon would wear having trapped an unsuspecting soul.

As he urged his horse forward and continued down the path, he tossed a command over his shoulder, "And wash the fish smell from you in time for my visit."

Sachi stood momentarily frozen, stunned by this stranger's pronouncement. She couldn't believe it but, at the same time, she sensed it was true. She did something she hadn't done since she was a little girl. She lifted her skirt, freeing her knees, and ran home as quickly as she could.

CHAPTER SEVEN

Sachi spoke to Father that night and the next morning trying to dissuade him from promising her in marriage to this man she knew she could never love. Father would not speak to her other than to confirm that Koji Takahashi had proposed marriage after seeing Sachi in the village. Sachi tempted Father's wrath several times by imploring him not to marry her to this man who looked so cruel and hated the very smell of her world. She pleaded for him to reconsider and, in desperation, added, "Mother would never make me marry this man. You know that."

Father's dark eyes narrowed sharply and the lines on his weathered face deepened. He raised his hand to her and yelled in quick, angry bursts, "Not another word. I know what is best. Your mother would do as a good Japanese woman does. She would do as I tell her. It will do you some good to have a strong husband to break you of these western ways."

Sachi instinctively raised her own hands in self-defense to shield her face. She had never learned her mother's art of timing and persuasion. She continued to try and dissuade Father, "But Takeo is going to send for me. He will write from America…"

He stepped within inches of her, his hand raised even higher, and said, "You will never go to America. Forget about Takeo Watanabe. Do not disgrace me by speaking of this again."

Sachi did not want to be deliberately disobedient. Daughters did as their fathers commanded or they brought disgrace to the family, but to have to marry Koji Takahashi was more than her heart, still tender from the loss of her mother, could bear. She knew Father could not afford a *baishakunin*, a matchmaker. While Mr. Takahashi could, it was apparent he was looking for a bargain and he thought he had found one in Sachi.

The next afternoon, while she served tea and sake to Takahashi and Father, they talked of the arrangement as if she were not even in the room. The conversation began with discussions of the weather, the village, and required pleasantries. Father then ordered Sachi to bring the sake and after a drink, the negotiations began.

Takahashi started, "I will offer you 50 yen for her."

Father said, feigning shock at such an offer, "She is worth much more than that."

"Perhaps, she is pretty in a country way, but she comes with nothing."

Sachi's face reddened in part from embarrassment and, partly, in anger at being bartered over like a bundle of fish.

Father responded, "She comes with an education."

Takahashi dismissed him with a wave of his hand, "An education does not ensure a good wife or an ability to bear sons. Those are the things I would be willing to pay for, but with this one...I am taking a risk."

Father said, "She is strong. She can do much work. She can do the work of a man."

"I do not want a man," Takahashi countered.

Sachi poured more sake, leaned in, bit her lip and then whispered to Takahashi, "Are you sure?"

He pushed her hard causing the sake to spill onto the old wooden table. It began to drip through the small cracks onto the floor.

"I heard she was impertinent," he said, speaking to Father and still not addressing her directly. "You obviously have not rid her of that quality as a parent so I will be forced to do it as a husband."

He turned to Sachi who was on her knees mopping up the sake, roughly grabbed her chin and thrust her head up to look at him. "Learning when you are older is even more unpleasant, but learn you will."

He released Sachi and looked at Father, "60 yen and no more. You send her to me."

The men stepped outside without acknowledging Sachi. She continued to wipe up the spilled sake as Father tried to calm Takahashi and increase the price. The door remained open and Sachi could hear the two men.

Father attempted to sooth Takahashi. "She can be a difficult girl, but her mother was the same until we were married and then she was a dutiful wife."

Takahashi said, "She may have been a dutiful wife, but, by the looks of it, she was a poor mother. She did not teach her daughter the importance of silence and humility, but I will."

Anger, as she had never known, rose up in Sachi. She ran and stood in the doorway, yelling, "You aren't fit to breathe my mother's name you arrogant, little flea. Father will have to kill me before I will marry you."

Father turned to her, his eyes large and his mouth open wide. His face was red with anger and Sachi knew she had insulted him and her ancestors. Her entire body trembled, but she was unafraid. She almost wanted a fight, some way to inflict on them the pain and humiliation they had inflicted on her today.

But Takahashi barely glanced at Sachi. He smiled slightly, turned to Father as he mounted his horse, and said, "I will be up north for a week on business. You shall send her to my home in seven days. I will send 60 yen by messenger upon her arrival."

He looked at Sachi, menacingly, and said to Father, "Do not kill her before our wedding day. I look forward to teaching her about marriage."

He rode away without a backward glance and Father turned to face her. His face was contorted in anger. His dark eyes and unkempt eyebrows narrowed in hatred. Sachi remembered the look he had given her as her mother searched in vain for her toy doll so many years ago. He had never hurt her physically, but like a monsoon gathering dark clouds to it and gaining power, Sachi always knew she was in Father's path and the day would come that he would land on her with all his force.

He marched toward her and, without hesitation, hit her hard across the face. She fell to the floor, telling herself she would not cry, but without her consent, her eyes began to water. Her face swelled immediately and her cheek felt like a hot ember.

"That remark cost me money, which I can ill afford."

Sachi spoke out, "But Father, he is not the kind of man I want to marry. Takeo will send for me. Mother..."

58

Father approached her again and kicked her several times. She turned to protect herself and the blows landed on her back and side. He clenched his fist and raised it threateningly. "You have dishonored your mother and me. This is a decision for me to make. Not you. You think I would send you to that pig in America. Never. You *will* marry Takahashi or I will kill you," said Father, wiping the sweat from his face with his dirty shirtsleeve. "He wants you, though I have no idea *why* he wants you."

"Because you certainly never did," Sachi said, the words sprung from her lips, like prisoners who had waited years for this chance to escape. "Go ahead and kill me. I meant it. I would rather die than marry a man I despise. I won't live like my mother did."

Father looked like Sachi had impaled him with a spear. He stood perfectly still for a moment, his face contorting from rage to what almost appeared to be pain and Sachi imagined the power of her words sinking into his sake-soaked mind. He let out a sound like a death rattle and stumbled outside.

Sachi slowly sat up and hugged her knees tightly to her chest, wishing her arms were wrapped around her mother. She was accustomed to Father's harshness, his tirades, but he had never struck her before today and she had never fought back with such hurtful, angry words. Father had promised her in marriage to Koji Takahashi and she wanted to die.

Dishes still remained on the small table where her future had been bartered away; a fair price negotiated over a cup of sake. She raised herself up from the floor, heavy with despair, and picked up the teapot and the sake placing them on the counter behind her.

Her hands shook as she set them down carefully, not wishing to damage the few items of value Father owned. He owned everything in the small house, including her. A sick feeling swept over her and her limbs felt heavy. Every move required extra effort it seemed.

She walked to the kitchen counter and slid open one of the four cabinet doors. Behind the large pots was a small red clay jar where household money was kept. It was almost empty. Since her mother's death, Father had been less interested in fishing and more interested than ever in drinking and sleeping. She took what was left and started to the village to get something for dinner. Even in the midst of her despair and fear, Sachi did as she was raised to do. Father would expect something to eat.

As she walked the path that strode along the cliffs, she hardly felt the cool ocean breeze on her hot, swollen face. The sea expanded and contracted daily like a woman laboring to bring forth life, each morning bearing treasures on its shores, starfish, shells, and the skeletons of sea-born animals. She stood and closed her eyes, listening to the hush, hush of the ocean as the tide was drawn in and out, rhythmic and soothing. It sounded like a mother comforting a child, her mother comforting her.

Sachi could hear the waves crashing and thought how easy it would be to throw herself from the cliffs into the ocean. If the cliffs didn't kill her, she would just swim until she could no longer. She would probably drown, but that was a prospect more appealing than marriage to Koji Takahashi. She could jump and maybe her mother would appear as an angel to catch her and fly her away. Then she remembered her mother had not converted to Christianity. She and her mother were headed to two different places. Certainly God had worked out a way for them to be together. For what would Heaven be without her mother?

CHAPTER EIGHT

In town Sachi purchased eggplant from Mrs. Yamio who looked at her cheek, knowingly, sadly. She patted Sachi on the arms as she handed her change. "Are you alright Sachi-chan? Your face…"

Sachi immediately lifted her hand to her cheek to hide the swelling, but it was too late. Sachi felt Mrs. Yamio's eyes on her and searched for an explanation. She said, "It's nothing. It's just Father…I didn't want to…"

She stopped and the tears welled up in her eyes. She could think of no words and was embarrassed by the older woman's intense gaze. Mrs. Yamio nodded and whispered, "Shhh…It's alright. I know. Opinions can be dangerous for a woman, especially if they were not the right ones."

Sachi lowered her gaze, bowed, and left without another word. She hurried past the post office, anxious to return home, only so that no one else would ask about her cheek. Mr. Yakusho, the postmaster, stopped her and asked her to come inside. She looked to the ground and held her hand next to her cheek.

He said, "Wait just a minute here. I have a letter here for your father. Would you give it to him?"

"Certainly," she said.

She was surprised and curious. It was unusual for Father to get a letter especially since he could not read.

"It's from America," the man announced, also curious.

He handed the envelope to her and asked, "Who does your father know there?"

Sachi's heart jumped and she forgot about hiding her swollen cheek. There was no return address on the envelope, but one of the postmarks was San Francisco.

Sachi let a smile break across her pained face and said, "I do not know, but thank you."

Before he could ask anything more, Sachi left the post office and walked quickly home, hiding the letter in her skirt pocket, holding it in as if it might jump out and run away. She rushed home so as not to anger Father any more by being late, but she knew the letter had to be from Takeo Watanabe.

As she walked she thought of when she had first learned about America. The missionaries painted a picture of America where things were pure and delightful. Differences were accepted and dreaming was encouraged for everyone, even women. In Japan women had dreams, but they were dreams for their country or family. In America, women could also have dreams for themselves.

That night while Father slept, Sachi pulled the letter from her pocket and read it by candlelight.

Dear Sachi,

I hope this finds you well. Please read this to your father. I sincerely hope it is acceptable.

Dear Mr. Suzuki:

I hope you remember me as well as I remember your daughter Sachi. I now live in California, United States of America and I am doing well. I have a farm and am in need of a wife. My first thought was of Sachi for I always found her to be a hard worker and a pleasant person. I have booked passage for Sachi and her mother on a ship leaving from the Nagasaki shipyard on November 9th. I hope this will prove to be convenient for you. If not, it is exchangeable for an open ticket so she may use it at any time. As soon as Sachi and Mrs. Suzuki arrive here we will send you money as we can. I have little extra and with the cost of the boat trip and the enclosed is all I have at this time. It is for Sachi's trip and anything you might need while Mrs. Suzuki is with us for a few weeks. I hope to see her soon.

Respectfully,

Takeo Watanabe

Sachi's heart pounded as she read the letter several times and marveled at its arrival. Surely her mother was watching over her like the guardian angels they talked of at the missionary school. She read the letter once again, counted the money, then blew out the candle and spent the rest of the night in bed, contemplating, too excited to sleep.

When she arose in the morning, she had a plan. The passing of the next two days was slow, like a stubborn mule refusing to budge. Father spoke to her only if something needed to be done or he was hungry and wanted to eat. Several times when she was not quite fast enough for him, he raised his hand, but he did not hit her. Sachi supposed he did not want to mark his daughter before sending her to Takahashi.

That evening Father returned home late. He entered the house and tossed a large fish on the table for Sachi to clean and cook for supper.

"I went into the village today," he said, looking tired and drunk.

Sachi was afraid to breathe. Except for selling his catch, Father usually sent Sachi to the village. She prayed that he did not go into the post office.

"Why?" Sachi asked casually.

"I had little to sell today, but Chiba said the postmaster told him there was a letter for me."

Suddenly Sachi felt like her head was too heavy for her neck to support. She put her elbows on the table and her head in her hands. He knew and now her life was over. She would never see America and she would be married to a hateful man, a man just like her Father.

She started to rise to retrieve the letter she was sure he would ask to see. He would be angry, so angry he might hit her again and again. Maybe he would make good on his threat to kill her. She began thinking of her mother and trying to still her mind so his loud words would not hurt quite as much.

"I want you to get it tomorrow," Father said.

Sachi stopped and looked at Father. His face needed a shave and his clothes were filthy. He sat on the floor waiting for Sachi to serve tea and prepare the fish.

"Tomorrow?" Sachi asked, all thoughts leaving her mind.

"I went, but Yakusho had already gone home. He does not keep the hours of hard-working fishermen. You will pick up this letter for me tomorrow and read it to me when I return home."

Sachi sighed deeply letting the tension ease from her body. She rose to prepare the fish and plan her escape.

Father left early the next morning and she packed the minute he left. She carefully wrapped her grandmother's tea set and the wedding kimono, which had belonged to her mother. She took the small vinyl covered bible, a gift from her missionary teacher, as well as her mother's hair comb and brush which had become hers when her mother died. She wrapped up dried fish, seaweed, and some bread and rice. It was all she could carry in the bag that had belonged to her grandmother.

Sachi wrote Father a note on a piece of scratch paper from her old school journal with a pencil stub she found in the box with a few of her old school supplies. Opening that box and seeing the used pencils and darkened erasers almost brought her to tears as she thought of leaving her home, the home of her mother and her ancestors.

She rubbed the back of her hand hard across her eyes. There was no time for tears right now. She had to implement her plan quickly and if she had to cry, then let it be on board a ship headed for America.

Sachi knew Father would be unable to read the note, but he would find someone to read it to him in the village. She wasn't sure exactly when the boat was scheduled to leave and didn't want Father taking from her this one chance.

The note read: "I have accepted your decision regarding my marriage. I am leaving early for Mr. Takahashi's home. Forgive me for not being enough. I will dishonor you no longer. Goodbye, Father."

Escape sounded like such a desperate word, but she knew that was what she was doing. Escaping like any living thing would do when it fears for its life. Next to the note she placed half the money Takeo sent.

Before leaving she glanced out the window and gazed one last time at the view. This was one of the precious things that belonged to her mother and her. Like the kimono and the hairbrush, she wished she could take that window with that view and pack it up in her bag. It was the one thing in this house, in this entire village, she would surely miss.

She stared at the ocean, fixing the picture in her mind. Sachi noticed dark clouds gathering in the distance and realized rain might come soon. She began to panic. Father could arrive home early. She said a quick prayer and left the little house on the cliff.

Sachi did not look back, but walked directly to the path leading to the road to Nagasaki where her ship was docked. She was able to find a ride to Nagasaki with a kind merchant and his wife. Sachi told them she was going to visit her sick grandmother and was determined to get there before she died. The couple said they admired her courage and willingness to walk so far to pay her respects to her dying grandmother. They were happy to offer her a space in the back of their horse-drawn wagon. Sachi felt a twinge of guilt about her lie, but the farther she got from Koji Takahashi and Father the better she felt.

When she arrived late that morning, she was told the ship for America would not leave until the next morning at 10:00 a.m. She spent the afternoon in the shops along the streets of Nagasaki admiring the store goods, paper lanterns, beautiful, colorful silk kimonos, foods of all kinds and she wondered when she would have money to buy things like this. She ate dried fish with the bread she had taken from home and stayed that night in the shipyard station. She was tired from lack of sleep over the last several days along with the anxiety of her escape and the possibility of getting caught. In the dark of the station, sitting up on a hard bench and trying to stay alert for strangers or Father, she fell sound asleep.

CHAPTER NINE

Sachi awoke early in the morning to the movements of the shipyard. Men yelled out to one another, loading freight on board the two large ships in port. Bells clanged and ship horns sounded preparations to sail. Dozens of smaller boats docked and sailed in a way that seemed chaotic and haphazard to Sachi. Some unloaded their catch while others were just leaving. Several small boats nearly collided and the men hurled threats and insults at one another.

The smells of fish and salt were familiar smells of home, but the smells of the city, the food and activity were foreign to her. She was anxious to board. The more familiar smells reminded her of Father, as if she sensed his very presence. As she thought of Father everything seemed to take on a dark cast, the cloudy skies, the looming ships, and the murky water of the dock.

The grayness seemed to envelope her like a fog, smothering her, threatening to suffocate her. She walked to where her ship was docked and a young woman, also traveling on the same ship, informed her the departure time was delayed an hour.

Sachi felt herself deflate knowing another hour could make all the difference. Father would surely have taken her note to town by now to have it read to him and he was likely to run into Mr. Yakusho inquiring about his letter from America. It wouldn't take Father long to realize she would never marry Koji Takahashi willingly and that Sachi was headed for America. The closest port for ships bound to America was Nagasaki, and she felt Father was headed here even now. Her mind began racing, but the mule of time slowly plodded forward.

She studied the faces of those around her looking for Father. She saw only the welcome sight of strangers bustling about or waiting as she was waiting. Everything else seemed a blur as she waited for the ship's crew to begin boarding. There had been little in her life that was important enough for her to wait in a line. Her thoughts drifted to the last time she had waited like this. It was many years ago when her mother had taken her to Kyoto to be blessed by a famous Taoist monk. They stood in the hot sun for several hours in a long line of people snaking around the gardens of a large pagoda, waiting to receive the life-changing blessing. All Sachi remembered of the meeting was the small, bald man in brown robes sprinkling water on them and mumbling words that she was told were a prayer especially for her and her mother. But there was not the same urgency to that wait as there was no fear Father would appear at the pagoda for a blessing.

All thoughts of her mother and the past were swept away as Sachi noticed the crew beginning to board passengers on her ship bound for America. Sachi moved with the crowd up a gangplank. She felt nervous and jumpy. If only the people would hurry and board. Suddenly she felt a hand grab her left shoulder. She startled and turned to see it was an elderly gentleman.

"I am sorry miss. This plank is moving about and throwing off my balance," he said, embarrassed.

Sachi smiled with relief that it was not Father and said, "Oh that's alright."

Sachi was about to turn back around and continue up the gangplank when she scanned the crowd out on the pier one last time. That is when she saw him. Bile immediately rose in her throat, hot and burning. She let out a cry.

The old man behind her kindly asked, "Are you alright? Did I bump you again? I am so clumsy on this ramp."

She shook her head and clenched her teeth together so to keep her panic within. Father, in the distance, was marching toward her ship. She hid her face with her shawl, and hunched over so to disappear in the midst of the crowd. Though they were boarding, the ship was not scheduled to leave for another 20 minutes. He had time to find her and force her back to the life that would kill her, if he did not do it first.

She saw fury and determination in his quick strides and purposeful march, gaining speed and strength with each step. He was moving faster than she'd ever seen him move before.

The line to board inched along, but finally she felt her feet hit the metal deck of the ship and she hurried to the closest railing, peering down at the dock. She didn't want Father to see her, but she needed to know where he was. Sachi scanned anxiously for Father, but couldn't find him. The gangplanks were removed and the ship's horn blasted with an impending urgency that Sachi felt to her core.

Suddenly she saw him, and worse, he saw her. He was on the dock, close to the ship, craning his neck upward, searching the faces of those on deck. The intensity of his every movement sent a chill throughout her body.

"Sachi," she saw his lips move, though she could not hear his voice. As he yelled, the ship's horn bellowed long and strong, announcing its departure, drowning out Father, and the ship began slowly pulling away from the dock. She saw his face redden as he screamed now in a state of pure panic, realizing she was sailing away before his eyes and he was unable to stop her. She saw him look about, yelling, trying to find an official or officer with enough authority to stop the ship.

Like a spectator watching as a volcano erupts from a distance, she was stunned at the fury she saw in his eyes, his face. She knew at that moment he would have killed her. She turned her face into the wind, looking ahead, out into the harbor and the vast ocean beyond. She imagined America. She knew she would send Father money as she could. It would arrive at the post office. He would receive it, curse his ungrateful daughter, and accept the money. It was what her mother would want her to do and what any respectful daughter would do, but she knew she would never see him again.

As the ship pulled away, a young Caucasian sailor hurried by. She stopped him and, in her best English, asked, "Ship was to go in more, oh, fifteen minutes, yes?"

He looked at her quizzically and then smiled and said, "Well, strictly speaking we are late, but we loaded up quicker than anticipated and got out a little early."

She smiled brightly. The young man returned her smile and said, "Sometimes you just get lucky."

She cocked her head and looked at him quizzically. It was an American word she'd never heard before.

"Lucky?" she repeated.

He laughed. "Lucky. Like when you meet a pretty girl or the sun shines when it looked like it was going to rain or when you get out 15 minutes earlier than you thought, you understand? Lucky."

She smiled back and said, "Ah, in Japanese, *kichi.*"

The man smiled again, nodded to her and, as he walked away, she whispered to herself, repeating his words, "Sometimes you just get lucky."

CHAPTER TEN

Crossing the Pacific Ocean, leaving one world for another, took two weeks. Ironically the longest leg of Sachi's journey occurred just one mile from San Francisco at Angel Island where Sachi spent three weeks being processed for entry into the country.

When she disembarked on the island, Sachi was given a number, #5108716, to identify her for processing, which often took weeks or months. A few unlucky individuals, with relatives in the eastern part of the United States who couldn't travel to the west, lived on Angel Island, in limbo. Many were sent back to the country from which they came, forced to leave with just a glimpse of "the land of milk and honey".

From the island the detainees could see the city of San Francisco, its skyline, its ship traffic, and its night lights and, to Sachi, it felt close enough to touch. For those who were accepted, the view was inspirational, but for those who were detained months on end or who were sent back to their homelands, it was a visual taunt, a beautiful cruelty.

She observed the people, her fellow immigrants, most of whom were Chinese, but some were Japanese, Filipino, and Russian. She felt strange being among so many who were so different. Their clothing, language, faces, and even the smell of each person was different from the others. She realized this was the texture of America and it would take some getting used to.

When Sachi arrived, she and a group of other women and children were led down a path lined with large oak and pine trees. Through the trees she could see a meadow and grasslands with purple and yellow wildflowers blooming. The colors seemed more vivid than the colors at home. Perhaps, she thought, because she had been at sea for so long. She breathed in the air, the smell of the land. She felt the solid earth beneath her feet, unmoving, and the sun on her face. She was free, free of the ship and the sea and all the bonds of home.

The group was quiet, perhaps sensing the same freedom, as if walking on holy ground, Angel Island. Even the name implied heavenly purpose.

They were led to the Administration building, a large multi-storied barracks with bunk beds and wash basins, where the women and children would live. The men were taken to a separate barracks. Sachi's feeling of freedom disappeared when she noticed armed men standing at the doors allowing them to enter.

The windows of the Administration building were covered with steel mesh, which Sachi later learned was to prevent escape. She suddenly felt caged in. The feeling of restriction and panic was growing and Sachi tried to ignore it, focusing instead on the other women around her.

Sachi placed her bag under her bunk and glanced around the room. A Japanese woman who looked about thirty was lying on the top bunk. She gave Sachi a quick nod and then returned to the magazine she was reading. It said Life on the cover and there was a picture of a blonde woman in a low-cut dress, smiling seductively.

Sachi turned and sat on her bottom bunk. She looked around the room and marveled at the beds. There were dozens of them in this one room. They were permanently placed, bolted to the floor. Sachi thought to herself futons were much more practical and required less space than beds, but space was obviously not a concern for Americans.

Two Japanese women, one older and one who looked to be Sachi's age, stood by the set of bunks next to Sachi. They whispered to one another, looking nervously around and still holding their bags as if they were deciding whether to stay or go. But, of course, there was no place else to go.

Sachi smiled and bowed her head slightly. The women exchanged whispers and the youngest woman approached Sachi.

She bowed to Sachi and Sachi rose, bowing to her as well. The young woman asked, "Excuse me please, but my mother and I were wondering…well…do you know why there are men with guns at the doors?"

Sachi shook her head and said, "I do not know. Perhaps it is to protect us."

Before she could say anything else the woman reading the magazine laughed loudly, vulgarly, and said, "I can tell you why they have guns and it is not for our protection."

Sachi and the young woman were embarrassed and both lowered their eyes to the ground, standing silent at such rudeness from a stranger.

"Ladies, you can look up. I'm not making fun of you."

Sachi and the young woman raised their eyes. The woman in the top bunk had rolled to her side and was facing them, propping her head on her elbow. Her dark hair was cut short and Sachi thought she had a look of experience and fatigue that seemed greater than her years.

"Listen, I know this place. It's home. I have been here almost two years now."

Sachi's eyes grew wide and she drew in a quick breath. She couldn't believe someone would be here for two years. The word slipped from her lips before she could stop it, "Why?"

The woman smiled sarcastically, "Good question. My dear relatives who were supposed to sponsor me suddenly moved to the other side of this huge country and have not yet managed to save enough money to come back for me. So now I sit and wait in this dump until they can come and get me out or, if they do not…"

The smile faded from her lips and she finished, "…Well, I will have to return to Japan."

Even though the words were spoken with a tough, sarcastic tone, Sachi noticed a deep sadness in the woman's eyes. Sachi could see she was hurt and felt forgotten. The woman's words suddenly frightened Sachi to her core. What if Takeo did not come for her? What if Yoshida talked him out of marrying her or he found someone else in the meantime? She could not return to Japan. Sachi's stomach was suddenly tied into knots and she wanted nothing more than to lie down on her bunk. She was tired and now worried. She wanted no more information from the woman above her.

But the young woman next to her asked, "I am sorry. But why do the men have guns if not for our protection?"

The woman on the upper bunk sat up, swinging her legs beneath her. She said, "They are not for our safety and comfort. They are guards to make sure no one here tries to short cut the processing procedure and get into America illegally. You try to get away and they will shoot you."

While Sachi wondered if anything pleasant ever left this woman's lips, the young woman next to Sachi began to visibly shake. She walked back to the older woman standing behind them and whispered to her. Sachi looked up at the woman still swinging her legs and smiling on the upper bunk.

Sachi said, "You make this place sound like a prison more than a processing station."

The woman sneered, "It is. Don't you know what is right next door to this island? Alcatraz. I could throw a stone and hit it from here practically."

Sachi raised her eyebrows and shook her head. "I do not know this place Alcatraz."

The woman resumed her prone position, picked up her magazine, and said, "It is a prison. And you will get to know it. It is just like here."

*　*　*　*

During Sachi's second week on the island she was called into testify, part of the processing procedure which had also included a full health and medical examination. A matron called out her number and then led her from the Administration Building to a smaller building. The matron was an elderly woman with a constant smile who wore soft, white shoes and a large cross around her neck. She led Sachi down a brightly lit hallway and stopped in front of the last door on the right. She smiled at Sachi and signaled, wordlessly, for her to open the door.

Sachi hesitated. She had already undergone the medical and health exam, including the embarrassment of being checked for lice as if she were livestock. It was a humiliating experience and she wondered if further humiliation waited behind the door. She turned the knob and entered to find a small, dim room. Two men sat at a desk, one Japanese and one Caucasian, both dressed in dark suits with ties and white shirts. A guard directed her to stand before them.

"Number 5108716, uh....Sachi Suzuki. Is that right?" asked the white man.

They glanced at papers in front of them on a small table. The Japanese man looked up at her questioningly when she failed to respond immediately.

She spoke quickly, "Oh...yes. Yes. My name is Sachi Suzuki."

"Why are you here?" he asked.

She answered, "I don't know. The matron brought me and said..."

The Japanese man shook his head, and said, "No. No. Why are you here, trying to get into America?"

Other women in the Administration Building had warned her of this questioning, this interrogation. They had warned her that witnesses also testified as to why the immigrant had come to America and ensured they had a place to stay. Witnesses were usually questioned first, so Sachi knew Takeo and his mother, Yoshida, had probably already testified. The men were interrogators and she knew if her answers did not match the answers given by her witnesses, she would be sent back to Japan.

"To marry Takeo Watanabe," Sachi said firmly.

"Where do you come from?"

"Tanchoichi, Japan."

"Describe your village."

"It is a fishing village like many others," said Sachi, unsure what they wanted to hear.

"How many steps from the village pathway to your home?"

"What?" Sachi asked, certain she had misunderstood the question.

When he repeated it, she faltered. She wondered how he could possibly know the answer to that question when she did not and wondered why it would be of any importance. She considered guessing, but what if Takeo or Yoshida had given a different answer?

She took a deep breath and finally said, "I do not know. I never counted them."

The questions continued for an hour. Some made sense to her like how long had she known Takeo and how she had learned English, but others made no sense. They asked how many pairs of chopsticks her family owned and what they ate most often for dinner. These were the questions that scared her most because there was more room for error and she wondered what they considered to be the "right" answers. Sachi left the interrogation feeling confused and frightened. In Japan, she had thought the most difficult part of her journey to America would be crossing an Ocean, but that, Sachi was beginning to realize, was the easy part.

The following week was torture for her. Sachi waited each day with a group of prospective immigrants as numbers were called to inform them who had been selected to go ashore. As each day passed and her number was not called, her heart sank a little more. She imagined being called back to the interrogation room and accused of lying because she'd forgotten the ceremonial chopsticks her mother kept wrapped up and hadn't included them in her answer. Nightmares filled her sleep as she imagined being sent back to Koji Takahashi or Father. She decided she would throw herself from the ship first. She could not go back.

Finally, on the seventh day, two matrons came to announce the names of those who would be departing for America the following day. The women and children in the barracks all gathered around the matrons to listen. It was quiet and the men with guns stood behind the matrons, a constant reminder that they were going nowhere without permission.

The matron with the list of numbers began reading. As she called each number there was a cry of joy from somewhere in the crowd. Each woman had her number memorized. In these barracks, Sachi had learned it was more important to know your number than your name. As the matron reached the end of her list, the tension among the women increased and the cries of joy for those who were called became louder.

Then, like the distant invitation of a ringing bell, Sachi heard the matron call her number. It sounded somehow louder than the other numbers and reminded her of the call to school years ago. She took it to be a sign from her ancestors, from her mother: she was right where she was supposed to be.

The matron repeated it to be certain and Sachi felt her heart, which had been so heavy these past few weeks, lift as if it would spring from her chest. The matrons finished their job and walked out of the barracks. Sachi returned to her bunk to dream of what tomorrow would bring and her eyes fell on her bunkmate. She was hidden behind the same magazine. She heard sniffling and knew the woman was crying at again being left to sit and wait and wonder if anyone would come to claim her. Sachi wanted to reach out to her, but could think of no words to comfort her. Sachi's good fortune at being processed in less than a month would not help this woman feel better. Sachi remained silent and crawled into her bunk. Tomorrow she was going home.

CHAPTER ELEVEN

San Francisco - 1923

Sachi stood on the deck of a small, crowded ferry headed across the one mile stretch of water from Angel Island to San Francisco. A strong, cool wind came off the water, leaving the taste of salt on Sachi's tongue, as the ferry skimmed across the choppy waters of the San Francisco Bay. Seagulls and pelicans swooped down searching for crumbs and discarded bits of food then escaped back up into the blue. People moved about the ferry, so excited they found it impossible to keep still. As the cityscape before her came closer with each passing moment, the anticipation and sounds of the passengers grew.

The ferry pulled into Pier 39 and Sachi searched the faces of the crowd on the dock, immediately catching sight of Takeo. He was positioned at the front of the crowds making Sachi think he had been waiting a while. Maybe he was the first to arrive. She watched as he nervously checked the buttons on his shirt, making sure it was tucked tightly into his pants. He pulled the front of his suit coat around his large middle and tried to button it, but the coat was too small and Sachi thought she detected a faint look of frustration in his face. He pulled out a handkerchief from his pocket and wiped his brow and the back of his neck. It was a cool morning, but Takeo was sweating.

Sachi marveled at the fact that Takeo looked nervous. She had been so focused on her own fears she hadn't considered Takeo may have the same feelings. She found herself smiling at the thought that she could have this kind of effect on a man. She watched as he shoved the handkerchief back into his pocket and began searching the faces of the passengers.

Passengers surged for position closest to the gangplank exit and Sachi was suddenly jostled toward the back. She held tight to her bag and patiently waited for the people to disembark. She had waited this long. A few minutes more would make no difference.

When she finally stepped onto the dock much of the crowd had dispersed away from the ferry. Takeo stood before her, wiping his brow again. He hurried to her and stopped, bowing as deeply as he could. Sachi did as well, keeping her eyes to the ground in diffidence.

Takeo spoke in Japanese, "Welcome to America, Sachi. We have been waiting for you."

Sachi responded, her eyes still lowered, "I hope you were not inconvenienced by having to come and get me Watanabe-san."

"It is an honor," he responded.

They both stood facing one another in silence. Sachi's long dark hair was piled on top of her head making her slightly taller than Takeo. His clothes were ironed and neat. He was heavy, which Sachi interpreted to mean prosperous. Sachi wore a long black cotton skirt with a white cotton shirt that fit almost like a tunic. She pulled the heavy black shawl tighter around her shoulders. The breeze off the bay was chilly and Sachi began shaking. The cold had not bothered her until now. Perhaps it was nerves she thought.

"Oh, uh, here, let me carry that," Takeo said, stuffing the forgotten handkerchief in his back pocket and awkwardly grabbing the bag from Sachi.

"Thank you," she said.

Again they stood in silence. Someone bumped against him and it seemed to awaken him. He said, "Well, we have a long ride home. Let us get something to eat before we leave."

Sachi responded in English, "That would be very nice."

Takeo said, "You do speak English."

She smiled shyly. "Yes. I practice my English good for people on ship. I work to talk better to people in America."

Takeo nodded solemnly, "It is good for you to know English. Life will be easier here for you and it will be good for you to teach it to our children as well. They will be Americans speaking English."

Sachi's face reddened at the mention of children. Having children seemed to belong in the distant future, far from where she stood at the moment. She looked into Takeo's eyes just long enough for her to see he had softness in his face that came not from his corpulent outside, but rather a kindness deep inside. He was not a handsome man, but that was unimportant. He had rescued her from a life she did not think she could bear and she would spend the rest of her life in service to him as his wife and the mother of his children. She was grateful and from that gratitude love and desire might grow.

Her glance moved from his soft dark eyes to two men standing just behind Takeo. She had not noticed them before, but now they stood together staring at her. She bent her head so as not to look them in the eyes. That would be rude.

As she turned her eyes toward the ground she heard one man say loudly to the other, "Another boat load of Jap bimbos."

"Come to make more Japs over here. Go home," the other said. "Go back to Nipville."

Sachi did not understand their meaning, but sensed they were trying to convey something important. Perhaps she was supposed to do something and didn't understand. They sounded angry, barking. Maybe she needed to move. She raised her eyes and looked into Takeo's face questioningly.

Waiting for direction she saw the softness in his face had hardened. His jaw was set tight and the kindly eyes had turned steely. She had done something wrong and had angered him. The last thing she wanted to do. She was always so clumsy, fumbling at the wrong time, doing the wrong thing. Was it possible he could send her back?

She hesitated for a moment, unsure of what to do or say. Takeo took her bag in one hand and her arm in the other.

He said sternly, "We should move."

They walked together, side by side, past the two men who were still staring, nasty sneers on their faces, faces which seemed to her so strange, almost cartoonish, with their large noses that took up almost the whole of the face and those wide, round eyes, much too round for their small pupils.

Takeo gripped her arm even tighter and they moved past the men. Sachi panicked thinking he was taking her to send her back home. She could not go back without knowing what had incurred his anger. Maybe she could make it right, correct her mistake. She would promise to do better and learn more quickly. It would never happen again.

Speaking his name for the first time that day, she said, "I…I don't understand Takeo."

He loosened his grip on her arm and as she peered at him, his face seemed to soften just a little, but the steeled jaw and angry eyes remained. Still he did not speak.

"Did I do something? I know I have much to learn about American ways. I learn quickly. If you just tell me…"

"Yes. You will learn quickly, "he said, distractedly, almost as if to himself. "And what you will learn is that there are people, Americans, who do not want you here. They think you should stay and marry in Japan. They think… "

Sachi's first thought was they all somehow knew she had fled Japan. She thought of Father and the dishonor she had brought to his name and his house by breaking his promise of her marriage to Koji Takahashi. Did they know about that? Had Father gotten word to Takeo? Perhaps in America that was something that could keep you out? They had not asked any direct questions about those arrangements at Angel Island. They did not ask if she were promised to another man.

91

"I did not know. Takeo, I am sorry. I do not wish to bring dishonor to you, but I cannot go back. I cannot marry Koji Takahashi. I will do what is done here in America for such dishonor, but I cannot go back, even if the Americans do not want me here."

He stopped, his eyes narrowed, and he tightened his grip on her arm.

"What do you mean you were to marry Koji Takahashi?"

Sachi drew in a deep breath, unsure where to start. She looked into his eyes, pleading, and suddenly the words tumbled from her lips like cherry blossoms from the trees in a strong wind. "Father promised this man, Koji Takahashi, I would marry him. I told Father I could not. He was a small, mean man. I told him of your promise to send for me, but Father was insistent. So when I received your letter and the money I...well...I just boarded the ship and came."

Takeo stood silent for a moment lost in thought. Sachi held her breath and looked down at the wooden planks under her feet. Here they stood at the entrance to the docks. People bustling around them, coming and going, and yet she felt frozen in time, held to this spot as Takeo considered her words.

"Where is your mother?" Takeo asked.

The question was so unexpected that Sachi looked up as if she had not heard him correctly. "What did you say?" she asked.

"You said your mother would come with you and we did not testify for her. Was she also for this marriage to Koji Takahashi?"

"No," Sachi lied. "My mother was against that marriage. My mother...she is very happy for me. She just couldn't come with me."

She did not know why she didn't tell him about the earthquake and her mother's death, but the words of truth would not come. It seemed too intimate to share with this man who was little more than a stranger to her. She was not ready for the kind of closeness sharing a death would bring and she did not want him to feel sadness for her on this day.

He looked at her as if trying to decipher her thoughts and then said decidedly, "I told you when I left for America with my mother I would send for you. That was a pledge. A pledge that was made before Mr. Takahashi even knew there was a Sachi. Therefore, you did not dishonor your father or yourself. You honor me by remembering and honoring that pledge."

Later they would laugh at how Sachi could think the whole of America would know of her and her life in Japan and how the entire country would not want her here. But today she smiled at him and they walked down the street together.

The shops, people, and activity energized Sachi. She had felt isolated and alone and now she was walking with the man she would marry in the country she was certain she would love. She breathed deeply, taking in the unique perfume of San Francisco, the ocean combined with the smell of coffee brewing, sourdough baking, hot dogs grilling, and flowers for sale. People hurried on their way to obviously important destinations.

White and grey gulls playfully swooped and dove at anything resembling food. She stopped at a shop to look in the window.

In Tanchoichi there was one store to sell many things. In America, there were many stores that sold only one thing; clothing in one, shoes in another, bread, flowers, jewelry. Each item had its own store. There was no shortage of space in America. So many things to see it was like looking through a kaleidoscope and trying to focus.

She felt the same dizziness when looking up at the tall buildings. Japanese buildings were shorter like sumo wrestlers sitting back on their heels. American buildings were towering structures. They seemed to swagger amidst the skyline, competing against the others like cowboys out of the old west. The buildings in America were like the mountains in Japan. Everything was large and grand and dizzying here.

Suddenly a woman rushed from the store in front of her, speaking in a harsh tone, spitting out the words, "No Japs", and pointing feverishly to a sign in the front of the store. It was a poster with the picture of a white man in a suit. His graying hair was slicked back making no effort to hide his receding hairline. His large nose topped a scraggly moustache and beard that matched his graying hair. He did not look happy in the picture, but solemn and serious. Above his picture were the words "Keep California White."

Takeo looked at the woman, shook his head, and taking Sachi by the arm, walked away without responding to her. Sachi could hear the woman still yelling at them. She wondered if she had again made another misstep. Takeo had the same icy stare as at the shipyard. Perhaps one did not look in store windows in America without being invited.

They walked to where Takeo had parked on the street. Takeo opened the passenger door of a black car. He motioned for her to get in and placed her bag in the back of the car. She had heard of cars, but, at 17 years old, she had never ridden in one. No one at home owned one. She was nervous and excited and watched his every move as he went to the front of the car and cranked something then got behind the wheel and started the engine.

"We will eat in Japan Town," Takeo announced.

Sachi nodded. She did not know what Japan Town might be, but she was too busy readying herself for the ride. Her left hand clutched the seat and her right tightly gripped the door handle, anticipating the speed. He looked at her, his brow in a frown and then laughed out loud, but said nothing. As the car turned into the street and began to pick up speed, Sachi realized they were protected from the wind and the ride was calm and smooth. As if they were in a time machine, in a matter of minutes they entered another world.

"This is it," Takeo announced. "This is Japan Town."

The buildings were not as grand as the ones Sachi had seen earlier. They were smaller and made of wood and brick. Some were topped with elaborate roofs and curling edges like the pagodas in Japan. She could easily read the advertisements in the shop windows. Everyone around her looked like she did; they were almost all Japanese. They parked the car and walked to a Japanese restaurant. She heard her native tongue spoken by everyone around her. It had taken almost five weeks for her to go from Japan to America, but it had taken a quick drive down the street to go back again. She immediately felt at home.

Takeo ordered in Japanese, "We will have hirame, rice and ale."

He glanced at Sachi and added, "And also tamago."

Sachi smiled as she sipped her tea. Tamago was one of her favorites, a sweet egg custard wrapped in dried seaweed. She had hoped her first meal in America would be more American like the hot dogs she heard about from people on the ship, but she did not let her disappointment show. This meal was a feast, her first time eating in a restaurant. There would be time for American food later she thought. There would be a lifetime.

"Why does America have a Japan town?" Sachi asked as she sipped her tea.

To her it made little sense to travel thousands of miles from Japan only to end up in a restaurant that could have been in any large Japanese city, eating the same Japanese dishes. Were the Japanese so loved by the Americans that they had a town named for them?

Takeo smiled, but there was a shadow of melancholy on his face. He said, "The Japanese people find comfort in it. They find strength and support in a community of their own people. Japan Town simply formed itself out of necessity and homesickness, I suppose. It is a place a Japanese person can be sure of. We know we will be served a meal or are welcomed to buy food or other goods. That assurance does not always exist outside Japan Town."

Sachi was not at all sure what he meant, but she sensed anger in Takeo's words and sadness. They sat silent, sipping tea. The restaurant was only half full and all of the patrons were Japanese.

After their meal was served and they began eating, Sachi asked, "Are all whites so quick tempered? I noticed the men at the shipyard and the woman at the shop. I'm sure I was doing something wrong, but the looks on their faces - they were so angry. I was hoping you would tell me what I did wrong and how I might correct it so I do not dishonor you here in America."

Takeo looked at her softly for a moment and then said, "You did nothing wrong, Sachi. It's as I told you. Some Americans just do not want Japanese here. Unfortunately, you have seen those kinds of people before you have met the others. Japanese are not welcome in all places. We are not welcome in many of the schools. We are not welcome in Golden Gate Park here in San Francisco. We are not welcome in many restaurants. That is part of the reason Japan Town is so important to many Japanese."

Sachi considered this and asked, "Is the sour-faced man on the poster important here in America?"

"The poster?" Takeo asked.

"The one in the woman's shop."

"That man is trying to get Americans to choose him as their leader. This man, James D. Phelan, is a leader, the mayor, of this city, San Francisco. He wants Americans to choose him to be a Senator for the state of California so that he can go to Washington D.C. and help make laws and rules for the United States. That poster was a way for people who pass by to see his name and picture, to remember him and to choose him."

Sachi was confused, but pressed on, "But why was the woman pointing to the poster. Does she want you to choose him?"

Takeo shook his head as he lifted his rice bowl and took a bite of rice with the hirame. He swallowed and answered, "No, no. I am not American. I cannot vote. Only Americans can vote. The poster was her way of telling us we were not welcome in her shop. The poster said, "Keep California White". She did not want us near her business. She only wants to have customers who are white, not Japanese. Do you understand?"

Sachi thought the business of a shopkeeper was selling and certainly American money from a Japanese person was just as valuable as the same amount from a white person. It did not make sense to her. She shook her head and answered, "No. I do not understand."

Takeo simply answered, "You will."

CHAPTER TWELVE

They left Japan Town and the wind from the speed of the car seemed to blow all negative thoughts from Sachi's mind as they raced down the road. They left the movement, the hilliness, the largeness of San Francisco and headed toward the farming communities where everything was green, lush, and welcoming. The land flattened out and Sachi was amazed at how far she could see. She had never been on land where there were no hills or mountains and being out now in the farming communities reminded her of her travels across the Pacific. That is how America must be - vast as the ocean.

Takeo said her second day in America was to be their wedding day. She was surprised at the urgency of the wedding, but assumed it would be awkward for Takeo to have her in his home for an extended period of time without being married. Perhaps he felt he had waited long enough. Takeo explained his father had died the previous year from a heart attack brought on by exhaustion. The exhaustion occurred from working their farm night and day. Takeo shared with her how his father rose every morning well before sunrise to begin work. There were no holidays or vacations, simply work.

As they drove the hours toward home Takeo grew silent. Sachi thought back to the day when he left their village with his father many years ago. He was filled with self-confidence and even boasted to his friends about how much money there was to be made in America. Now he was quiet and Sachi noticed his hands were marked with work, tough, dry, and weathered. Even his face seemed much older than when she had seen him last, only six months ago. His smile was not as quick as she remembered, but she knew he was a kind man and she vowed to be a good wife to him. She owed him her life.

Sachi, watching Takeo operate the car so effortlessly, asked, "Is it difficult?"

"What?"

"Driving."

Takeo smiled and said, "Oh no. I will teach you. Put your hand on the wheel."

He reached over and, taking her left hand in his, gently placed it on the steering wheel. At the touch of Takeo's hand, Sachi felt the calloused skin of his palm from hard work and clamminess from nerves. There was no excitement in her at his touch, but she expected that would come and it did as he placed her hand on the wheel before him. She was exhilarated. She felt the vibrations of the vehicle as if she were feeling its heart beat. She was driving, almost. Her eyes grew wide and she drew in a deep breath.

Takeo misinterpreted her response as fear. He said, "It's nothing to be afraid of. You will get the hang of it someday."

He smiled, patted her hand, and removed it from the wheel. She wanted to tell him she was not afraid, but thrilled. She wanted to learn more, but he looked so self-satisfied and protective of her she said nothing. There would be plenty of time to learn to drive she thought.

Sachi asked, "Will you tell me about…?" She stopped, realizing she did not even know the name of the place she would be living.

"Will you tell me about your village?"

Takeo smiled and said, "Orange Grove is much larger than Tanchoichi. It is not a village, but it is not like San Francisco either. It is a town and most of the people around are farmers. It has a post office and *two* stores, a temple, a church, a feed lot, a clothing store, a drug store, a bank, a gas station. It has everything really. It has grown a lot the past few years. We are almost there now."

Sachi was listening and looking out the window watching the countryside fly by. A few minutes later they passed a sign and Sachi could not help reading it aloud, "Welcome to Orange Grove."

They entered the town and it was as Takeo had described. There were many businesses and people walking from place to place. There were cars parked on the side of the road and several horses tied up to posts. Not everyone traveled by car in this country Sachi thought to herself, but she was happy Takeo owned one and decided it must be, like his large waistline, a sign he was prosperous.

As they drove out of town toward Takeo's farm, Sachi noticed three small wooden shacks with several women sitting outside. The shacks, situated to the right of the road, were almost hidden by several large trees. There were no fields around these shacks and they sat on a small hill. The women appeared to be idle. Sachi might not have even noticed them if she had not been eagerly taking in every detail of her new town.

"What are those women doing?" she asked, pointing to the clump of trees.

Takeo said quickly, "They are not women you will ever know."

Sachi continued to look at Takeo. He drew in his breath and spoke slowly, "They entertain men. Do you know what I mean?"

Sachi thought for a minute and asked, "Like the Geisha?"

She had heard of Geisha at home and had even seen one once. The Geisha woman she had seen was beautiful with graceful carriage and confidence. Her kimono was turquoise with a greenish embroidered pattern toward the bottom that made Sachi immediately think of the ocean. Her hair was beautifully coiffed and her skin was painted white with deep red lips. Her neck, the most sensual part of a woman's body, was exposed just slightly.

These women were not like the woman she had seen. Of course, she knew there were different levels of Geisha as well. The one she had seen was very expensive according to what she overheard people say in the village. It was quite an experience when the Geisha stopped into town with the gentleman who was there for business. They stayed only a few hours, but long enough for many people to get into town in time to view this beautiful creature like artwork on display. Sachi had admired her beauty, her clothes, and her tiny feet. She knew what many Geisha did to acquire that lifestyle.

"Yes." Takeo answered. "Sort of like Geisha, but without the skill of Geisha. These women do not serve tea and dance and sing and converse like Geisha. It is..."

Finally he said, "Let's just say it all translates the same."

"But this is America? Is this kind of thing allowed in America?"

Takeo looked quizzical and asked, "It is not allowed under the law, but it is ignored. Why do you think America would not allow it?"

Sachi said, "Everyone knows America is a great land where religion and morality are respected. In school, the missionaries taught us America is a Christian country where freedom and kindness are deeply valued. I thought America would be this way, pious and kind and...and...holy."

"You have been in America four hours. You have seen the men at the docks, the woman at the shop, these women living as they do. Does this seem kind and holy to you?"

Sachi shook her head slightly. Takeo watched the road ahead and then loudly said, "America is not kind and holy. America is a country of many people and everyone is struggling to compete, to reach this thing they call the American dream. You will meet a few people who are kind, just like at home in Japan. You will also meet people who are not, just like at home."

They drove in silence the remainder of the journey and Sachi was grateful. She was lost in her own thoughts and the view of the countryside speeding by her until Takeo announced, "Here we are."

Takeo's farm was a lush, green 30 acres and the house was a five room wood structure, but it looked like a palace to Sachi. The house smelled of fresh paint. There was a large barn to the right where chickens scratched freely in the dirt and a milk cow languorously wandered at her will. The strawberry fields and grape vines were in the back and between the house and the field was a large vegetable garden. Even in the midst of winter there seemed to be growth and life everywhere she looked.

Takeo drove the car down the small dirt path leading from the main road to the house. Sachi pulled open the car door and waved the road dust from her face. She gazed around, visually taking in her new home, while Takeo retrieved her bag and then escorted her up to the house.

Yoshida Watanabe sat on the porch in a small wicker chair, rocking back and forth. She looked smaller than Sachi remembered and her gray hair was pulled back. Her mouth was puckered in a tight grimace and her eyes looked larger behind wire-framed glasses. She was sewing something Sachi could not make out, a small piece of cloth that barely covered her lap. The rocking seemed as important as the sewing and Yoshida did not stop either task as they approached.

Takeo set the bag on the porch and introduced Sachi to his mother. They had known one another in Japan, but the introduction was formal as if they had never met before.

Sachi bowed deeply to Yoshida Watanabe and said in Japanese, "It is an honor to see you again."

Yoshida remained seated, rocking and sewing, but bowed her head toward Sachi in acknowledgement.

Yoshida said in English, "It is good you have finally arrived. We can use much help. Takeo, does she speak English?"

Takeo answered, "Yes. Her English is quite good. As are her manners."

Yoshida snipped, "It will need to be."

Takeo added, "And, of course, you speak Japanese mamma-san."

Yoshida snapped, "I know what I speak."

Takeo, gently chiding his mother, said, "Then speak to her about what she knows, not to me. I have work to do."

He looked at Sachi and said, "I will put your bag in my room. You will sleep there tonight and I will sleep in the living room."

Yoshida interrupted, "She may sleep in my room tonight."

Sachi suddenly felt like a piece of new furniture, a couch or a lamp. The residents were arguing over where to place it and where it would look best.

Sachi added, "Your mother is right. There is no need to put you out."

Takeo raised his voice just slightly and said, "Is this how it is to be with two women in the house now? Both of you in disagreement with what I say? Mother, we have discussed arrangements. Sachi, you will sleep in my room. It will soon be our room and I want you to feel comfortable there."

Both women bowed their heads to show their submission and discomfort in reference to the marital bedroom. Takeo's remarks of women in the house reminded her of Father and she vowed to watch her words and not to argue with him again.

Sachi felt as if her feet were planted into the ground along with everything else at this farm. She stayed, watching even after the swinging screen door closed and he had gone inside.

105

Sachi knew it was her destiny, as her mother and grandmother before her, to go to a new home and live in submission to her in-laws, but Yoshida was not going to make it easy for her and sat quietly sewing for several minutes. Sachi shifted feet waiting for an invitation or even an order, anything that would take her from this spot in which she felt rooted. Her knees began to tremble and she thought for a moment she might faint from the excitement of having reached her destination, but she was unable to move.

Yoshida finally nodded toward the only other chair on the porch, a straight-backed cane chair, and said, "Since you are staying with us you might wish to sit down. There are many things I need to tell you."

"Thank you," Sachi said as she accepted the invitation, to sit, such as it was, and sank gratefully into the chair.

Yoshida began, "Now I know you were educated at that missionary school. I knew your mother, of course, a fine woman, but always looking to go beyond her station."

Sachi dug her nails into her palm at this criticism of her mother and thought to herself that Yoshida had come to America in an attempt to go beyond her "station". She did not mention her mother's death and instead bit her bottom lip and remained silent as Yoshida continued.

"Since Takeo and I have been alone for the last while the work has been difficult. I have worked the fields alongside my son, but age is coming to me and I cannot do all I once could. We must work hard here, harder than most. That is why we sent for you."

Again Sachi sat quietly. The old woman made it sound as if she had sent for Sachi as much as Takeo and as she listened she learned it was likely true.

"It is well past the time for Takeo to take a wife. He needs a wife for himself, but more importantly he needs a wife to work beside him in the fields as I have done, and to bear his children, so that they may also help with the farm and sustain this family."

Yoshida laughed a laugh without humor, "There are few Japanese American women who would marry a Japanese man, not that Takeo would consider that. There are laws forbidding marriage between whites and Mongolians, which is how they refer to all of us. Mongoloid races. But Takeo would not marry one anyway. American women or Japanese women who have been raised in America are both the same. They are spoiled and unsuitable for this life. They would expect to be treated as a guest in their home, not working in the fields like a farm hand. Of course, most of the Japanese women who are here are married. That is why they were sent for in the first place. We had no choice, but to send for someone in Japan and Takeo mentioned that he thought you would be a hard worker, particularly since you are a big, strong girl. Not one of those delicate flowers that wilt in the heat. You will bear many children and right away, mind you. Takeo has put off fatherhood much longer than he should. And, at some point, when we have made enough money and return to Japan, you will go with us since it is your home as well."

Each sentence Yoshida uttered stunned Sachi. She sat dismayed as her future mother-in-law laid out her life for her in a few minutes and with as much thought as if she were a dairy cow. "Now you will produce five gallons of milk each day and seven calves and then when that is through you will pull the plow and then be put to pasture and then you will die."

But it was this last sentence that compelled her to speak.

"Return to Japan?" she repeated.

Seemingly unaware of the panic in Sachi's voice, Yoshida said, "Of course. That's why we came here to America, to make money and return home. You will find that is what most Japanese have in mind."

"But don't you like it here?"

Yoshida grunted and raised her eyebrows, "It is not Japan. We agreed before leaving home we would come to America. We would come and work hard and make a little money so when we return home we can live well. That is why Takeo is forcing this confusing language on me so we will succeed in this place. It is the only reason I agreed to come here with Takeo in the first place. Many of the women of my generation have not even bothered to learn this language because they know they are going back and will never have to use it again, but Takeo insists we learn English."

Sachi again was quiet, feeling dispirited by her mother-in-law's words. She was tired from her journey and the excitement of the day. She would talk to Takeo. Surely he didn't send for her just to return. No. Her mother-in-law must be mistaken or perhaps simply homesick.

Yoshida continued her sewing, not missing a stitch since Sachi's arrival. Sachi watched her rock in rhythm with each push and pull of the needle. It was hypnotic and after many minutes of silence Sachi was on the verge of dozing off.

Yoshida suddenly stopped rocking, stood, and said, "We may as well begin. The kitchen is yours. I will show you where everything is. You may make us a cup of tea and we will discuss the meals you are to prepare each day. Most likely you do not know how to cook, but you will learn."

Sachi opened her eyes, stirred from her dreamy daze, and said, "I was hoping we could discuss the wedding tomorrow."

Yoshida ordered, "In the kitchen, over tea, and after I have explained the meals to you."

Sachi followed Yoshida into the house. The front room or living room, as she was to learn its name, was for listening to the large radio in the corner or visiting with guests. The cooking and eating were done in the adjoining kitchen, a completely separate room. As Sachi passed through the living room she stopped to admire the porcelain figurines on the sturdy wooden table in the opposite corner from the radio. The couch and two chairs faced one another in the middle of the room and there were two paintings hanging on the walls. One was a floral garden with many colors and one was of a man fishing in the sunset in a small boat on a lake. She thought of Father then quickly brushed the thought from her mind.

Sachi smiled at the little porcelain figures. They each stood about six inches tall and were made of delicate, shiny, white china. There was a porcelain boy holding a lantern and he was turned, just so, facing a smaller porcelain girl holding an umbrella. A girl with flowers stood alone, smiling. A boy sat cross-legged, fishing pole in hand, with his dog sitting next to him while a little girl stood beside him holding up a string of fish. There was a mother holding her baby high in front of her, looking at him, smiling. And there was another statue of a mother reading while her daughter rested in her lap. These beautiful, white, porcelain figures were without color, but each was carefully detailed with tiny fingers and toes and faces. They were expressive and looked like little dolls to Sachi.

She leaned over, her hand outstretched, to touch one of the statues, the mother and daughter. She wanted to feel the cool, smooth porcelain on her fingertips. Yoshida stopped her.

"No one touches these, but me," she commanded. "You will dust and sweep this room. Dust everything, that is, but these. I will do that myself."

Sachi pulled back her hand and nodded. Like all good Japanese wives, she had escaped Father's demands and now she would do as her mother-in-law and husband demanded. She followed Yoshida into the kitchen to make tea.

CHAPTER THIRTEEN

The next morning Sachi stood looking out the small bedroom window at the sun rising to greet her wedding day. She slept fitfully even though she was tired. She feared oversleeping and wakening to Yoshida's scowling face telling her to rise. Sachi lingered at the window only a moment before getting dressed to fix breakfast for her new family.

She hurried to the kitchen to begin making tea. Yoshida had not yet risen, but Takeo had already milked the cow and collected eggs. He stood in a t-shirt and overalls washing his hands at the sink. A bucket of fresh milk stood by the table and six eggs sat on the counter.

Sachi smiled and bowed her head slightly as she entered the kitchen and waited for Takeo to finish before she approached the sink to put water in the kettle.

The prior afternoon Yoshida explained the meals and everything else expected of Sachi. She was responsible for the kitchen and helping Takeo in the fields as well as keeping the house clean and caring for the animals. Yoshida would help her with the laundry and the shopping as well as incidental chores like sewing. Yoshida did not like cooking much and was happy to give the job to Sachi on the condition that the food was good. If not, Yoshida made it clear she would take over that job and it would be a great dishonor for Sachi.

There were no words spoken between Takeo and Sachi that first morning and no superstition about seeing the bride on the wedding day. Sachi bustled around the kitchen frying eggs and sausages while Takeo sat and watched her. To an outside observer they might appear as a couple married for many years. There was a comfortableness that existed on this first morning. Sachi knew they could marry and work together.

Yoshida rose at the smell of breakfast and entered the kitchen breaking the serene silence. She explained that after breakfast they would dress for the ceremony to be held at 11:00 a.m. in the local Buddhist temple. Sachi was not asked where she would prefer the ceremony to take place, but it was of little concern to her. She could easily slip on the glove of Buddhism for this one day. She had a lifetime to convince Takeo to convert or, at least, allow her to attend the religious ceremony of her choosing. Religious freedom was one of the promises of this country. Like love and passion, it would be a promise kept to her eventually. All things were achieved through patience.

After breakfast Sachi went to the bedroom to dress. She pulled out her mother's white silk wedding kimono, *shiromuku*, which she had carried half way around the world. White signified the beginning of a journey and Sachi thought perhaps she should have been wearing this on the ship to America since that was truly the beginning of her journey. She put on the *tabi,* the pure white split-toe socks to wear with her *zori* sandals. She put on the under garments and then wrapped the kimono around herself. After all these years of thinking some day she would wear her mother's kimono it felt strange, not familiar as she expected.

Yoshida knocked loudly. Sachi made sure she was fully clothed except for the obi before allowing Yoshida into the room.

Without a word Yoshida took Sachi's *obi,* a thirteen-foot long and 12 inch wide piece of silk, and constructed an almost- perfect *taiko-musubi*, a drum bow, in the back, which puffed out beautifully like a small satin pillow. She placed in Sachi's hand an abalone hair pin in the shape of a fan for the back of her swept up hair.

She said, "I wore this on my wedding day. I thought you would use it today."

"Thank you," Sachi said, accepting it gratefully and smiling slightly at her soon to be mother-in-law.

Yoshida did not return the smile. She glanced at Sachi from head to toe and declared, "This will have to do."

Yosida left the room and closed the door. Sachi stared into the mirror hanging on the wall over the dresser. The kimono was beautiful. The shoulders were snug and it did not have *furisode,* the long-flowing sleeves of the unmarried woman's kimono. The kimono was a bit tight as she was a little larger than her mother had been, but it fit well enough. She thought of what her mother must have looked like on her wedding day. She wondered if she had felt the same apprehension, uncertainty, and nervousness.

Sachi wanted her mother in the same way she'd wanted her as a child, to calm her and tell her everything would be fine, and to tell her she was beautiful. Sachi had never felt more alone. These people were not hers. There was no one from her previous life to escort her into her future life. No one at the temple would be there for her today.

She stopped thinking of her mother and instead put in her mind the image of Koji Takahashi. To steel herself she recalled quickly what life with him would have been like and the tears ceased. She drew a deep and steady breath as she counted her blessings. She was here, in America, where her mother had wanted her to go. She was far from Takahashi and about to marry a man who by all accounts was good and someone who would take care of her.

Yoshida knocked on the door again. Sachi blinked the tear residue away and answered.

Yoshida stood in a cotton blue dress with faux pearl buttons trailing down the front. Her hair was pulled back from her bare face in a tight bun clasped in place with several tremulous bobby pins and one looked on the verge of escape. Sachi thought to say something, but before she could Yoshida said, "Don't keep us all waiting. It is time to go."

Sachi ignored the escaping bobby pin and followed Yoshida from the room. Takeo stood in the living room in black trousers and a dress shirt. On a hanger he carried a long, black, silk coat.

Takeo did not move as Sachi entered the room. Sachi could not look into his eyes. She felt self-conscious in the white wedding kimono as the center of attention and she looked at the wooden floor. From the corner of her eye, Sachi saw Takeo staring at her for a moment, but then he bowed and said, "Sachi, you look…"

A car horn honked loudly outside, interrupting him.

Yoshida said, "That is Duke. Where is my pocketbook? "

Takeo didn't finish his sentence. Instead he pointed to the large black pocketbook on the table and led the way from the house followed by Yoshida and Sachi. A voice boomed from a car outside. A large Japanese man with thick black hair and lively eyes sat in the driver's seat, honking and smiling broadly. He waved at the trio as they approached the car. Takeo opened the passenger side. Yoshida climbed slowly into the back seat and said, "Duke, stop all this racket. You're scaring the animals."

The man laughed and said, "It's Takeo's wedding day. It's a day for loud noises."

He stopped honking as Takeo climbed in behind his mother, squeezing into the back seat, leaving Sachi to sit next to the noisy stranger since her kimono was not made for climbing into the back of cars. She knew it was more practical for her to sit up front, but Sachi still felt isolated, as if the man she was to marry chose riding next to his mother over her. This was not a good beginning.

Takeo said, "Sachi, this is my best friend and my best man, Dyuke Satamora. He prefers Duke."

Duke nodded his head and smiled.

"Soon to be Sachi Watanabe, I presume, from the get up," he said, pointing at her kimono.

Sachi did not understand.

She repeated, "Get up?"

She started to rise in her seat and Duke burst out laughing. Takeo put a hand on her shoulder from behind keeping her in her seat.

Duke shook his head and said, "Your get up. Your kimono, what you're wearing. In America we sometimes say your "get up"."

Sachi's face burned with embarrassment over her lack of understanding. She did not like this man and would stay as far away from him as possible.

Yoshida said to Duke, "Sachi is not interested in your American phrases. Speak in Japanese if you can't speak English without your useless slang."

Sachi was thankful for her mother-in-law's words, but Yoshida added, "Sachi, you're going to have to learn not to be so gullible."

Sachi said nothing, staring at the floorboard and her feet. She wished she could jump out of the car and go… Where? She had nowhere to go. She had no one else besides the mother and son in the back seat of the car. She continued to try and keep Koji Takahashi in her mind. He was the alternative and it strengthened her resolve. Funny, she thought, that she would be thinking of the man she despised on her wedding day in this new country. She wondered how he reacted when he found out she had gone. She smiled to herself thinking of how angry he must have been.

Duke interrupted her thoughts and said, "I wasn't making fun. You look beautiful. It's been a while since I have seen kimono and it makes me think of my family back home. I hope a wife will help with that. I'm working on the wife part and then you all will be coming to fetch me for my wedding."

Sachi nodded politely and counted another blessing: she did not have to marry Duke. She pitied the poor unsuspecting girl who did.

Duke continued, "The *baishakunin* here has shown me several prospects. Several appeared to be very ugly or not photogenic, but either way I'm not inviting them out. You have to think about the children, your future, you know those kinds of things."

Takeo chided his friend, "Beauty means little, Duke."

Duke laughed, "You're one to talk. You have the most beautiful girl in Orange Grove."

Sachi blushed in spite of her dislike for Duke. It was nice to receive at least one compliment on her wedding day even if it wasn't from her husband-to-be.

Yoshida interrupted, "It is not proper to discuss such things with a young lady, especially on her wedding day."

Duke ignored her and continued, bubbling with enthusiasm, "The *baishakunin* writes to her and, if she is agreeable, she comes. In fact I have already selected my bride and she will be arriving in a few months. We will work, have children, and then we can own our own land. The farm will really be ours."

"There are ways around that," Takeo said. "Watch that dog!"

Duke swerved in the road just missing the large golden-haired dog oblivious to the danger he had just avoided. Without missing a beat, Duke continued, "Yes, like you did. Borrowing the name of Bob Goodman. You put *your* land in *his* name hoping he will not change his mind or be found out

No, thank you. I will wait until I have a son and buy land to put in his name. I will just keep leasing for now."

Takeo said, "Lease? You mean sharecrop. Come on, Duke. You have to share more than half what you make with the owner."

Duke laughed, "Only until my son…"

Takeo was growing frustrated, "Duke, we've gone over this. The owner may find someone who is willing to work a little harder. He may get rid of you and put someone out there who can make more money. There is no security in sharecropping. You must think to the future. My borrowed name is only temporary until my own son can own the land, but in the meantime the borrowed name is safest."

Duke looked over at Sachi and grinned as he said, "I have been slower in my success than Takeo."

Takeo said, "You would be more successful if you spent more time in the field and less time…" he hesitated, looking at the women in the car and finished with simply, "…other places."

Yoshida yelled, "*Abunai.* Duke! The stop sign!"

Duke slammed on the brakes and Takeo continued, "You are working for another man. You are an *Oyatoi Gaikokujin*, a hired foreigner."

The women drew deep sighs. Yoshida said, "You crazy man. I can drive better than this."

Duke ignored Yoshida's comment and said, "You have had help along the way. You have had your parents. It is harder being alone."

He paused, suddenly realizing the serious turn the conversation had taken without his notice, much like his driving. He smiled and said, "I guess we are all working for the white man for now. The American government has already stopped Japanese laborers from immigrating here and rumor has it they are working on stopping all Japanese, including women and children. That's why I am hurrying to get my bride over here quickly."

Takeo said, "Yes. You must plan your future."

Duke, dismissing his friend's concern and pulling to a stop in front of the temple, said, "Ah, my friend, this is your day to think of the future, not mine. Let's not discuss such things on your wedding day. This is a day for enjoyment and celebration, not work. We get too few of those days to let this slip away."

"Finally something sensible comes from that man," Yoshida said. "Now, let me out of this crazy car."

The wedding ceremony was short and simple. It was a blur to Sachi. In no time at all they were hustled into the social room at the temple for a small reception. There were a dozen people who witnessed the ceremony, friends of the Watanabe family.

The first people Sachi met were the only white people in attendance, Mr. and Mrs. Goodman. They farmed 100 acres next door and Sachi remembered this as the man

119

whose name Takeo borrowed. Takeo worked the farm and paid the mortgage and taxes, but legally Bob Goodman owned the farm.

He was a tall, thin man with light red hair and a quick smile. Sachi wondered how much power he had over their farm. Could he take it if Takeo suddenly displeased him? Sachi knew she must be nice to this man who held their futures in his name. His wife was a talkative, short woman, with long brown hair tied in a bun on her head, perched under a hat of green netting.

She shook Sachi's hand vigorously and kissed Takeo on the cheek quickly in congratulations. Sachi was immediately uncomfortable with the public display of affection and stiffened involuntarily. Mrs. Goodman took no notice.

Instead she smiled brightly and said, "Sachi, please call me Sarah. I am so happy Takeo has such a beautiful wife to take care of him and now Yoshida has a daughter as well. I know she is happy about that."

Sachi glanced at Yoshida in her blue dress serving food at the reception table and talking with another older woman Sachi had not met yet. Next to the older woman were a young man and a younger woman holding a baby. She doubted Yoshida was happy about having her as a daughter, but she smiled at Mrs. Goodman and nodded politely.

Mr. Goodman kissed Sachi softly on the cheek. Sachi was again uncomfortable with the familiarity, but did not turn away knowing it would be rude.

Mr. Goodman said, "Congratulations you two. I know it won't be long now till there are little Watanabes running all over that farm. It'll be nice to have little ones around."

Duke and a woman who looked a little older than Sachi approached the group and asked if Takeo could be excused to step outside with him for a moment.

Mr. Goodman said, "Certainly if it's okay with his new wife. You'll have to start asking her permission now, Takeo."

Sachi nodded to Takeo and the group laughed at the notion that Takeo would have to ask permission of Sachi for anything.

Duke said, "Sachi Watanabe, this is Ikuko Fujimoto."

Because she was one of the younger women in attendance Sachi had noticed her earlier. Ikuko was small with short dark hair lightly framing her face. It wasn't until Sachi looked at her closely to talk that she noticed Ikuko appeared to have one eye out of sync with the other. Sachi had known of an old man in a nearby fishing village that suffered from this. Some superstitious people called it the "evil eye", but she had also heard it called "lazy eye".

But Ikuko's small dark eyes were anything but lazy. They seemed to catch every detail in the room as they moved quickly from person to person. Her mouth seemed continually in motion as well and her laugh was steadily interspersed between her words like mortar filling in the spaces between bricks. Sachi could not help be feel happy to see her. Ikuko's youthful presence seemed like an oasis in the desert of so many older guests. Sachi bowed to Ikuko who laughed and grabbed Sachi's hand, pumping it up and down. Both eyes fixed on Sachi in friendliness.

She said, "First off, no more bowing. We shake hands over here and congratulations."

Mr. Goodman, smiling, said, "Well, if I know Duke those boys probably went to have a celebratory drink. Prohibition hasn't slowed Duke down. But I guess a man does need a strong drink on his wedding day."

Ikuko leaned over and whispered with a smile, "It's us women that could use a strong drink on our wedding night, don't you think?"

Sachi blushed and smiled. This funny stranger with the funny eye was alluding to the most intimate part of her life. She was shocked and embarrassed.

Mrs. Goodman asked, "How old are you Sachi?"

"18 in just a few months," Sachi answered.

Anxious to remove the focus from her, Sachi asked, "Do you have children?"

Mrs. Goodman said, "Yes. My daughter is in Kentucky working with the volunteer nurses program for the poor unfortunate children there. My other daughter is married and lives in New York with her husband."

Mr. Goodman said, "Takeo has met my girls. In fact, they both left about the time Takeo and his father arrived here. We were good friends with Takeo's father and, after he died, we tried to help Yoshida as much as we could."

Mrs. Goodman took her husband's hand and added, "You're too young to learn this yet, but it's hard losing the one person on earth you belong with and who belongs with you."

Sachi thought of her mother, but couldn't tell Mrs. Goodman that age had little to do with loss. There was silence for a moment and then Mr. Goodman said, "But when those babies come you will need Yoshida, I'm sure. It's nice to have help with babies."

Sachi's smile faltered a moment. Mrs. Goodman, perhaps noticing, said, "Come on, Bob. No talk of babies on the wedding day. Much too soon for that. Let's get some punch. Maybe, if we're lucky, Duke has spiked it."

He laughed and followed his wife. Sachi overheard him say, "You are so bad."

Sachi was glad Mrs. Goodman had stepped in. She was already tired of hearing that she was expected to produce babies on demand. It seemed to be all anyone could talk to her about. She was left standing alone with Ikuko thinking babies would be the subject of this conversation as well. A woman like this probably had lots of little ones, she thought.

As if reading her thoughts, Ikuko whispered, "Get use to it. It's all the old ones talk about. Babies. They don't want to talk about making them, just having them."

"How many children do you have?" asked Sachi politely, resigning herself to the topic at hand.

"See him?" Ikuko pointed to a large man, who was much older than she. His face looked like Japan itself with a mountainous white moustache like the snow on Mt. Fujiami. He must have been 50 years old, at least 25 years older than Ikuko. Sachi nodded.

"Edo, that's the only baby I have," she laughed. "My husband. My baby. Two in one. I have to feed him and comfort him and someday I'll probably have to change him as well."

Sachi covered her mouth as she stifled a laugh imagining this large man in a diaper with small Ikuko having to change him.

"We've tried, but no luck so far," Ikuko said, a more somber look clouding her face.

Sachi said, "Everyone talks as though I should have a baby tomorrow."

"I know. Don't rush it. Babies, I mean. A young woman has a lot to learn about herself and being a wife before she is ready to be a mother, don't you think?"

Sachi smiled, knowing she had found her first friend in this country.

Two hours later Duke drove them home though it was clear he had too much to drink. Mr. Goodman was right. Duke's wedding gift had been a bottle of sake, most of which he drank while toasting Takeo's marriage. His drinking didn't seem to have an effect on his driving, Sachi noticed, mainly because it was never very good to begin with.

Yoshida spent the night with the family friends and as Duke drove Sachi and Takeo home he talked to Sachi about his car. His speech was a little slurred and Sachi didn't understand everything as he rambled, "This is a 1918 Cadillac. Fits seven people if I need it to. Cost me some money, but it's worth it. V8 engine. Fast. What'd ya think of that? And look at this."

Duke pulled a lever to the side of the wooden steering wheel and the wheel tilted upward then down then up again.

Duke smiled broadly, his eyes clouded from drink but the sparkle of enthusiasm could not be dimmed. He continued, "See that? It's called a 'fat man wheel'. First of its kind. You know, so if you're fat, you can tilt the wheel up. You lose a few pounds; you can tilt it back down. Takeo, you should have one of these in your car."

Duke laughed loudly at his own joke.

As they pulled up to their drive and the couple exited from the car Duke yelled out, "Enjoy this time alone. It may be the only night you ever have without ol' mama-san lurking about."

Then he added gleefully, "Just wait. I'll be next."

The couple stood apart watching Duke drive down the path from their house his red taillights blinking in the dark like a Morse code good-bye.

Sachi did not know what was expected of her or what to do next. Takeo turned to look at her and then said, "Let's go inside, my wife."

They both smiled shyly at Sachi's new title and walked inside their home together. Sachi had looked forward to this evening thinking that marriage, the mere ceremony, would magically help her to feel a part of something, a part of someone. She finally thought she would belong with another person and she was anxious for the wedding night, hoping it would seal that feeling like a wax stamp on an envelope, seal it up tight.

They walked into their bedroom together. Takeo did not speak and they kissed only briefly, lightly. He was at first gentle and tender, unsure perhaps. He smelled of sake and cigarettes and something sweet. Sachi was anxious, too anxious. As he fumbled with her obi Sachi began to undo it herself, trying to help him.

He stopped and looked at her questioningly for a moment. As if her eagerness to consummate their marriage troubled him. She stopped untying the obi and looked into his eyes, but she could not make out what he was thinking. He resumed his efforts and she left it to him.

As they continued Takeo became less gentle and more fervent, but without emotion. Takeo did not speak, but moaned and grunted and the whole process amazed Sachi. She felt almost detached from it as if she were watching rather than participating.

Sachi had some pain and bleeding. The second time was a little easier but less interesting for Sachi. She enjoyed the physical closeness, the touching and holding, but she did not feel the intensity that Takeo was obviously feeling. She wondered at his shuddering and groaning on top of her, as if he had lost control of himself. She was glad she did not react in this way. She examined Takeo's round, large body in wonder; the covering of soft, fleshiness belied the powerful muscles beneath. She felt Takeo's large calloused hands on her body and the weight of his being converging with hers. She felt small and delicate next to Takeo's large, robust body. She liked that feeling.

Early the next morning she rose from her marriage bed to begin her new life. She gathered the eggs and eyed the cow suspiciously thinking how surprised Takeo would be if she came in with a pail of milk, but she knew nothing about milking a cow and decided the beast looked cantankerous that morning. As she considered this, Takeo entered the

126

barn in his long johns and pants. He smiled and said good morning to her. He kissed her lightly on the lips and she returned the greeting.

At the breakfast table Takeo addressed her and the *gohan*, the meal, in the traditional Japanese manner. They were words she had not heard spoken in a long time. It was a way of showing respect and appreciation for the one who had cooked the meal. Father said them when she was a little girl, as did most traditional Japanese families, but gradually he had stopped.

Sachi set the eggs, rice and vegetables, her first meal cooked as a married woman, before her new husband. Takeo bowed his head and said, "*Itadakimasu.*" (Thanks to the one who prepared this meal.)

When he finished eating he bowed his head again and said, "*Gochiso sama deshita.*" (It was quite a feast.)

She was a woman who had lain with her husband. Her childhood was over. Now they were one and she could ask what she had wanted to ask since her arrival.

Sachi began clearing the dishes in front of him and asked, "Do you plan on returning to Japan?"

Takeo looked up at her, his brows furrowed, and said, "What? No. I'm not going back to Japan."

Sachi turned, placing the dishes in the sink, her back to Takeo, and said, "Your mother says we are leaving."

Takeo said, "My mother wants to return to Japan and so she has convinced herself that I wish to return as well. If you had not come, I might have gone back with her. This is not an easy life for a married man. It is almost impossible for a bachelor."

Sachi turned and faced her new husband, "But I did come."

"Yes. You and I will start a family. Perhaps we already have," Takeo smiled slightly at this thought and then continued, "Our children will be Americans and Japan will seem as strange to them as America first seemed to me. I want my children raised on American soil.

Sachi continued, "But your mother..."

Takeo interrupted, frustration edging his words, "What is this? My wife wants to discuss my mother on the first morning of our marriage? When I brought my mother here I promised she would return to Japan, someday. It was the only way to get her to agree to come and now, with my father gone..."

He let the sentence hang like a thread from a spider's web dangling in the breeze. They would not be returning to Japan. Sachi drew in her first deep breath in her home. She smiled at her husband and turned to do the dishes, feeling full of hope and promise. America was where she would finally belong.

CHAPTER FOURTEEN

Orange Grove - 1924

In the six months since her marriage Sachi's life had taken on a familiar rhythm. She worked hard in the fields alongside Takeo. She cooked, cleaned, mended, washed, obeyed Yoshida, and attended temple with her new family. She even had a best friend. Her friendship with Ikuko had grown starting two days after Sachi's wedding. Ikuko had stopped by to say hello and welcome her formally as a married woman into the community.

Sachi was shy and felt somewhat awkward entertaining a stranger in her new home. Yoshida had seen Ikuko's car coming and said, "Bah, no class to this flighty girl. She does not call before coming to our house. Just dropping by. No sense this one."

Sachi found that what Ikuko lacked in sense she made up for in sense of humor. Sachi opened the door to Ikuko and asked her to enter and sit down. She was not quite comfortable with her role as wife and mistress of a house, but Yoshida appeared with tea and biscuits and then sat to talk with them. Ikuko visited pleasantly enough at first. She commented on the wedding and how radiant Sachi had seemed in the beautiful snow-white kimono. She talked about the mild weather and the heat that was inevitably to come. She talked of a sale at the store on canned peas. Finally Ikuko looked at Yoshida and asked, "Mrs. Watanabe, would you mind if Sachi showed me your garden?"

Sachi was surprised and Yoshida looked a little taken aback as well. It was well-known that Yoshida, as many Japanese, could grow anything, even those plants that were

129

best suited for other climates. The three women knew it was proper for Ikuko to ask Yoshida to show her garden or wait for an invitation, but Ikuko made it clear in that one question that she had come to visit Sachi, not Yoshida. She also made it clear to Sachi, though she might be foolish and not so proper, she was brave.

Yoshida paused before answering and Sachi thought perhaps she would refuse to let Ikuko examine her garden, but that would have been more improper, refusing a guest in her home.

Instead Yoshida said, "If that is what you would like. It looks like it might rain soon. This is still my winter garden so things are somewhat bare. I'm sure Sachi won't know what everything is..."

Ikuko interrupted, "Oh, I know a bit about plants and I have heard so much about it."

Yoshida waved her hands as she dismissed them and said, "Do as you wish. Go and see the garden. I will take care of these."

She picked up the tray with the tea things and walked into the kitchen.

Sachi spoke up, "I will do those when I return, if you like."

Yoshida ordered, "I will do them. You show Ikuko the garden, but hurry back as we have much work to do today and we are behind already."

In seconds they had transformed from three women visiting to one woman chastising two little girls. As they walked out the front door and around to the back toward

Yoshida's garden Ikuko giggled and said, "I guess that was meant for me. Just dropping by like this."

Sachi smiled and graciously said, "You are welcome any time."

Ikuko smirked, "Any time there's not work to be done and if you listen to the old ones, there is always work to be done. That is why I came today. I'm here to save you."

Sachi raised her eyebrows and asked, "From what?"

Ikuko smiled and said, "From working to death, from your mother-in-law, from boredom. You and I are going to be good friends, Sachi. I'm a few years older than you. I've been here a while. I will show you the ropes."

"The ropes?"

Ikuko linked her arm with Sachi and said, "It's a saying. It means I will show you how to get along here. There is much work to do, but there are wonderful things to see in America. This is a big land with all kinds of people and places. San Francisco is only a few hours from here. We will go someday and shop at the large stores that hold everything you can imagine and some things you can't. We will go to the museums with the beautifully painted pictures containing every color in the world and sculptures of nude men and women. We will jump on a streetcar and ride up and down the hills with the wind in our hair and go to the plays in the grand opera house with the large crystal chandelier that is bigger than our houses. We'll eat crab and sourdough bread on the wharf and watch the large ships come in from all over the world bringing more people and more things. We will have grand adventures in our friendship. We will walk down the streets and people will admire us and wish they were friends with us because we will be having so much fun."

Sachi smiled shyly and said, "I would like that."

Sachi did not think she knew how to have fun. It was not something that was encouraged, but she had read about such fun and friendships in books. She had never had many friends and certainly never a best friend. She had grown up lonely, thirsting after friendship and belonging, and Ikuko was suddenly a well of cool water.

She also had many questions about the things that happened in her daily life in America and wanted a confidant, someone with whom she could share things without fear of critical judgment.

They reached the garden and Sachi, pointing toward the first row, said, "This is Yoshida's garden. That is Butter lettuce growing there and those are dakius there. I think that is…"

Ikuko interrupted with a laugh.

She said, "The garden was only an excuse. I've seen enough lettuce and onions and vegetables growing in the ground to last a lifetime. I just wanted to talk to you. Get to know you and," she hesitated as if not sure how to phrase it, "I thought that perhaps, as a young newlywed, you might have some questions about…oh…things."

"Questions? Oh yes. I have lots of questions," said Sachi, happy her new friend understood. "I wanted to know if there is a library in town. I don't want to ask Yoshida. I don't think she would like it. But I imagine a place like America has a large library. I also want to know about…"

Ikuko laughed again. Sachi wasn't sure why and looked at her questioningly.

Ikuko said, "Library? That's your big question? In less than a week, you have moved to a new country, are living with a new family, married a man you hardly know, spent your wedding night together, and your first question is where is the library? I learned to read in missionary school too, but, believe me, I haven't had time or really much interest in picking up a book since then. The library?"

Sachi looked down, ashamed. Obviously she wasn't asking the kinds of questions Ikuko expected and she found it to be a failing on her part. She felt stupid again and wished she knew the right things to ask, questions that showed she was an exciting person and not so dull.

Ikuko stopped laughing and said gently, "I'm sorry. Stupid me. Sometimes I have a way of saying things… I didn't mean to laugh at you. I just thought maybe you had questions about your wedding night."

Sachi's face burned with embarrassment at the mention of this most intimate part of her new life.

She asked, "Why would I have questions about that? It is the same for all people, I expect."

Ikuko knelt down and absently rubbed the leaves of an artichoke plant between her fingers and said, "It can sometimes be difficult, particularly the first time. Perhaps there

133

was pain or fear or shame. Sometimes a man, well, he can be in a hurry and too...forceful."

Sachi's eyes remained on the ground. She did not like speaking about such things especially to this woman she hardly knew. She had no questions about that part of her new life. It was something wives did and she knew it was the way to pregnancy and children. She did have questions, but she hardly let herself think about the questions sometimes floating in her mind much less give voice to those errant private thoughts and to a complete stranger. Is this what best friends talked about?

Sachi's eyes remained on the ground. She wasn't sure she liked this vivacious new friend feigning interest in Yoshida's garden in order to pry into her physical relationship with her husband.

Sachi said, "I have no need to talk to anyone about ...that."

Ikuko stood, brushing her hands together to remove the specks of dirt as well as the topic at hand, said, "I know it is personal and it is new. I just thought, well, if you ever do have a need to talk to someone, feel free to call on me. Somehow I don't see you being able to have a heart-to-heart chat with Yoshida about this artichoke plant much less marriage."

Since that first awkward conversation in the garden, they had talked many times. Ikuko's words flowed as water from a babbling brook refreshing Sachi's spirit. It was like having the radio on. Sachi would just sit and listen. Ikuko's talking seemed to have the opposite effect on Yoshida, who much preferred the quiet, and so on those days when Ikuko came to their home Yoshida busied herself in her garden or the kitchen.

Over the last six months Sachi did as she was told in every regard, but each Sunday as they entered the Buddhist temple Sachi looked longingly at the small Japanese Methodist Church practically next door. Father had always dismissed anything having to do with religion and, as a result, Sachi's religious training at missionary school was Christian and not Buddhist. She wanted to go now, but she did not know how to approach her husband.

One Sunday morning after Temple rites Sachi was talking to Ikuko in the social room. Tables and chairs were set up around the room and people stood in line for the coffee and tea service. Doughnuts and cookies were on a table next to the coffee and a group of children and Edo, Ikuko's husband, were gathered around. The room was filled with the noise of conversation. People wanted to talk after remaining silent for an hour at temple ceremonies.

Sachi moved closer to Ikuko and lowered her voice, "I want to attend church, but I have not mentioned it to Takeo. I am not sure how. I don't think he would like it."

Ikuko thought for a moment and then said, "The Japanese woman is in an interesting position, particularly here in America where independence and the individual are held in high esteem. We are raised to know our destiny, submissive service to our husband and his family. Some might think we Japanese women have no ability to influence what takes place in our lives and our homes. Is that how you feel, Sachi?"

Sachi nodded, "Yes. Takeo's desires come first. It is the best way to ensure the unity of the family."

Ikuko smiled and shrugged as she said, "Maybe. At least, that's how we were taught, isn't it? Unity is important, but so is happiness. When are you happy?"

The question surprised her and she thought for a moment before answering, "I don't really think much about happiness. I am happy to be here in America. I am happy when I am reading."

Sachi paused as if unsure and said, "I am happy to have you as a friend."

Ikuko smiled and said, "Me, too. But there is an art to being a good Japanese wife and still attaining a level of individual happiness and influence over your own life."

Ikuko looked around the crowded social room, which was crowded, and took Sachi by the arm leading her to the empty Temple. The smell of incense hung in the air adding an almost ancient, mystical quality to Ikuko's words.

Ikuko said, "Has anyone ever talked to you about the art of...let us call it womanly persuasion."

Sachi shook her head.

Ikuko started, "When you want something you must talk to your husband about it at just the right time and in the right way. If you yell and demand the minute he steps in the door at night, chances are he will not be agreeable. But, if you speak in gentle whispers asking for just this one little thing, particularly in the blanket of night when he is asking you for one little thing, an equitable trade can be realized where all parties are satisfied. Do you understand?"

Sachi raised her eyebrows in disbelief and whispered, "Are you talking about at night before we…before he and I, you know?"

Ikuko smiled and nodded.

Sachi said, "What if he refuses?"

"Then, in your sweetest, kindest voice, you say, 'That's perfectly alright, my love. If that is your position on the matter, then I accept it. You are my husband and you know best.'"

Ikuko placed her hands on either side of her head and began rubbing her temples.

She continued, "And then you say, 'Oh dear, all this discussion has given me a headache. I'm sorry, sweetheart. I must just be tired, I guess. Goodnight.'"

"Then you give him a soft and lingering kiss on the cheek, just enough so he can get a sense of you, and then you roll over to go to sleep."

Sachi asked, "That's it? Won't he get mad when I…roll over?"

Ikuko said, "Not so much mad as frustrated. And it is this frustration women have used for centuries to influence their lives and families."

Sachi shook her head and said, "Why can't we just talk? Why can't I just say what I want to do and have it be okay?"

"Sometimes that works depending on the man, but you also have to consider the mother. You have Yoshida to contend with in all this decision-making. She wants you at

Temple so you have to decide how best to convince Takeo you should be able to attend church. One more thing. Do not wait until afterward to ask. If Takeo is like Edo, he most likely falls asleep within seconds. Timing is important."

Not for the first time in their conversations did Sachi think of her mother who also had tried to teach her the importance of timing in all things.

Ikuko continued, "Lovemaking and all its negotiations is an art just as much for the man as the woman. Try it. You'll see."

The next Sunday Sachi began attending the Methodist church with Takeo. After services they stopped at the Temple to pick up Yoshida. When Takeo announced to Edo that he was now attending the Methodist Church with Sachi, Ikuko leaned over to her friend and whispered, "You see. Not everything can be learned at the library."

CHAPTER FIFTEEN

WASHINGTON, D.C. - 1924

Steve Gordon, Democratic Senator from New York, removed the papers from his briefcase and set them in two piles before him on the large table. The small conference room belied the importance of the meeting, but it was the only one available on such short notice. Meeting rooms on Capitol Hill required the advance notice of transatlantic cruise ship reservations these days. The Senator arrived early for meetings. He thought it gave him an edge as he welcomed others into the meeting upon their arrival, as a host would greet his guests. It placed him in a position to take charge, sometimes. He hoped it would work today. He was meeting with several Senators including Republican Senator Robert Danburn of California. Danburn was an anxious little man and it was a testament to Danburn's political power that this meeting was called so quickly.

Calvin Coolidge, just recently inaugurated as President, had asked Gordon to attend today and report back to him. During his tenure as Vice President Coolidge had come to trust Gordon, as much as he did any Democrat. And now as President, since Harding's recent death in office, he turned to Gordon.

Gordon missed President Warren Harding. Theirs was an instant friendship from the moment they met even though they were on opposite sides of most issues. After a long day of politicking they often had a drink and, sometimes, played poker in Harding's private quarters. Coolidge never participated. Perhaps he was never invited. Gordon respected and admired Coolidge, but he'd loved Harding and it had been a difficult six months since his beloved president's death.

He'd agreed to attend this meeting as a favor to the President, but he thought his own constituents could care less about Japanese immigration into California. He knew little about it other than the research and history he'd read over the last few days between committee meetings, hearings, constituent meetings, and phone calls. Gordon knew it was not his words needed today, but the words of others. He would soak in what was said and wring out the information for the President in a brief, but concise report to be delivered in two days. Having the ear of the President sometimes required more listening than speaking.

It was cold as Washington tended to be in February and Gordon rose to turn up the thermostat. He felt the symptoms of age coming on as if it were a disease. At 62 years old the cold pierced him more quickly than when he was younger maybe because the fire in his gut was not as strong as it had once been.

As he moved back to his seat three other Senators on the committee entered; Connally, Bushnell, and Peters. The senators greeted each other complaining of the cold, sipping tepid coffee brought in from their last meeting, and took their seats.

Moments later Senator Robert Danburn entered with three male associates trailing behind him. Gordon thought the associates always looked the same as if they were manufactured from some Ivy League factory for up-and-comers with potential that would never be reached. Danburn's slicked-back black hair and gray eyes seemed to match his mood today as he bustled into the room. His custom tailored suits were cut to look American when, in fact, he made several trips to Europe each year to purchase his wardrobe. He wanted to give the impression of buying American, but preferred the ostentatiousness of hiring a European tailor.

Danburn took a seat and his associates positioned themselves around him as if in protection of their employer. Danburn had his young pups in tow at each meeting, press conference, hearing, or just walking down the hall. Gordon decided they probably wiped his butt. On second thought, he probably had to wipe theirs. Gordon had seen this kind of political swank before and knew these young men were with Danburn to emphasize his importance and to help him with his thoughts when he became flustered or disorganized. They were also there as scapegoats to be fired if something went wrong, flushing a man and his political career away with Danburn's own accountability. Gordon disliked Danburn's manner of swooping into a room and trying to take over all power and authority. He immediately felt confrontational and reminded himself he was simply there to gather information and opinions. He took a deep breath and a long sip of his cold coffee.

Gordon took his seat, checked his watch, and said, "It seems we are waiting for one more person. Maybe we can give him just a few more minutes."

Danburn, tapped his gold-plated pen on the table as if sending out Morse code and demanded, "Who are waiting for? By my count we're all here."

141

Gordon, speaking to everyone at the table, said, "Joe Preston. He's an expert in the area of Japan and immigration. He lived in Japan for a number of years and has acted as a liaison between our government and theirs. He has his Masters degrees in International Relations and Economics. I thought it might be a good idea to have him talk with us. Help give us some perspective on the issues."

"I live in California," Danburn said curtly. "With due respect, I have all the perspective I need on this issue."

Gordon replied, "Correction Senator. You're *from* California. You *live* in Washington, just like the rest of us. And *I* require more perspective."

Senator Bushnell from New Hampshire rubbed the back of his neck, already sore from sitting through two previous meetings earlier in the morning, and said, "I 'd like to hear from an expert, get some numbers, statistics, that kind of thing, before we make a decision here. Besides I thought we stopped Japanese immigration about 16 years ago."

Danburn said, "That agreement stopped male laborers from immigrating, it did not, however, stop women and children. The men already here are simply sending for brides and creating multitudes of Japanese American citizens. That's the problem."

A voice came from the doorway, "How exactly is that a problem?"

All heads turned. The voice belonged to a small man in his forties. His light brown hair receded like a wave rushing back to the ocean leaving a sprinkle of sand colored freckles on his nose and forehead. His green eyes sparkled behind thick black-rimmed glasses. His white dress shirt was rumpled and his tie crooked, but his suit was neatly

142

pressed and shoes shined. He held a small leather folder in his hands.

Danburn looked back at Gordon and said with a hint of distain, "Your expert, I presume."

Without waiting for Gordon's reply Danburn turned back to the man in the doorway and said, "Maybe if you'd arrived on time…"

The man interrupted and, without apology, said, "Traffic. I'm Joe Preston. You're talking about possibly ending all immigration from Japan and most likely doing irreparable harm to U.S./Japanese relations. I'd like to know what you see as the Japanese immigration "problem."

Danburn snapped his fingers at the associate beside him and ordered, "Newspaper."

The nervous young associate shuffled quickly through a stack and handed Danburn a section of newspaper. It all appeared rehearsed since the associate knew exactly what to retrieve. Gordon chuckled to himself and remembered how he had trained the family's cocker spaniel by saying "Newspaper, boy, newspaper. Good boy."

Danburn held it up and demanded, "Have you seen this editorial in the Chronicle? It says the Japanese are the cause of the depressed wages for American farmers. They are gathering more and more of California's agricultural wealth leaving the American citizens to scurry for crumbs under the Japanese table of agricultural prosperity."

Preston dismissed the editorial with a wave of his hand as he took a seat next to Goodman and said, "Are you saying Californians are angry that the Japanese are working harder than they are and reaping the benefits of their labor? Come on. The so-called

143

Gentleman's Agreement of 1908 ended immigration of Japanese laborers. Now you want to stop the Japanese who *are* here from bringing over a wife? Your constituents would be a lot more upset if these Japanese fellows started marrying white girls."

Danburn warned, "If they try, they'll end up in jail. In California we have laws against that sort of thing."

Preston said, "Of course, you do. So then what is the problem with sending for an ethnically similar bride?"

Danburn shook his head and pointed at Preston, "I thought you were the expert. It's more than that and you know it. The Oriental situation has been simmering in California for years now. Every time we try to fix things out there the damn Japanese find a way around it. We need to do this thing now before things get out of hand. And make no mistake. They're headed that way. American citizens in California are tired of the Japanese laborers and their brides who are experts in growing red strawberries, purple grapes and yellow babies."

Senator Bushnell said, "It sounds like simple prejudice to me. *Sour* grapes, if you will."

Several men chuckled, but not Danburn or his staff. Danburn's face reddened and a vein throbbed in his neck as he raised his voice trying to force his point home to these men.

He said, "This is a matter of national security. These Japanese are allowed to continue to create Japanese American citizens when it is a fact that their allegiances, morally, culturally and fiscally, are to Japan. The majority of these immigrants have plans to return to Japan with a pocketful of American money. That is what California wants ended. Out in California we see what's happening. We have a clearer view of the Pacific than the rest of the country and I'm telling you if the Japanese are allowed to continue in this manner, it won't be long before they've taken over the entire agricultural community. The California economy is based on its agriculture."

Preston directed his comments to the other Senators ignoring Danburn and his contingent of aides. He spoke calmly, as if delivering a college lecture, and said, "Legislating against an entire group of people is not the answer. Things don't go our way and we try to legislate protection of one class of people over another. First, we toss the Chinese out of California mining where they were doing pretty well. California tells them they have to be certified to mine by passing a written test given only in English. Keep in mind that most of these men can't write their native language much less English. We effectively send them packing because we don't like the competition. But then when we need our Transcontinental Railroad built suddenly somebody remembers how expert those Chinamen were with the blasting rock and guess who we invite back to do one of the most dangerous jobs we've got and for less pay, of course."

Danburn smirked looking directly at Preston, "We're not talking about the Chinese. We're talking about the Japanese."

Preston shook his head and laughed a laugh without humor, "Chinese miners. Japanese farmers. It's the same situation. The same prejudiced thinking. Do you think the

American public, the white American public, which you claim to represent, give a damn about the difference between Chinese and Japanese? All they know is some foreigner with slanty-eyes is doing well and they're not. Instead of changing what they do, they figure let's get rid of the successful guy. The unsuccessful always blame the successful. The difference here is they have a powerful Senator who's apparently bought into this idea."

Danburn retorted, "And apparently we have a Jap-lover who would protect the rights of the Japanese over his own people. Just how long did you live over there, Preston?"

Preston paused examining the challenge in Danburn's eyes, sizing up his verbal combatant. Refusing to take the bait, he said calmly, "The point needs to be made that if the United States enacts a law that no Japanese person can immigrate here, we are basically saying to the Japanese that they are not welcome in our country. We are saying others are welcome, but the Japanese are not good enough. It will be taken as an insult to the Japanese people and the Emperor."

Danburn said, "Who gives a damn?"

Preston exhaled loudly as if trying to explain a complicated issue to a small child and said, "I don't know if you are as aware of what's happening in Japan as you claim to be about what's happening in California, Senator, but Japan is in the midst of its own industrial revolution. What took Europe 150 years to accomplish looks like the Japanese may do in 40 or 50 years at the rate they're going. The Japanese economy is suffering. It's a small island with limited resources. They are beginning to build quite a military-industrial complex and they are looking to us. They were our allies just a few years ago in the Great War. America is their model in many ways. We have a responsibility to them."

Danburn jumped to his feet and shouted at Preston, "A responsibility? To the Japanese? No sir. My responsibility is to the voters of California. Maybe you need to re-examine your priorities."

Gordon interrupted, "Have a seat, Bob. Listen, I need numbers, numbers and a little history. Preston, in a nutshell, what exactly is our history with Japan?"

Preston didn't open his briefcase and didn't take his eyes from Goodman. This was the man he had to convince. Danburn was a lost cause on this issue. He couldn't see or accept the possible long-term effects that might come from entirely halting Japanese immigration into the United States.

Preston began, "In 1894, we gave Japan most-favored nation status and promised the Emperor to give Japanese the rights and protections of U.S. citizens. We helped open up Japan with our promises and, therein, lay our responsibility. The Emperor, of course, grew a little miffed and somewhat skeptical when that very same year the San Francisco school board attempted to segregate "Orientals" from the schools. The government managed to stop that, but it was a sign. Then in 1901, a U.S. Industrial Commission report stated that the Japanese are more servile than Chinese, but tricky, unreliable and dishonest. Do you think that helped pave the way for better relations? No, because within four years of that report we have a number of groups who have formed against Japanese.

"In 1908, we have the Gentleman's Agreement with Japan, which we previously discussed. Japan reluctantly agrees to discontinue issuing passports to Japanese laborers for the U.S. and Hawaii, but a provision allowed for the immigration of wives, children, and parents. The Japanese were not thrilled with this, but they accepted it. No more Japanese laborers coming over to take away our American jobs, just some women and children. Of course, the anti-Japanese contingents like those Senator Danburn claims to represent don't like that because it means the birth of Japanese children who were now Americans with all the rights and responsibilities of citizens. Just about 10 years ago, 1913, we legislated the Alien Land Act. The Japanese can work the land. They just can't own it. No alien can. The Japanese grow millions of dollars worth of produce in California. The Japanese are a large part of why California's agricultural economy is thriving. They help feed millions of people. They work hard and they keep to themselves."

Danburn, unable to tolerate Preston's lecture any further, interrupted, "And they have found ways around the Alien Land Act. That's how they earn their reputation for being tricky and dishonest. They put the land into a citizen's name either their children's name or a borrowed name from a sympathetic Jap-lover. It's this kind of trickery that has given the American public the view many of them have of the Japanese. They see these Japanese come here and succeed. They figure if the Japanese weren't on the land, they would be and maybe they are right. I'm telling you these people are not citizens and if our citizens do not want them here, then they need to go home."

Preston said, "And I'm telling you if we end all Japanese immigration, Japan will feel disgraced and humiliated in the eyes of the world. We will be giving in to the prejudice of one group of people. Is that really the message we want to send? I have studied the Japanese. I have been to California many times. The Japanese work hard, tirelessly. They are the epitome of the Protestant work ethic. They are simply living the American dream like our ancestors. They come to this strange land from another country with the understanding that if they work hard, they might succeed. They are the kind of people we want as citizens."

Danburn shook his head in frustration and said, "In California we don't want them as citizens. The Japanese have to expand to survive and if we allow them to continue to gain a foothold in the California agricultural industry, there is no telling what they will set their sights on next. We must stop all Japanese immigration into the U.S. and now."

Gordon checked his watch and stood up, indicating the meeting was coming to an end. He had heard enough. He needed to move to his next meeting and a warm cup of coffee. Each Senator promised to call Gordon later in the afternoon with their recommendation for the President.

Danburn stepped toward Gordon and, before leaving the room, and said, "One more thing to throw into your report to the President. The number 13. Californians vote. Not Japanese. He might want to keep that in mind if he hopes to hang around."

Danburn turned and walked out the door trailing his associates behind him.

Preston looked at Gordon and asked, "13?"

Gordon shook his head and said, "With the election coming up next year and Coolidge running for the Presidency, Danburn is reminding me of California's 13 electoral votes."

CHAPTER SIXTEEN

Sachi's main luxury came after church and supper on Sundays when she settled down with books she borrowed from the small library in town. These small freedoms were made possible when Takeo fulfilled his promise to teach her to drive. He thought she should learn for practical reasons, although Yoshida didn't think it proper for a young woman to go without a chaperon into town. All kinds of evils lurked there. Sachi thought perhaps Yoshida was afraid a demon would jump out from the grocery shelves, but she was now a married woman. She could handle a demon or two. In the end, Sachi knew, though Yoshida would never admit it, she would eventually realize Sachi's driving ability had advantages.

Sachi delighted in the freedom driving brought even if it was just to go into town and get groceries. Usually Yoshida accompanied her, but Sachi loved it best when she was alone. She could sing and think without interruption.

Her first time alone in the car she lost all consciousness of driving, flying down the dirt road, dust trailing after her. The speed and serenity made her feel independent, powerful, in complete control. She was so distracted by her newly discovered power and driving so fast she failed to see the truck coming at her from the opposite direction. The driver of the truck blasted his horn and swerved to avoid her. She yanked the wooden steering wheel hard and spun the car in a 180-degree turn. In a spray of red clay road

151

dust, Sachi bounced into the field next to the road, hitting her head on the steering wheel as the car lurched to a stop. The engine continued running and dust was everywhere.

Sachi felt something warm on her forehead and when she touched it drew back blood mixed with the red dust. She looked in the mirror and saw she was covered with dirt, her hair was windblown, and a small trail of blood wove its way from just above her hairline to her right eyebrow.

The driver of the truck ran over and stuck his head in the open passenger window. He was a white man of about 21 years of age with dark brown hair and a matching, well-trimmed moustache. Many men with moustaches she had seen looked unkempt, as if something had crawled up on the man's face, but this was flattering to the face of this blue-eyed man with the tanned skin.

"Are you alright?" he asked, breathing rapidly.

Before Sachi could respond, he noticed her forehead and ran over to the driver's side of the car to help her out. He held her arm to assist her and she stiffened at his touch, the touch of this strange man. He was tall, taller than she'd realized from inside the vehicle and much larger than she first thought. Not heavy like Takeo, but muscular and imposing. He pulled out a clean white handkerchief from his back pocket and began dotting at the blood on her forehead. She felt like a small child when her mother use to tend to her scrapes or bumps. It was endearing and much too familiar for Sachi.

She felt no panic. Something about this man was calming and she realized neither of them was really hurt. She gently took the handkerchief from him and said, "I am fine. I apologize for my driving. I still have much to learn apparently."

He sat down into the driver's seat of her car and, for a moment, she thought he was going to drive away. Instead he turned off the ignition.

"Where are you going in such a hurry?" he asked sternly as he checked her car for damage.

"Nowhere. I mean, into town, but nowhere to be in such a hurry."

He smiled, his large, white teeth shining from behind the dark moustache. "It's the weather. It seems the more beautiful the day, the faster the car. All drivers learn that lesson at one time or another. I'm Jack Albright."

He rose from the driver's seat and held out his hand in greeting. Sachi took it, her hand lying inside his firm grip. She still had not gotten use to this manner of greeting. It was an odd, intimate custom, touching one another, touching strangers. Bowing was more respectful and more efficient.

"I am Sachi Watanabe," she said.

She wanted to leave, but he continued, "Watanabe? Are you related to Takeo Watanabe?"

"Yes," she said. "I am his wife."

He looked surprised, just for a moment, and then shrugged his eyebrows. "I didn't know he'd married."

She stood still daubing her head and feeling the arrival of a headache. She walked to the driver's side of her car to get in and said, "Well, I must be going. I still have shopping to do."

He stopped her, taking her face in his hands, and examined her cut. Her heart pounded and she could smell peppermint on his breath. He smiled wide and released her.

He said, "I guess you don't need a doctor, but be sure to put something on that when you get home. You wouldn't want an infection to set in. And slow down."

They waved good-bye and Sachi felt a strange sensation in the pit of her stomach. She wished she could sit a while with this stranger and she did not know why. Maybe it was just nerves combined with hunger, but she found herself holding his handkerchief for the rest of the ride into town. She pictured his concerned face towering over her. She could still feel his hands on her cheeks, his eyes on her face. Was this the kind of demon her mother-in-law was worried about?

Later that afternoon she sat with Ikuko, both sewing on the front porch while Takeo worked and Yoshida rested inside.

Ikuko was talking about last week's ladies meeting at Temple. They were Buddhists in Japan and had remained so mainly at Edo's insistence. Ikuko could do perfect imitations of all the older ladies, particularly the ones who seemed to put on airs. She was in the middle of a story about Mrs. Kuzuki's weekly tragedies in the kitchen.

Ikuko rattled on, "They were hard as rock these muffins. I mean you could barely choke down a bite. I think she may have cooked them days before, though she swears they were fresh. I mean how else do you make muffins so hard no one can eat them? She tries American cooking all the time and apparently isn't getting any better. Of course, Charlie Shimmer would be happy to have even Mrs. Kuzuki cook for him. You know Charlie."

Sachi shook her head, trying to place him in her mind, but unable to do so. Ikuko said, "Oh, you know. Charlie Shimmer. He lives across the road from us."

His face flashed before her eyes, bucked teeth and skinny. She nodded her remembrance. Ikuko continued, "He's a good-natured man, but not known for thinking before he speaks. Something we have in common, I suppose."

She laughed at herself and continued, "His most memorable achievement in his twenty-nine years was proposing marriage six times to six different women. He was rejected six times. Of course, he wasn't very bright about it. He asked all six women at different times on the same day.

"Can you believe it? I mean especially living in Orange Grove where the only thing more plentiful than the grapes is the gossip. It didn't take long for word to get around. That evening when Charlie returned home from the fields there stood the group of six angry proposees. It's said, 'That hell hath no fury like a woman scorned.' On that evening six scorned women stood on Charlie Shimmer's front porch and unleashed their collective fury. Edo happened to be with Charlie that evening because Charlie had borrowed some tools and Edo wanted to get them back. Anyway, Edo said their words hit Charlie like bullets from a machine gun, pouring from their mouths, suddenly, undecipherable, until he no longer heard anything but tone. Then it stopped. They walked away directing their weapons of words toward one another and leaving him standing stunned, speechless, and very much alone. All six women ended up marrying other men and Charlie remains a bachelor."

Sachi enjoyed listening to Ikuko's stories. They were always filled with vivid descriptions of people and places. She talked often about her trips to San Francisco, shopping, sightseeing, meeting relatives at the dock. She talked of the museums, stores, and restaurants. Ikuko was entertaining and Sachi often thought she should be on one of those radio programs, but the only Oriental voices ever heard on radio were thick with stupid-sounding accents intended to be comical.

Even though Sachi was becoming close to Ikuko she still had told no one of her mother's death. She started to tell Takeo one night and then again to Ikuko one day when she asked of Sachi's family, but she could not form the words and she realized she had never spoken them. Someone had told Father and Father had told her, but she had never said the words to anyone. It seemed in this new place that just as she knew her mother's spirit lived in heaven she could pretend that her mother never really died, but was in Japan living as she always had.

As the months went by she began to almost believe her fantasy that her mother still lived and sometimes she would even forget for a moment and wonder how her mother was doing. When Yoshida asked about her family Sachi lied and said that they were doing well. She said Father would always be angry with her for leaving and that is why she didn't hear from them. Yoshida suggested that at least her mother might visit someday and Sachi sighed, "Yes. I would like that very much."

Ikuko interrupted her thoughts and brought her back to the present.

"Sachi, did you hear me? I asked if Duke is coming for dinner tonight."

Sachi smiled at her friend, glad to be distracted from thoughts of her mother and her own lies, and answered, "Yes, with his new bride. He's in San Francisco today to pick her up. He already went to Angel Island as her witness. He received word a few days ago that her processing should be complete and he arrives there today to meet her. She will stay with us until they get married in a few days."

Ikuko said, "I knew he sent for her, but I didn't know she was arriving today. Well, Duke will finally get what he wanted. He is the only bachelor I have known to go on and on about getting married. He's a little wild. I think marriage will calm him."

She leaned toward Sachi and whispered, "Or should I say regular sex will calm him down. I think his new bride is going to be busy in the boudoir for quite a little while. I may not actually get to meet her for months. Crops will rot on the vines. Farm animals will go hungry."

They giggled at Duke and his new bride locked up in their bedroom for months. But Duke did not arrive for dinner that night. They waited two hours past the time he was expected before they sat down to eat. Although Takeo said nothing Sachi knew he was worried about his friend.

Yoshida was angry and chalked it up to Duke's insensitive nature. "He probably wanted to show off for this girl and took her around the city, lost track of time, and ate dinner without a thought to us."

"He was very excited about having Takeo meet his new bride," Sachi suggested, "Maybe she arrived later than he thought."

Takeo quickly held on to that possibility and said, "That must have been it. Those ferries are delayed all the time."

Sachi fell asleep that night and dreamt of her mother. Her mother stood before her in white holding a little boy in her arms. She began tossing the little boy into the air. They were both giggling and smiling. Suddenly everything began to shake and her mother couldn't hold her footing. She was trying to remain erect, but couldn't. From nowhere the ground split open revealing a black abyss below. Her mother tried to hang on to the little boy, but she was losing her footing. Just as her mother and the boy were to plunge into the abyss below her mother threw the little boy at her. Sachi screamed, "Mother-r-r-r." She tried to catch the little boy, but before she could she was awakened.

Someone was pounding at the front door. Takeo was already out of bed and putting on his robe.

She heard Yoshida by their door whispering, "Takeo. I think it's Duke."

Takeo answered the door and when Sachi entered the living room she saw Duke standing in the open doorway with a bottle in his hand. Sachi noticed it was almost empty and Duke appeared to have been fighting. His clothes were rumpled and dirty. He had a black eye and there was a small spot of blood on his white dress shirt. His upper lip was swollen, but he didn't appear to be in any pain.

Duke announced loudly, "I'm here for dinner. Why you're not even dressed. No matter. Let's eat. I'm starving."

Duke looked around and smiled, "I know, I know. I'm a little late, but I have a good excuse. I was stood up. Stood up by the United States government. Can you believe it?"

Takeo reached for his friend's arm and led him to the sofa. Takeo said, "Sit down, Duke. What happened?"

Duke did not sit down, but quaffed the last gulp of liquor from the bottle he'd obviously not shared with anyone else. Then he stared at it and said to Yoshida, "I am so sorry, Mrs. Watanabe. I meant to bring this for dinner and somehow, I don't know, I just drank it all up. I know it's not legal, but I have a little place I can get a drink from time to time."

He placed his index finger over his pursed lips in feigned secrecy and then laughed at himself. He continued, "And, of course, with my new bride and all I thought this would be okay. We could celebrate with just a little drink. Just tonight. "

Yoshida was not pleased with the midnight interruption and remained silent, her arms folded and her face cross.

Takeo asked, "What do you mean, 'stood up by the U.S. government'?"

Duke smiled and said, "Yep. My bride was almost here. Just a mile off the coast in fact. She could have jumped in the water and swam from Angel Island to my waiting

159

arms. But guess what? The U.S. government sent her packing. Told her to go back home. She wasn't welcome here. I guess they told her 'We're full up on Japs over here. Don't need any more. Thanks for stoppin' by. Go on home'."

Takeo pulled his friend to the sofa and took the empty bottle from his hand.

"Listen to me," he said. "What happened? Why did they send her back?"

Duke stopped for a moment and looked at Takeo. His swollen lip began to tremble and tears formed in his dark eyes. Takeo snapped, "Sachi, fix some coffee for Duke. Mamma-san, I need a cold cloth and a blanket."

The women left the men alone, but Sachi could see them from her position in the kitchen. She could hear the pain and tears in Duke's voice. Duke sobbed, "They told me at the dock. It's new. A new immigration law. No more Japanese."

Takeo shook his head, "No. It's just no laborers. No Japanese men. Women and children have always been allowed."

Duke lay back on the sofa and closed his eyes, causing more tears to flow down his tired, swollen, face. He said, "No. Not anymore. It's new. No more Japanese. No more Japs over here. We don't want 'em. Nobody wants 'em. Nobody wants me. "

When Sachi returned with coffee Duke was lying on the sofa. Yoshida had placed a blanket over him and Takeo removed his shoes. Sachi took the cold cloth and gently wiped Duke's face. Duke opened his eyes for a moment and looked into hers. He whispered, "That's better. I knew it was a dream. Just a dream."

And he fell into sleep.

160

Takeo said, "Well, I don't know that he'll remember any of this in the morning, including how he ended up with a bloodied mouth and black eye, but maybe that's best."

Yoshida asked, "What was he saying 'no more Japanese'?"

Takeo sighed, "There's been talk...talk about not allowing Japanese women and children into this country. But I thought it was only talk. I did not think they would...No matter. We will deal with it in the morning. There must have been a mistake."

CHAPTER SEVENTEEN

Duke woke up the next morning and, though he looked awful, he said nothing about his departed bride, the fight he'd obviously been in, or the hang-over he was most certainly suffering. He sipped tea in weary silence. Takeo's gregarious friend had never been still for more than a few seconds, but this was the quiet of a man who had given up.

Sachi and Yoshida prepared breakfast as the two men sat at the table sipping tea. Duke certainly looked defeated with his left eye nearly swollen shut and bruised face and knuckles, but it was not the physical beating that disturbed Takeo. His friend had been in plenty of fights. It was the beating he'd taken within. He planned and waited so long for a bride and now the United States Government told him he could not bring a bride from Japan.

Takeo broke the silence and said, "Duke, we will contact the Japanese embassy. There must have been a mistake."

Duke shook his head, "I don't remember much of last night, but I do remember being told no more Japanese are being allowed to migrate to the United States. Women and children included."

Takeo pressed, "But we need to go and verify what has happened. Certainly there is an explanation."

Duke looked as if he were tired of talking and said, "Takeo, it's been in the papers. The government has hinted that this might happen. And now it has."

Takeo said, "But if you don't marry…"

163

He stopped, but too late. Duke finished his sentence for him, "That's right. If I don't marry, I won't create any Japanese Americans and, hopefully, I won't stick around. I'll go back to Japan where I belong. With my own kind. That's what they're hoping, anyway. I can't even think of how my Liana will explain this to those at home."

He lowered his head and took another sip of tea. Sachi felt ill and embarrassed. She thought of the poor girl on the ship having to go back home in disgrace, sent away by a country that would not allow her entrance because it did not want her babies to be citizens. Duke was a good, hard-working man who wanted nothing more than to have a Japanese bride to help him raise his children in this land he had come to love. She placed breakfast in front of Takeo. Yoshida sat down and sipped the tea she had poured for herself.

"And here I sit bringing this burden to your door. I should have gone home last night, but I just couldn't face that house alone, not last night," said Duke.

"Nonsense. You came right where you should have come. We are your family." Takeo said, then, hesitating slightly, he asked, "Are you going back?"

Duke, trying to seem cheerful, smiled a lopsided grin with his swollen face and said, "Hell no. I won't go back. I'll just change my plan. That's all. I either have to marry me a white woman, which they'd really love, or…" he looked at Sachi as she placed breakfast in front of him and smiled slyly, "I'll have to wait until one of our Japanese lovelies suddenly becomes available."

Sachi bowed her head in embarrassment and walked over to the sink.

Duke stood and walked over to where Yoshida sat. He knelt down and took her hand in his. He continued, "In fact, I believe there may be some nice Japanese women available that I have not considered. What do you say, Mrs. Watanabe? Ready for another go around?"

Duke laughed, almost as if he were feeling like himself again, as Yoshida snatched her hand from him. She stood up to take her dishes to the sink and said, "Good Grief. I wouldn't have anything to do with you even if I were in the market for a husband, which I am not. You must still be under the influence of that illegal liquor you brought in this house last night. When you sober up you'll decide to go back to Japan and we will probably be ready to go with you."

Sachi cringed at the thought. She looked quickly at Takeo who acted as if he hadn't heard his mother's remark, concentrating on Duke and smiling at his friend's laughter. She knew it would be hard from him to tell his mother that, despite what he had said, he had no intention of returning to Japan.

And there were things Sachi, too, did not tell. She never told her husband of the near miss car accident or the meeting with Jack Albright. She didn't want him to worry every time she took the car out alone, but deep down she felt it was more than that.

She was learning to trust herself and her intuition. There were things she could keep for herself and even more than that was an overwhelming gratitude that she had made it into America. Six months later and she would have been as Duke's intended bride, heading back to Japan and death or, worse, a life of humiliation and entrapment.

165

Several weeks later Sachi learned that the dream of her mother tossing the baby to her foretold her pregnancy. She knew what her body was telling her even though she was young and had never been pregnant. The town doctor confirmed it and as she drove to the market she smiled at the doctor's words.

"Mrs. Watanabe, you're going to be a mother."

Mother. The very word, though foreign in its use as applied to her, was a comforting word. It produced feelings of acceptance and protection. She smiled all the way to the market.

Everything had changed. The world looked different now, filled with even more color and warmth. Mr. Grimshaw, the usually acerbic large man who owned and operated the market, looked almost winsome today. She pulled items off shelves absently, disregarding Yoshida's list that lay on the floorboard of the car outside. She was a wife and soon a mother. She could shop without a list of demands from Yoshida. As she turned a corner she ran into another shopper.

"Excuse me," she said, interrupted from her daze.

"We've got to stop running into one another," a deep voice said.

She focused and realized it was Jack Albright. Suddenly all thoughts of motherhood left her mind and she became inexplicably embarrassed.

"I…" she started. "I was thinking of other things. I wasn't paying attention."

He laughed. "Well, I have to admit, I wasn't paying attention either. My sister is visiting for a week and asked me to stop and pick up baking powder and almond extract.

166

Those aren't items I keep in the house. I'm not even sure what you do with them. I can't seem to find them."

Sachi offered, "I can show you where those are."

As they walked over to the baking section Jack talked of his sister visiting from St. Louis and how much he enjoyed having her there.

"The life of a bachelor can get pretty lonely, not to mention my sister's cooking is out of this world. I don't know what I'll do when she leaves."

Sachi smiled and thought of Duke. They should have him over more often, especially now. She had heard from Takeo that Duke was spending more time drinking and fraternizing with the women on the hill than farming.

She handed Jack some baking powder and turned to get the almond extract. As she reached toward the shelf, it began to shake. The ground shifting beneath her felt like a ship on the ocean. She tried to maintain her balance as the entire store shook and several bottles fell from the shelves and broke on the floor. She heard Mr. Grimshaw shout, "Earthquake."

At the same moment, Jack Albright pulled her to him and put his arms around her, positioning his back toward the glass bottles on the shelf behind them to protect her.

She felt nauseous immediately and thoughts of her mother's last moments flooded her head. She began to cry. The quake lasted only 15 seconds, but it seemed much longer than that to Sachi. There wasn't much damage. No one was hurt and the building appeared to suffer no structural damage. Mr. Grimshaw immediately began taking

167

inventory of the few broken items. Sachi, along with a few bottles from the shelves, were all that had been upset.

Jack continued to hold her close even after the quake ended. Trying to comfort her, he said, "Mrs. Watanabe, this is California. We get earthquakes once in a while. They're usually little tremors that hardly ever do any real damage."

Sachi continued crying. She could not stop and she could not move. She was not crying out of fear of death. She thought of her mother and her new baby. Images and buried emotions flooded her mind, overwhelming her. She cried thinking of her mother's last few moments, the confusion and fear she must have felt. She cried thinking her mother had no one around to try and protect her during her last few moments on earth, nor during her entire lifetime. Father certainly had not protected her from life's harshness.

Jack released her, led her to a chair by the back door, and asked if she'd like some water. She shook her head.

Mr. Grimshaw yelled from several aisles over, "Is everything okay back there? Somebody hurt?"

"No," Jacked yelled back. "We're fine."

He turned to Sachi and said, "Mrs. Watanabe, it's okay. You're all right."

"I'm not all right…"

"Do you want me to take you to a doctor?"

"No. I've just come from the doctor. It's just my mother. My mother is dead."

Jack Albright's eyes widen and he made no reply. Sachi stopped crying as she uttered the words. It was the first time she had spoken of her mother's death. The words came, as if poison drawn from a deep wound.

"Father told me she was dead, but I didn't believe him. Ever since...since I was a child I had learned he did not speak the truth. So I waited. She was life to me and I never considered she might die."

Jack knelt patiently besides her, listening to the story of her mother's death and how she had pretended her mother was still alive.

When she was finished, Jack reached out and took her hand in his. He said, "I can talk a blue streak about farming and weather and fertilizer, but I don't know what to say. I am so sorry. I know what it's like to lose a parent. I lost both of mine when I was young. I was lucky though. I had my sister."

Sachi thought Jack looked like he wanted to hug her or pat her on the back. She told herself it was just a manner of comforting another here in America, but in Japan, touching and physical contact was not their custom, especially between married women and single men. Even her hand in his was too familiar, too intimate. It stirred something inside her and Sachi didn't like the strength and uncertainty of that feeling. So as not to offend Jack and to give her hands something to do, she pulled her hand away, took a tissue from her purse, and dried her tears.

She sighed, tired from crying, "I feel I have just lost my mother today...just as I have learned I am to become one."

He looked at her confused for a moment and then, with realization, asked, "A baby?"

"A baby boy," she said thinking of her dream.

She looked away. Amazed that she sat here telling these secrets to a stranger, a man she didn't even know. She told him before her own husband or her best friend. The fact hit her, but the words had bubbled up so naturally. She rose from the chair as if afraid something else might tumble out of her mouth if she sat there any longer.

"I can't believe I have told you all this. I mean, I haven't told anyone yet. I shouldn't..."

He interrupted, assuring her, "Don't worry. You only told me because of the earthquake. You've had quite a shock today. You need to go home and rest. Don't worry. I'll keep your secrets. No one, but you and I will ever know you told me first about your mother and your son. I am quite honored really. "

"Well...there's no reason to be honored. I didn't mean to tell you any of this," she snapped and hurried past Mr. Grimshaw, who was ordering his clerk to clean up the spills and complaining about how he would recoup this loss, though it was only a few dollars worth of items. She forgot to buy the things needed for dinner that night, but she didn't care. She had to get out of the store and away from Jack Albright. They would forgive her forgetfulness when she delivered the news about the baby.

As she drove home she felt a strangeness, a vulnerability, as if she had butterflies in her stomach and couldn't catch her breath. She pulled over to the side of the road, opened the car door, and suddenly threw up. She attributed all the emotion to her pregnancy. That must be it.

She did not want to tell Takeo right away. She wanted to hold onto the information, the knowledge of her baby in her. It was almost like uttering the words of her mother's death. She knew once she told Takeo of the baby, life would be different. Maybe not right away, but she would no longer be a young bride. She would be instantly transformed into that next phase of life: mother.

CHAPTER EIGHTEEN

But there was no waiting. Takeo and Yoshida knew she had been to the doctor twice. Yoshida was waiting for her when she returned home. As she walked up to the porch Yoshida sat in her rocking chair, sewing and rocking. All movement stopped and Yoshida asked, "Well, what did the doctor say?"

Sachi did not want Yoshida to know before she told her husband, but then she thought of Jack. Takeo would not be the first person to know anyway and she could think of no way to avoid Yoshida's question. She said, "I am going to have a baby."

Yoshida smiled, returned to her rocking and sewing, and whispered to herself, "I knew it."

Then as if she realized she had forgotten herself, she looked up at Sachi and said, "And the things for dinner?"

Sachi opened the screen door to go into the house and said, "I forgot them. I'm…I'm sorry. I'll go tomorrow."

"I see," Yoshida said. "Well, the baby is good news. Finally. We were beginning to worry."

Sachi stopped at the door and turned back to her mother-in-law, feeling a sudden surge of anger. She asked, "We?"

Yoshida continued to rock and answered, "Yes. Takeo and I."

Sachi felt like a prize cow being bred for its off-spring and the owners were starting to worry whether their investment would pay off. Sachi said, "Takeo never mentioned any worry to me."

Yoshida smiled slightly again and shrugged her shoulders. Sachi went into the house. She felt vulnerable. The doctor had said pregnancy could make a woman highly emotional, but Sachi knew it was not the pregnancy. This baby inside her was the one thing in her life she knew, without uncertainty, was real and strong. She hoped this pregnancy would bring her closer to her husband so she would feel a part of him and their life together, but Yoshida had a way of casting doubt in her mind.

When Takeo arrived home, Sachi had planned exactly how she would announce the impending arrival of their first child. This announcement would be her first official act as a mother and it would be her gift to Takeo. He had wanted children for so long and now she was able to make his dream come true. It was a powerful, wonderful feeling and suddenly the vulnerability she'd felt moments before vanished. It was replaced with excitement.

She heard the back door screen close and she rushed to the kitchen to greet him. He was breathing hard as he sat on the stool by the door and removed his boots. He looked up at her. His sun-browned skin was dry and his hands and fingernails were caked in dirt.

He asked, "Why do you look at me like that?"

Sachi smiled broadly and Takeo's face lit up in a way Sachi had not seen before. He asked, "Does that smile have something to do with your doctor's visit today?"

Sachi began to nod her head when Yoshida entered the room.

"Sachi is pregnant," she announced as she busied herself with dinner preparations. "We will have a baby here soon. There is much to plan."

Takeo, still smiling, walked toward Sachi. Sachi turned to Yoshida with her eyes wide and burst into tears. Takeo stopped short of her with a look of confusion on his face.

Sachi ran out the front door. The warm wind was blowing slightly as she ran to the barn. She stopped, leaning against an old bull pine tree, and began to sob uncontrollably. She knew Yoshida intentionally ruined this moment with her husband. She had tossed out the news as if she were tossing out dishwater. How could she expect to have love grow with this man? How could she expect them to get closer with Yoshida right in the middle of them?

A few minutes passed and Takeo quietly walked outside. He stood next to her and touched her shoulder gently and only for a moment.

"I am happy to hear of our baby. This is wonderful news."

Sachi remained silent.

"Mamma-san says that we must learn to accept your outburst of emotion. She says women carrying babies often act this way, weak and out of control. It is okay."

Sachi felt the anger surge again. "Why don't you ask me what I feel? Mama-san can't speak for me, though apparently she thinks she can. How could she blurt the news to you of our baby?"

Takeo looked confused again and said, "Does it matter, my wife? The fact remains the same. You are having our baby."

"Of course it matters. It was not her place to tell you. It was mine."

Takeo nodded his head in tacit agreement.

"She is excited for us. She has wanted grandchildren for so long."

"I don't care. You tell her she was wrong. I will tell her nothing more. And why are you speaking to your mother about your fears of your wife not being able to get pregnant? That is wrong as well."

Takeo said, "My mother should not have shared that with you. I simply thought I had waited too long to try and be a father. I didn't want to upset you."

He was quiet for a moment.

Sachi filled the silence with her words, "I have something else to tell you. I… I have been unable to say these words for many months, but I think this baby has strengthened me somehow, contrary to what your mother says. It is something about my family in Japan I have not shared with you. I told you they were fine and Father is fine, but… you know of the Kanto earthquake?"

"Of course," Takeo said. "The newspapers reported over 100,000 people died."

"Almost 143,000." Sachi said.

Takeo's jaw tightened, but he remained silent and looked toward the ground then back to his wife. She knew it was not respectful to correct her husband, but she did not want those deaths discounted. Each life was important and when so many go together, it is easy to speak of them as simply numbers without meaning.

Sachi struggled to find and speak the words living inside her all these months. She looked into Takeo's eyes. He was waiting patiently.

Sachi said, "My mother...

Her eyes filled and overflowed as she spoke the word mother. As if the tears were the oil greasing her words so they flowed smoothly from her lips, she said, "My mother was one of the people who died that day. My mother is dead."

Sachi longed to be held, to have her husband put his arms around her and comfort her just as Jack Albright had tried to do. She longed for her husband to tell her it was all right and she was a brave woman for getting through this. She wanted him to thank her for telling him even though it hurt almost more than she could bear to say the words, but he did none of those things. He stood as if planted in the ground.

He was quiet a moment and then asked, "Why did you lie to me? Why didn't you tell me right away?"

Sachi continued crying, but said, "It hurt too much. I couldn't say the words. When I came here I could pretend she was still alive, living back home with Father. But now...It's hard to pretend anymore. I mean the earthquake today. The baby. Everything. It just came out."

Takeo walked to her and held her hand. He patted it gently and said, "Yes. That's right, the earthquake today, and the baby. I am sorry to hear of your mother's death, but it was a long time ago now."

Sachi found herself thinking of Jack's firm grasp on her hand, connecting them, assuring her he was there and not going away. Takeo's grip was slight and he patted her hand gently and only for a moment.

Sachi turned and looked up at the sky as if talking to her mother and not her husband, "It feels like it just happened, just today."

"It's alright," Takeo said. "I am not angry."

Sachi turned and leveled her gaze at him. He was still in his dirty work clothes and he smelled of earth and sweat. She was amazed at his lack of concern for her feelings and his apparent interest only in the fact she had hidden her mother's death, not in the death itself. She flashed to Jack Albright's face, his compassion and sympathy. When she looked at Takeo's face she saw nothing. He wanted to be done with this conversation and go in to dinner. She marveled that a stranger showed more understanding and concern than her own husband.

Incredulous, she repeated his words, "You are not angry?"

Takeo shook his head and said, "No. Not now."

Sachi raised her voice slightly and asked, "Why? Is it because I am having your baby? Is that it? As if hiding my mother's death was an offense against you?"

Takeo nodded, "In a manner. I mean you lied to me. A wife should not lie to her husband."

Sachi said, "Don't you understand? How could I tell you the truth? I was lying to myself, pretending. This is very difficult for me. You have no right to be angry."

Takeo looked confused and mumbled, "I thought... I am sorry about your mother. I...I just...please do not upset yourself this way. It is not good for the baby. Come, have something to eat."

Sachi's tears stopped. She had gotten more sympathy and understanding from Jack Albright in the middle of a grocery store than here alone with her husband. His concern was not for her and her feelings except in how they might effect his child.

"I am not hungry," she said stubbornly.

"Well, I will have mamma-san fix you some tea."

"I will fix it myself."

"No, no. You need to rest. I will make your tea. I think I can do that, maybe. I will try. Whatever you want. Just come inside and eat something. No more tears. What's done is done. We will speak no more of it."

Sachi said, "I'll be in shortly."

Takeo walked inside to start her tea. Sachi's heart ached, but along with the pain she felt a new sensation, power. She suddenly felt brave and she realized this pregnancy gave her power. She felt this power surge through her. She didn't know where this feeling came from. Maybe it was the beginning of her maternal instinct kicking in and causing deep feelings of protection. She knew the balance of power was shifting within the Watanabe home, even if Yoshida did not yet realize it. She wanted to get even with the old woman for all the remarks about her mother, her marriage, and her clumsiness. She had not made Sachi feel welcomed in the role of new wife and Sachi decided she had the power to make the old woman feel uncomfortable in the role of new grandmother.

She stood staring into the distance planning how she could shift this balance of power, if she wanted, when a familiar brown truck appeared headed toward their farm.

It was Jack Albright. He pulled into the Watanabes' drive, exited his vehicle, and looked around before walking toward her. Sachi's heart leapt into her throat and she wasn't completely sure why. He had said he would keep her secret of the baby boy and her mother's death and the near-miss car incident weeks earlier. She had failed to tell Takeo of that as well. He would think she lied about all things. She was afraid of his anger. All it would take is one slip. Certainly he hadn't come out here simply to betray her, but what would Takeo think of her confiding in him. If he found out, he would not understand, she was sure of that. She could not explain it.

She walked toward him and, even with the setting sun in her eyes, she could see his bright smile. At the very moment she was beginning to feel brave and in control, he showed up, making her feel vulnerable and uncertain.

Jack smiled and said, "Good afternoon, Mrs. Watanabe."

Sachi knew she should be polite, but something within her was seething and Takeo would be upon them in a matter of minutes. She said quietly with a nod of her head, "Good day, Mr. Albright. Why are you here?"

Albright smiled again feigning shock at her sharp tone, "I am here in part on business and in part to check on you. How are you feeling?"

"I am feeling fine. As you can see."

He stared at her a moment too long and said, "Yes, I see."

She was confused by his look and he immediately looked away, toward the fields and the house. He seemed embarrassed and she was not sure why. She was the one to be embarrassed.

She continued, "There is no need to check on me, really. I am fine."

Jack fixed his gaze upon her intently and said, "You ran out this afternoon so quickly. Considering the state you were in, and how fast you've been known to drive, I just wanted to make sure you made it home."

Sachi could not meet the intensity of his gaze. She felt inexplicably guilty and, when their eyes did meet, she looked instantly to the ground as if his eyes had burned hers, like looking into the hot sun.

She said, "I apologize for speaking so sharply to you. I know you were simply trying to help me and thank you for that, but I don't think you should…"

Takeo stepped up from behind, interrupting her, and said, "Hello, Mr. Albright. I see you've met my wife."

She bowed her head slightly toward him, not lifting her eyes from the ground. She felt the blood rushing in her ears and waited for his next words.

"Oh yes," he said still smiling. "I saw Mrs. Watanabe in town today at the store."

"Oh?" Takeo said. "I did not know that."

He smiled again and said, "Yes. During that earthquake. Some things fell from the shelf very near where we were standing. Mrs. Watanabe was kind enough to show me where the almond extract was kept."

Sachi simply nodded.

Jack continued, "Oh, yes, and I believe we may have passed each other on the road once or twice."

Sachi nodded nervously and said, "Perhaps. I only take the car to town every so often."

Jack smiled, "Well, be careful. There are some crazy drivers out there."

He turned his attention to Takeo and said, "I just wanted to stop by and see what you've been doing out here. It looks good."

Takeo was anxious to talk of his farm. Sachi remained rooted to her spot as the two men walked toward the fields. She glanced at Jack's truck and saw the words California Department of Agriculture printed in white lettering on the side of his truck door. That was his "business."

She watched the two men talk. The wind brushed back Jack's brown hair, cooling his glistening forehead. He closed his eyes for a moment facing the breeze and smiled into

182

the wind as if in silent thanks. He removed a short pencil from behind his ear and absently licked the point before jotting down his notes on the clipboard he held in his hand.

As she watched them, noticing how very different they were from one another, she realized she was attracted to Jack in a way people are when they see things that are the complete opposite of themselves. He was a curiosity to her. He was one of the few white men she had studied up close beside Mr. Goodman, their neighbor. Jack was young and his laugh was loud and strong. He threw his head back enjoying that moment. That was the way Americans laughed.

It was a kind of laugh she wanted. She imagined herself at an American party. Everyone dressed in expensive gowns and suits. She stood holding a glass of champagne, something she had never even tasted. Interesting people surrounded her and she threw her head back at some wonderfully funny joke. In this image Takeo was not with her, but Jack was. The image disturbed her immediately.

"What are you doing?" a voice demanded bringing her back to reality.

She turned and saw Yoshida standing behind her.

"I am thinking," Sachi mumbled, embarrassed to be caught in her daydream, wondering if Yoshida could somehow decipher her thoughts.

Yoshida said, "Well, come inside and think. We have peas to shell for dinner. If you want to daydream, shell peas while you do it."

Sachi was instantly embarrassed, "Daydream?"

Yoshida said, "Women having babies do it all the time, stand around thinking of the baby and daydreaming the day away. I guess you'll do less work than ever now."

Sachi ignored the insult, thankful Yoshida thought she was daydreaming of her baby. This added to her guilt, however, dreaming of parties when she should be dreaming about her baby.

She was still angry with Yoshida, but as she sat down at the table in the kitchen and began shelling peas she was not thinking of that. Yoshida acted as if nothing had occurred. She began preparing lemonade at the sink. The last of the warm June sun and a light breeze poured through the kitchen windows.

Sachi asked, "What is the California Department of Agriculture?"

Yoshida said, "What? Where did you see that?"

Sachi continued shelling peas and said, "Outside on that man's truck."

Yoshida answered, "It is where Mr. Albright works. He comes and inspects the fields, monitors how different farmers do things differently, gives advice. When Takeo takes harvests into town, Mr. Albright is there to inspect and make sure things run smoothly. Of course, he is there, too, when other crops come in: grapes, artichokes, lettuce, all kinds of things."

Sachi asked, off-handedly, "Is he a good man, I mean, at his job?"

Yoshida turned from the sink and looked at Sachi as if sizing her up.

"He is young and has only been in our area a year or so, but he has a reputation for being honest and respectful, qualities which can be difficult to find in a young person these days. I would say he is a good man," Yoshida added, "at his job."

Yoshida finished making lemonade and Sachi shelled the last pea when Jack and Takeo entered the kitchen. The door creaked and Jack seemed to fill the doorframe. He followed Takeo's lead and removed his muddy boots.

Yoshida said, "Sit down, Mr. Albright."

She handed him a glass of lemonade and poured one for Takeo. Sachi would have liked a glass, but Yoshida seemed to have forgotten about her with the arrival of men in the kitchen and so she sat with the bowl of peas in her lap. She stared at the little green balls, which looked to her as if someone's green pearl necklace had come unstrung.

Takeo sipped his lemonade while Jack Albright finished off the glass in three gulps. Yoshida was immediately at his elbow with the pitcher. He drank half the glass and then slowed. Sachi saw Yoshida shake her head in a tsk, tsk sort of way undetectable to anyone else.

Sachi knew these large Americans did not have the refined manners of the Japanese. They took in life like Jack Albright took in his lemonade, quickly and in large gulps, while the Japanese took in life slowly, mindfully.

Yoshida asked, "Mr. Albright…"

He interrupted, "Call me Jack, please."

"Of course," Yoshida said. "Jack, have you met Takeo's wife, Sachi?"

Jack nodded, "Yes. I saw Mrs. Watanabe at the store this morning. As I was telling Takeo, she was kind enough to help me find some almond extract my sister wanted. And then the earthquake began."

"Oh?" Yoshida asked, looking at Sachi who still had her head down. "Sachi, I thought you said you forgot to go to the store today?"

Sachi did not know what to say. She sat motionless staring into the bowl in her lap. Her fingers tightened around the edges and she felt as if she were going to be sick.

Jack interrupted, as if swinging in on a vine, and said, "Mrs. Watanabe forgot her groceries as did several people. The earthquake upset many people this afternoon. "

Takeo changed the subject and said, "Jack says our strawberries are the best he's seen so far and the weather looks like it will let them produce all season this year. I have to say I agree. I think the fertilizer change we talked about this winter has helped a great deal."

Yoshida looked again at Sachi as if unsure and then turned back to the sink.

Jack smiled and nodded agreement at Takeo's words. He said, "I am very impressed with what you have managed to do here. From what I understand, the last owner was unable to grow much of anything."

Takeo said, "Well, proper soil preparation is important, but continued feedings are also important. The earth gives back to you what you give to it, like a child to its parents."

Jack looked at Sachi and said, "Speaking of children, congratulations, Mrs. Watanabe. I understand you will soon be blessed with a baby."

Sachi felt her face burn once again and she was sure everyone was looking at her. Why did her stomach churn each time he gazed at her? She stared at the peas in the bowl and started to sweat.

As if he could read her mind and to clarify, Jack said, "Mr. Watanabe just told me while we were outside so I thought congratulations were in order."

Sachi's heart pounded in her ears and her throat was dry. Why didn't Yoshida pour her a glass of lemonade? Sachi nodded her thanks for his good wishes.

He asked, "Boy or girl?"

Yoshida interrupted, "Mr. Albright, Sachi doesn't know if…"

Sachi interrupted her mother-in-law, and without taking her eyes from Jack's face, she said, "It's a boy."

He raised his eyebrows, smiled, and nodded.

Yoshida dismissed her, "I think it will be a girl. Look at the way you carry yourself. You're not showing much yet, but your stance says it is a girl."

She looked at Yoshida and repeated with a deliberate voice, "Nonetheless, it is a boy."

Takeo verbally stepped in the middle and said, "Boy or girl. I will be happy with either one. Healthy is what matters."

Suddenly Sachi jumped up from the table, repeated, "It is a boy," and then clamped her hand over her mouth and ran out the back door.

Jack stood up. Takeo looked at his mother and asked, "What happened?"

Yoshida appeared unconcerned and continued dinner preparations, She said, "Morning sickness. Sit down Jack. Will you stay for dinner?"

Jack sat slowly back down and nodded.

Yoshida continued, getting in the last word, "Good. Well, I hope Sachi is right and it is a boy. That would be best, but I think it will be a girl and I haven't been wrong yet."

CHAPTER NINETEEN

Sachi gave birth to a baby boy, choosing an American first name and a middle name to honor Takeo's late father. The first American Watanabe was named William Masato Watanabe.

Billy arrived one cold December morning after a quick labor of only a few hours. Mrs. Goodman, who helped deliver many babies in town over the years, delivered nine pound Billy to his mother's arms, while Ikuko stood beside them. Ikuko had wisely assigned Yoshida the job of caring for Takeo and they waited in the living room.

Billy was a large, robust child who seemed anxious to enter the world. Sachi's muffled moans and grunts were quickly replaced with Billy's loud, frantic cry as both mother and son were propelled into new lives.

With no previous experience caring for babies, Sachi felt much like a helpless child herself those first few months. Yoshida was full of advice and, as she often pointed out, experience, which made Sachi feel even less competent. Sachi missed her mother at her wedding and many times since her mother's death, but this, having her first child, was another reason to grieve the loss anew. Particularly since Sachi was forced to rely on Yoshida's advice, which many times was good, but given in such an insistent, officious manner Sachi began to resent it.

During one particularly difficult day, Billy cried constantly. After making sure he was dry and fed, Sachi held him tight and rocked him back and forth as he continued wailing. Yoshida entered the bedroom and insisted, "Sachi, you must leave him in the cradle until he stops crying."

Sachi was tired to the bone and uncertain of what to do. Obviously what she was doing wasn't working and she considered maybe Yoshida knew what was best. Sachi raised her voice to be heard over the baby, "I feel like maybe he will quiet down soon. I don't think I can just leave him alone to cry."

Yoshida shook her head and spoke with such authority Sachi felt she must know what was right. Yoshida warned, "Don't listen to me, but if you continue to cater to him in this indulgent manner he will only grow up to be a weak, difficult, spoiled child."

Sachi did not want to spoil him so, fighting every maternal instinct she had to hold him tight, she obeyed Yoshida's command and put Billy in his cradle leaving him to cry himself to sleep. But he refused to sleep and his crying grew more insistent. Each time Sachi rose to go and check on him, Yoshida cautioned, "Let him be. Do not let him win this."

Finally, after an hour passed, Sachi could no longer tolerate the crying. Her breasts leaked from the sounds of her baby's misery. She rose from her chair, entered the bedroom where Billy lay screaming in his cradle, and picked him up. His face was beet red and little tufts of black hair were matted with sweat to his head. His dark eyes were no longer filled with tears, but with a strong emotion Sachi immediately recognized as anger. It was a kind of reaction she would never have expected in a baby. As she drew him near to her chest, he flailed as if fighting her closeness. She thought perhaps he was feverish. Sachi thought of all the illnesses that threatened babies - polio, whooping cough, measles, and mumps. Suddenly a fear over took her that she had never experienced. She sat on the bed and cradled her boy, rocking him and whispering as he cried.

Yoshida stood in the doorway and said, "Now you've done it. Now he will know that if he cries long enough you will eventually come. He has won."

Sachi held him tightly to her chest and yelled at Yoshida, "No. You have lost. Now get out. Get out of here."

She would never have spoken to Yoshida with such anger to defend herself, but she was a mother now protecting her baby. Yoshida's eyes grew wide and she rushed from the doorway. Sachi heard the back door slam and she knew Yoshida was going to talk to Takeo, but Sachi did not care. Right now the only thing that mattered was for her son to know she was there. Fifteen minutes passed and, finally, gradually, Billy quieted. He didn't sleep, but gurgled a bit and accepted Sachi's breast for feeding. As he suckled taking in the milk, he looked into his mother's eyes and all was forgiven.

Takeo entered the room, sweaty and muddy from the fields. He gazed at his quiet son receiving life from his mother. Sachi looked up ready to defend herself. She was so tired, but she was ready to take on Takeo if need be. Thankfully, he did not say anything. He stared at them for a moment and then quietly closed the door, leaving her and her infant son to their sacred work, giving and receiving life. She knew from then on her maternal instinct was more than just what she thought. It was more than just her voice. It was the collective voices of herself and her mother and her mother's mother, all of the people who had come before her. And it was the voice of God. She would begin listening to this voice.

When Billy cried Sachi picked him up immediately. Yoshida bit her tongue, but her eyes and expression gave away her feelings. Sachi did not care. Sachi had been raised to be submissive to her in-laws, but this was America, not Japan, and Sachi was no longer only a "Japanese girl". She was a Japanese woman living in America and she liked the power she felt surge in her from migrating into motherhood and womanhood just as she had migrated to America.

In many ways that week was a blessing. Yoshida was hurt and angry with her and, in turn, did not speak to her, which meant she did not order her about or give unsolicited advice. If Sachi entered the room, Yoshida left if she could. At meal time, Yoshida ate quickly and then went to her room. Sachi liked the silence.

One evening after dinner, Duke arrived. They had seen little of Duke since his bride was returned. He refused dinner invitations saying only that he was too busy. He smelled strongly of alcohol and his clothes were dirty and rumpled. He did not look like the Duke of their first meeting.

Billy was almost eleven months old. He smiled and gurgled as Duke held him. Sachi suggested they sit on the couch, especially since Duke appeared to have been drinking and Sachi was concerned Duke might drop Billy. She stayed close by and watched him intensely, but Duke was gentle and careful and he seemed to snap out of his drinking haze as he stared at Billy, his tiny feet and hands, his beautiful face and wispy dark hair.

192

Duke held him as if he held babies every day and had many children himself. Billy struggled and wriggled. As Duke handed Billy back to her she thought she saw tears in his eyes.

"You are very lucky," he said to Takeo. "He is a beautiful boy with a good mother."

Takeo smiled and said, "And he is a land owner. We have put this farm in his name. Now it truly belongs to the Watanabes."

The smile quickly left Takeo's face and he looked down. Sachi realized he knew he had sounded boastful and was ashamed. Duke did not seem to notice. He smiled at Sachi and she smiled back, thinking how sad it must be to return to his home alone and quiet, especially after visiting his best friend with a new baby.

Takeo changed the subject and asked, "How are things over at your place? Are you getting ready for harvest in a few months? Any problems?"

Duke simply shook his head and laughed, "Things are great at my place. No problems. Not me."

There was an awkward silence that had never existed before.

Sachi offered, "Duke, we have not seen much of you. I wish you would come for dinner. How about tonight?"

Duke said, "I have been very busy. I can't tonight. Things to do. But soon. We will do it soon."

He turned to Sachi and handed her a small box.

"This is a present for Billy. Maybe he can use it when he is old enough to marry. And if marriage does not come to him, you tell Billy he can sell it and just live it up like his Uncle Duke."

Sachi opened the small box and inside was a beautiful opal ring. The opal was large and milky white with a tinge of pink. It reminded Sachi of cow's milk. Thick and pure with a crimson drop from blood that sometimes appeared. It would be the height of rudeness to refuse such a gift even if it was extravagant. Sachi looked into Duke's eyes, searching, questioning.

Duke nodded. "It was for my bride, but that is not to be now. I will watch you and Billy and your children yet to be born and I will think of you all as the family I might have had. But tell Billy he must use it for a great adventure whether it is marriage and family or something a little less strenuous like climbing Mount Everest or hot-air ballooning to Hawaii."

Sachi kissed Duke softly on the cheek and said nothing. Duke looked into her eyes and smiled.

Takeo said, "Duke, you will have need of that. We will hold it for you. Life has a way of changing in a day or a minute. You never know what turn karma will take."

Duke nodded and said, "You're right, Takeo. Life can change in the blink of an eye."

It was the last time they ever saw Duke.

Two nights later Ikuko and Edo arrived unexpectedly in the middle of dinner. It was apparent Ikuko had been crying and Edo was somber. His hair was ruffled and he looked

194

drawn and tired. His large nose and the outline of his eyes were red. Ikuko's eyes were red as well containing traces of tears.

"Takeo, we have had some sad news and felt we should come right over. Not wait until the morning," Edo said.

Takeo asked, "What is it?"

Edo sighed heavily and said, "Duke. Duke was found dead this morning."

Ikuko began to cry again and Edo continued over the sounds of her weeping.

"He was by his car. A sheriff deputy found him late this morning. He'd gone off the road just north of town. You know where I mean?"

Takeo knew as did everyone else in the room. He was going to or leaving the ladies on the hill.

"He hit a tree off the road. He must have been going pretty fast. The whole front end of his car was smashed in. The sheriff said he'd been drinking pretty heavily. He was found a few yards from the car face down in a large puddle of water and mud."

Sachi cried out at the description of Duke's last seconds on earth. It hurt her to think of the kind, funny, boisterous man dying, alone, in a mud puddle on the side of the road. She thought of the animals she saw from time to time dead on the roadside. To think Duke ended his life in such a manner made it even more painful.

Takeo was stunned and kept repeating, "How can that be? How can that be?"

195

Edo shook his head sadly and shrugged his shoulders. Takeo looked about the room

wildly as if he did not know what to focus on or how to react. He looked toward Yoshida

and said, "Mother, he's gone. He was like my brother and he is dead."

Yoshida sat next to him on the couch and tried to comfort him by placing her arm

around his shoulders. He began to cry quietly, silently. Sachi would not have even known

he was crying if she didn't see the tears fall from his eyes. He made no sound or

movement, trying desperately to contain himself.

Sachi wondered at her husband turning to his mother for comfort instead of her, but

she told herself Yoshida had known Duke much longer. Billy was asleep and Sachi found

herself wishing he were awake, giving her someone to hold in her arms, someone to

comfort her and to be comforted by her. Edo held Ikuko. Yoshida held Takeo. Sachi sat

alone feeling empty and out of place. Poor Duke. All he'd ever wanted was to be

accepted and loved and to have a family. Just like her.

Edo continued, "I was in town this evening and ran into Sheriff Malloy. He told me

what happened, wondered if I knew anything. I told him I didn't know anything other

than Duke has been depressed this last year or so ever since, well, once immigration

ended and his bride was sent home.

"When they found him he was pretty badly beaten up, too. I mean he had a swollen

eye and lip. His knuckles were bloodied as if he'd been fighting, which knowing Duke,

he probably had been. The question is how he got into the mud puddle. The sheriff isn't

quite sure. He apparently wasn't thrown from the car so the sheriff figures he must have hit the tree, gotten out of the car and walked a little ways, then collapsed from injuries or a drunken stupor, drowning in the mud puddle. Anyway, the thing is, well... some people in town are already speculating that maybe he was murdered. Some people think he was killed by vigilantes out here who don't like the fact that Duke was messing around with a white woman, a married white woman. I don't know who she is, but that's what they are saying."

Takeo shook off his mother, his grief turning quickly to anger, "Who is saying that? That is not true. Duke would never do something like that. He respected marriage."

Edo continued, "The sheriff talked to a neighbor, the Hammonds, who said he wandered around at night after drinking all day. They said they even found him in their barn one morning after he tied one on. Then I guess they talked to the bartender at The Backwoods who said Duke had been in the night before and gotten into a fight with someone. They didn't know who it was. Probably a drifter. I guess that's where he got all the bruises and cuts, you know, from a fight last night. They said it was all an accident. They aren't investigating any further."

Takeo stood and walked to the front door to look out at the dark, scanning the night sky as if searching for Duke.

Takeo asked, "What do you say Edo? Do you think it was an accident?"

Edo shrugged, "I think Duke wanted to die. Now whether he drank himself into a mud puddle and drowned or whether he fooled around with a white woman and was killed over it I don't know, but I think either way Duke wanted it over. If he didn't do it himself, then he was just as happy to have someone do it for him. Haven't you noticed how depressed he was this last year and it had gotten worse over the last few months?"

Takeo shook his head and said nothing. Billy began to cry from their bedroom. He was hungry.

Yoshida said, "Well, with the baby coming and all the activity around home maybe we weren't as attentive to Duke as we were before. Certainly marriage and family require a lot more time."

Everyone looked at Sachi and nodded quietly. Sachi felt she was being blamed. That somehow if it were not for her and Billy, Takeo would have noticed his friend's depression and tried to save him from himself. She was angry at Yoshida for directing all the blame toward her and again at Takeo for not standing up for her. She did not know how to react. She looked away and her eyes fell on Yoshida's prized porcelain collection. The little figures all stood perfectly poised and dust free waiting to be admired. Sachi, feeling full of sadness and hurt, felt like throwing something against the wall. She imagined what would happen if she stood up, walked over to the cabinet, took out one of Yoshida's precious porcelain figures and smashed it against the wall.

Without a word she stood up, walked past the cabinet, and went quietly into the bedroom to feed her child. While the milk flowed from her breasts for Billy, tears flowed from her eyes for Duke.

CHAPTER TWENTY

Duke's death was ruled accidental and no further investigation was undertaken. Takeo took many months to recover from the unexpected death of his best friend and it wasn't until almost nine months later when Sachi gave birth to their second son that Takeo seemed happy again. They named him Mitchell Dyuke Watanabe.

Unlike Billy, Mitchell took his time arriving and was more than two weeks later than expected. He and Sachi were in the throes of labor for three days. While Sarah Goodman continued to check Sachi and the process of her labor, Ikuko tried to make her comfortable and also keep Yoshida at bay.

Those 72 hours were filled with whispered concerns, loud encouragement, relinquishing moans of exhaustion and grunts of concentration and determination. The heavy smell of life anticipated hung in the air. Sweat, wet cloths, wet sheets, water by the bed, everything seemed wet. Sachi's thoughts were random, the thoughts that come unexpectedly to a mind dealing with a body in pain. She had started with confidence, having done this all before, but that confidence like everything else, except her baby, had left her body, seeping out with the hours of sweat.

Finally, just as Sachi thought she could longer go on, Mitchell arrived. At 5 pounds, he was as frail as Billy had been robust. At birth, he was not breathing and Sarah quickly sucked the deadly mucus from his nose and mouth. He did not cry right away and when he did it was more of a soft whimper than a victorious, loud wail, as if he didn't want to disturb anyone.

As with Billy, they had many visitors over the next several months. Ikuko came almost daily to hold Mitchell and to play with Billy. She sometimes brought a cookie or a white rock crystal or something "interesting" for her "silly Billy". Billy loved his "Auntie Cuckie" who made him laugh and played all the funny games with him. Sarah Goodman stopped by often particularly the first few weeks to check on Sachi more than Mitchell. Sachi enjoyed Sarah's visits. She was a kind, quiet woman with a pioneer determination about her, the kind Sachi had read about in novels. Sachi imagined her with a sunbonnet reining in a team hauling a covered wagon.

Jim Goodman came over, as did Edo. Both men took quick peeks at the baby as Takeo presented him, ruffled Billy's hair, and asked, "How is it being a big brother?"

Then they retired to the porch for a congratulatory drink or smoke.

One afternoon Yoshida's friend, Seda Kusuki, came for a visit carrying a large wicker basket covered with a blue cloth. Ikuko entered Sachi's bedroom and announced Seda would be coming in soon to see her and the baby.

"She's brought a basket of something," Ikuko whispered. "I just hope for your sake she hasn't been baking."

Sachi thought of the muffin story Ikuko loved to tell and laughed. Several minutes later Yoshida and Seda came in with a covered tray. Yoshida took Mitchell from Sachi and Seda laid the tray next to her on the bed.

Seda greeted Sachi in Japanese, as she had not learned any more English than on the day she arrived in America. Sachi wondered if perhaps she spoke English, but found it

200

convenient to pretend otherwise. She politely inquired into Sachi's health. Sachi answered in Japanese and inquired as to her family. Then Sachi asked Seda if she would like to hold Mitchell.

She quickly snatched the baby out of Yoshida's arms and spent the next ten minutes gurgling and cooing to him in Japanese.

Six weeks after Mitchell's birth and about the time Sachi was finally able to move around without any discomfort, there was a knock on the door. Takeo and Yoshida had taken Billy into town for ice cream and to watch a baseball game organized by one of the Japanese clubs in town. The Japanese clubs were becoming more common and a way for the Japanese people to socialize and participate in activities from which they would be excluded otherwise.

Mitchell was asleep and Sachi planned on stealing this time to read, something she had little time for with the arrival of children. *The Last of the Mohicans* sat unopened on the coffee table. Sachi had gone to the library right before Mitchell's birth, but the librarian told her the books she wanted were not lent out. When Sachi inquired as to which books she might borrow, the librarian snapped, "None of them. You may read them here if you like."

"But I have a library card," said Sachi, pulling it from her purse.

The librarian was an older, stiff woman with a lisp that slipped words between her thin lips like letters under a door. She said, "Nonetheless, you cannot remove books from this library."

201

Sachi knew this feeling. She had felt it at home as a girl and she sometimes felt it in America being Japanese. It was a feeling of powerlessness. There was nothing she could do and she accepted it as she accepted the setting of the sun each evening and the rain in the winter. It simply was. But she had learned there were often other roads leading to the same destination. She would find another way.

She stopped at the store on the way home and bought *The Last of the Mohicans* even though she knew it was a selfish indulgence. But she knew if she couldn't read, something inside her, something vital and alive, would shrivel up and die. She would get books as she could.

The Last of the Mohicans was an American story filled with romance and Indians and adventure. It lay on the coffee table calling to her like an old friend and she was anxious to sit down with it when she heard the knocking on the door.

Assuming it was Ikuko, Sachi opened the door planning on telling Ikuko she was tired and needed to lay down, but it was Jack Albright. Sachi automatically tied her robe tighter and tucked her long dark hair behind her ears.

Before Mitchell's birth, Sachi saw Jack many times when he came to the farm to talk with Takeo. Jack and Sachi always spoke, friendly, but protective, innocent and aware, and it seemed to Sachi the unspoken words were the loudest. Jack arrived to check on the crops, discussing the latest techniques, fertilizers, or pesticides with Takeo. They would inevitably come into the house for something to drink, and sometimes Jack stayed for supper. He always accepted the invitation to stay. The discussions were thoughtful and interesting when Jack was around, and Sachi found herself listening carefully to his opinions on everything from music to art to politics. On occasion she offered an opinion and Jack always considered it, turning it over in his mind. It was something she was not used to. Father had never wanted to hear her voice an opinion and Takeo never discussed anything with her except the farm, the house, or the children. He was traditional and his opinion was the opinion of the house.

Sachi knew her feelings for Jack were different than anything she'd felt before and she told herself they stemmed from a developing friendship much like her warm feelings for Ikuko. But she knew there was a difference. Jack seemed to understand her, He did not judge her and he never betrayed her trust.

This Saturday visit was unusual and Sachi was caught off guard. She was unsure whether to ask him in or tell him to go. Since the earthquake several years ago, they had never spoken alone. Jack looked handsome, but nervous and tired. He spoke quickly.

"Good afternoon, Sachi," he said. "I know this is a surprise and I noticed your car is gone. I thought maybe no one was home, but I have had this gift in my car for two weeks now. I've been meaning to drop it off and congratulate you and Takeo, but things have been…hectic, busy lately. Anyway, I see you're not dressed. I'll just leave this for you and come back another time."

Sachi smiled and felt a sudden, surprising calmness juxtaposed to his nervousness.

She said, "Takeo took Billy and Yoshida to the baseball game in town. It's just Mitchell and me. Come in. If you don't mind waiting, I'll go get dressed and then make us some tea."

Jack sighed, as if grateful for the invitation, and entered the house. Sachi went to her bedroom and quickly dressed into a dark brown skirt, green blouse, and dark green cardigan sweater. She didn't feel like stockings and instead put on her slippers. She felt strange dressing in her bedroom while Jack sat on the other side of the wall, alone, with no one else in the house. She checked Mitchell who was sleeping soundly in his cradle by the bed. Somehow her mood had changed. She felt lighter and in the mood for company.

She entered the living room, picking up one foot to show him her footwear and laughing at herself, she said, "I'm keeping the house slippers."

Jack chuckled and said, "They match perfectly."

Jack followed her into the kitchen, bringing the copy of *The Last of the Mohicans* he'd thumbed through while waiting.

"This looks brand new. Did you buy this?"

Sachi did not look up. She simply nodded. She did not want to discuss the humiliation of being turned away at the library, but Jack pushed on.

"Was this a gift?"

Sachi shook her head.

"I thought you liked borrowing books at the library."

Sachi's face was red, and she realized he was not going to let this go.

As she tied her apron around her waist she said, "They won't allow me to borrow books anymore."

Jack thought for a moment and then said, "Late fees?"

Sachi shook her head again and said simply, "Japanese."

Jack looked struck and was quiet a moment. He said, "I am sorry. That's not right. I could…"

Sachi shook her head, dismissing his offer again, and said, "You could do nothing. People think as they think. Give it time, but let's not talk about that now."

Jack attempted to change the subject. "Have you read this yet?"

"Just getting started," Sachi said, "I've been a little busy myself here lately."

Jack laughed, "I'd say so. Is the newest one asleep?"

Sachi nodded, "He's in the bedroom."

She felt odd using the word bedroom with Jack. It seemed too intimate a word to use. It was strange how words took on new meanings with him. She put on her apron and continued to prepare the tea telling herself she was being silly.

Sachi noticed Jack watching her pad around in her house slippers, preparing tea and biscuits with homemade strawberry jam. He seemed to have relaxed, she thought, and looked like he felt comfortable in the warm kitchen with the winter daylight filtering through the window.

"So how is he? Mitchell, right?"

Sachi smiled at the mention of her baby's name. She sat down after putting out the biscuits and tea things.

"He's wonderful. We gave him Duke's name as a middle name. It was very hard on Takeo to lose his best friend, especially in such a shocking, unexpected way."

Jack nodded, "Like when you lost your mother, I suppose."

Sachi looked at him quickly searching for signs of meaning in his words and decided they were only meant as sympathetic kindness. He watched as Sachi poured the tea, delicately, carefully. She didn't spill a drop. Little did he know it had taken her these last years to gain confidence in this and to feel the calmness and serenity one should feel when serving tea.

Jack sipped the warm drink, something he had learned over the last two years from dining with the Watanabe family. Sachi thought of the first time she watched him gulp his lemonade and smiled to herself. It seemed he was never in a hurry when he sat in their kitchen, eating or drinking, talking and laughing. He took his time now.

He spoke calmly and clearly as if stating the weather forecast, "I have recently lost someone I loved. My only sister."

Sachi's eyes grew wide and she automatically reached out to touch Jack's arm in comfort and compassion and whispered, "Oh, Jack. I am so sorry. What happened?"

Jack did not move his arm and his eyes searched her momentarily. He breathed in deeply, as if preparing himself, and then looked out the window, to the fields.

"She died two weeks ago. She wrote a few months ago saying she'd taken a bad fall at home and broken her leg. She was bed ridden for quite a while, I guess. The doctors weren't sure it would heal properly. They did what they could, but they weren't sure she'd walk the same again. I thought that was the biggest problem that lay ahead for her. Walking a little different.

"Anyway, she developed pneumonia and four days later she was dead. Her husband, Andy, called the day before she died. I asked him how serious it was and he said he thought she was getting better. She was in the hospital. They were taking care of her. He didn't really see a reason for me to come and said I should plan a visit after she recovered so she could enjoy it. I thought I had plenty of time with her. I told him I'd wait and the next day he called and said she was…dead."

He began to cry, but continued speaking, trying to catch his breath between sobs, as if he'd just run a long distance, "The worst of it is I didn't get to say goodbye. There have been so many things I wanted to tell her. She raised me after our parents died. She took a job cleaning floors at night and waitressing during the day just so I could go to school and get an education. She was the strong one, pushing me through life when I was scared and pulling me through when I was stubborn, which was all the time. She was my family. The only person in this world who meant anything to me and now I am alone. I'm all alone."

He broke down in sobs, holding his head in his hands. His body heaved, rising and falling with each cry, the movement of mourning. Sachi stood and walked over to him, leaning down and wrapping her right arm around his shoulders. Automatically, without thought, physically needing someone to comfort him, to hold him, he turned, wrapping his arms around Sachi's waist and burying his tear stricken face into her red gingham apron. Sachi placed her hands on his head, smoothing his hair back, holding him and allowing him to hold her.

She didn't say anything. There was nothing to say. She didn't want to tell him it was okay or that things would be all right. Sachi knew right now Jack felt things would never be all right again. She also knew when someone tells you things will be okay, you lose trust in that person, not believing them or their words, knowing they just don't understand. And she did understand. It would never feel okay.

Slowly the cries diminished to whimpers and the whimpers became sighs. Jack held fast to Sachi and looked up at her.

He sniffled and said, "You are the only one."

Suddenly, as if his mouth had betrayed him, he let go and pulled a handkerchief from his pocket to wipe his eyes and blow his nose. Sachi removed her apron and laid it across the counter. Then she took her seat, waiting for him to explain his remark, but afraid it contained serious meaning, hoping it was just the ramblings of a wounded man and hoping it was not.

He looked at her, his eyes red and puffy, and perhaps even more brilliant blue by contrast.

He said quickly, "What I mean is you are the only one I thought of when this happened. I knew you would understand how I felt without me having to explain it. I mean, you lost your mother and weren't able to say goodbye. I thought you would know."

Sachi nodded, feeling tears well in her eyes, and said, "Yes. I know what it is to lose the one person who is everything to you. I know that feeling of being left completely and utterly alone. Tell me about her, your sister. What did she look like?"

Jack began describing his sister and talked about her life. Sachi knew it felt good to talk of the person you'd lost. She had learned that the hard way. She knew he needed to talk about her. Even though it was painful, like childbirth, a tiny piece of that person was reborn in the talk, alive again, if only for a moment. Jack talked for an hour and Sachi listened quietly, just nodding her head or asking a pertinent question here or there.

Then he talked about the loneliness and said, "She lived across the country, but at least I always knew she was there. She was my connection and now I feel so alone. People say it goes away and you go back to normal, but it never went away after my parents died. It's still there. Only worse now that my sister is gone."

Sachi shook her head and said, "It never went away for me. Once you lose that person you are left with vulnerability, a knowing of what it is like to be alone. Maybe you close yourself off to everyone so you never have to experience that kind of pain again. Or, if you're lucky, you develop a greater appreciation for the people around you."

Jack said, "I have no one around me."

Sachi drew a deep breath and said, "Then Jack, it's time you started looking around you. A man eventually creates his own family. There are probably many wonderful women that you come in contact with every day."

Jack looked at Sachi for what seemed a long time and finally said, "Yes. Some days."

Sachi leaned forward, knowing this was talk of an intimate nature, but also wanting to soothe Jack's troubled heart. He was reaching out to her and he was alone. Jack had tried to comfort her when she talked about her mother. She wanted to help him now.

Sachi said, "You will always miss your sister and your parents, but you can start to fill that emptiness inside and find someone who will love you for all your wonderful traits, your kindness, your sense of humor, your love of the land. There is a woman out there who would be perfect for you."

Jack said quietly, "I know there is."

Sachi asked, "It's not my place to ask, but do you have someone in mind?"

Jack nodded.

"Then you must approach her when the time is right. You might find she feels the same."

Jack shook his head, "No. She couldn't possibly."

He looked at his watch and said, "I have taken much more of your time than I intended, but Sachi, I am so thankful you were here and that you were alone this afternoon."

As if on cue, a cry from the bedroom interrupted Jack and Sachi smiled, "Well, almost alone."

"Yes," said Jack, rising from the table and walking toward the front door as Sachi followed behind him. "I must go. Thank you again, Sachi. What can I do for you? I would like to do something special."

"Oh, no," said Sachi. "You must not do anything."

He nodded and then, as if suddenly remembering something, he said, "I know. I will bring you books. I have a whole collection at my house courtesy of my sister who worked hard to try to educate a very stubborn brother. I will bring you books to read and you will tell me what you think about them. Yes, it all seems right, doesn't it?"

He stepped outside and turned, grabbing Sachi's hand. Her eyes grew wide, but she didn't pull away.

He kissed it softly and said, "You don't know what you did for me today. I really needed to talk, but more than that, I just needed to know there was someone out here who would listen."

Sachi drew her hand back and watched him climb into his truck to leave. Mitchell's cries and her own leaking breasts drove her to the bedroom to feed her son. She picked him up and held him close, her full breasts filling his empty stomach.

Sachi never told anyone of her afternoon with Jack. When her family arrived home late that afternoon, Sachi was asleep on her bed, Mitchell lay sleeping to her right and *The Last of the Mohicans* lay unopened on the bed beside her.

CHAPTER TWENTY-ONE

Sachi had much for which to be thankful. She had been in America 16 years. Her husband was hard working and her three children, Billy, 16, Mitchell, 14 and John, 8 were healthy, happy American citizens. She was not allowed to become an American, but her children were and that was something no one could take away from them, she thought. They had even built on a third bedroom to accommodate their growing family.

Yoshida insisted each child maintain Japanese citizenship as Japan allowed dual citizenship. Sachi was against it for many reasons. She saw this as Yoshida paving the way for their return to Japan. She wanted her boys to be Americans. There was no need to deny their Japanese heritage, but there was no reason to pretend that they might someday go live in Japan, a place that was as foreign to them as Africa or Switzerland.

Takeo, as with all things, eventually sided with his mother, asking, "What could it hurt to have the best of both worlds, to be accepted in both worlds as a citizen?"

So after each birth Takeo applied for and received Japanese citizenship for each of his children.

Life plodded along like a good plow horse, back and forth, without change of course. Farming and raising a family demanded a large degree of practicality and true love was not the measure of one's life. For a farmer, children were life, not only for the man, but for his livelihood and his farm. A farmer was a grower outside his home, inside his home, inside his wife.

Sachi loved Takeo, but passion never reared its fiery head. He was a caretaker and like a brother to her. She was like his farmland to him. He planted his seeds deep within the beloved soil and marveled at the way it all grew so strong and full of life, but he did not accept her as an equal. He never shared his fears or sat back and laughed with her. He was a serious man of serious ways and there was no time for laughter or mirth in raising the crops or the children.

The urgency of her escape had diminished with time in Sachi's mind and her previous life was a dim memory. Ironically, she could no longer remember her mother's face and she could not forget Father's, no matter how hard she tried.

Thankfully, there was little time for much backward reflection in Sachi's life. With growing boys the focus was on the future and the concerns of the here and now. Every evening at dinner the weather was discussed. Would there be too much rain this season or too little? Would hot weather come too early and burn the crops or would it come too late and effect production?

After the weather, Takeo talked to his children about respect for elders, about controlling anger, and maintaining dignity. Saving face and working together, these were the important things in life.

One day John came home from school and told the family the Lion's club was offering a medal to the person in the second grade who carried the best marks for the semester. John was an excellent student and he had worked hard that term determined to win the medal.

The day the semester ended John announced at the dinner table that the medal had been awarded to Susie Carter. He began to cry. Through his tears, he looked up at Sachi and asked, "Why? Why did she get it? I'm smarter than her and my grades were better."

Sachi felt a sharp pain deep in her heart as she searched for words to comfort her son.

Before Sachi could answer, Billy said, "Aw...that's the way it is John. No sense crying about it. They're probably going to have the newspaper come out and they want some little white girl representing their school. Not some Japanese kid. There's nothing you can do about it."

Sachi was surprised at Billy's comments so cavalier and, unfortunately, most likely true she thought. Mitchell rose to put his plate in the sink, but Yoshida intercepted it and took it from him. Mitchell smiled at his grandmother and said to John, "Who knows. Maybe it doesn't have anything to do with how you look. Maybe your grades weren't good enough. Have you thought of that?"

"But they were," John insisted. "I know it."

Billy asked, "So did you ask the teacher about it?"

John shook his head and looked down in his lap. "No," he answered. "I was too embarrassed. I didn't want to cry in front of everyone."

Billy punched his brother playfully on the arm and said, "Well then stop blubbering about it. You have to learn to stand up for yourself and if you don't, then quit whining."

215

Takeo sat back from the table and repeated the advice his father had given him, advice he had given the boys dozens of times. He said, "We are rivers. We simply go around the obstacles and flow forward."

As he spoke, his hand weaved back and forth like a snake or a fish in water. "You are a river. Just go around it."

Sachi and Yoshida remained silent and both began clearing the table. Sachi had felt the sting of prejudice, but it hurt much more when her children were treated unfairly. She worried most about Mitchell. He was small for his age, thin, frail looking, but at 14 he already had big dreams. He wanted to go to college and medical school. Sachi feared that opening himself to the wider world would bring more disappointment and pain than he could manage and she would not be able to comfort him. John was still young and she didn't worry as much about Billy. He was strong, handsome, and ready to take on the world and the family farm. He had no aspirations outside Orange Grove, but Sachi knew pain could be found anywhere.

After dinner, Sachi and Billy accompanied Takeo to town. While Sachi went to the market for a few things, Billy and his father went to the feed store. When Sachi found them they had just finished placing their orders and loading up. She stood behind Takeo and Billy as they talked to the owner, Mr. McDonald. For 20 years Mr. Mac, as he was called, ran the feed store. He was a rotund man, heavy and tall. His hands were large, meaty, and rough as burlap from years of working with hay, grain, fencing, and tools. Many of the men talked to him at length, especially during the slow winter days. Only men were involved in conversations about changes in feed, what worked for better egg or milk production, and weather, always the weather. Billy stood quietly at his father's side, listening and learning.

But on this particular day, as Billy helped his father with supplies, Mr. Mac addressed him directly. Sachi knew Billy would see this as a sign that he was growing up and being accepted into the community of men. She smiled at Mr. Mac for showing her son this kindness. He smiled back at her.

As they stood at the counter Mr. Mac asked, "So Billy, how old are you now?"

"Sixteen."

"Sixteen?" Mr. Mac said. "Well, son, you're darn near a man. What do you plan to do when you finish school? Are you looking at the service?"

Billy looked at his father and then nodded, "Of course, sir, but after that I hope to work with my father on his farm. I've learned a lot over the years. Eventually, when my father thinks I'm ready, I'd like to take over."

"Nothin' wrong with farmin'. It's good to take over the family business," Mr. Mac said absently as he figured the costs of the items.

Billy continued, speaking excitedly and, Sachi thought, encouraged by Mr. Mac's attention, "There's a plot next to us that, with a little work, could make good farm land. I'm hoping to grow, you know, expand the farm. Maybe get a bigger tractor, one of those threshers and grow corn or wheat back there. I think…"

Mr. Mac smiled and shook his head, "You people. Always thinking of expansion, aren't you? Must be in your blood."

Billy smiled, looking unsure of his meaning, he asked, "What do you mean?"

Mr. Mac laughed, a friendly, reassuring, salesman laugh, "Oh nothing. You have some big plans there. You're going to take over the world, right?"

Sachi saw Billy's face redden and knew he was embarrassed. He remained silent and carried some of the supplies to the truck. Mr. Mac added the items and presented Takeo with the bill. Takeo paid and began loading the last of the items on the truck outside.

Mr. Mac shouted out, "See you next week, Watanabe."

Takeo did not reply. Sachi knew what Takeo's silence meant. She sat in the middle with Takeo driving on her left and Billy looking out the open passenger window on her right. It wasn't until they were in the truck that he spoke to Billy.

Takeo asked, "Do you know what Mr. Mac meant by 'you people'?"

"I guess he meant young people maybe always thinking of growing, getting bigger. I didn't mean to sound like I was bragging. I just….I don't know," Billy mumbled, his eyes remaining on the landscape passing by.

Takeo said, "He meant Japanese people. He meant Japan has become more and more aggressive and is trying to expand, like the war with China right now. Most Americans see China as the victim and Japan as the offender. That's what he meant by expansion being in your blood."

Sachi watched as Billy considered his father's words. He sat up looking forward. His jaw was set and flexed with anger. He spit out the words, "I am an American looking at his future. Not Japanese looking to go to war. Besides, isn't expansion also the American way?"

Takeo nodded, his voice calm, "Yes, but you are missing the point. Don't make the mistake of denying your Japanese heritage. You are an American, but you are Japanese too. You are both."

Billy shook his head stubbornly, "No. I am an American. I cannot be both. I can't have loyalty to both countries equally. America is my country. I know nothing of Japan other than what you and mother and grandmother have told me. I didn't ask for Japanese citizenship. I don't want it. I have no intention of ever living there."

Takeo was silent for several minutes. Sachi looked at Takeo out of the corner of her eye and raised her brow. She wanted to turn to Billy and tell him Japanese citizenship had not been her idea and that she agreed with him, but she would not show disrespect to her husband in front of her son.

With a slight edge in his voice, Takeo said, "Well, let me tell you something about this Japanese heritage you apparently have come to despise. It is a heritage of thousands of years, not a few hundred. Like the Poplar trees, Americans look like they spring up on their own, from nowhere, but if you trace their roots back you find the main tree, the main country from which these Americans have sprung. They are almost all rooted in another country."

Billy interrupted, "Father I don't want any more Japanese wisdom. I know where you come from. I've heard the stories of the fishing villages and I know some of the language and the stories and everything else. I want to concentrate on my future. I don't want to think Japanese. I want to think American."

Takeo said, "Then think about this. Even water cannot enter. Do you know what this means?"

Sachi elbowed her husband lightly and said, "Takeo. Let's change the subject."

She knew where Takeo was headed with this statement and she did not want him dissuading Billy from his ideas of what it meant to be an American.

Billy did not answer his father, but sat and waited for an explanation.

Takeo continued despite Sachi's objection, "It means only some are included. The rest cannot get in. Even water cannot enter. You will find America is this way."

Billy spoke to his father exasperated, "You got in. Mother got in. Grandmother got in. What are you talking about?"

Takeo sighed deeply, adjusting his large frame in the driver's seat, tired of the day and this conversation.

He sighed, "You don't see it yet, but you will. I am not talking about getting into the country. I am talking about being accepted as an American into this society, but you're right. Enough of my Japanese wisdom. You, like all young, will have to learn on your own."

And Billy did learn. On the evening before Ganjitsu or New Year's Eve of 1941, the Watanabes threw a small gathering at home as they did every year. Ikuko and Edo were there as well as the Goodmans and Jack Albright. These were the friendships which had endured.

New Year's Eve dinner was *miso* soup, steak, *soba* (noodles), pickled cabbage and *dashiki* with rice and salmon. Yoshida said steak was too expensive, but Sachi insisted they splurge just this once and she knew Jack would appreciate steak. They made apple pie and chocolate cake. The food, like the people who ate it, Sachi thought, reflected the best of American and Japanese.

Jack was now a close friend of the family and had dinner with them weekly. He had never married. When Yoshida or Takeo asked, he talked about this woman or that, women he dated for short periods and then, for a hundred different reasons or no reason at all, just stopped seeing.

He sometimes brought Takeo sake, flowers to Yoshida, and toys for the boys, but every month, without fail, he brought books for Sachi. He often brought books focusing on the American lifestyle or American thoughts, sometimes classics or love stories or murder mysteries.

Yoshida frowned upon this and said to Sachi, "It is not proper for a man to bring you gifts."

Sachi responded, "They are only to borrow. I give them back. They are not gifts."

But she knew they were gifts in so many ways. They were wonderful books by American writers like Mark Twain and Ralph Waldo Emerson and European writers like Victor Hugo and Herman Hesse and Jane Austen. Unlike Yoshida, Takeo never seemed to care and was glad Sachi had someone to share this interest in reading as long as it didn't interfere with her duties as wife and mother.

Jack arrived early this New Year's Eve and sat with Takeo drinking sake as they discussed farming. When Ikuko and Edo arrived, they played with the boys for a while and then Ikuko helped with dinner while the men talked.

After dinner Jack complimented them on the steak and Sachi was glad she made the choice despite the expense and Yoshida's objections. Yoshida gave her a look, which Sachi could not decipher and decided to simply ignore.

After dinner they played *Fuku Warai*. Players took turns being blindfolded and placing paper cut outs of facial features on an outline of a face drawn on a large white sheet. The other players shouted out verbal directions to the blindfolded player like "higher, lower or to the right" so the blindfolded person tried to create a proper face. Each time the blindfolded player had gone through the eyes, ears, nose, mouth, moustache and hair, the eyes were often where the mouth should be or the ears were on top of the head. The player creating the closest thing to a normal face won.

John had given it a try and the face he created had a mouth in the middle and no ears.

Jack said, "That kind of reminds me of Mrs. Schaffer. All mouth and no ears."

Everyone laughed.

"You would think someone with that much money wouldn't have time to gossip like she does," Yoshida said, unaware of her own propensity to gossip.

Ikuko shook her head, "And what about that dog of hers?

Yoshida interjected, "Pookie."

Ikuko continued, "Yes. Pookie. It goes everywhere with her. I've even heard her call it her "baby." But I guess after the mystery of what happened to her husband, Pookie's all that is left to her."

John looked up from the paper face on the floor and asked excitedly, "What happened to her husband, Auntie Cuckie?"

Ikuko gave Sachi a quick look. Sachi shrugged as if to say go ahead and Ikuko began, much to John's excitement. He loved hearing a story.

"Well," Ikuko started, "Mrs. Schaffer is at the center of Orange Grove's greatest mystery. Or rather, her husband is. A few years ago Mr. Schaffer was found at his desk, hunched over, and he was pronounced dead by the coroner. He was transported to the mortuary where his body was left on a table until morning. Sometime in the night, the body disappeared and it was never recovered. He is still considered dead because the coroner had determined it and it was considered theft of a dead body. Some thought maybe he suffered a temporary coma or condition that made it look like he was dead and when he awakened in the morgue he decided to take advantage of his new found freedom and flee Orange Grove and Mrs. Schaffer even at the loss of his fortune. Others think he haunts Orange Grove to this day. "

Edo said, "From what I hear, it would have been worth the loss of a fortune to be rid of Mrs. Schaffer."

As the game of *Fuku Warai* ended, Sachi rose announcing it was time for John to go to bed. At ten years old it was well past his bedtime, though he insisted he was not tired and wanted to stay up until midnight. Billy and Mitchell were going into town to watch the fireworks display.

"Mother, please just let me go into town with Billy and Mitchell," John pleaded.

Sachi shook her head, "No. In fact, I wish you'd all three just stay home tonight. It's not a good night to be out late."

Mitchell insisted they would watch him carefully. Ultimately, it was Takeo who relented. She was countermanded yet again and felt the surge of anger at not having her decisions or opinions matter to Takeo. As she always did, she swallowed her anger. It would not be right to contradict her husband, particularly in front of guests. Takeo made both Mitchell and Billy promise to watch over John and come home immediately after the fireworks display. They were to be home by 12:30 a.m. They quickly promised, grabbed their jackets, and headed to the car. Billy and Mitchell hopped into the front and John tagged behind, jumping into the back seat just as the car pulled away.

Edo smiled as they drove off and said, "They'll have a great time. I remember being that age flying off to see the New Year's celebrations and fireworks in our village in Japan."

Takeo lit his pipe and said, "Yes, me too, though with each New Year it seems my memory of that age dims. Life in Japan seems like so long ago."

Sachi offered everyone tea and Ikuko and Yoshida joined her in the kitchen to help prepare it.

Ikuko started to boil water as Yoshida got the cups from the cupboard. Ikuko asked, "Don't you worry about the boys going off like that especially at night by themselves? I mean, with the war going on between China and Japan I have heard our people are being attacked because most believe the Japanese are wrong and they hate us for it."

Sachi nodded and said simply, "I would have liked them to stay home tonight, but Takeo, well, he knows best."

She didn't need to say anymore. Ikuko understood the way of the Japanese man. She had one of her own. She knew Sachi's opinion did not carry the weight of Takeo's and certainly Sachi could not go against her husband in front of guests.

Ikuko nodded, playing the game, and said, "I'm sure Takeo knows best. But I do worry about the boys with such anger pointed toward the Japanese right now."

"They're not Japanese," Sachi quickly corrected her. "They are American."

Ikuko shook her head and quietly said, "Do you think most people make a distinction between Japanese and Americans who happen to look Japanese?"

Sachi took the tealeaves from the cupboard and, as if trying to convince herself, said, "I just know what I've read and heard on the radio. I know there is violence in the bigger cities, but we haven't heard anything happening around here. People around here aren't like that."

Ikuko raised an eyebrow and warned, "Yet."

Sachi put her hands on her hips and said in a voice louder than she intended, "What do you want me to do, Ikuko? Takeo said they can go and I could not stop them. Do you want me to sit here all night with visions of harm coming to my boys? There is nothing I can do about it."

Yoshida looked sternly at the two women and whispered, "Shhh. They'll hear you."

Just then Takeo entered the kitchen and demanded, "What is going on in here?"

The three women remained silent and continued making tea as if he were not in the room. Takeo shook his head and they could hear him as he went back to the living room. He said, "Onna sannin yoreba kashimashii." To Jack and the Goodmans he translated, "If three women visit, noisy."

Ikuko said, "I'm sorry, Sachi. You're right. There is nothing to be done. I just think of the boys as my own sometimes and I worry. But I know you worry, too."

Sachi smiled at her friend and they both stood basking in the good feeling of friendship and forgiveness.

Yoshida said, "Bah. Enough of this. Sachi, prepare the tea."

After the tea was prepared Ikuko and Sachi served it to everyone. The men spoke of the economy and politics while Yoshida sat quietly in a corner of the sofa next to her son, hand-stitching and only half-listening.

Edo said, "The fact of the matter is most people are sympathetic toward the Chinese. They see Japan as the aggressor and the Chinese as simply defending themselves."

Jack interjected, "From what I've read Japan has been building their military and sometimes when you have it, it's too tempting *not* to use it."

Edo said, "But they have to be careful. Using their power to subordinate the Chinese will only cause other countries to hate them."

"Or fear them," Takeo interjected.

Tom Goodman said, "And depending on your ultimate goal, fear may be a useful weapon. Of course, the United States won't be bullied or scared."

Jack said, "I agree. The Japanese government needs to take a more diplomatic approach in obtaining the things they need."

Takeo sat forward, tapping his pipe on the ashtray, and said, "Japan tried diplomacy. Japan opened itself up to the west only to be treated like barbarians time and time again. The U.S. promises to treat Japanese citizens as their own, but they do not. We are looked upon with suspicion and distrust for no other reason than we look different and we have some different ways. We are not honored in this country. We were asked to join this world party and now we are treated like an unwelcome guest. The Emperor will not allow that to continue indefinitely. Japanese honor is at stake in Japan, in America, and around the world. Just this last year the United States terminated all commercial treaties with Japan leaving them without things like oil. What do they expect Japan to do? They must survive."

Edo added, "America has chosen sides and it is against the Japanese."

Without thinking Sachi blurted out, "But that was because Japan signed a pact with Germany and Italy."

All eyes turned to Sachi. Women, like children, were to be silent on matters of politics and business. This was a social breach, but Sachi did not care. These were important matters and she had read much in the newspaper about what was happening. It interested her and she continued since no one stopped her.

"I mean, how can America sit back while Japan signs with Italy and Germany, two countries who are at war with Europe? How can America sit back and wait for Japan to move in from one side and Germany and Italy from the other?

Silence was her answer. Takeo's face had turned red, but he said nothing, staring at his wife as if she were a stranger.

Jack broke the silence and said, "I think Sachi is correct. America has come to regard the attempt at expansion as a threat to American safety and territory and interests. And because of that, violence against Japanese here in America has increased. Even Chinese and Filipino people feel the need to distinguish themselves as such so as not to be mistaken for Japanese and risk being beaten up or worse."

Takeo refused to acknowledge Sachi's input, ignoring her, and continued to speak to the men, "The United States is punishing Japan by cutting off resources it desperately needs simply because it does not agree with Japanese policies. America will not war against Japan and if it does, it will be caught short, only because it underestimates the Japanese. Americans think the Japanese are backwards and uncivilized. We are not."

Jack interrupted, "You speak like you are one of them, Takeo. Are you Japanese or American?"

"I would be both, but America does not allow me to become one of its own. So I sit on the sidelines. I pour my sweat and my life into America's land and I raise my family on that land. Still I am viewed with suspicion and not allowed the privileges that accompany most hard-working people who live in this country. I would like nothing better than to become an American citizen."

Jack continued, "But where do your loyalties lay?"

The room was still as the words hung in the air like soap bubbles ready to burst at the next sound, the next breath.

Sachi again breached etiquette answering for her husband, wanting to make it clear to Jack that their loyalties were the same as his. She said, "Our family loves Japan. It is where we come from. It is where our ancestors lived and died, but our loyalties now lay with America because our children are American. Our future is America."

Yoshida could no longer bear her daughter-in-law's interruptions. She said, "Sachi. You forget yourself. Mr. Albright asked your husband about his loyalties."

Sachi's face reddened at the embarrassment of being chastised by Yoshida in front of their guests. She wanted to go into her room and hide from their gazes. She knew that within minutes she might even cry in part from embarrassment, but in part out of frustration at not being able to voice her opinion without chastisement as if she were a young child speaking out of turn.

Jack interrupted, "That's quite alright. I would like to hear what Sachi thinks."

He looked at Sachi and with a kindness in his voice and his eyes said, "Tell me, as a Japanese woman who chose to come to this country and bear her children here, raise her family, what is your view of this country?"

Sachi glanced at everyone watching. Yoshida went back to her sewing, knowing it would be the height of rudeness to say anymore since Jack, being a guest, had directly asked her opinion. Takeo looked down at the ground as if he, too, were embarrassed at his wife's words.

Ikuko smiled as if in on some private joke and Edo looked at the ground as well, as if he were embarrassed for Takeo. The Goodmans politely waited for Sachi to reply. She began slowly as if her thoughts and her voice were a frozen mountain and Jack's interest and questions were the warmth of the sun, melting the freeze away, and as she spoke the words came quickly and more easily. She forgot her place and became lost in self-expression. The trickle became a flood of words and opinions.

She said, "I believe America is slow to move maybe because it is so big and it takes much to move something so large. America might have sympathized with Japan. I mean, Americans certainly felt the need to expand across this great stretch of land taking it from those already there, the Indians, because they needed more room and more resources. Certainly, America as much as any country in the world would understand Japan's need to do the same. But there should be a different way, a better, more peaceful way than just marching into another's country and taking what it wants. Perhaps Americans fear Japan because they know the need for expansion and the danger when dealing with a government that must expand at all costs."

The sound of a car pulling up outside ended the conversation. The boys had arrived home earlier than expected. Sachi, still holding her teacup, got up and went to the window.

"It's the boys," she said, relieved that they were back safe. However, what she saw caused her to forget everything, including the cup in her hand. It fell to the floor with a loud crash and shattered at her feet. She ran out the front door.

Billy was out of the driver's seat. By the outdoor light of the moon and the indoor light of the car Sachi could see why her boys had returned so early. Billy's left eye was starting to swell and there was blood on his forehead and shirt. Mitchell sat in the passenger seat with his head back, holding a bloody cloth to his nose. Sachi could make out John in the back, but he was turned around looking out the rear window as if searching for something. Everyone poured from the house as Sachi ran toward Billy. Instead of running to her, Billy grabbed a nearby shovel and turned toward the road.

Just as everyone gathered around the car to see what had happened to the boys, a large sedan filled with young white men pulled off the road into their drive, spraying gravel as they stopped. A young man stuck his head out of the passenger window and yelled, "Go back to Japan, you damn nips. Better yet, go to hell where you belong."

Dusty, John's new dog, was rigid and barking, running up and down the drive as if to protect his owners. Sachi couldn't make out who was driving and the car was unfamiliar. John had scrambled over the back seat, out of their car, and was clinging to Sachi's leg. Takeo and Edo helped Mitchell out of the car. Sachi barely noticed any of this as she was focused on Billy. He was running toward the car of boys wielding the shovel. The boys in the car yelled more profanities at him daring him to get closer. They started throwing bottles and cans that barely missed him, but none of this seemed to frighten Billy and it didn't deter him. His anger seemed stronger than anything else. Finally, a well-aimed bottle hit him in the knee. He stumbled and started to fall amidst the whoops and victory cries emanating from the car. But, as if these same whoops buoyed him to stand, he gathered himself, and once more proceeded toward the sedan.

Sachi's hands went to her chest and in her loudest voice she screamed, "No, Billy. Come back."

There was the sound of a gunshot. One shot from the darkness. The whoops died down and the car sped off as quickly as it arrived. Sachi couldn't breathe. She couldn't think. She watched her oldest son as he turned toward her looking confused, but not frightened. She scanned his body quickly, but could see no gunshot wound.

Someone approached and passed on her left. It was Jack. He held a gun in his hand and Sachi quickly realized he had fired into the air to scare off the car full of young men. Sachi brushed John aside, unaware he was crying, and rushed for her oldest son. Jack was helping him walk to the house. Billy was limping and bleeding from a gash in his head.

232

Sachi positioned herself on the other side of Billy. As they passed Takeo, Sachi turned to him and said, "This is why I didn't want them going out at night alone. You let them do this."

Takeo looked as if he'd been slapped. He said nothing, but Sachi could see his anger beginning to grow. At the moment she didn't care. Her fear was dispersing replaced by her own growing anger.

Once inside the women checked the boys over and treated their injuries, which were less serious than they first looked. As they did this, the men sat, and Mitchell told them what had happened. His breathing was shallow and it seemed he couldn't get the words out quickly enough.

"We were waiting for the fireworks to start and Billy took John to get a drink. I was waiting and two older boys came up to me and started calling me names and tried to get me to fight them. But when I refused to fight they started beating me. Billy came back with John and…"

John interrupted, no longer frightened, and jumped up with breathless excitement, "And Billy whomped em' good. He beat up both those boys until they just ran off."

Sachi was examining Billy's knee which was a little swollen and slightly bruised. Billy turned from his mother and toward the men. His anger seemed to fill the room. "They were cowards, both of them. They took off yelling that they were going to get help. I knew we were in trouble. I mean Mitchell won't fight and John is too little."

John put his hands on his hips, indignant, "I am not!"

Mitchell said nothing and looked at the ground. Billy raised an eyebrow and continued, "We were heading home and I realized they were following us. There were six of them in the car, driving wild and fast, all over the road. I think they were trying to get in front of us and block us."

John interrupted again, "Billy almost lost control of the car three times."

Billy shook his head in disgust at his little brother, "I did not. I was keeping them from getting by us. I just wanted to…to kill those guys."

Takeo rose from his seat and silently stared out the window.

Edo asked, "Jack, where did you get that gun?"

Jack smiled, a bit embarrassed, "Well, I keep it in the truck. Just in case, you know. I've always kept it, but never had a need for it. Until tonight, that is."

Sachi, bandaging Billy's forehead, said, "Thank God you had it tonight and thank God you were here, Jack. I don't know what would have happened if you hadn't stepped in."

Takeo turned his head quickly from the window and glowered at his wife. Her words were meant as a comment of thanks to Jack, but Sachi could see they had the unintended effect of making Takeo feel even worse. She knew she had only reminded him he had not been the one to protect his sons.

Jack said to Takeo, "You should go to the Sheriff in the morning and report this."

Edo shrugged, "What's to report? Do you think the Sheriff will spend ten seconds trying to find some white kids who got into a fight with some Japanese kids when the Japanese are the ones complaining?"

That night Takeo refused to sleep with Sachi and instead slept in the living room. He did not speak to her the following three days and Yoshida said little unless it was about meals, the house, or the boys. Takeo worked outside though there was not much to do in the fields during the winter months. He repaired the barn and cared for the animals, walking the fields as if checking and rechecking. He went into town for supplies or conversation or just to have a place to go.

Takeo might be angry, but Sachi was scared and angry, too. Watching her sons threatened and hurt had that effect on a mother. Takeo had Americanized some, particularly for his livelihood and his sons, but where his wife was concerned he seemed not to want to change at all. Sachi knew she had spoken sharply to him in a heated moment when she was afraid for her children, but that was not all. She knew there was more to her feelings than that. Changes had come over Sachi as they were coming over the world.

CHAPTER TWENTY-TWO

Sachi went to town alone to shop and go to the bank. It was a cold, rainy afternoon and she was glad to enter the bank's warm building. As she waited in line, Jack Albright entered, shaking his umbrella and himself in the entryway. He walked over to her smiling and said, "They say the rain is going to let up soon, but I don't see any sign of it."

Sachi looked past him, out the window and said, "I hope so. I have to go shopping in this."

"And I have to go out to farms in it," Jack smiled and continued, "I'm glad I ran into you here. I really enjoyed dinner the other night. How are the boys doing?"

Sachi smiled back, conscious of the people around her. She said, "They are fine. Billy took the worst of it, but he is doing very well. Just some cuts and bruises – thanks to you."

"Listen," Jack said. "Will you wait for me a moment by the front door when you're through?"

Jack got in line. There were several people between them and Sachi finished before Jack. She stood at the door feeling the breeze as people entered and exited. She wondered what he wanted to discuss. Probably the last book he'd brought over, but she had yet to read it. The holidays had kept her busy.

She thought again of how handsome he looked. He had aged well, not putting on extra weight and the lines in his face seemed purposeful. He had long since shaved the

237

moustache he first wore when they'd met and his lips were thick and smooth. Today he wore a wool overcoat that hung to his knees and made his thin frame look more muscular than it was, at least more muscular than she imagined him to be.

As she always did when Sachi thought of Jack, she let her thoughts get just so far before stopping them.

Jack finished with the teller and approached her. He asked again, "So the boys are okay?"

Sachi smiled, trying to minimize the effect that attack had on her family, "Yes. John is afraid to go outside now, but he will get over that soon enough. When the weather gets warmer, I'm sure. And Billy, he's still so....so angry."

Jack's face turned a shade more serious as he asked, "And you. Were you in trouble?"

Sachi at first tried to feign surprise. She started, "Why would you think…"

She stopped. This was Jack. He knew them well enough by now to know how things were done. She nodded.

He sighed and said, "I thought so. I did a lot of thinking after the other night. I thought you were magnificent. I enjoyed hearing your opinions and the things you've read about. I thought a lot about…anyway, I wrote down some of what I've been thinking. I want you to read it when you are alone and have a chance."

He handed a sheet of white paper folded in half. She started to open it and he said, "No. Not here. It's…It's not something to be shared."

238

She looked at him with the same feelings of excitement and fear that she'd carried with her all these years. He excited her and she was aware of that, but her fear was greater. She was afraid the words on that small paper could end their friendship. Next to Ikuko, he was her closest friend and, in some ways, understood her better than even Ikuko, appreciated her differently.

"Jack," she said, starting to hand him the paper. "I don't think..."

A familiar voice entered the bank and said, "You don't think what?"

It was Ikuko and she seemed to size up the two of them standing in the bank. She immediately noticed the paper Sachi was trying to hand to Jack. "What's that?" she asked.

Sachi turned red giving herself away immediately. She had no idea what the note contained, but she knew it must be something intimate and personal since Jack asked it not be shared. Sachi could think of nothing to say.

Jack laughed, calmly, smoothly, and said, "Ikuko. I am surprised at you. Did you not send a thank you note to the Watanabes for the wonderful dinner the other night?"

Ikuko looked from Jack to Sachi and said, with suspicion, "Oh, so it is a thank you note?"

Jack feigned surprise and said, "Of course. And why are you so curious? What did you think it was?"

It was Ikuko's turn to blush. She said, "Oh nothing. I thought maybe it was a note saying, 'This is a hold up.' I thought maybe you two were planning to rob the place."

Jack said good-bye and left. Ikuko invited Sachi to tea and Sachi slid the unread note into her purse. The rain was still falling, so they hurried along the street to the restaurant under Ikuko's one umbrella and holding their rain hats tight to their heads. Over tea and sandwiches they talked about the boys and dinner and the fact Takeo wasn't speaking to her. But Sachi was no newlywed anymore and she knew the marital battles ended eventually either by direct effort from the warring parties or simple fatigue and collapse of resolve to keep it going.

Ikuko sipped tea and over her cup said, "Jack looked handsome today, don't you think?"

Sachi said, "Did he? I didn't notice."

"Really?" Ikuko smiled.

"What's that suppose to mean?" said Sachi overly defensive.

Ikuko just smiled and shook her head. "It means nothing," she said. "I just wonder if you are getting old not even noticing a handsome man anymore."

"It's just Jack," Sachi said. "I don't think of him as handsome or ugly or anything. He's just Jack."

"Really? And do you think you are just Sachi to him?"

"Of course."

"Let's at least be honest here. Don't you wonder why he hasn't married? He hasn't even gotten engaged. He's at an age where he should have children of his own. I mean the man must be 36 or 37."

"39," said Sachi, wishing she hadn't spoken as soon as the words left her lips.

"Excuse me. I stand corrected. He's 39. He dates and dates and dates, but he can never get interested in a woman. Don't you wonder why?"

"No," answered Sachi firmly, wanting to discuss anything, but the topic at hand.

Ikuko smiled slyly, "Do you think he's, you know, one of those. Maybe he doesn't particularly like women."

Sachi's eyes grew wide with anger and disbelief, "How can you say a thing like that? Of course he likes women."

Ikuko asked, "How do you know?"

Sachi sat wordlessly for a minute and then answered, "I just know."

Ikuko nodded her head and said, "I know you do."

Sachi said, "Stop these little word games. There is nothing going on between Jack and me if that is what you mean. We are friends and nothing more."

Ikuko placed her hand over Sachi's and leaned forward. She looked somber and said, "Keep it that way. No matter what happens, keep it that way. Friends."

Sachi snatched her hand back, angry at her friend's insinuation, "Of course. You and I have been friends for over 17 years. What kind of person do you think I am?"

Ikuko smiled and said, "Loving, passionate, smart, things only a certain kind of man would appreciate. Takeo may not. But Takeo is your husband and the father of your children. Jack is simply drawing pictures on water: not tangible, not real, not for you."

241

After tea Sachi stopped at the grocery store all the while thinking of Jack's words in her purse and Ikuko's words at lunch. She absently selected food from the shelves. Her body worked, but her mind was somewhere else. She paid for the groceries and loaded the car.

The rain storm had bullied its way through the valley and left only some light sprinkles behind. Sachi sat on a bench by her car and removed Jack's note from her purse. She felt her breath catch has she anticipated what message he had for her. The paper was typed, single-spaced, unaddressed and unsigned. She read it slowly,

I have known for some time, perhaps from the moment I saw you behind the wheel of your car, blood trickling down your forehead that my feelings for you go beyond friendship. I have tried many times to change my feelings, control them, avoid them. I know to feel more than friendship for a married woman is wrong. It is more than that. It is sinful, but it seems there is nothing within me strong enough to combat this flood of thoughts about you and for you.

It seems my soul is willing to risk eternal damnation just to be near you, with you, in your presence. I have learned that the Japanese speak of a feeling of falling flowers and flowing water. This is the feeling I have with you and I think you have it with me as well. If I did not think so, I would not have chanced this letter.

I do not expect anything from you. I do not even expect you to acknowledge this communication in any way. I just wanted you to know my feelings and, if you can, someday, maybe years from now share your feelings with me.

Sachi sat, shocked by his words. She was not shocked by the content, but by the fact that he was willing to express them. She immediately wondered how this would change their relationship. In just a few minutes he had gone from loving friend to friendly would-be lover. But it wasn't instantly. This had existed for years.

As all these emotions and thoughts flitted through her spirit like fearful birds in a cage, looking for an escape, something caught her eye. It was a large puddle of water next to the bench that would hardly be noticed except to be splashed in by children or cursed by adults who accidentally stepped in it. Ikuko's words came back to her as she picked up a small stick from the ground and bent over the puddle next to her.

Sachi picked up the stick and began absently tracing shapes in the puddle, straight lines, circles, stars, and, finally, hearts. Before she could get the beginning started it disappeared. As Ikuko said, "...drawing pictures on water."

Sachi imagined what might happen if she went to Jack right now and told him she felt the same. Would they fall into one another's arms and kiss with a passion Sachi knew existed within her that had never been expressed? Would he offer to take her away to some romantic place? She allowed her imagination to drift to his thick brown hair and lips, his bright blue eyes and tall, tanned body. She felt her breath catching as she imagined his deep kiss and the feel of his body against hers. She told herself that feelings this strong did not disappear into the water of a muddy puddle.

"Bah," she found herself saying out loud, borrowing one of Yoshida's expressions. She tossed the stick in the puddle with a splash and said, "Ikuko and her nonsense."

She got in her car and headed for home. When she pulled into the driveway she shut off the car and turned off her imagination. The letter, her first and only love letter, was tucked into the pocket of her skirt. After unloading the groceries she went to her room and slipped it between the folds of cloth of her wedding kimono. The irony of hiding Jack's love letter in her wedding dress was not lost on her, but it was the only place Sachi could think that no one else would look. She placed it in its box and pushed it on the back shelf in the closet.

Finally on the fourth evening since New Year's Eve Sachi walked to the barn where Takeo was milking the cow. She stood in the doorway and watched. She knew he knew she was there, but he did not turn to look at her and kept at his task.

"Takeo," Sachi asked, "Will you ever speak to me again?"

He continued the milking and after several seconds went by he answered, "I do not know."

Sachi said, "You will have to speak to me. There are things we should discuss from time to time, don't you think?"

Takeo said stubbornly, "Oh, so now you are interested in what I think?"

"I have always been interested in your thoughts."

Takeo sat back on the cold ground and sighed deeply. He said, "I do not know. I do not know anything anymore. My son does not want anything to do with Japanese. He is an American he says. My wife apparently thinks she is one of these American women speaking to guests in such a way and blaming me for something so terrible happening to my sons."

"Takeo, I was upset. I'm sorry. Of course, it wasn't your fault. Sometimes I say what's on my mind without thinking."

Takeo shook his head, "But not in front of guests. Not in such a way as to disparage Japan and oppose your husband."

"I'm sorry, Takeo," Sachi said. "I am sorry you felt I was arguing with you and blaming you."

She walked over and sat on the cold ground next to him adjacent to the cow, still waiting to be milked. The cow lowed every so often and the smell of hay and manure filled the barn. It was not an unpleasant smell and Sachi did not notice it.

She said, "Takeo, I would never intentionally embarrass you. You must know that." She placed her soft hand over his chubby, calloused one.

"Do not do that to me again. I will not lose face in my own house. We will speak of it no more."

He put his hands on her shoulders and gently pushed her on her back. He crawled on top of her and began kissing her neck, roughly and quickly. She felt his weight and struggled to maneuver herself under him so that she could breathe more easily. He stroked the top of her head absently, but roughly as he pushed her legs apart, pulled up her skirt and pulled down her underwear. She heard him unzip his pants and the cow mooed again, upset at being forgotten.

He pushed himself inside her despite the dryness, pushing up and down. He gripped her breasts as he pushed deeper and within minutes he was finished. He lay on top of her, gasping for air, sated. The pushing and pulling of their usual lovemaking was over. He stood up, zipped his pants, and gripped the cow's udder. Sachi dressed herself quickly and left Takeo to his milking.

That night Sachi had a disturbing dream that woke her in the middle of the night struggling to breathe. In the dream she was flying, soaring above green trees and forests. She was proud of her ability to fly and she knew she could escape anything by just taking flight. If she positioned her arms a certain way, she could turn at a different angle. She saw their house below her, and she swooped down to rest there. As she stood on the porch she saw in the distance huge waves headed toward her. These waves were as tall as buildings and seemed to reach the sky. She craned her neck to look up at them, but she was unafraid. They were beautiful, awe-inspiring waters. They came closer and closer and suddenly the house was engulfed in giant waves and an ocean of water. She ran inside her house for protection. Her family sat in the living room. They were trapped. They were sinking and there was no way out without drowning. They were too far below the surface and the waves were too powerful. Her flying could not save her or anyone else.

She woke up wondering what the dream meant. It felt so real and vivid. She knew the water in dreams represented change of some kind. What kind of change could be coming that would effect her whole family and her home? She thought of Jack and vowed that he would not be the change that destroyed her family.

CHAPTER TWENY-THREE

Despite having expressed his true feelings, Jack came for dinner the next week at Takeo's invitation. He arrived on time as usual and showed no signs of awkwardness though Sachi thought he looked pale and a little tired. Jack brought a book for Sachi and flowers for Yoshida.

Sachi was uncomfortable and remained quiet throughout dinner, afraid of speaking directly to Jack in fear that she might give herself away.

"But Father, the Kias, well, they're more political," Billy said during dinner.

Takeo responded, "They are Nationalistic. They are loyal to Japan. Pass the rice."

Sachi handed Takeo the rice and reminded John to use his napkin.

Takeo continued, "I don't think it wise for you to be involved with such a group, especially now when we know the FBI is making lists of Japanese citizens and our loyalty is being questioned. Why make trouble when you could just as easily be involved with the Japanese American Citizens League? They have a more moderate bent and are looked upon more favorably by the white establishment."

Billy said, "You say that because you are one of them."

Takeo nodded and said, "That's true, but what I am telling you is also true. You must not be rash in this regard."

Mitchell pushed some squash around on his plate and said, "The JACL is not about warring against the whites as the Kias would have us do. It is about working together."

Billy sneered, "You mean assimilation. The JACL would be white if they could. 'Yes, sir and no, sir and aren't we the quiet, good little minority that never steps out of line.' Makes me so mad. We need to show the whites we'll fight if we are pushed anymore."

"Billy," Sachi warned, looking at Jack and then back at Billy.

Billy hung his head for a moment and said, "Sorry, Mr. Albright. I didn't mean you."

Jack nodded and smiled. He said, "I know. I enjoy hearing what you think, Billy."

She sensed Jack appreciated the fire in her oldest boy and his willingness to stand up for what he thought was right. Perhaps he had been like Billy when he was a teenager, impetuous, out spoken, enthusiastic. Sachi smiled at Jack and then quickly looked away, afraid it would be misinterpreted, but she was not quick enough to escape the gaze of Yoshida.

Takeo bit into a chicken leg, letting a little grease slip down the side of his mouth then wiping it with his napkin as he said, "Billy, just last year you told me you didn't want to be Japanese. You wanted to forget about Japan and think American. Remember?"

Billy, who had eaten little, said, "During the last year I have seen and heard things I did not recognize as prejudice before. It is becoming clearer to me in some of the people I know and the news I hear and the laws that have been made against the Japanese. And Father, I am thinking like an American. Americans don't let anyone push them around. They stand up and fight for what is right and prejudice against the Japanese is not right."

Takeo said, "Be patient. In the meantime I don't want you associating with the Kias anymore. You stay clear of those boys. They'll just bring you trouble. Remember, be a river. Go around the obstacles and move forward."

Takeo's greasy hand cut the air, back and forth like a snake. Billy sighed deeply and absently played with the food on his plate deep in thought. He knew his father's advice to be a river was the end of the conversation.

John said, "Hey Billy, will you play ball with me? Mom, can we play ball?"

Sachi said, "I guess so. It's still light out, but as soon as it starts to get dark you come in and do some reading. And feed Dusty."

"Alright," John said as he jumped up from the table.

Takeo stopped him and said, "What do you say John?"

John sat back in his seat and said, "Can I be excused?"

Takeo nodded and John took off to retrieve his mitt and ball and the dog food.

Billy and Mitchell excused themselves. Mitchell went to his room to read and Billy and John went out back to play ball.

Yoshida asked, "Jack, are you feeling alright? You've been awfully quiet."

Sachi was grateful for the old woman's question. She had noticed his relative silence, but had been afraid any inquiry by her would be misinterpreted as too familiar or insightful.

"Oh, I'm fine," said Jack pulling a handkerchief from his back pocket and wiping the sheen of sweat from his brow. "Just a little warm is all."

251

Yoshida bustled about collecting the dishes and said, "Well, you and Takeo go outside. There's a nice breeze blowing and Sachi can bring your drinks out there."

The men went outside to smoke and sit on the porch. Yoshida washed dishes and Sachi brought out coffee for Jack and tea for Takeo as she did each time Jack ate with them. Over the years it had become almost a tradition, coffee and a cigar for Jack, tea and a pipe for Takeo.

"I seem to have lost my pipe," Takeo said as Sachi stepped out on the porch. "I think I may have left it in the barn last night."

Sachi, not wanting to be left alone with Jack, said, "I'll get it for you."

Before she could set down the tray Takeo was at the bottom step, "I'm not sure where I left it. I'll go. Just pour me some tea."

Twilight had arrived and the brighter stars could already be seen on the darkening expanse of sky. It was a mild March evening an example of the very weather that attracted so many to California. Just as Yoshida had said, a light, warm breeze drifted over them.

Sachi began to pour Takeo's tea. The boys played catch in the distance with Dusty running back and forth between them.

Jack cleared his throat and said, "I hope you enjoy the book I brought. It's a poetry anthology. I thought you might like it."

"I'm sure I will."

Jack asked, searching for a topic of conversation that would put them both at ease, "Do you have any books in Japanese?"

Sachi, her back still to Jack as she finished pouring the drinks, said, "I have just two. They are storybooks, but many of the stories I learned in Japan are stories passed on from generation to generation. They have most likely never been written down. If they were, it wasn't until recently."

She handed Jack his coffee and continued as she stood at the railing looking at the evening sky, "My mother was a wonderful story teller and she shared with me many Japanese legends and tales. Of course, I share them with my boys. They like the ones with giants or ogres the best, at least they use to when they were little. They are getting too old for the stories now, except occasionally John."

Jack smiled and looked from Sachi to the sky, "I don't think I know any Japanese stories. I'd love to hear one."

An old story popped immediately to mind. Sachi hesitated telling him and looked around. Yoshida was still in the kitchen and Takeo had disappeared into the barn.

She looked at Jack's face and began, "In Japan on July seventh we celebrate the Festival of Tanabata. People write their wishes on strips of paper and hang them on bamboo trees. This tradition comes from a story about a young man who finds a robe of feathers. A beautiful girl, Tanabata, asks if he has seen the robe. He lies to her and says no. She says if she cannot find her robe of feathers she will be unable to return to the heavens and will stay earthbound. The boy is so in love with her that he lies again.

Eventually the two marry and one day she finds the robe, where he has hidden it, in the beams of their home. She puts it on and starts to rise to heaven telling her husband he must weave 1000 pairs of straw sandals and place them around the bamboo tree before they may see one another again.

"Finally he finishes and the bamboo tree grows into the sky. He climbs to the top, but he had woven only 999 pairs because he was in such a hurry and he stopped short of heaven. Tanabata missed him so much that she pulled him up. Her father was angry and told the young man that he must complete another task. He must guard the father's melon field for three days without eating one of the melons. The young man grew so thirsty that he broke his promise and opened a melon to drink. Water poured from the melon creating a large river and immediately the two lovers rose to opposite sides of the river and became the stars Vega, the weaver star, and Altair, the cow herd star."

Sachi looked into the sky again and said, "To this day her father allows the two stars to meet only once a year on July 7. Otherwise they spend eternity facing one another across the Milky Way, shining brightly."

Jack looked at Sachi as shadow and light met in the moments of twilight and said, "It's a beautiful story, but sad that two people who loved each other could not be together."

Sachi drew in a deep breath and looked at Jack. His blue eyes were almost gray without the sunlight. He seemed so serious and her heart beat faster as she looked at him knowing his was probably doing the same.

She said, "I chose to tell you that story for a reason. It symbolizes many things. When I was younger I thought of the sadness of unrequited love. As I get older, even now as I tell it to you, what seems to jump out at me is that a relationship built on lies and deceptions is destined to end badly."

Sachi looked out toward the barn and saw Takeo headed back to the house with his pipe in hand. He waved it at them and spoke loudly, "I found it."

Jack nodded to Takeo and then said to Sachi, "I see. Perhaps you are right. Destiny is a funny thing. One never knows what twist or turn life will take. I guess before July seventh I will have to find a bamboo tree on which to hang my wish "

Sachi shook her head and said, "Jack, life doesn't work that way. Besides, it's just a fairy tale."

Takeo stepped up and asked, "What's a fairy tale?"

Sachi said, "I was telling Jack about the Festival of Tanabata."

Takeo smiled and lit his pipe, sucking hard until the tobacco burned brightly. "Oh yes. It has been quite a while since I heard that story."

He handed Jack his matches and Jack lit his cigar.

Sachi handed Takeo his tea and excused herself saying, "It is dark now. I must get the boys inside."

The following week Jack called and canceled dinner. Yoshida took the call, but didn't mention it until two days later at breakfast. The boys were getting up and Takeo was finishing his eggs. Sachi's meal sat, untouched, and she was becoming frustrated at her inability get an answer from her mother-in-law that satisfied her.

"He just isn't feeling well, that's all," said Yoshida dismissively.

Sachi couldn't help but wonder if this was the beginning of Jack pulling away from her. She'd made it clear that, regardless of their feelings for one another, there was no future for them and yet he had become a part of her life. She realized this as she contemplated his not being there even if only for dinner.

Sachi asked, "What is wrong with him?"

Yoshida shrugged and said, "Probably just a cold."

Takeo said, "Maybe more than that. He has not been around town for at least a few days."

"It's not like Jack to miss work," Sachi said, "I think I will drive over to check on him."

Takeo nodded agreement, but Yoshida eyed her suspiciously and said, "He's a grown man. He can take care of himself. Call him if you are that concerned."

Sachi picked up the phone and dialed Jack's number. Her hands were clammy and she felt her throat go dry. She didn't even know what she would say, but she had to know he was okay. There was no answer on the other end of the line. She turned to Yoshida and Takeo, who was pulling on his work boots, and said, "I'm going."

The boys rushed into the kitchen all at once, like a wave of noise hitting the room and drowning out all other thoughts and conversation. Takeo said good bye and went to the fields.

As they were preparing breakfast for the boys, Yoshida, ever concerned about appearances, spoke to Sachi in a low voice so only she could hear, "Well, for heaven's sake, if you're going, take Ikuko with you. A woman alone visiting a bachelor at his home doesn't look proper."

That afternoon Ikuko and Sachi drove to Jack's home. Sachi had never seen this part of Jack's life and she was curious. She asked Ikuko to repeat the address and they scanned the numbers on the houses until they found his. It was a small house crowded on either side and from behind by other small houses. But there was a large oak tree in the front yard and two vehicles parked in the drive. One was Jack's truck and the other was a car Sachi did not recognize. She parked on the street. She and Ikuko removed the two large baskets they'd brought from the back seat containing teas, herbs, and food. They climbed the three steps to the front door and knocked.

A minute went by and Ikuko said, "We could see if it's open and just let ourselves in."

As Sachi considered this they heard footsteps on the other side coming toward them and the door opened. A woman, about thirty-five, stood before them. She held a large amber bottle in one hand and a spoon in the other. She was, by most standards, pretty, with blonde hair pinned just behind her neck and dark green eyes. She wore a matching

257

eggshell-colored skirt and jacket and a grim look on her face. Ikuko and Sachi stood, surprised, unable to speak.

Sachi's first thought was he is married. She felt her heart sink and she did nothing to curb it. Her reaction disturbed her as much as the thought that Jack had lied all these years. He couldn't be married.

Ikuko found their collective voice and said, "Hello. We are here to see Mr. Albright. Is he in?"

The woman said, "Yes, but he's not well I'm afraid. Are you…friends?"

Sachi answered, inexplicably irritated at the woman's question, "Yes. We're friends. And you are…?"

The question hung for a moment like the ringing of a bell, clear and with purpose that was lost on the woman before them. Ikuko turned, almost imperceptibly, and looked at Sachi out of the corner of her eyes. She knew her friend too well and its purpose was not lost on her. At that moment, Sachi did not care. She had to know who this woman was in Jack's life and why they'd never met.

The woman answered, "I'm Janice Stoddard. I was just dropping off some medicine for Jack. He's got a pretty bad case of pneumonia, but he won't let me get him to the hospital."

"Pneumonia?" Ikuko repeated.

Janice said, "Yes. He's had it a few days now, but when he missed his appointment, the doctor asked me to check on him."

While she still didn't know who this woman was exactly, at least, she'd confirmed it was not his wife.

"He is going to be okay?" Sachi asked.

Janice shook her head and answered, "I don't know. He needs to be in the hospital, but he refuses to go."

"His sister," Sachi said aloud.

Ikuko and Janice looked at her, questioningly.

"Does he have a sister?" Janice asked.

Sachi shook her head. "He doesn't talk about it, but his sister died years ago of pneumonia...in the hospital."

Janice said, "Please come in."

Sachi and Ikuko entered the darkened house. The living room was sparsely furnished with a couch, one chair, and a lamp and radio on a table in the corner. The beige curtains were drawn and there was a small brown throw rug in the middle of the floor. It was a sad, little room to Sachi, lonely and bare, without warmth or personality. It could belong to anyone or no one.

Janice said, "Since you seem to know Jack so well I'm hoping, well, I'm just the doctor's nurse checking on his patient. I really can't stay, but the fact of the matter is that he refuses to go to the hospital and he needs someone here to care of him. Can you stay?"

Sachi immediately said, "Of course, we'll stay."

While the nurse gave information to Ikuko on what medicine to give and when, Sachi entered Jack's bedroom. The room was dark and as her eyes adjusted she could see the double bed with one night table and a bathroom to the right next to a closet. The walls were bare except one small hat rack over a four drawer maple dresser. She could also make out a still silhouette in the bed. She stepped closer and gazed down at Jack. He was asleep. His mouth parted slightly and his breathing was labored. He looked small and thin under the white sheets and blue comforter, like one of her boys. A sheen of sweat glistened on his face. She bent over and, almost instinctively, placed the top of her hand on one cheek and then the other. They were rough and unshaven with days of stubble. Then she brushed the hair from the top of his head and felt his forehead. He was burning up.

Sachi walked out of the room and went into the kitchen where Ikuko stood alone, unloading the baskets. The nurse had gone. Sachi found a kettle and began heating water for some of Yoshida's special tea made from herbs grown in her garden. Sachi found a bowl in the cupboard and filled it with water. There was no ice in the ice box so Sachi asked Ikuko to order a block of ice and also to call Yoshida and tell her they would be staying with Jack until he was better.

Sachi said, "Ask her to make the miso soup she makes when the boys are ill. Maybe Takeo can bring it over this evening or tomorrow morning."

Ikuko said, "You are not staying here all night?"

It was more a statement than a question.

Sachi answered, "Of course."

The two women stared at one another for several seconds and Sachi anticipated an argument about the appearance of her staying all night alone with a single man. She steeled herself.

Instead Ikuko said, "Then I better call Edo, too. I'm staying with you."

Sachi smiled, relieved that she could save her energy, and rushed to Ikuko to hug her tightly.

Ikuko pulled away and shook her head, "Alright now. We have lots to do. I'll call Yoshida and Edo before I leave here and then go get the ice. I may have to drive by the house if no one answers. You give him some tea and two teaspoons of that medicine. I'll be back."

Sachi reached in her skirt pocket and handed the keys to Ikuko. Ikuko left the room and Sachi could hear her dialing the phone. Sachi removed her hat and set it on the table. She readjusted the pins in her hair to keep it out of her face and removed her suit jacket. She rolled up the sleeves to her white shirt and searched for a tea cup and spoon.

A few minutes later she entered the bedroom. She sat on the edge of the bed, as she'd done many times for her own sons, and dipped a cloth in some cool water, laying it gently on Jack's feverish face.

He began to stir and, without opening his eyes, whispered, "Sachi."

"I'm here," she said, stroking his head and holding the cloth on his forehead.

His eyes opened. They were rimmed in red and bloodshot. He looked exhausted and immediately began coughing. She removed the cloth, helped him sit up, and waited for the coughing spell to subside. His chest was bare and heaved with the work of trying to clear his lungs. He had the same tan of all men who worked a majority of their day in the sun, tan forearms and a pale chest and abdomen. Sachi had never seen a white man without his shirt and she marveled at the way the dark hair broaden from the chest and tapered toward the stomach like an arrow pointing…She stopped, ashamed of her thoughts.

"Where did you come from?" he asked when he could breathe again. "How did you…?"

Sachi said, "Shhh. Don't talk. Save your energy."

She fed him two teaspoon of his medicine from the large amber bottle and then gave him the cooling tea to sip.

"What's in this?" he asked.

"I'm not entirely sure, but it is what Yoshida makes when the boys are feverish or have congestion. It always helps them," Sachi said. "I understand you refuse to go to the hospital."

Jack looked at her hard for a moment and said, "No hospital. My parents died in the hospital. My sister…well you know. I just can't…"

His coughing started again. Sachi grabbed his tea and set it on the table. His coughing sounded so deep and so painful and as he labored he grabbed onto Sachi's arm, squeezing it tightly as it were a life line keeping him from drifting away. She held onto his hand as if holding him in place, willing him not to go anywhere. Eventually the coughing subsided and he began to glide into sleep. Sachi cooled his brow with the wet cloth and said, "I know. Don't worry. You will stay here and I will stay with you. No hospital."

She thought he had fallen asleep and didn't hear her, but he squeezed her hand as he drifted off and whispered, "I knew you would come."

Jack slept and Sachi's back began to ache from sitting in the same position. She rose and stretched and went to brew him more tea. As she walked out of the bedroom she passed by a closed door. Curious, she opened the door and peeked inside. A bright smile crossed her face as she examined the room.

The room was covered in wall-to-wall bookshelves containing hundreds of books. Here were all the books Jack had brought to her over the years in his own little library. There was a large desk sitting in front of the only window and a large leather chair sat behind it. It smelled of cigar and peppermint, just like Jack. She crept slowly in the room and pulled the chair from behind the desk. The blinds were closed and it was dim, but she could see his ash tray with two half-smoked cigars and a half filled cup of coffee from some previous morning. A book lay on the desk, turned over, marking where he left off, and stacks of papers sat in three neat rows. The entire house had seemed so bare and empty and in contrast this room felt so full. Sachi knew this is where Jack lived. This room was him.

263

Sachi slowly slid into the leather chair, aware that this is where Jack sat every evening, maybe, from time to time, thinking of her. The leather was cool and soft. She felt connected to him. She didn't know how long she sat there, but she heard the front door open and the sound of footsteps entering the kitchen.

Sachi felt interrupted, as if she were doing something she shouldn't. The feeling disturbed her, but she had no time to consider it. She stood, pushing the chair in, grabbed the coffee cup, and left the room quietly closing the door behind her. Sachi entered the kitchen to find Ikuko putting ice in the ice box and warming water for more tea.

"Well, I had to drive home, but I told Edo and Yoshida where we would be for at least the next few days," Ikuko said. "Edo was fine, though he complained about what he would do for dinner. I told him to go to your house and eat whatever Takeo and the boys eat. Will do them good. They'll appreciate us more when we get back. How's he doing?" she asked, nodding toward the bedroom.

Sachi shook her head, placing the coffee cup in the sink, and said, "He's burning up with fever and coughing terribly. I'll take him some more cool water and more of Yoshida's tea. What else can we do?"

"Sleep is the best thing for him right now," Ikuko said.

The evening passed slowly. Sachi pulled the leather chair into Jack's bedroom and spent most of the evening bathing his head with cool water and whispering prayers over his sick body. Ikuko mixed tea, made a list of things to get at the market, and fell asleep on the couch toward midnight.

Sachi awoke in the morning curled up in the leather chair having fallen asleep sometime early in the morning. She opened her eyes and looked at Jack expecting him to be asleep. He was awake and staring at her. He didn't say a word, but smiled and closed his eyes, falling again into a deep sleep. She didn't move, exploring this moment of waking up next to Jack, seeing his face last thing in the evening and first thing in the morning. Once the sound of his heavy breathing told her he was sleeping soundly, she stood and checked his fever. He was a hot as ever and his sheets were soaked through.

She walked into the kitchen. Ikuko had written a note saying she'd gone to check on the families and get things from the store. Tea was brewing on the stove and she prepared some for Jack. She got a bowl of warm water, a bar of soap, Jack's razor, and some cloths from the bathroom. She sat on the edge of Jack's bed.

She picked up the warm, wet cloth and vigorously rubbed the bar of soap on it. She pulled the sheet down from his chest to his waist and stared, unsure where to start. She picked up his right hand and rubbed the cloth across his knuckles, slowly, gently, not wanting to wake him. She cleaned his hand and slid the cloth between each finger. She worked her way slowly up his tanned forearm to his elbow and the muscular upper arm. She felt her breathing quicken and her senses heighten. She looked into Jack's face and his eyes were open. He was looking at her as he had moments earlier, as if in a dream. What surprised her was his awareness of her touching him, this intimacy, did not stop her. She did not pull back, but continued exploring each arm, each hand and finger, tenderly, with her memory working in sync with her hands. She knew his body even

265

before she touched it. She knew what it would feel like and she wanted to always remember. Her eyes stayed with his as she placed the cloth on his chest and slowly wiped the sweat and illness from him. She pushed up his pajama legs and washed his lower legs and feet. Once she was finished bathing him, she helped him into the leather chair, while she changed the wet sheets on his bed.

She went into the bathroom, running hot water into a bowl, and came back to him. He sat in the chair and she on the edge of the bed. She rubbed the bar of soap in her hands, working up a thick lather, then took his face between her hands and lathered the areas of stubble. She had never shaved a man before, but she had seen Takeo do it. She slowly worked the razor across his face, first one cheek and then the other. She placed her fingers on his lips to pull his upper lip down. His eyes did not leave hers. She moved the razor, slowly, gently, freeing him from the discomfort of the prickly little hairs. He lifted his chin to her and she worked the razor slowly down.

Suddenly there was the sound of a door slamming. Ikuko was back. As if brought back from a trance or caught in the act of something forbidden Sachi jumped and a small trickle of blood trailed down Jack's chin. But he did not flinch. His eyes remained steadfast on hers.

She whispered, "Oh, I am so sorry."

He smiled and shook his head as if to say, "Don't be."

266

She placed a washcloth on his chin then helped him back into bed, between the clean sheets, and covered him with a light blanket. No words had past between them. He didn't need to say anything. She could feel it.

In washing his arms, and legs, and chest, in shaving his face, she felt more alive and connected to him than she ever had with Takeo. In some ways, she knew the body of this man more intimately than that of her own husband. When she and Takeo were physical she was never allowed to explore his body, there was never enough time and it seemed pointless in so many ways. When she touched Takeo she did so because it was part of what they did, but she did not feel the kind of pleasure she felt in simply bathing Jack. Takeo never stared into her eyes for the length of time and with the longing look that Jack had. There was something erotic and mystical about it. It was something that went beyond her five senses and touched the deepest part of her spirit, a place she'd never known existed until this moment.

Maybe it was because Takeo had never been vulnerable to her before. He'd never needed her in this way. He'd never been completely alone with no one else to care for him. He'd always had Yoshida. But both Sachi and Jack knew what it was to feel alone and exposed in this world, to deeply need another person. The thought hit her suddenly, like the earthquake years ago, and it shook the depths of her soul. This was being in love. She didn't recognize it immediately because she had never been in love before, but she knew it just as she knew that with this new found elation and passion she would feel an absence, a perpetual longing, for the rest of her days.

Suddenly, as if exhausted, she fell back into the leather chair, staring at Jack, tears streaming from her eyes. How could giving one bath to Jack make her feel more alive and aroused than all the years of loving Takeo? As the tears slipped out she realized it was because she loved Jack in a way she would never love Takeo and she made love with Takeo in a way she would never be able to do with Jack. She cried at the sadness that this bath was one of the most erotic moments of her life and it was over, never to happen again. And now, like the young lovers of the Japanese fairy tale, she would spend eternity looking over at Jack, unable to touch him again.

The next day Jack's fever broke and he began to improve. It took several weeks, but he started regaining his strength and was back at work. He and Sachi never spoke of their time alone, but Sachi could see the reflection of that tenderness in his eyes every time they met, every time they shook hands.

She did not know how their friendship would survive, but she knew that she could not let him go from her life. Right now, with times so tenuous and uncertain, talk of war and prejudice filling the papers and conversations, she had helped him survive. Tensions were high in Orange Grove and around the world. Even in the midst of her own family. Jack, in some way, was helping her to survive as well.

CHAPTER TWENTY-FOUR

Oval Office of the President of the United States Franklin Delano Roosevelt
December 7, 1941

Texas Senator Tom Connally, recent head of the Foreign Relations Committee, stood in front of the president's desk with General Douglas next to him. He pointed his finger at Douglas and, in a drawl as thick as an oil gusher, said, "The attack was *suppose* to occur in the Philippines. That's where your guys put the first attack. The Philippines. Not in our own backyard."

The General, still stung from the loss of men and the sneak surprise, was not able to answer quickly enough for the Senator.

"Well, General?"

The General said, "Senator Connally, they changed strategy. There was no evidence to suggest this is what they were thinking."

New York Senator Jetter possessed a deep voice, which belied his small stature. At five feet six inches he was the shortest man in the room. He had been pacing about and suddenly stopped next to the six foot four inch General, yelling up at him. "Isn't that the business of the military? To anticipate the worst-case scenario and prepare for it? And how can there be no evidence? Hell, we broke the Japanese code months ago. We were hearing everything they had to say to each other."

Senator Connally said, "Obviously not."

269

Jetter continued, "It doesn't make any sense. I know we terminated our commercial treaties with them last year and we have essentially stopped all trade with them because of their continued aggressive expansion in the Pacific, but the bottom line is we're not in the war. Why the hell would they want to drag us in? This doesn't help them in any way."

Roosevelt, who had been quietly sitting behind his desk up until now, said, "Well, we're in it now, by God. They obviously think they can beat us. Maybe they think that like Europe we will be willing to give up a little territory to avoid war or that we will re-enact trade agreements. It's worked for Hitler so far. They think they can start by taking Hawaii."

Connally turned to Douglas and said "General, it's public knowledge you believe we should have been in this war long ago. Is it possible you kept this information, hoarded it away, so that we might be dragged into this fight?"

The General looked at Connally like he might attack him. Instead, he walked across the room, his impressive military decorations and medals jingled just slightly like the gun belt of an old west cowboy. He marched back over to where Connally stood by the President's mahogany desk. His jaw was set and eyes narrowed, creating a deep line between his eyebrows that was as sharp as the creases pressed into his pant legs.

He stood toe-to-toe with the Senator and said, "I've just lost over 1100 people under my command and hundreds of civilians. There are people dead, people I was responsible for protecting. We've lost up to 200 planes. They've destroyed the Arizona, the Oklahoma, the Downes, the Cassin, and about 14 other ships. We had eight battleships lined up like sitting ducks. That's what they were after. I have wanted in this war for a while now because I thought the sooner we got in it the more lives would eventually be saved. For this country, today ranks right up there with the worst days we have faced as a nation. For me personally, this is the worst day of my life. You can accuse me of incompetence if you like, but don't you dare accuse me of intentionally causing this or contributing to it in any way. That is when this will go from a discussion among gentlemen to a bar brawl real quick."

Connally banged on the President's desk in frustration and said to Roosevelt, "Then how did they catch us with our pants down, Mr. President?"

Roosevelt muttered, "I don't know, Tom. I just don't know."

****

They received the awful news that afternoon. Charlie Shimmer, the buck-toothed bachelor who lived next to Ikuko and Edo, delivered the news to the Watanabe family like a careless paperboy tossing the newspaper, trying to hit the porch, but not worried if it landed in the bushes.

Charlie stopped by the Watanabe house just as the family arrived home from church. Sachi said hello and then went into the house with the children trailing behind her and Yoshida following slowly. Yoshida had begun attending church years ago in order to worship with the grandchildren. Lately, she had complained of the aches and pains that

271

come with age. Sachi wanted to start the Sunday meal and turned on the radio as she walked into the kitchen just as she did every Sunday. She noticed Takeo's pipe sitting by the sink. She knew he would miss it so Sachi picked it up and walked to the front door. His tobacco and matches were on the table in the living room so she grabbed those as well and stepped outside.

She handed them to Takeo and he smiled gratefully. "Thank you."

She stood a moment enjoying the breeze as Takeo filled his pipe, lit it, and offered Charlie a light for his cigarette, which he accepted.

Charlie took a drag from the cigarette. Sachi started to head back inside. Charlie exhaled, shook his head, and said, "You folks are in some trouble now. You heard about that bombing, didn't ya?"

Sachi stopped and turned back toward Charlie. Takeo took the pipe from his mouth and said, "We've been in church all morning. What bombing?"

"Damn Japs," Charlie said. "Damn Japs bombed Pearl Harbor, Hawaii this morning. A surprise attack, sneaky sons-a-bitches."

Sachi stared down at her shoes, the black sling backs that she usually wore to church on Sundays. She was angry at his language, but she wanted to know more.

"But why," Takeo asked. "Have you heard why? America has remained neutral in this war. Why would Japan bomb America? "

"I don't know," Charlie said, "I was thinking maybe you could tell me."

"Me? Why would you think I could tell you? I didn't hear about this until just now."

"I was just asking. I thought maybe you'd heard something from your kin over there or maybe…"

Charlie let the sentence hang like casting a fishing line to see what would bite.

"Maybe what?" Takeo said indignant. Sachi searched Charlie's face trying to decipher his meaning.

When Charlie didn't answer, Takeo shook his head. Takeo said, "I know only what you have told me."

"Oh, well. Just askin'. I'm sure there'll be more on the radio, some announcement or something 'bout what's going on."

After a minute of awkward silence and not wanting to seem rude, Sachi asked, "Would you care to stay for supper?"

"Oh, uh, no thanks. I better get going. I got some things I gotta do, but, uh, thanks anyway."

"Maybe another time," Takeo said, looking relieved the man was going on his way.

The three boys were in the front room. Mitchell sat on the couch listening to the Dodgers versus the Giants playoff football game. Billy and John were tossing a baseball between them. Dusty had somehow gotten into the house and was excitedly running back and forth between Billy and John.

The commotion stopped as Takeo and Sachi entered the house. Takeo had a strange look on his face. Sachi had never seen him look so unsettled, so unsure. Billy must have noticed, too.

"What's wrong?" he asked.

"The United States has been attacked. Japan has bombed the United States at Pearl Harbor, Hawaii."

Takeo stood in shock, stunned at his own announcement to his family, as if it were the first time he were hearing the words himself. The boys stopped and turned to their father waiting for his next words.

The football game played on the radio as if everything were still the same. Yoshida entered from the kitchen wiping her wet hands on the yellow apron tied loosely on her waist. She still wore her Sunday clothes. She looked at her quiet family and frowned, "What is going on in here? Too much noise drives me crazy, but too much silence is worse. That's when I know something's wrong."

Yoshida glanced quickly at her porcelain statutes and Sachi knew she was checking to see if the boys had thrown the ball accidentally breaking one of the treasured pieces. They looked intact. She looked back at Takeo waiting for an answer.

"Well, what is the matter?" she asked impatiently.

Takeo looked past his mother, out the kitchen window to the fields beyond, and in almost a whisper responded, "Our countries are at war."

CHAPTER TWENTY-FIVE

As awful as Sunday, December seventh had been, the following day was even worse for the Watanabes. It started when Sachi went into town to get groceries and was told the store would not sell to her. Mr. Grimshaw, never a man to smile, said it was his patriotic duty not to sell to sneaky Jap bastards or any of their kin. He said this in front of Mitchell and John and ordered them out of his store.

Sachi said nothing and went to the smaller Japanese owned store down the block, which offered less, but at least she could get staples. The atmosphere was somber and fearful. No one chatted or laughed. The few Japanese customers gathered their orders and left quickly. After paying for the groceries she went to the bank.

Sachi wrote out a withdrawal slip and stepped up to the teller, an older woman with blue horn-rimmed glasses and a thin-lipped smile. She took the withdrawal slip and looked up the account.

"I'm sorry." She announced loud enough for the other customers to hear. "That account has been frozen."

"Frozen? What do you mean frozen? By whom?"

She tossed back a wave of auburn hair and loudly announced, "Our government," with the emphasis on "our".

Sachi asked, "What? I don't understand? Why?"

She shrugged her shoulders and with a self-satisfied smirk said, "Well, Mrs. Watanabe, I am not the United States government, but I believe it probably has something to do with your people bombing our country. All the Jap accounts have been frozen."

Sachi was stunned, "When can I get my money? How are we to live without money?"

"I don't know. You can check back next week maybe." She looked through Sachi and said, "Next."

Again Sachi said nothing. There was nothing to say. That afternoon Ikuko and Edo came over and said the same thing happened to them. Their accounts were frozen and Mr. Grimshaw had posted a notice saying he would not sell to any Japanese.

Edo said, "Apparently it's happening all over California."

Then late that afternoon, after Ikuko and Edo had gone, three men knocked on their front door. John was wrestling with Dusty in the living room when he heard the knock. Sachi entered from the kitchen.

"I'll get it," he yelled, racing toward the door, with Dusty nipping at his heels. He opened it to find three men, officious and somber looking. One of the men ordered, "Get your parents, young man."

They entered the Watanabe home without invitation.

John turned to his mother. Sachi looked at the three dark-suited Caucasian men in her home. Everything, but their height appeared the same; dark suit, white shirt, dark tie, short hair, clean shaven, steely eyes and a business-like air.

"Where is your husband, Ma'am?" the tall one asked.

"He is outside. John, go get your father and Billy, please."

John ran out the back door with Dusty following. The tall one, obviously the leader, motioned to the shortest one with a jerk of his neck in John's direction. The short suit brushed aside Sachi and followed John out the back door.

"What is this about?" Sachi asked. "Who are you?"

Before the agent responded, Yoshida came out of the kitchen, drying her hands on her worn yellow apron, and said, "Sachi, who was that man?"

She looked at the two others in the living room and asked, "And who are you?"

The tall one flashed what appeared to be a badge, but he flashed it so quickly it was difficult to tell.

He answered, "We're with the Federal Bureau of Investigation. FBI. We're here to see the man of the house."

"Why?" Sachi asked as Mitchell walked from the back bedroom where he'd been reading.

The man said, "Let's wait for your husband. Why don't you all have a seat?" he said motioning to the couch as if this was his home and he was inviting them to stay a while. It was an order, not a question.

Yoshida sat on the couch and Mitchell sat on the floor by her feet looking up at the two men. Billy and Takeo entered with John and the short FBI agent following.

The tall one said, "Mr. Watanabe, please take a seat with the rest of your family."

Takeo remained standing and said, "Who are you and what are you doing in my house?"

"We're FBI and we are here to search the premises for contraband."

"Contraband?" asked Takeo. "There is no contraband here. What do you mean?"

The tall one continued, "By Presidential Proclamation 2525 signed yesterday by President Roosevelt all alien enemies shall be liable to restraint, removal and/or arrest upon search of the suspected alien's premises and the seizure of contraband. My men and I will begin our search and, if we don't find anything, then we will leave and you people can go about your business."

Without saying another word the men began searching the living room and kitchen. The Watanabe family watched in fear and disbelief as the three FBI men searched through their things. The living room was first and done quickly. They were told to stand while the sofa was searched and then, when nothing was found, they were told to sit down again.

One agent walked over to Yoshida's porcelain statute and started to pick one up. Yoshida jumped to her feet and said, "Those are just my statues. Certainly the FBI has no interest in them. Please…"

The man turned on her quickly and ordered, "Take a seat. Now. We'll tell you what is contraband and what isn't."

He picked up each of Yoshida's statues, the statues she would never let anyone touch, and looked beneath each one. Sachi could see Yoshida physically recoil at his touch as if his fingers were running over her very body. When he was satisfied they contained no contraband he set them down and moved to the kitchen.

Takeo and Yoshida sat looking like the statues as if devoid of all energy or will. Billy, Mitchell, and John sat on the floor. Sachi could not stand to sit. She followed the tall man into her bedroom and watched as he dumped drawers and rifled through her life.

These strange men touched their clothes, their under garments, their personal papers, family pictures, their eating and cooking utensils, their books and private mementos.

Two of the men yelled from the living room to the tall one in Sachi's bedroom, "We're going to check the barn."

The tall man yelled back, "Okay."

Then he turned to Sachi and said, "What are these books in Japanese?"

She shook her head, "They're only story books."

He sneered, "Sure. We'll need these."

He threw them on the bed. He began to search the closet. He pulled out Takeo's samurai sword removing the sharp blade from its sheath.

"A weapon, huh? What's this for?"

He didn't wait for Sachi to answer before throwing the blade on the bed and resuming his search of the closet.

She explained, "It's my husband's. Well, really his father's. It was passed down through several generations. It's not a weapon. It's a family heirloom."

As she spoke the man reached back and grabbed the box on the top shelf. He opened it and unwrapped the kimono. Jack's letter fell out. She had forgotten the letter was there until the man reached for the box. She reached for it as it fluttered in the air, but he got it first. He read it, then sneered and whispered, "Looks like this was written to you. A love letter? We're finding all kinds of juicy little secrets about you Japs. Who is this from? It's obviously not from your husband since he says you're already married, but he doesn't sign his name. Smart fellow."

Sachi reached for the letter and asked, "May I have that? It is of no interest to you."

The man held fast to the letter and said, "I'll determine what's of interest to the FBI and I think this just might be. A woman who would have an affair is capable of anything."

Her eyes grew wide and she whispered afraid her family might overhear, "How dare you? An affair? I am having no such thing. It's simply a letter from a friend."

"Then I'm sure your husband knows about this friendly letter."

Sachi panicked. She was afraid Takeo would see the letter and it would crush him. He had enough to worry about with everything that was happening. Their whole lives were coming apart at the seams and this would hurt him further. Why hadn't she just torn up the letter? Why did she keep it? It was the only love letter she'd ever received and she kept it for sentimental reasons, reasons she now cursed.

A voice came from the living room, "Hey, Tom, look what we found in the barn."

He exited the room with her letter still in hand. She followed him.

The two others were standing over a large box. Sachi recognized it as one of the many boxes of Duke's stuff they stored in the barn. It was a box that for the first few years they'd kept in the house and then as their family had grown and the pain of Duke's death had eased, they put his things in the barn never able to completely get rid of them.

The tall one asked, "What'd ya find?"

"Well, first we found this short wave radio sitting on a work bench out there."

Takeo said, "That belongs to my son, John. He has an interest in this. It is not contraband."

"We'll decide that, Watanabe. Sit down."

"Then in this box here we found some maps," the third suit said. He pulled some cloth from the box and, as if announcing he'd discovered the enemy spy plans, he said, "Look what we have here. The flying meatball."

It was a Japanese flag, white with a large red sun in the middle. Duke had brought it over from Japan. His father gave it to him so he would remember Japan and now it was being used against the Watanabe family.

The third suit handed the tall one a book. He said, "We'll need to take this, too."

Mitchell jumped off the floor and yelled, "Hey that's my journal. You can't take that."

The tall one narrowed his eyes at Mitchell and said threateningly, "Boy, you better take your seat, now."

He looked at the journal and said, "Yeah, it's filled with blank pages. Could be invisible writing in there. That's one of the articles we have to confiscate. These are all on the list issued by the president: weapons, short wave radios, cameras, books, maps. These Japanese books will need to be looked at, too. All this property must be seized and confiscated. We'll examine it and if there's nothing there, I'll see if I can get it back to you."

He looked at Takeo and said, "Are you a member of the Japanese American Citizen League?

Takeo said, "Yes. It's just a group of…"

The short one said, "We know what it's a group of. It's a group of Japs just like you."

Takeo tried to explain, "But we are Japanese who wish only…"

The tall one interrupted, "Save it. Taco Watanabe, you'll have to come with us."

Takeo sat as if unable to move. He said nothing, sitting in disbelief.

Sachi, standing by the bedroom doorway had believed they would take what they needed and just go. She didn't think they would need to take Takeo.

"No," she yelled. "You have taken our money and our possessions today. You cannot take my husband."

The tall one walked over to Takeo and the short one moved toward Sachi.

The short one said, "Mrs. Watanabe, don't make this hard. Think about your boys here."

The tall man, appearing to remember the letter, handed it to Sachi. As if punishment for her outburst, he said, "I guess we have enough here without that. Keep your letter."

He looked at Takeo and said, "I guess all wives should have a few secrets. Taco Watanabe you are being detained under Presidential Proclamation 2525 as a suspected alien enemy to the United States of America."

Billy interrupted, "His name is Takeo Watanabe."

John feeling empowered by his oldest brother's voice stood up and shouted at the men, "And he's no enemy to the United States."

The tallest man turned and focused his laser eyes on Billy and then each of the boys in succession. He said, "Careful boys. We know about all of you. You're American because you were born here, but you chose to be Japanese citizens. We know your folks here applied and received Japanese citizenship for you all. Now why do you think that is? Why would you need Japanese citizenship if you were not planning on returning to Japan? And if we all have our way, that is exactly where you'll be going."

Takeo looked shocked at the man's words and Sachi was not sure if it was at the announcement that his wife had a secret, that he was being taken from his home, or that his family might be sent to Japan. It was too much to absorb all at once. He simply let out a breath that he seemed to have been holding the entire time the FBI was in his home.

Yoshida began to cry and wail. Billy sat stoically. Sachi knew he was seething with anger and trying to control it for the sake of his family. John began to cry and Mitchell sat, looking as if he were fighting back tears.

Sachi cried, "No. What are you doing? We let you search the house. We helped you and now you are taking my husband? Why?"

One of the men stepped in front of her, threateningly, "Stand back and don't make this worse. You could find yourself arrested as well. You wouldn't want that. Your children need you here. We are investigating potential spies. If your husband is innocent, he'll come back home. If not, he'll be tried."

"But we have done nothing. We are just farmers. We love America. Really. We would never…"

They picked up the box and escorted Takeo outside. Sachi did not know what to do. She stood in the doorway stunned as they put Takeo in the car. The sun was setting and the reflection off the glass on the car door blinded her.

She yelled, "Where are you taking him?"

The only reply was the cloud of dust that rose as they sped off.

Ikuko came by early that morning. She said she had not slept. The FBI had taken Edo after finding "explosives" in his barn, two sticks of old dynamite he had used years earlier to crack some large boulders on the property. The dynamite was so old and

284

weathered Ikuko said it probably would not even work now, but it was all they needed to take him away. She was in town earlier and heard FBI agents had picked up most of the Issei men the previous night.

Sachi and Yoshida worked through the night scrubbing the house from top to bottom trying to wash away the fingerprints and germs of the men who had entered her home and taken their privacy, their husband and son, and their security. United in their work, they washed each dish and planned on washing all the clothes. It was something to focus on – a job to do, a place for their minds to be.

The next morning Ikuko sat in the kitchen. Yoshida was cleaning one of the bedrooms and Sachi swept the kitchen floor, listening to Ikuko who had no one now that Edo was gone. There was no laughter in her voice and the brightness in her eyes had dulled. She was frightened and alone.

Sachi asked, "Why don't you stay here with us for a while?"

Ikuko shook her head and said, "You don't have enough room. Besides Edo will be home any day once they realize what a mistake they made. I want to be there when he gets home. Maybe even today. And when Takeo gets home he will not want company here."

During that first long week they were notified Takeo had been sent to Lincoln, Nebraska for questioning and it could be months before they saw him again. Ikuko's husband was sent to New Mexico and could eventually end up in Nebraska as well. Rumor had it their men would not return until after the war, if then. It had all happened so

285

quickly and without warning. There were few Issei men left to speak for the Japanese. The FBI had effectively silenced the already quiet Japanese voice. The women who were raised in Japan to submit to their husbands and in-laws were now left to make major family decisions without support.

Sachi's first thought was for her children. If they were to survive this ordeal, then they must be protected as much as possible. She could not protect them from the arrest of their father. Then it hit her - the borrowed name and the children's citizenship. The borrowed name was the one thing her husband had done years ago to "get around" the Alien Land Act. That small action could be his undoing. She felt it might be all they would need to accuse him of breaking the law and send him back to Japan. Then they could claim the entire family, all Japanese citizens, would be sent back to Japan. To her children, Japan was a foreign country.

The papers were filled with anti-Japanese sentiment and storeowners began refusing service to anyone with a Japanese face. The Japanese papers, and there were only a few, rallied against the taking of Japanese from their homes without warrants and without due process arguing that though many of the Japanese were not citizens by birth or naturalization, they still should be accorded the same legal proceedings as American citizens. They warned Japanese and Japanese Americans to be careful.

That week she did not hear from Jack. He did not visit or call her to see what was happening. She wondered where he was and thought perhaps he was feeling as everyone else, that they were Japanese and they were the enemy. The fear of war, of destruction and extinction, was everywhere and the hysteria grew.

Sachi was plunged into a day-to-day existence that seemed like a death struggle. Every morning she woke and wondered if today they would release her bank accounts so she could buy food. They had few supplies left and were rationing the essentials amongst themselves to make them last as long as possible.

Ikuko finally accepted the offer to stay with them. Her loneliness accentuated her fear and she had come to expect the worst, though what that might be no one could say. Like the necessities of sugar, flour, rice, and tea, hope was in short supply.

CHAPTER TWENTY-SIX

EAST COAST - Washington, D.C. - January, 1942

Francis Biddle was the Attorney General of the United States, having been just recently been appointed by President Roosevelt. As Attorney General he was also the head of the Department of Justice as well as the FBI, which gave him authority even over J. Edgar Hoover.

Francis Biddle had never known life without money and privilege and he had come to expect his life to follow a certain path. He finished law school at Harvard, served in the Navy, and worked for the Justice Department. He served as a judge for the Circuit Court of Appeals for the Third Circuit. He also had worked tirelessly on the Roosevelt campaigns, the only president he'd ever voted for. His father's east coast money and influence had played no small part in having him appointed to the post of Attorney General, particularly at so young an age, but his shared interests with the President were what drew them together as political teammates. They both enjoyed a background of money and privilege, which allowed them to acquire extensive educations and amounts of influence first through their families' accomplishments and then through their own.

His parents taught him his responsibilities were to God, his family, and then his country. His father worked hard and amassed a fortune in the stock market and oil. His mother taught him of the principles of democracy and freedom, the American dream, and outlined his destiny for him. He was to serve his country for himself and his countrymen.

If he did so, the masses would repay him in kind.

Biddle was also raised with a strong sense of right and wrong, though his mother often claimed he was born with it. He refused to play games with other children if they attempted to violate or change the accepted rules. He respected his father, but did not admire him because he played fast and loose with rules claiming they were for everyone else and made to be broken. This contributed heavily to Biddle's own sense of right, wrong, and fair play. He often stood up for his younger, weaker brother who was not a high achiever and had plans for his life other than his mother's strategic destiny. His brother eventually moved to New Orleans after breaking with his parents to play Jazz in the French Quarter. Biddle talked to his brother occasionally and he was happy.

Though his brother was a free spirit, Biddle felt the added weight of expectations for his brother shift onto his own shoulders, increasing his burden. He had just recently begun to feel that weight lift, along with a new surge of power each morning as he walked the streets to his office as the country's youngest attorney general. This was the part he'd studied for so many years and now he had achieved it and was enjoying it. His young wife was pregnant with their first child. Everything had fallen into place.

Blue blood flowed beneath his pergamenous skin providing it with a lucid glow like the traces of illumination cast off neon light. His brown hair, trimmed just above the collar, was neither too long nor too short, graying, just slightly, along the temples. His bright, clear blue eyes looked larger in the black-rimmed glasses he had worn since an early age. Francis Biddle always did things right. He did not make mistakes and prided himself on this. Roosevelt had selected him for his stands on individual rights and his exceptional legal record as well as his unqualified political support. Biddle was most fanatical about not infringing on the rights of any United States citizen and had won almost all court cases he'd tried involving violations of civil rights. As a judge, when needed, he always came down on the side of the individual. His country was at war. There was the war in Europe, the war in the Pacific, and the war at home. He sat in his Department of Justice office in Washington, D.C. several thousand miles from where all the wars, most of them anyway, were being fought.

WEST COAST - Los Angeles

General John Lesesne DeWitt was the polar opposite to Francis Biddle physically, philosophically, and in all other ways. He was 61 years old and at the end of a long and, until this point, mostly undistinguished career.

Raised by a poor family who lost their farm during the depression in the 1890s and found themselves waist-deep in poverty, DeWitt was no less a portrait of the American dream than Biddle, just in a different frame. He had immediately joined the army and risen through the ranks fighting in the Great War and now found himself as the Commanding General of the Western Defense Command, which included the states of California, Arizona, Oregon, Washington, Utah, Nevada, Idaho, and Montana.

Leaving his poverty-stricken family at 16, DeWitt joined the military and had been with them ever since. The military protected him from the next great depression and other societal discomforts. Unlike many Americans at the time, he always had a job and he never had to worry about his housing, meals or, later, his family.

Recently he'd served several years in the Philippines where he acquired some knowledge of the area and culture along with some of the prejudice of the masses there against the Japanese. Those who knew him called him a "competent bureaucrat." The insult was lost on DeWitt who found bureaucracy necessary and, at times, enjoyable. He loved writing memos and insisted on all communications being in memo form.

The first conversation to take place between the unwavering Biddle and the officious Dewitt occurred by telephone on December 8, 1941. Both men, like the rest of the country, were still in shock over the attack just a day earlier. The conversation was short, concise, and immediately illuminated the differences between them.

Dewitt rolled a fresh cigar between his thumb and forefinger as he spoke. It was a habit he had taken up while in the Philippines and he felt it gave him an air of authority.

He said, "We have to conduct mass raids on the homes and businesses of the Japanese in this country. It's the only way to check for and seize contraband. They're not going to come up and give it to us. We have to flush out the spies and mass raids are the best way to do that. The FBI has compiled that list of potential alien enemies. They've had it for months now waiting to use it for just this contingency."

Biddle said, "I don't like it. The FBI is already detaining potential alien enemies. You can't do mass raids without search warrants. It's as simple as that."

DeWitt said, "If we have to get a John Doe search warrant, it simply serves to alert the enemy and they have plenty of time to hide the evidence. We need authority to conduct mass raids where we feel it's needed."

Biddle said, "We must proceed swiftly, but cautiously in this regard. We are talking about not only alien enemies, but also American citizens. The Issei are aliens, but their children are not. They are entitled to the protections of the Constitution."

DeWitt sighed in frustration and said, "I understand that, but you're in Washington. Here, in California, things are in a panic. There are blackouts, sirens, drills and not just out of fear of Japan. There are rumors that the Mexican army is ready to overrun us as well. The air raid sirens send people running for cover. There are a lot of people saying we should arrest all the Japanese, everyone that even looks Japanese, right now."

Biddle's assistant, Thomas Rowe, entered and handed Biddle a phone message and some pieces of opened mail. Biddle looked them over without much thought and said to DeWitt, "The constitution cannot be ignored because we are at war. If anything, we need it now more than ever."

DeWitt said, "I agree and I'm not sure that arresting all Japanese, Issei, Nisei or Kisei, is the answer, but I'm telling you that is what I'm hearing from my staff, the public, and the media out here. The Japanese are aggressive and cunning by their very nature. We need to avoid violence from war hysteria right here in California. We need to be able to pinpoint the alien enemies. And we need to start putting together a plan to lock them all up. Not just for the country's security, but for their own."

Biddle declared, "Fine. I agreed with the suggestion that we officially register all alien enemies right away and go ahead with those raids, but remember the Nisei are

American citizens and they have rights. Coordinate matters with the FBI. I understand they are already detaining people, but I will not agree to arrest an entire group of people without just cause, particularly when a large portion of that group consists of Americans. It's not going to happen."

CHAPTER TWENTY-SEVEN

Mount Gearhart, Oregon was a popular campsite and Reverend Archie Mitchell was popular with the children of his church. Mrs. Mitchell made the county's best potato salad and Reverend Mitchell was always up for a game of stickball. Maybe it was because they did not have children of their own, but the Mitchells, newly married just two years earlier and hoping to conceive, seemed to have boundless energy for their young charges and boundless patience.

It was a late August morning, a day made for picnics and stickball. It was the kind of lemonade-can-advertising day filled with sunshine and the future, created for exploring, watching clouds, and examining bugs. The Reverend pulled the car into an area and let his young wife and the five parish children out of the car. Mrs. Mitchell yelled after the children to stay close.

"I'll bring the picnic baskets. Here," he said, handing her a large blanket. "I'll park the car and be right back. Find a good spot."

She stuck her head through the open passenger window to take the blanket from the front seat. A tendril of her brown hair had sneaked off from the rest pulled tight in her customary bun. The heart-shaped locket he had given her upon their engagement swung back and forth from her neck as she leaned over to take the blanket.

She smiled, "We'll find the best spot in Mount Gearhart for a picnic."

"And stickball," he laughed. "You know how the children like it."

"I know how you like it."

"That I do."

He leaned toward her and puckered. She kissed him quickly and smiled, almost shyly, particularly for a woman who was already married two years. No longer a newlywed, really, but inside she still felt like one.

As he parked the car and took the picnic basket out of the trunk he thought how grateful he was to be away for the day. A day outside with children always provided him with relief from the duties and burdens of his ministry and relief from the war.

Everything it seemed was centered on the war, winning it, conserving for it, talking of it, and praying about it. He believed in the war effort and did everything he could, recycling and going without. He was a tall, thin man with glasses from all those years of reading and studying. He usually didn't eat much except on days like today when he found himself ravenous, almost insatiably hungry. Today he could be just another man enjoying his wife's potato salad and playing stickball with children. The fact they were not his children mattered not at all.

He drew the fresh mountain air deep into his lungs and started a brisk walk toward the area where he had dropped off his wife and the children. Suddenly he fell to the ground as it shook. An explosion rocked the earth and the very airwaves, causing him to put his hands to his ears, both picnic baskets swinging from each arm.

Ahead he saw what looked like thick, dark fog rising from the trees. He ran to the spot where his wife and the children were to be and momentarily, he could see nothing through thick, rising dust. Breathing in the hot fumes, coughing, and calling his wife's name, Archie tried to find some sign of life, but there was no response. As he walked toward the center of the explosion he saw small fires blaze around him, singed trees, twigs, and branches, and, in the distance, one of his wife's shoes, a small, brown leather Oxford, lying in the blackened dirt. He spotted a baseball nearby and then body parts, inanimate things like the shoe and the ball and the trees and the twigs. There was a foot and an arm and it took several minutes for him to realize his wife and the children had been killed, blown apart by something evil and unknown. He stood near the center of the scorched earth crater with the picnic baskets containing his wife's fried chicken and potato salad, unable to move and still calling their names, knowing they would not answer.

He looked up into the sky hoping another one of these mysterious explosions would engulf him as well, but nothing came. The sky looked exactly as it had minutes earlier, promisingly bright blue with a few lazy white clouds wandering by. The sun shone as brightly as before. The only differences were the birds were silent and his wife and the children were dead.

The FBI coroner said it was a Japanese bomb that had been sent along with about 300 others attached to balloons. The Japanese floated these bomb-carrying balloons toward the United States. Some landed in Canada and some in America. None had caused fatalities or casualties of any kind until now. These were the first and the only. The FBI man speculated his wife or one of the children happened upon the bomb. They were intrigued by it and probably disturbed the undetonated bomb connected to a parachute-like balloon. The coroner marveled that the bomb had not exploded on impact when it hit the ground. The Japanese had planted a bomb in his own back yard. They had taken from him his wife, his only family, and his entire future.

The FBI impressed upon him the need for secrecy in this matter. Japan could never know even one of their bombs had been successful. They must never know they had achieved a successful attack on the continental United States.

CHAPTER TWENTY-EIGHT

Sachi spent the morning working at church and then went to Kitashima's to spend her last few household dollars on tea, rice, and sugar. She placed the groceries in the car, but instead of driving back home she locked the car and wandered the streets feeling the warm sunshine and looking in the store windows. Orange Grove had changed dramatically since the first day she had come to town twenty years earlier. There were more stores, more people, and more businesses. Main Street was lined with cars and fewer trees. There was even a small bus station at the north end of town.

The weather had warmed and Sachi removed her cardigan sweater, folding it over her arm. She reached the bus station, crossed the street, and headed back on the other side. Sachi tried to empty her mind of all the worries that had weighed so heavily these past few months. Sachi took her time, enjoying the feeling of being alone. She neared Hank's Diner. The smells of apple pie and coffee wafted from the open windows. A sign out front advertised the Meatloaf Lunch Special. Sachi sat down on a wooden bench outside one of the open diner windows to rest. It was lunchtime and she could hear the clinking of silver wear and glasses, but within seconds she suddenly heard familiar voices.

It was Jack. She heard the frustration in his voice and he said, "Listen Charlie. We're not at war with our neighbors."

She turned slightly, just enough to peer in the side of the widow, and saw Jack sitting

with Charlie Shimmer, Buck Toller, and a man she did not know. All four men had plates

of meatloaf and cups of coffee in front of them. Sachi quickly turned her head so as not to

be recognized.

Charlie Shimmer sounded as if he had just taken a bite of meatloaf. "You can't really

trust any of em' Jack. I heard about this group of Jap farmers down toward Bakersfield.

They were mowing arrows into their corn fields and crops and things so that the Japanese

pilots could see these arrows when they were in the air and know where things were like

our utilities and gas storage and munitions stations or armament facilities, stuff like that."

Jack laughed. "I heard that rumor, too, Charlie. Do you really believe it?"

"'Course I believe it," Charlie said. "You don't know what they're capable of Jack.

Not all of em' exactly, but I mean the sneaky ones. The ones who are against us and it's

hard to know who's with us and who ain't."

Buck Toller was a short, balding man whose wife left him three years earlier. He was

a farmer like almost everyone else and Sachi knew him from church. He spoke, almost

with glee, Sachi thought. "I heard about that one Jap farmer had the nerve to put the

flying meatball on his tractor and drive around his fields displaying it. Disgusting. But he

learned his lesson or should I say those Japs around him learned. Group of decent

American boys went out one night and beat hell out of him. Killed him. Took the flag and

burned it right there next to his body."

Jack said, "I don't understand killing a man over a flag."

A fourth voice, one unfamiliar to her, said, "It ain't just over a flag. Look at all those battles those Japs have been winnin' lately.

Charlie added, "Yeah, and I heard a rumor from a cousin of mine up there in Oregon who said they had an explosion last week. Nips sent bombs over here tied to helium balloons. A pastor, his wife, and three kids were killed by one up in Oregon.

Jack's voice contained disbelief as he said, "I haven't read anything about balloon bombs in the papers."

Charlie replied, "And you won't either. Can you imagine what would happen if those bastards thought their trick worked? Our skies would be filled with balloons. I don't understand how naive you are. God-fearing Americans all across this country are concerned about everything Japanese, particularly their flag. You should be concerned, too, unless, of course, you are one of them Japanese sympathizers. Don't think we don't know how tight you are with those Watanabes."

Sachi felt her stomach tighten further and knew she should get up and leave, but she was held to the bench partly out of fear of being found out. She realized these men thought Japanese people were sneaky and spying. What would they do if they found her sitting there listening? She knew she should go, but she had to hear what Jack would say. She wanted to hear him stick up for her and her family. She had to know.

She heard Jack's voice filling with anger. "What's that suppose to mean?"

Buck Toller said, "Nothing unless you care more about the Japanese than your own kind."

301

"What is my own kind?"

Charlie answered, "If you don't know, then maybe you've got bigger problems."

"Just because I have dinner with Japanese friends once in a while is no need to question my loyalty, Charlie. And just because you are afraid is no reason to begin hating all Japanese including your neighbors who have been living here for years."

Buck laughed, "This didn't just begin. I haven't liked the sneaky Jap bastards since they started taking over the farms around here and using those paper names as a way of getting around the law."

Jack said, "I have to work with everyone who farms in this valley. It's my job. I want America to win this war and I am against Japan as much as anyone. I just don't think we should punish the people who are here."

It was not the impassioned protective declaration Sachi was hoping to hear from Jack. It sounded more like she and her family were just another Japanese family that he had to work with whether he wanted to or not. She drew in a deep breath trying to rid herself of the nausea she suddenly felt.

Buck said, "The papers spell it all out for you in black and white. All the editorials say the same thing. Japanese are Japanese no matter where they live. Even Lippman said it and ya know I got no use for Lippman. You gotta choose sides here."

In a tone filled with suspicion, Charlie said, "Unless there's another reason you been havin' dinner with the Watanabes so much. That Sachi Watanabe. I know she's a good…what shall I call her? A friend of yours? Or is it more than that? She's fine for a Jap."

She heard something carefully measured in Jack's voice as he responded. "Say her name again and I'll crack your head."

Charlie's voice told Sachi he caught something in Jack's voice as well, "Hey. No need to get so upset Jack. I'm just sayin'…"

"Hank, where's that coffee?" Buck interrupted him. "You said enough, Charlie. Don't accuse Jack here of bein' interested in another man's wife, particularly a Jap broad. No, Jack. We know that ain't true, but come on. You gotta know that friendship ain't gonna buy you no friends around here."

"I'm not looking at buying friendships. I just want to do my job."

Buck said, "Can't be that way no more. We gotta get rid of the Japs around here. Move em' out. We can't take chances right now. We're at war."

"Yes, I guess we are," Jack said.

Sachi heard a change in the position of his voice and the sliding of chair legs on the concrete floor. She knew he was leaving. She quickly rose from the bench and walked away.

CHAPTER TWENTY-NINE

It was one of those March days that only come to California. In the middle of winter, the sun decided to visit and show off for a while raising the temperature to 77 degrees.

Sachi thought about asking her children to be right home from school as she had done every day since the bombing. John and Mitchell always obeyed, but Billy sometimes came home late filled with excuses about work or school or helping out one of the neighbors. Sachi was afraid to check out his stories for fear she would learn he was lying to her. She felt stupid and knew if Takeo were here, Billy would not dare to make up stories or stay out late. He needed his father at home.

But with the unseasonably warm weather, Sachi allowed the children a little more freedom. The warmth of the sun made her feel safer. Perhaps things would be okay. She told the boys they could play with their friends after school. Mitchell went to the home of another Japanese boy in his class and John was going to stay after school and play baseball with some boys.

Yoshida was in her garden, working the soil, but mainly sunning herself. Ikuko had gone to visit friends. Sachi was in the kitchen chopping vegetables when she heard the front door screen slam shut. Her back was to the kitchen table. She heard the plastic seat on the kitchen chair gush out air from the weight of her son and John said, "I'm home."

"What are you doing home so early?" she asked without turning around.

"I don't know. Nothing to do I guess."

Sachi still did not raise her head, concentrating on the vegetables in front of her, happy John was home and wondering when Billy would decide to show up and what story he would manage to concoct this time.

"Are you hungry?" she asked.

"No."

Sachi sighed and wondered if he was ill. He was always hungry when he returned from school and he must have come home early because he wasn't feeling well. She hoped it was nothing that would require medicine or a doctor's visit. How would she pay for it? Would the doctor even see him?

"Mom, I'm an American, aren't I?"

"What?" She asked, continuing to chop. Something in her son's voice caused her to look up. As she did, still chopping, she saw her son's lovely face, perfect in every form, marred with a large black eye and a small trickle of almost dried blood dropping down from his nose. She winced from the pain. She could actually feel it. Sachi grabbed a dishcloth and went to him.

"How did this happen?" she asked

"They said I couldn't play baseball with them. They said baseball was an American game and since I'm a stinkin' Jap, I can't play an American game. Only Americans can."

She winced again, as much from the pain from the words as the pain from looking at his injuries.

"I told em' I was American as any of them. I was born right here. But they said it didn't matter. I looked like a dirty Jap so I am one."

He began to cry at the final words, but continued through his tears and the black eye seemed to grow larger by the second from swelling, "I am American. I am. I can't help how I look. I want to look like them, like an American."

Sachi lifted the dishtowel to his face to wipe his tears and the blood under his nose when she noticed there was already blood on the cloth.

"Where did this come…?" She started, but as she looked at her hand she noticed she had cut herself in her concern to care for her son.

"Mom" he cried out. "You cut yourself bad. Grandma-a-a-a."

Sachi said, "It is okay. You're grandma is in the garden. Do not disturb her over this silly cut."

As she looked she saw it was deep, but she didn't want to take time to look at it. She wanted to talk to her son, tend to his wounds, not her own.

"I need to get Grandma." He said hesitating by the back door.

"No," said his mother. "This is okay. It will heal. Just get me the iodine and the bandages out of the cabinet."

John went to the cabinet and retrieved the bandages. Sachi unwrapped her hand again and examined it carefully. It was still bleeding.

John stood next to her, calmly watching as she examined her cut.

He said, "It looks bad, Mom."

He looked gingerly at her wound as if, by looking too closely, he might hurt her. She applied the antiseptic, which stung. As she winced, she noticed John wincing as well. She tried to smile as they wrapped the finger in the bandage. She marveled at how she always thought it was just parents who experience the pain when their children are hurt. She realized children, too, experience the pain when their parents are hurt.

"Here I am supposed to be taking care of you and you're taking care of me," she smiled at him.

He had wiped away the dried blood under his nose. The black eye stood out against his pale skin. She went to the freezer and took out a piece of meat and told him to hold it on his eye for the swelling.

She said, "John, you are American. Those boys… well, those boys are just saying things they hear from their parents. Their grandparents or great-grandparents all came to America from different places like Scotland or England or Mexico or anywhere in the world. It just so happens your family came from Japan."

She handed him a cookie and said, "The swelling will go down very soon."

He brightened at the treat and said, "I hope not. I want Billy to see it. He thinks he's the only one around here who can get into a fight and get a black eye."

Sachi said, "John. I won't have you talking like that. You know better. It is not a thing of glory to go around town sporting an eye such as that."

"I bet Tom Drucker's mom must be tellin' him the same thing right about now."

"Tom?"

"Yeah. He gave me this, but I gave him one, too."

She shook her head and turned back toward the vegetables with a slight smile on her lips. Maybe her children would learn from all this and become stronger. Maybe they all would. Surely this was as bad as things could get. They would survive this.

When Billy returned home that evening, Sachi said nothing for a few minutes. She took his dinner from the oven, where she'd kept it warming, and set it on the table.

He slumped into the kitchen chair and began eating.

"Where have you been, Billy?" she asked.

"School" he said.

"School was dismissed four hours ago," she reminded him. "You almost stayed out past curfew."

"Curfew. Who cares? The curfew was set to make sure I'm not doing anything to topple the American government. As if plotting to overthrow the government only occurs at night."

Sachi said, "That curfew is for your own protection, too. You don't know what to expect right now. These are dangerous times. Besides, if you don't care about yourself, think of me and your grandmother. We have enough to contend with without you getting yourself arrested or beaten up or…"

She could not finish the sentence and tears filled her eyes. She blinked them back, but not before Billy noticed.

"I am here, okay? Besides I was looking for work. You know, a part-time job or something. Couldn't find anything, of course. No one wants to hire a Jap," he stopped as he looked into his mother's face, a beloved Japanese face.

He breathed deeply as if to rid himself of the feeling and continued.

"Anyway, I couldn't find anything so I stopped by a friend's house and then came home."

"You were at one of those meetings, weren't you?" Sachi said, raising her voice. "Those Kia's, trying to stir up more trouble, as if we don't have enough already. They are going to be your downfall. Stop associating with them."

Billy raised his voice as well, "At least they're doing something."

"Doing something?" Sachi looked at him, incredulous, "And just what are they doing? They are talking tough and complaining."

Billy became indignant, "At least they are not sitting still for this kind of treatment. Not like those old women at the Japanese American Citizens League who think they can talk and talk and that will accomplish anything. It won't. It hasn't. Dad has been gone almost three months. He missed Christmas and New Year's, our birthdays. They have taken away our lives and without proof of anything."

He took a deep breath, lowered his voice, and said, "Besides I wasn't at a meeting today. Not today. I was looking for work and there is none for a Jap."

Sachi said, "Stop using that word. It is insulting. Perhaps you are mistaking a lack of available jobs on prejudice. Anyway, it's just as well. I need you here after school. We have a business here to run until your father returns. It will be harvest time soon and I will need you then. Your father will need you."

Billy threw out a laugh filled with sarcasm. "Do you think father is returning? Wake up, Mother. Father is in prison. He probably will be sent back to Japan. And I know you've heard the talk about imprisoning the rest of us. We're all going to jail and then to Japan. Father sure won't be here in time for harvest and we probably won't either so I wouldn't spend too much time worrying about it. We won't be here to reap what we've sown."

Sachi shook her head, "You don't know that, Billy. You might be right about your father and me, but not you and your brothers. You are American citizens. They can't send you to Japan. You've never even been there. We have no family there."

Yoshida entered the kitchen in her worn yellow robe and matching slippers. Sachi remembered giving those to her for her birthday almost ten years ago. The robe was extra large and fluffy and though she complained of its size and said it was simply too big and heavy, she wore it every day.

Yoshida muttered as she put water on the stove, "I hope they do send us back."

"No," said Sachi. "That's not going to happen."

"Well," Yoshida said. "The children might be better off. They wouldn't be hated for simply looking Japanese. They wouldn't come home with black eyes and broken spirits."

Billy asked, "Who's got a black eye?"

311

Yoshida said, "Your brother. A fight at school today. Kids wouldn't let him play baseball. They are trying to break his spirit. Those…Hjukin."

"Yoshida. No one's spirit is broken."

Yoshida spat out her words, "Those boys are akuma from jigoku.

Sachi shook her head. "They are not devils from hell. They are boys who are repeating what they've heard at home. What they hear everywhere."

Yoshida said, "I see. So it's acceptable."

"Of course not." Sachi shook her head. "None of it is acceptable. But going to Japan is not our answer. Do you really think our children would be less hated in Japan? They would be more hated. The minute they opened their mouths they would be branded Americans. Over there Americans are the enemy. I know you want to go back Yoshida. You always have, but this is not the way."

Billy said, "No. The only way for us is to fight what they do."

Sachi looked at her son puzzled and asked, "Fight what who does?"

Billy pushed his plate away and looked at his mother. He said, defiantly, "These whites. They aren't going to get away with this. We need to stand up to them."

Sachi said, "I know the Japanese American Citizen League is trying to negotiate with the government. They have opened our bank accounts back up. That is something. I think the JACL will do what is right and in our best interest. They simply want to make it clear that we are willing to prove our loyalty to our country if called upon. That should be enough. Certainly, they won't take everything from us. "

312

Billy scoffed, "Mother, what do you know about it? Most of the men, the Issei like father, were taken away and arrested. That leaves families like us, children and women and young Nisei men like me. We are Americans, but we have two voices and neither one is very strong. We have no political or cultural or financial clout. They will make us go even though they know it is wrong. They just don't know what else to do to calm their fears. And are we to go like sheep? Are we to be responsible for protecting them from the consequences of their hatred and fear and prejudice? No. I think we should fight them. We should not have to go, but they will make us because they are afraid. It is coming."

Sachi said, "Billy, they cannot make us go anywhere. Your father will be home soon and…"

Billy stood shouting at his mother in frustration, "Are you blind? You read the papers and listen to the news. We are going to be removed and imprisoned. They will take us away as they did Father. He isn't coming home soon. Don't you see it? Are you that stupid?"

Billy stomped from the room and out the front door before Sachi could think of what to say. She stood shocked at her son's harsh, loud words. Yoshida sat at the table with her tea and stirred it silently for a moment.

Then, matter-of-factly, she said, "I told you picking him up as a baby would come back to haunt you. He thinks he can get away with acting anyway he pleases."

Sachi clenched her fists and let out a loud, frustrated, "oh-h-h-h-h."

It took all her self-restraint to walk from the room without saying something hurtful. Billy later apologized, but the pressure and hardships were taking their toll. Things were changing within Billy and within the family.

CHAPTER THIRTY

February 1942

President Roosevelt had read the memo in front of him from the Western Defense Command, General Dewitt to Secretary of War Stimson. It read in part:

"Hostile naval and air raids will be assisted by enemy alien agents signaling from the coast …Sabotage can also occur to power, light, water, and sewer… The Japanese race is an enemy race and, while many second and third generation Japanese born on United States soil, possessed of United States citizenship, have become "Americanized," the racial strains are undiluted. The very fact that no sabotage has taken place to date is a disturbing and confirming indication that such action will take place."

Roosevelt faced Stimson as they sat late that night drinking coffee and discussing the Japanese situation. Roosevelt, holding the memo in front of him, said, "I am not too sure of the logic presented here, but…"

He sighed deeply and continued, "Harry, I am overwhelmed with the war effort, domestic matters, and working at winning this war. I am too busy to spend the time it will take for me to become knowledgeable enough about this situation to make the evacuation decision. If those directly responsible and presumably most knowledgeable about this recommend evacuation see this as being essential, then those are the people we should listen to and that's what we need to do."

Three days later President Roosevelt signed Executive Order 9066.

Now therefore by virtue of the authority vested in me as President of the United States, and Commander in Chief of the Army and Navy, I hereby authorize and direct the

Secretary of War and the Military Commanders whom he may from time to time

designate, whenever he or any designated commander deems such actions necessary or

desirable, to preserve military areas in such places and of such extent as he or the

appropriate Military Commanders may determine, from which any or all persons may be

excluded, and with such respect to which, the right of any person to enter, remain in or

leave shall be subject to whatever restrictions the Secretary of War or the appropriate

Military Commander may impose in his discretion...

With that the futures of Japanese and American citizens of that ancestry were changed forever.

CHAPTER THIRTY-ONE

WESTERN DEFENSE COMMAND AND FOURTH ARMY

WARTIME CIVIL CONTROL ADMINISTRATION

PRESIDIO OF SAN FRANCISCO, CALIFORNIA

INSTRUCTIONS

TO ALL PERSONS OF

JAPANESE

ANCESTRY

LIVING IN THE FOLLOWING AREA:

All that portion of the counties of Sacramento and Amador,

State of California, within the boundary beginning at a point at

which California State Highway No. 16 intersects California State

Highway No.49 approximately two miles south of Plymouth;

thence southerly along said Highway No. 49 to the Amador-

Calaveras County Line, thence westerly along the Amador-

Calaveras County Line to the Amador-San Joaquin County Line;

thence northerly along the Amador-San Joaquin County Line to

the Sacramento-San Joaquin County Line; thence westerly along

the Sacramento-San Joaquin County Line to the easterly line of

the right of way of the main line of the Southern Pacific Railroad from Lodi to Sacramento; thence northerly along said east-

erly line to its crossing with California State Highway No. 16;

thence easterly along said Highway No. 16 to point of beginning.

Pursuant to the provisions of Civilian Exclusion Order No. 92, this

Headquarters, dated May 23, 1942, all persons of Japanese ancestry,

Both alien and non-alien, will be evacuated from the above area by 12

o'clock noon, P.W.T., Saturday, May 30, 1942.

Yoshida and Sachi stood outside Kitashima's small market, the only place they could

shop for food now, and read the order in disbelief. Yoshida did not read English, but

Sachi knew Yoshida was embarrassed, angry, and insulted to have such attention drawn

to her in public in this manner.

She tugged at Sachi's arm. Sachi waved her off as she stood and read it. It ordered all

Japanese people to report to local Civil Control Station for further instructions and

registration. The notice informed them they would be evacuated in nine days. They could

take bed linens and clothes and only two suitcases per person. There would be no pets

allowed and no "contraband", including sewing needles and tools.

Sachi heard stories of others on different parts of the west coast who were evacuated

as early as three months ago in February. But like death, disease, and the traumas of life,

it was always difficult to believe, until it happened to you.

318

She walked as if in a daze up to the stand where Mrs. Kitashima was spraying some vegetables with water. The stand was filled with delicious looking late spring produce, onions, artichokes, lettuce, carrots, and traditional Japanese foods like Dashiku not sold at Mr. Grimshaw's down the street.

Yoshida and Sachi did not speak until they got up to the counter where Mrs. Kitashima totaled up their purchases and said, "I guess you've seen the notice. The time has come."

Sachi nodded. "It is convenient they placed it right outside your stand."

Mrs. Kitashima said, "I guess they figured that would get the information out more quickly to the Japanese since they're not allowed in Grimshaw's anymore. But these are posted all over. Didn't you notice them coming into town today?"

Both women shook their heads.

"Well, they've only been up since late yesterday afternoon. I don't know what we're going to do. They want us to leave this. Just walk away from it as if it were nothing, meant nothing. How do you do that? Walk away from your home where you have lived most of your life, where you have borne your children and raised them?"

Yoshida said, "You go back to Japan if you can. That's what we would do if I had my way, but they have my son so I cannot go back."

The three women stood, as so many women, held to a place, to a destiny, by their children and decisions made by men. They bowed to Mrs. Kitashima and said goodbye.

319

At home Sachi put away the groceries then looked out the window at the fields just beginning to yield the precious strawberries - plump, red gems peeking out from under the large, green guardian leaves. She, Yoshida, and the children had worked hard to make sure this crop was healthy. They had planned and looked forward to picking day and now she had nine days to pack up her life, dispose of her belongings, and leave her home.

This was war and many were making sacrifices, but it seemed so unfair America was willing to sacrifice all Japanese families.

Yoshida entered the kitchen, interrupting Sachi's thoughts. Sachi brushed away tears and walked to the sink to begin making tea. Yoshida brought in the suitcases. They only owned three and even those were hardly used. There had never been much reason to leave their home before now. Planning was so important in a situation like this, but there was little time to plan.

Sachi looked around the kitchen and realized how much they owned. She had never thought about it before, but the thought of trying to decide what to bring was overwhelming. There was still a mortgage on the house. They had little money and would need every bit of it since they didn't know where they would be going or what conditions would be like when they got there.

Sachi spoke first, "I am going to the bank tomorrow. I will close out the accounts. I guess we should make a list of the things we might need, though I'm sure I don't know. I wish we knew where we were going. I wish we knew when Takeo was going to come home. He may come home and not even know where we are. I wish..."

She stopped. Wishing was a waste of thought and breath. There was no bamboo tree to attach paper wishes. There was no planning how to avoid this. There was only planning on how to do it best.

She continued, "While I am at the bank I will talk to them about the farm. Maybe there is some way we can put off the payments. I mean if we are back in a few months, that would be plenty of time to get next year's crop into market and pay off our debt, at least some of it. Maybe the bank will allow that. I will talk to someone."

Yoshida looked tired. She said, "Sachi, do you think the bank is going to allow all the Japanese farms to miss payments? We don't know how long we will be gone. Who knows if we'll even come back? What if they really do send us back to Japan? The house is gone. The fields are gone. All we can do is hope to sell it for a fair price in the next week. As it is, the crops are just lying out there in the hot sun. They will rot soon. We can't do it all. Not everything works out like it should. Don't think that any bank is going to help you, to make this easier for you. They will not."

Sachi was angry. Why did her mother-in-law always have to be so negative, so sure she was right and nothing would work as Sachi planned?

"I am going to try," she said resolutely. "If it doesn't work, what have I lost?"

Yoshida said smugly, "If you look like a beggar, you are one. You lose face."

"Lose face?" Sachi said. "We are being kicked out of our homes and told we are alien enemies. I think losing face is the least of our concerns."

Yoshida's eyes lit up and she said, "They can take your home and your things, but no one can take your honor. That you keep or you give away, but it cannot be taken. Do not give away your honor, Sachi. It may be all we have left."

Sachi couldn't think about honor right now, though it was how she was raised. In Japan honor, saving face, was the most important thing. To lose face was to lose everything. In the past many Japanese had committed suicide by *hari kari,* a stomach cut, in order to maintain their honor and dignity. She touched her stomach as she dressed thinking of ancestors that might have committed the last deadly act on themselves for less than this. She wondered if it would come to that and if she would be glad.

CHAPTER THIRTY-TWO

She left for the bank the next day and stood in line. There were many Japanese customers all withdrawing their savings. Sachi stepped up to the first available teller and cringed. It was the same teller who had embarrassed her on the day after the Pearl Harbor bombing. Her auburn hair was tied in a tight bun, as if, it too, had been inducted into the war effort where now all things, even hairstyles, were deadly serious. Her green eyes did not flash recognition. Her face held the tension of a clenched fist, etched in lines with pinched lips and a scowling brow.

Sachi spoke first, "I would like to close…"

The woman sighed as if she were the one being interrupted and not Sachi. She said, "Yes, I know, close your accounts. Bank books?"

Sachi handed her the bank documents, and, as she was processing them, Sachi quietly asked, "Can I speak to the manager?"

Without looking up the teller said, "The manager is at lunch."

Sachi fingered the ruffle on her best dress. It was a thin crepe material and as she rolled it nervously in her sweaty palm the crepe grew more wrinkled and damp.

Sachi lowered her voice. She was nervous and did not want to be overheard. Takeo had always taken care of business and Sachi was unsure of the procedure, but determined to ask. "Is there anyone else I could speak to about a loan?"

The teller stopped and looked up at Sachi incredulous. Her large eyes and cruel smile gave vision to Yoshida's words. The woman spoke loudly with an incredulous tone, announcing Sachi's request to the entire bank, "You want a loan?"

The teller spoke to her co-worker on the next stool as she worked on the papers closing the Watanabe account and counting out the little money that was left.

"Did you hear her? She's leaving in a week, but she thinks we'll give her a loan."

Sachi continued to look straight ahead, afraid to look at anyone else in the bank, embarrassed at being there and being the brunt of this woman's attack.

Sachi said, "Please, whom would I speak to…?"

The teller's painted red lips spit the words at Sachi, "Forget it. Do you think this bank stays in business by making loans to people who can't pay them back and will probably never be here again? Do you people think we are going to do anything for you or make anything easier for you?"

Sachi looked her in the eye and let go of the ruffle on her dress. Sachi refused to let this woman intimidate her. This was too important and Sachi knew she had no other choice. She raised her voice slightly and said, "I will be back here. I don't know when, but I am coming back. Now I would like to speak to someone…"

The teller interrupted again. "You are being arrested in a week. I mean, let's face it. That's what it is. They are calling it protective custody, but everyone knows it's simply to round you people up and keep you from hurting America anymore. Just like you Japs did in Pearl Harbor. Yeah, I heard about the hundred of Japanese cars lining streets so rescue vehicles couldn't get at our ships and our men. No one knows where you are going and no one cares. We can only hope they send you and all your kind back to where you came from."

Sachi raised her voice to the woman, desperate, and asked, "Do you not see that my family is losing everything? My children are Americans. I simply want to speak to someone to see if there was any way I can save my home. Don't you have a heart?"

The woman did not back down and Sachi witnessed the depths of her hatred. "I have a heart, Madam. And that heart goes out to those boys who were savagely attacked and killed at Pearl Harbor. My heart goes out to their families. At least you still have yours, for now."

As she said the last threatening words she handed Sachi her money and loudly stamped the account books in red ink "closed".

Sachi said quietly, "My heart goes out to them as well."

As she turned to walk away, she heard the woman sneer behind her, "Yeah I bet it does, dirty Jap."

Once outside, Sachi walked quickly along the sidewalk unaware of which direction she was going. The tears she had held back for so long now blurred her vision and she could only make out smudges of people walking by.

What a fool she had been to think the bank, the American bank, would wait for payment from a Japanese family that did not even know where they were going or how long they would be gone. How foolish to think she would be treated with respect for the years of business she had done with them. How silly to think that they would loan her anything. She had learned her lesson. She would not venture out of the Japanese community unless forced to. She would not subject herself to that kind of humiliation again. She would not ask anyone for anything ever again.

She realized she'd parked at the other end of the block and turned to go back toward her car. As she turned she bumped into a man who was following her closely. Her purse fell out of her hand and the contents spilled out.

The man, irritated, said, "Hey, watch where you're going."

He kept walking. She stooped down to pick up her things when she noticed another man picking up things that had scattered, including her billfold with all of their money. How could she be so careless? Her heart leapt into her throat and she shouted, "Those are my things. Give them to me."

"I was just helping," the man said as he handed her the items.

He handed her back her lipstick, papers, and billfold.

"I don't need any help," Sachi responded curtly, tears still staining her face.

"Ok. Ok," the man said, looking startled and backing away.

Sachi knelt over her purse checking the contents. She felt a twinge of guilt over her rudeness to the man. She was not like that, but, she quickly told herself, there was no room right now in her for guilt or sorrow toward anyone. She would take care of things without anyone's help, somehow.

She stood quickly, turned without looking and walked into another large man. The air was knocked out of her momentarily and she gasped slightly clutching her purse as she fell backward. Before she hit the ground two arms reached out and grabbed her, righting her on her black high-heeled pumps. She did not look at the man as tears streamed down her cheeks.

As she started to hurry past him she whispered, "I'm sorry. So sorry. "

He reached out and gently grabbed her arms.

"Sachi. It is me," the deep voice said.

She looked up and through the watery haze in her eyes she recognized Jack Albright. He was tan even in this early season and he wore a suit and tie making him look even more handsome Sachi thought. Her cheeks burned with embarrassment at her clumsiness, her tears, and her thoughts.

"I must go," she said vaguely, wanting to go and not wanting to go at the same time.

"You are upset. I hurt you?"

"No, no. It's other things. It's nothing."

Jack took her elbow and began to walk her down the street to a restaurant. As he did he said, "Let's have some coffee. I have time before my appointment. And I was coming to see you today anyway. I have...well...something I wanted to talk to you about."

His strong arm guiding her down the street felt good. It was nice not to have to make the most simple of decisions like where to walk. It was a relief to be directed if for only a brief moment and to see compassion in a white face rather than anger.

327

They entered Hank's diner and Jack began to guide her to the nearest table. It was covered with a bright yellow tablecloth and white napkins. Jack pulled out a chair for her, but before she could sit down a voice from the counter said, "Hey. You can't bring her in here, Jack. We don't serve Japs. Didn't ya see the sign outside?"

Sachi was horrified. In her state she had forgotten to even look for a sign and certainly Jack was not use to having to look. She should have known and began to berate herself for letting someone else take control if only for a moment. She looked at the short man in the white apron standing at the counter. She had seen him before. He was big-bellied probably from eating his own cooking every day. He had sparse patches of gray hair. His large nose was red and his brown eyes were small and quick.

Sachi worried for a moment that Jack might get angry, but as she looked over at him he was grinning.

Jack said, "Come on, Hank. This poor girl has had a bad day and she just wants a cup of coffee."

Hank shook his head stubbornly. "I ain't servin' no Jap. And where's your loyalty? Here you are havin' coffee with one of em'?"

Jack laughed, "Loyalty? I can guarantee you this woman didn't bomb Pearl Harbor. Can't we just get two coffees?"

Hank said, "She didn't, but I bet she knows them that did. Best I'll do for ya is give ya two coffees to go. And that's only because you are one of my good customers, Jack.

Otherwise I wouldn't even do that. She can't stay in here. What about my other customers?"

Sachi glanced quickly around and the only customer was a young man seated at the counter reading a paper and showing no interest in their conversation.

Jack shook his head and the smile left his face. He said, "Well, your other customer doesn't seem to care much unless you're also including the flies, but fine. Give us two coffees to go."

Hank poured two coffees and Jack laid a quarter on the counter.

Hank said, "That fly comment wasn't necessary. You know I run a good clean place here."

Jack said, "Well, I thought so until today."

He took the coffees and they walked outside. He handed one to Sachi who had never acquired a taste for coffee, but said thank you anyway.

They walked to the end of the street where Jack's truck was parked and got in. He drove out of town a few minutes and pulled into a vacant dirt lot off to the side.

"So," Jack said. "What happened today?"

"Oh, nothing," said Sachi. "Just a bad day."

"Something happened."

"I went to the bank to see if they would extend our mortgage payments or work something out so that we would not lose all we have worked for over these years. You know we must leave next week."

"Of course," said Jack solemnly. "Everyone knows. It's posted everywhere. I'm sorry. I wish…"

He did not finish his thought and Sachi thought it didn't matter. She was tired of wishing. She had been wishing for months since Takeo was taken. Wishing did nothing but remind you of what you did not have.

He continued, "So what did the bank say?"

"The teller said…well, she said many things. None of them nice and all of them boiled down to no."

Jack nodded and stared into his cup of coffee. His strong jaw flexed several times and he rubbed the edge of the paper cup with his thumb. He looked thoughtful as if deciding how to proceed.

He asked, "So what will you do?"

Sachi shrugged slightly and said, "Nothing. Try to sell, I guess, but we will not make much money I am sure. We need the money, but this is our home. It is the only home my children have known. It has been my home for almost 20 years. It has been Yoshida's and Takeo's longer than that. We persuaded the land to give us a living. That land contains the sweat of my husband, his parents, me, and even my children. That land is ours."

Sachi caught herself blushing, surprised at the strength of her emotion. She didn't realize how passionately she felt about her home and the land until just that moment. Jack looked at her and she realized it was a look of admiration. She knew he felt the same about land and family and home. He turned and looked out the window, unable to hold her eyes. She wished he would just start driving. They could go away together somewhere. But it was a momentary flash in her head and it could certainly never happen. She was married, and more than that, she was committed to honor and to her family. Jack turned back to her.

"Do you trust me, Sachi?"

"Trust? Well…"

Jack interrupted her. He turned, leaned closer to her and stared deep into her eyes. He whispered, "Don't just say, 'yes'. I mean it. Think about it. Do you trust me?"

Sachi stared back into his blue eyes. His eyes reminded her of the sea, of the sky, of freshness and light and new beginnings. He was close enough that she could smell the coffee on his breath or was that her coffee? She wondered if he started the truck and just drove down the road and kept driving, would she try to get out or would she hold her seat and go with him? Just the thought of it caused her to catch her breath.

Sachi held her breath a moment and then said, "I do not know."

She broke his gaze and looked ahead through the windshield to the open lot in front of them. She could not look into his eyes as she said, "I'm not sure I even trust myself anymore."

Jack remained where he was leaning close and said, "I know how you feel. I want to do something for your family," then he corrected himself. "I mean for you. I want to do something for you, Sachi".

"There is nothing you can do."

"But there is."

Sachi turned toward him wanting him to offer her some escape some brilliant plan that would fix everything. Sachi knew what he felt for her. He knew she was alone and vulnerable and frightened. He turned away from her and slumped slightly over the steering wheel.

"Oh, Sachi. Maybe you shouldn't trust me. For five cents I would drive out of this town right now. If you asked me, I would take you so far away from here and I would never look back. We could go back east or to Mexico. We could go somewhere that would accept us together."

Sachi smiled as she often did at her boys when they expressed some plan or dream. The thought was beautiful, but it was simply a dream. She laid her hand on his shoulder and said, "There is no such place."

He turned and looked at her again. "I know. At least, not today perhaps, but someday….maybe…"

Sachi shook her head. She had too much to worry about and Jack's vision of some future for the two of them was more than she could think about now. She was a married woman with children in the midst of war, internment, and losing everything she owned. People were counting on her, including her imprisoned husband, children, and aging mother-in-law. This was no time for dreams, but somehow, if just for a moment, it felt good to think of something else.

She said, "Jack, there will be no someday."

Jack slumped back over the wheel a moment. He drew in a deep breath and then, as if a switch had been flipped, he sat straight up. His face had lost the sorrowful, dreamy look it held just seconds earlier.

He said, "Then just listen."

Sachi refused. "No, Jack. I can't think about the future right now. I have to make decisions concerning my boys and today. Today is what matters right now."

Jack grabbed her hands in his to still her. She felt his strength and passion radiating into her hands, her arms, her entire being. She was not strong enough to fight him. She didn't want to. Her resolve melted in the warmth of his hands.

"Let me take over your place. I will make sure everything is harvested over the next few months. I will keep up the house and the fields. I will take the money and make the mortgage and tax payments on the place for you. But it will require a lot of trust, trust in me. Do you have that?"

Sachi sat for a few minutes not looking at him, not knowing what to say.

"Sachi?"

She avoided the question. This plan was unexpected and not something she had considered before. She asked, "How would you be paid? You will be doing this and your job with the Department of Agriculture. How will you be paid for the time you spend at our home?"

"I'm not looking for money."

Sachi looked at him directly in the eyes. "Then what are you looking for?"

He smiled slightly and Sachi knew they were both thinking of the same thing. Both minds held the same image of the two of them together. It made her blush, but she did not take her eyes from his.

He said, "I'm looking to help you, Sachi. I love you and want to do what I can for you. It's as simple as that."

"You take half," Sachi said.

"Half?" Jack said. "No."

Sachi turned to him. "What you are offering to do is save my home. Right now, sitting with me in this car sipping coffee it is a noble, honorable, generous gesture you make. But, when you are working two jobs, in the hot sun for months or perhaps years, depending on what happens to us, you will begin to resent the work if you are not paid properly. You will come to think you cannot move away or do many of the things you might otherwise be able to do. If I am not paying you, more people will wonder…Takeo, Yoshida. They will wonder what has caused you to act in such a manner. I am not offering to pay you for your honor and generosity for I could not pay you for that. What I am offering is to pay you for your hard work, which this most certainly will be. It is the only way I can accept your kind offer."

Jack raised his eyebrows and said, "Well, if that is the only way, so be it. 50%."

Jack did not release her hands, but squeezed her tighter as if sealing the bargain. She did not move away, feeling the hard calluses, the roughness of his hands.

"You can trust me, Sachi. You will have something to come home to."

He drove her back to town in silence and dropped her at her car. He told her he would be over in a few days to work out the arrangements, but he knew her land as well as she did.

As she stepped from his truck, she leaned in and whispered, "In answer to your question, in this time that is so difficult and no one trusts anyone, I trust you, Jack. I trust you to do the right thing and I trust you as my... my good friend. And you have been a good friend, Jack."

Jack slowly shook his head and said, "No. We both know I have not been a good friend to Takeo, don't we?"

When Sachi arrived home tired and hungry, Yoshida was in the kitchen making tea. Sachi sat on one of the kitchen chairs with the red vinyl seat cushions she picked out many years ago. The sun poured through the window. The kitchen was warm and inviting. Sachi noticed the two cherry trees outside the window beginning to bloom. She would not be here to gather the sweet cherries and feed them to her children and her husband. For the first time Sachi thought of how hard it would be for Yoshida to leave her garden.

Sachi looked at Yoshida and noticed she was not wearing her house clothes, but rather one of her church dresses. This one was a green cotton shift with a short-sleeve jacket. The green complimented the old woman's watery eyes and gray hair. She wore a strand of faux pearls around her neck, the only jewelry she possessed. Her small gray sling-back shoes clicked on the floor as she busied herself getting the tea and cookies. As she set them before Sachi and sat down across from her, a half smile danced on Yoshida's face.

Sachi asked, "Have you been into town today?"

Yoshida shook her head and took a small sip of the hot tea. Sachi sipped from her tea as well to give Yoshida a chance to volunteer where she had been, but instead Yoshida asked, "What did the bank say?"

Sachi looked into the teacup, ashamed to look at her mother-in-law. She did not tell Yoshida of the details, the anger of the teller or her own comments. Sachi said, "The bank said no. They will sell the house unless we keep up the payments."

Yoshida asked, "But how are we to do that when we will not be here to work the farm? This is our time to make our money. Just look out there."

Sachi remained seated. It was a rhetorical statement. They were both aware of the crop ready to pick just outside.

Yoshida continued, "Is everything to rot in the fields? We are being called traitors for letting our fields go, but at the same time we are being sent away without notice, without time to plan, without time to gather our crops. We could have enough money in September, but not in the beginning of May. This is our important time of year and this is when they chose to send us away."

Sachi's eyes began to water. She had promised herself not to cry in front of her family, in front of anyone. This was the second time today she had broken that promise.

336

She ran the back of her hand on her face and dried her tears. Jack would make things all right. He would gather their future up for them.

Yoshida drew in a deep breath as if it was needed to change the subject. "I went to visit the Goodman's today."

Sachi responded absently, "That's nice."

That was why Yoshida was dressed up, Sachi thought. It must be nice not to worry about making the decisions. Sachi wondered how to approach Yoshida and tell her Jack Albright was taking over their home while they were gone. It had seemed so simple and right when she sat with Jack in his truck, but now, at home with Yoshida, she was uncertain how to begin.

Yoshida continued, "I offered to make them a deal."

Sachi looked up from her tea and fixed her eyes on Yoshida.

"What kind of a deal?"

Yoshida sat forward in her chair. "To sell them our car. Bob Goodman has needed another car for months now and he said he would buy ours. So I sold it."

Sachi understood how difficult it was for Yoshida to have gone to the Goodmans and asked them to buy the family car, her son's car. Takeo was so proud when they first bought the sedan and, even though it was used, you would have thought it was brand new. He took very good care of it over the years. Yoshida got up and walked to the counter where her purse lay. She took out $300 and laid it on the kitchen table. Sachi's eyes were wide in disbelief.

"I didn't think anyone would buy that car for more than $100."

Yoshida said, "I suppose they were a bit over generous because of our situation. But when Bob Goodman offered the $300 straight out I did not argue. I simply said, 'sold'. We will accept his generosity and be grateful, but our home. Our home I will not be able to sell so easily or with as much gratitude."

Yoshida eyes began to well up and Sachi could not take Yoshida's tears. Even her cutting remarks and criticisms were preferable to crying. This was the time.

Sachi said, "When I was in town today, after the bank refused my request, I...I ran into Jack Albright."

Yoshida blinked hers tears back in order to see better, searching Sachi's face for something, some sign.

Sachi continued, "He has offered... that is... he is willing to watch our home while we are gone."

Yoshida sniffled, pulling a tissue from her pocket and wiping her nose, she asked, "Watch it?"

"Yes. Watch it and work it. He will pay our mortgage and our taxes and then he'll divide the profits with us. He might be able to send us a little extra money if the crops do well. We will need money where we are going...wherever we are going."

"Um."

"What?" demanded Sachi, defensively.

"Nothing," Yoshida said sipping her tea. "I was just thinking how generous that was of Mr. Albright. I wonder why he would make that offer to our family and no other."

"Well, I don't know that he hasn't made it to other families. Maybe he has. He has many Japanese friends in the area."

Yoshida looked Sachi in the eye and said, "He has not offered to do this for anyone other than you."

Sachi felt her face redden, but she was tired of feeling embarrassed and guilty and worried. She blurted out, "So what? So what if he is doing it for me? It solves our problem and we can keep our home. I would think you would be grateful to him."

Yoshida remained in her seat and said softly, "I'm sure he is counting on the fact that you will be."

"What is that suppose to mean?"

"You know what it means."

Sachi felt as if she were in front of the woman at the bank having to defend herself all over again. She was tired of defending herself, her family. Sachi said, "It is a business deal, a business arrangement."

Yoshida shook her head and said, "*Abunai kankei.*"

Sachi threw her hands in the air and said, "This is not a dangerous relationship. It is a safe business liaison. He will watch over our place, take care of the fields, that kind of thing, until we get back. In return he will get 50% of all the profit from our crops. This solves one of our many problems."

339

Yoshida said, "This arrangement may create more problems than it solves. It might be better to give the entire house away than to give away your honor."

Sachi was exhausted and angry. She said. "I am not giving away my honor. I am accepting help from a friend. I am trying to save our home for our children. *Kodomo no tame ni.* This is for the welfare of our children. We can pay our mortgage and our taxes and Jack can make a small profit."

Yoshida stood to go to her room and said, "Just not too much of a profit, I hope."

CHAPTER THIRTY-THREE

Sachi was in Jack's arms, tight around her, safe and secure. He enveloped her like a cocoon until she felt she had crawled inside his very being. He was her armor against the outside world. She looked up waiting for him to kiss her, but the sun lit up the room and awakened her from the sweet dream. She lay for many minutes, her eyes closed, trying to return to that soft, safe place even if it only existed in her mind, but she could not conjure it again. All she could think of was the long, painful day ahead. Today she and her family would sell their things to strangers and neighbors. So many American families of Japanese origin in these last days were trying to make money quickly and yard sales had sprung up all over the area.

She didn't want to move. She thought of her children and, even then, it took all the energy she possessed to rise from bed and dress. She did not want to begin this day.

The afternoon before, Ikuko and the boys brought over two cars full of items and the rest Ikuko declared she was leaving behind in the hopes that Charlie Shimmer would take care of it. A few mornings prior Charlie approached her and offered to stay in her home and manage things. He would work the land, make the payments to the landowner, and she and Edo would have a home whenever they returned. Ikuko had only a few days to arrange things and she was completely alone and without any other choice it seemed. So she accepted Charlie's offer. At least it was something, she told herself.

Yoshida said, "You know you'd probably be better off selling the things now rather than relying on that man."

Ikuko's face was without expression or care. She said, "I can't sell it all and we do not own the land. Charlie Shimmer will keep his promise or he won't. There is nothing more I can do."

Ikuko seemed to have given up. She'd lost the enthusiasm and sense of humor that had always lived in her. She seemed to have aged overnight as if simply existing in a state of depression that no amount of cajoling or encouragement could relieve. The hardest part for Sachi was the lack of laughter within Ikuko. Ikuko, who had always found humor in anything, was so somber, now so quiet. Losing her husband, having to report to the internment camp, the indignity of the past few months was more than she could bear. Sachi couldn't remember the last time she'd heard the sound of her friend's laughter.

At the beginning of the day, Sachi gathered Yoshida, Ikuko and the three boys into the living room and ordered, "I do not want to see tears today. We can cry all night if we like once this is over, but today we will be strong. We will not let them see us cry or break down. If you think you might, then go into the house until you can control yourself."

And, with that, the yard sale began. Ikuko sold her first item, a tea set from her husband on their first anniversary. She began to cry and Sachi immediately went to her and commanded, "Into the house, now."

Ikuko was surprised at her friend's harshness. So surprised that it stopped her tears, at least until the next sale when she began to cry again, but one look from Sachi sent her indoors. With each sale came tears and a trip into the house for Ikuko. She would be in there a few minutes and then return, composed and dry-eyed.

Their lives lay exposed on shaky old card tables and blanketed ground. They did not know what they would need or how long they would be gone, but all families were in agreement that they needed to make as much money as they could as quickly as possible. With only a short time to take leave of most of their belongings, a yard sale was all that was left to most of the Japanese who were on their way to internment. Everything had to be sold. The Executive Order was clear, only two bags per person, and only that which you could carry.

It was a cool morning, but clear and the promise of heat hung in the air. Sachi placed the last item, the children's cradle, in the yard. She surveyed her home. Unpicked strawberries sat plump and ripening in the field. Her belongings and those of her children, husband, mother-in-law, and best friend lay strewn about the yard - Yoshida's china set for twelve, the children's bicycles, Ikuko's fancy clothes and hats from trips to San Francisco, and Sachi's wedding kimono. The furniture was for sale as well, but it was left inside so potential buyers paraded through the house as if it were a store. They discussed the items: too old, too ugly, not the kind of item they would have in their homes. Most walked around making comments carelessly, like tossing trash to the ground, not realizing their words hurt the people selling their most beloved possessions.

Yoshida carried out a box containing her porcelain statues and set them up carefully, neatly, as if she were decorating the inside of her home and not some broken down card table at a yard sale.

There was the boy holding his lantern and the girl holding an umbrella. She set up the girl with flowers and the children fishing. Sachi watched as Yoshida pulled each statue out of the box. Yoshida examined the mother holding her baby high in the air. A slight smile came to Yoshida's lips as if she were remembering something joyful. Then she put the statue on the table and the smile slid from her face. Sachi knew Yoshida had brought them from Japan, safely transporting them to America. She had kept them immaculate, unharmed, dusted each week, loved and cherished for many years. Sachi also knew why these statues were so dear. Yoshida's late husband had given her the one of the mother and boy when she was first pregnant with Takeo. He had also given her the one of the mother and daughter when she was pregnant the second time, before she'd lost the baby. They had been with Yoshida like good friends for many years and now they were on a wobbly, dusty card table as if they had no value.

All was laid out and in the morning as many people arrived looking over things, examining, commenting on the craftsmanship of this, finding fault in the quality of that, looking for a bargain, knowing the Watanabes, like all Japanese families, were motivated to sell. This was the time to get a bargain. These Japanese families had no choice.

Neighbors descended quickly and loudly, like hungry vultures on prey still clinging to life. Each item picked up and examined and put back as being not quite right was like

344

the peck of a vulture's beak tearing at Sachi's emotional insides. Everything exposed in the front yard of her home. Everyone knowing she was leaving with her family and why she was leaving.

Men looked in the barn at the livestock, the tools, and the equipment. The women examined the furniture, the household goods, the clothing. The children played with her children's toys. Everything examined and no one needing to ask permission.

Sachi caught sight of Mrs. Schaffer exiting her car. The sight of her reminded Sachi of the last New Year's Eve celebration when they had played *Fuku Warai*, talked about Mrs. Schaffer and her disappearing husband, and Jack had scared off a band of angry young men. Sachi marveled that only five months had passed since then and wondered at how much in her life had changed.

Mrs. Schaffer was a large woman with a penchant for small things. She carried her little Pekinese dog Pookie, with her everywhere she went. She donated hefty contributions from her late husband's estate to the church and libraries and scholarship funds so no one ever said anything about Pookie.

Yoshida's statutes had apparently caught Mrs. Schaffer's eye as Yoshida lorded over them, protecting them from the children who were allowed to run free while their parents looked inside at furniture or in the barn at tools. One child ran by the table knocking the mother and son statute on its side, unbroken, but Yoshida stood by the table, nervous and watchful, standing guard like a mother hen over her chicks in a yard full of predators.

Mrs. Schaffer asked Yoshida how much she wanted for the statues of the fishing children. Yoshida hesitated, clearly finding it difficult to place a dollar figure on something she cherished so much. There were ten figurines in all and she hoped to sell them together so as not to split up the porcelain family, as her own family was being torn apart.

Yoshida answered, "I was hoping to sell them as a group for $30. They are worth much more, but I think $30 is more than a fair price."

Mrs. Schaffer laughed in a superior manner, dismissing her immediately, "Oh no. $30? That is much too much. I will buy the fishing children only for say…50 cents."

She put down her Pekinese, who sniffed the ground, as Mrs. Schaffer fumbled through her change purse for the coins.

Yoshida stood her ground, "I'm afraid not. But thank you for the offer."

Mrs. Schaffer fixed her eyes on Yoshida and said, "Certainly it is better to sell at least one than none at all. Don't be foolish. I'm sure others will sell as the day goes on and most likely for less than what I am offering to pay you this minute."

Yoshida stubbornly shook her head and again said, "No, thank you. I will wait and hope to sell them all together."

Mrs. Schaffer shook her head as well and said, "I'll tell you what. I will be back toward the end of the day. You'll sell to me then. I'm sure."

Mrs. Schaffer walked toward Pookie and said, "Come on, Pookie" just as Pookie urinated on the side of a box of dishes. Mrs. Schaffer did not register anything other than glee at the fact that Pookie had relieved herself before getting into the car.

"That's a good girl, Pookie. Good girl."

She picked up her dog and walked to her car. Sachi and Ikuko stood by Yoshida.

Yoshida said, "Perhaps I should have sold her the one. I just don't want them separated."

Sachi knew she was talking about more than just her porcelain figurines. She spoke sharply to Yoshida and said, "We need the money. This is no time for sentimentality or holding on to things. We don't even know if we'll ever be back here. The next offer you get you take it. I know it's hard, but we have to sell these things and we only have a few days before we leave."

Yoshida looked at her and her eyes began to fill, "I know."

Sachi felt her own eyes start to water, but she had to get back to business. Ikuko was in tears and Sachi chided them both, "Stop that right now. None of that. Not here. We do not have time for emotion."

She yelled to John and William who were playing catch with an old baseball and their mitts, which were also for sale. Mitchell sat next to a box of books he was selling, re-reading an old Sherlock Holmes mystery.

She pointed to the box of dishes Pookie had wet and said, "Boys, get that box of dishes and wash them thoroughly. And put those mitts down. They are going to be sold."

The boys obediently started toward the box and put their mitts down the backs of their pants. Sachi started to tell them again to put them on the table for sale, but stopped herself. If they cared that much about their baseball mitts, she guessed they could take them wherever they were going to end up. It might keep them busy if nothing else.

A young woman approached Sachi's wedding kimono. Her eyes were large with appreciation for its beauty and detail. Ikuko was selling some of her clothing on the other end of the yard and Yoshida was busy with a family looking at furniture inside. Sachi approached the girl, as if she were a saleswoman in a boutique approaching a customer, and said, "It looks like it might fit you."

The girl who looked to be in her early 20's said, "It's beautiful. Is it your wedding kimono?"

Sachi nodded slightly not anxious to discuss any emotional attachment to the very items she was selling to these strangers.

"You must have been beautiful in it. It looks something like the one my friend, Jessica, wore at her wedding. Her mother was, I mean, is, Japanese. She left a few weeks ago."

There was sadness in her voice at the thought of losing this Jessica who was obviously a good friend.

The girl stilled herself for a moment and then said, "I would like to buy this from you."

Sachi took a deep breath and said as businesslike as she could muster, "$15."

The girl pulled out a $20 bill and a pen and a piece of paper. She gave the $20 to Sachi.

She said, "Take that. It is certainly worth at least $20. And if, I mean, when you come back here, whenever that may be, call me at this number."

She wrote down her telephone number and handed it to Sachi.

"When you come back you call me and I will have your wedding kimono to give back to you. I will keep it for you."

Sachi was puzzled. She did not know this girl and didn't understand her gesture.

"Why?" Sachi asked. "This is yours now. You bought it."

The girl smiled and said, "I bought it, but it is not mine."

She picked it up and walked to her car. Sachi stood with the $20 in one hand and the phone number in the other. She walked to Yoshida who was selling the boy's twin beds to a family with two young boys. Sachi handed her the $20 and told her and Ikuko of the young woman. The three stood quietly for a moment.

"Like an angel," Ikuko finally whispered, almost to herself.

Sachi heard the boys arguing as they came out the front door with the dishes they'd washed.

"You aren't even lifting," Billy accused John. "Come on. You're going to drop it."

John yelled back, "The box is wet and my hands are slipping. You didn't dry the dishes."

Just as he finished, the underneath of the box gave way and the dishes fell to the ground sounding like coins from a slot machine, breaking as they hit the hard ground. Only a few plates and one cup survived intact.

Sachi ran over and checked the boys who were fine, but horrified at what they had done. Both started talking at once.

"He wasn't holding it right."

"He didn't dry them."

Sachi let out a deep sigh, trying to expel the anxiety, frustration, and discouragement from her body. As if blowing it into the air might cause it to drift off into the wind and through the trees far away from her. She shook her head and said quietly, "Let's pick it up, carefully. Carefully."

Yoshida came over and said, "I'll do this. There's a man over there that wants to ask you about Takeo's tools."

She walked with the man to the barn. He was a tall, thin man, in his fifties with little hair on his balding head, smelling of sweat and tobacco. He said he was from the next county over and understood there were a number of these kinds of sales going on in the area. He wanted to hit as many as he could that morning and was in a hurry. When they entered the barn he pointed to Takeo's toolbox filled with most of his hammers, screwdrivers, saws, pliers and other tools. It was the toolbox his father had used. Many of the tools were purchased by Yoshida and the children as birthday or Christmas gifts. This was something she always thought one of her sons would take and use and pass along to his son and his grandson.

As she stood looking at her husband's past and her son's future she realized there was no way to put a value on it, but when the stranger offered $3 for the "whole kit and caboodle" she declined.

"My husband's tool box is certainly worth more than $3."

The stranger narrowed his mean eyes and said, "You'll be lucky to sell it for anything. Now I know you need the money. $3 is better than nothing and that's what you very well may end up getting today if you don't sell to me."

"I'm sorry. No. I will sell it for…"

"I'm not here to negotiate. It's $3 or nothing. Take it or leave it."

"Then I must leave it."

"Fine. Then I'll just take it."

The man closed the toolbox, picked it up, and began to walk out of the barn.

Sachi called out, "Wait. What are you doing? You can't take that."

The man walked up to her closely as a few of the bargain hunters turned to see the commotion.

He said menacingly, "I'm takin' this here tool box. You don't need it and can't haul it with you wherever you're goin'. You make any trouble, I'll say I paid you for it and it'll be your word against mine. Now who do you think they're gonna believe, an upstanding white American citizen or a Japanese alien enemy? And going to court. Hah,

351

if this even went to trial you wouldn't be here to testify. I'm taking this toolbox and I'm takin' it for $3. You're lucky to get that."

He slipped three one-dollar bills into her hand. She let the bills drift to the ground, stunned, feeling violated in a brand new way. As she watched the man load Takeo's tool box, her son's toolbox, into his old pickup and drive away, she felt anger surge in her as she had never felt. He drove away leaving behind the dust off his truck. She left his dirty dollar bills where they fell and walked slowly back to the house.

A large swarm of people had gathered around their things and a sudden image invaded her mind. She imagined all these people just taking what they wanted and leaving just as the man in the truck had done. What would be her recourse? Her husband had been taken, the community had turned against them, and the law had betrayed them. Sachi realized she and her family were completely without protection. The thought was more than she could bear at the moment and she forced it from her mind.

It was difficult watching other children go through her children's old clothes and toys, putting a price on the things her children had valued most of all. Mitchell sold all his books for just a few dollars, including his favorite book on the stars and planets and constellations. It was one Sachi had given him for Christmas last year, but it was a big, heavy book and not one easily toted around. He only kept two books: his paperback Dictionary and his hardcover copy of *The Three Musketeers*.

Billy and John kept their gloves and an old ball. Sachi sold everything except her old, vinyl-covered Bible, her mother's comb and brush, her wedding ring, and Duke's opal ring. Those were items easily carried and perhaps, wherever they were going, they might need something of value like the opal ring. Besides, Sachi rationalized, she would get nothing for it here. It was the only thing of Duke's they had, the only material evidence of his existence and memory. She would not sell that. Not yet. Not quite yet.

The Department of Agriculture truck pulled into their driveway half way through the afternoon. Jack stepped out of the truck and walked over to Yoshida and Ikuko who were straightening some of the clothes on the blankets.

"Good afternoon," he greeted them. "How are things selling today?"

Ikuko held up one of her sweaters she was selling and said, "Everything is marked down today. Lots of bargains. How about this?"

Jack smiled and shook his head, "Pink is not quite my color."

Ikuko looked sadly at the sweater and responded, as if talking only to herself, "No, but it is mine or was anyway."

Yoshida continued to fold clothes, straightening items that had already been straightened, avoiding Jack's look and his words. Jack noticed the distance between them and said, "Yoshida, I just stopped by to see if there was anything I could do. I think I know how to handle things here while you are gone, but do you need anything else?"

"No," Yoshida said. "I think you've done more than enough for us."

Jack smiled slightly and looked unsure of how to react. Sachi walked up and said hello. She was tired and hot, her hair was coming lose from its bun and her face shined with the work of the day.

Ikuko said, "Jack stopped by to see if we need anything else."

Sachi said, "No. I think we have managed to sell most of our stuff."

Jack looked around at the few people left going through items. He shook his head and said, "Were most of the vultures here pretty early this morning?"

Yoshida said, "I don't believe these people are vultures. They are giving us money for items we are freely selling. We have to have this money and so they are helping us. It is disrespectful to take their money and then refer to them as vultures."

"Sorry," Jack said. "I didn't mean to be disrespectful."

Sachi looked at Yoshida angrily and said, "Jack would you like some lemonade. Ikuko just made some in the kitchen. Will you help me serve it?"

"Sure," said Jack, happy to leave Yoshida's company.

When they were in the kitchen alone Jack said, "It's been hard on her, huh?"

Sachi knew he was referring to Yoshida and said, "Yes. It has been. In some ways it must be harder to see your son taken than your husband. She is old and from another world."

"So it is not just me?" Jack asked.

"Well," said Sachi. "To be honest she is concerned that you and I are such good friends. She doesn't think it proper and all."

"Oh," Jack said. "She is afraid something might happen between the two of us. Well, no fear. We are too honorable for that, aren't we Sachi?"

She nodded and said, "I hope so, Jack. My honor and my family are all I have left."

Jack quickly changed the subject and said, "Do you have a ride tomorrow to the train station?"

Sachi shook her head. "We were going to ask the Goodman's house this evening. They are coming by to pick up the car."

Jack said, "Then I will be here tomorrow morning at 7:30. I will bring breakfast, help you all load up, and take you to the station."

Sachi poured the lemonade and Jack drank his quickly, like the old days, as if there were no more time to relax. Sachi turned the water on in the sink to rinse the onions and lettuce Billy had picked from Yoshida's garden, which was still blooming. She set them in the sink to soak, plugging the drain, and letting the cool water run.

As she did this she found her words coming out before she could stop them. "A man came by today and stole Takeo's tool box. He told me he would give me three dollars and when I refused he took it anyway and told me there was nothing I could do about it."

As Sachi talked, the tears began to fall into the sink filling with water. After telling everyone all morning they could not cry, it seemed that here, in her kitchen with Jack sipping lemonade as if everything was the same, she could not hold back the tears or the words.

"The worst is he was right. There was nothing I could do. I felt absolutely helpless to stop him. He could have taken anything from here and no one would have done a thing. I was afraid to draw attention to him because I thought the rest of them might get the same idea and just start taking what they wanted. I can't believe my entire life has come to this."

"Sachi, I wish there was something…"

Sachi wiped her eyes quickly on her shirtsleeve and said, angrily, "This is no time for wishes. Nothing can be done except to wait and be patient. Hope this will end soon. Enough of my tears. This will pass."

She turned and noticed Jack had drained his glass. He set the moist glass on the counter and Sachi reached for it to refill it. Their hands touched and neither moved away.

She had known no other lover but Takeo and wondered if it was excitement or fear that rose in her chest causing her pulse to quicken and her heart to beat wildly. Jack approached her quickly, immovable and unstoppable. Sachi realized her fear came not from him but from within herself.

He said nothing and took her in his arms. He fastened himself to her, tight, strong, as if he would not let her go again. His lips, pressed against her own, were soft and tender, then they parted and he began kissing her deeply in a way she had never experienced before. At first she was passive, shocked at such intimacy, but soon she began to participate, feeling the flicker of his tongue and hers, the warmth, the wetness. They kissed long and hard, his hands moving from her face to her hair to the small of her back and to her neck. He was not pushing or pulling. He was exploring, feeling, and allowing her to feel as well.

Sachi wanted to let go of herself and allow this to take her over. She could forget everything that was happening in her life and her world if even for a few moments. She wanted him to pick her up and carry her off to some distant place away from all this reality just for a little while.

His right hand moved to her breast and she felt him grow more urgent as he positioned her against the wall. There was no air, no space, between her and him and the wall. They stood as one. Suddenly he stopped kissing and stood back from her. He looked at her deeply, intensely, as if he had never seen a woman before, as if he were concentrating to memorize every aspect of her being.

He whispered with tears in his eyes, "Sachi, you are so beautiful."

She drank in his words like water, not feeling embarrassed or strange. It felt right. She wondered if Takeo had ever seen her this way before.

He placed her back to the wall and kissed her again. She felt an excitement within her that she had never experienced. It was an urgent need, but her thoughts screamed out that at any moment someone might walk into the kitchen and she pulled herself free of him and moved away.

Her chest rose and fell as if she'd run in from the fields and she couldn't catch her breath. She stammered, "We must not. This is not right."

Jack stopped and dropped his head, a defeated man.

"That's not the problem," he said, his voice breaking. "The problem is it is so right. Like a dream."

Sachi touched his cheek softly and said, "The problem with dreams is they disappear when you wake up."

He looked up at her through his wisps of bangs that needed trimming. His bright eyes looked wounded and it hurt to look at him, but she knew she spoke the truth. He walked from the kitchen, said goodbye to the boys, Ikuko, and Yoshida, then drove away. Sachi watched through the living room window. She watched as he drove his old pickup truck, which seemed to travel on clouds of dust rather than wheels and yet, somehow, he was never dirty. It was one of the first things she had noticed about him years ago and it was to be one of the last she would see before leaving.

As if awakening she heard a sound from the kitchen and rushed back to realize the water had overrun the sink and was spilling to the floor. She turned it off and unplugged the sink to drain some of the water. As she mopped up the wet floor and counters with the dishtowel her dream of her house being flooded came back to her. Perhaps there was not such a difference between dreams and reality.

Sachi remained businesslike all day. She was possessed now and flew from item to item practically giving things away, anxious to be unburdened of these possessions for which she was responsible. Yoshida was powerless to stop her and simply watched as she sold everything around them; everything but Yoshida's porcelain figurines.

Toward the end of the exhausting day as Mrs. Schaffer and Pookie waddled up to the card table of figurines, they were all still there. Both Mrs. Schaffer and Pookie had the same snooty, "I-told-you-so" looks on their faces.

358

Mrs. Schaffer, in a superior tone, said, "Well, I see they are all still here."

There were more people milling about. The crowds picked up toward the end of the day as people hoped to get an even better bargain. Ikuko and the Watanabes were hungry and tired. They still had to pick up the front yard before going into their almost empty home.

Yoshida was stone faced as she responded to Mrs. Schaffer, "Yes. I wanted to sell them together, but…"

Mrs. Schaffer interrupted, "But they are all still here. I want to purchase those two figurines for my niece. She loves fishing and I think it would make an outstanding birthday present for her."

Sachi and Ikuko stood behind Yoshida and began picking up some of the items in the yard to put them back in the house. The sun would set within the next hour or so, the light would be gone, and this dreaded day would be over. They began folding some of the blankets that lay on the ground.

Yoshida hung her head, unable to look Mrs. Schaffer in the eye. Her voice was low, heavy with resignation. She said, "Yes. They are still here. I will sell you the fishing children for $2. That is fair."

Mrs. Schaffer said, "I'll pay you 50 cents. Just like I offered this morning."

As if she were making a purchase from a store, she asked, "Do you have a box?"

Yoshida shook her head no. She was tired, and she was not going to dicker over small change when these figurines meant much more to her. She picked up the boy and girl to hand to Mrs. Schafer when suddenly Sachi stepped to the table and said, "I'm sorry, but I simply don't understand, Mrs. Schaffer."

Mrs. Schaffer looked at Sachi and said haughtily, "What is it you don't understand, Mrs. Watanabe?"

Yoshida pulled Sachi aside and whispered, "Sachi, we need the money. Fifty cents is fifty cents. I know you've always thought me too protective of these silly things. Now let me sell them and be done with it."

Sachi looked into her mother-in-law's eyes and something hit her. She had never particularly liked this woman who had been so hard and demanding, covetous of her son, Sachi's husband. They had struggled for power these many years. Sachi viewed Yoshida as her adversary and suddenly it was as if she were seeing Yoshida for the first time, vulnerable, tired, without any control. Here stood this poor old Japanese woman who should be in the golden years of her life enjoying the success of her son and his children, having to sell her most cherished items in the front yard of her home that she would soon be leaving and to a woman who cared nothing for them, who was going to give them to a niece who would no more appreciate them than Pookie and would probably have them broken within the first five minutes.

And Sachi realized something else. This was not the first time Yoshida had sold her things to neighbors and strangers. She'd had to do it before in Japan when Takeo had come to get her. But Yoshida never mentioned it and never complained. Yoshida had been through this before and had managed back then to hold on to her most precious possessions. Sachi would not let it go now. Something in her snapped. Maybe it was the entire day of selling her life for pennies on the dollar.

Sachi said loudly to Yoshida, "We don't need the money this much."

She turned to Mrs. Schaffer and said, "I just don't understand. Is it that you can't afford to pay more than 50 cents for something that is obviously worth much more?"

"Of course, I can afford it. That's not the point."

"Then what is the point, Mrs. Schaffer? What is the point of taking advantage of my mother-in-law? Of my family?"

"Taking advantage? My word. No one forced you to hold this sale, I assume. Here I am helping you people. Giving you much-needed money for something no one else wants and you stand there accusing me of taking advantage."

People stopped shopping and looked at them. Large wisps of Sachi's long, black hair hung down. Her face was tinged from being in the sun all day and she was tired from not eating since breakfast. Sachi took the fishing girl from Yoshida and held the porcelain statue in her right hand, waving it about like an SOS flag on a ship going down at sea.

She looked at Mrs. Schaffer and, in a loud voice filled with exhaustion and frustration, said, "You didn't come here to help us. You came to get a deal, pick up a bargain from the desperate Japanese family. You waited until the end of the day hoping we'd be frantic enough to take your offer. But we're not that frantic. We're not as desperate as you'd like, Mrs. Schaffer. We are particularly not desperate enough to sell you something that has a value that you can neither see nor appreciate. An item

361

purchased for fifty cents from a desperate family at the most difficult time of their lives has no value, Mrs. Schaffer. I would rather see this cherished item be crushed into the dirt rather than go to you and your niece."

With that, Sachi took the treasured statue and threw it with all her might into the dirt at Mrs. Schaffer's feet. The figure cracked into five pieces. The arm proudly holding the string of fish broke off and flew by Pookie who sniffed it. The scarved head rolled under the table and the feet, body, and other arm scattered.

Everyone stood completely still for several seconds. Sachi was as surprised by her actions as anyone. She couldn't believe what she had done. She had destroyed one of Yoshida's treasured gifts. She hadn't even been allowed to dust them and here she had picked one up and deliberately destroyed it even before she really knew what she was doing.

Yoshida was the first to speak. She smiled slightly at Mrs. Schaffer and said, "Do you see anything else you like, Mrs. Schaffer?"

And Ikuko started laughing, laughing until tears streamed from her eyes, hysterical, pent-up laughter, infectious, as Ikuko's laughter had always been. Yoshida laughed and even Sachi started laughing, happy Yoshida was not angry, happy her friend Ikuko was laughing again, happy this terrible day was over and her boys kept their mitts and Yoshida kept her statue family intact with one casualty.

With her eyes wide in disbelief and shock, Mrs. Schaffer yelled, "You people are crazy. You deserve to be locked up, every single one of you. Come on, Pookie. Let's get out of here."

She gathered Pookie who was sniffing at one of the blankets. She turned and Sachi watched her large rear end waddle back and forth with Pookie's rear end sticking out from under her arm.

Ikuko whispered, "Those two bear a striking resemblance to each other, coming and going."

The women broke out in renewed laughter, Ikuko and Sachi hanging on to each other for support.

Ikuko, still giggling, said to Sachi, "You've been waiting 20 years to do that."

Yoshida gathered the broken fragments and tied them in a handkerchief. Not to repair them she said, but as a remembrance of that day and what they had been through and how they had handled it, if not with refinement and grace than at least with humor and dignity. Those were items much more valuable and would continue to be throughout the coming hard years.

CHAPTER THIRTY-FOUR

That night the Goodmans stopped by with a picnic supper as the boys finished storing the last cardboard box and old blanket in the barn. Sachi almost told them to leave the boxes where they were. Why store things if you might never return? But she could not. This was still her family's home at least for tonight and things would be in order. The Goodmans also brought a basket of food for the long train trip the next day as if Sachi and her family were simply going to visit relatives for a few weeks.

Sarah said, "You don't know how long you might be traveling tomorrow so take this with you. It's just fruit and sandwiches and things. And we will check on the place. Yours, too, Ikuko just until you get back, which I'm sure won't be long."

"And I know Jack and Charlie Shimmer will do their best. Not as efficiently as Takeo or Edo I'm sure, but enough," Mr. Goodman said. "Now, do you have a ride to the train station tomorrow?"

Yoshida shook her head and said, "In fact, I was going to ask you if…"

Sachi interrupted, "Oh I forgot. Yes. We do have a ride tomorrow so we won't have to bother you any further after all of your kindness. Thank you for everything. The supper was wonderful."

Yoshida shot Sachi a look, but did not dispute her. She knew who would be giving them a ride. They hugged the Goodmans good-bye and thanked them for everything. Sachi wondered if they would ever see them again.

Their belongings waited in the new suitcases by the front door ready for the morning. It was difficult to pack everything a person owned in two bags. Yoshida had carefully packed the figurines to take with her to the internment camp. In those few minutes at the yard sale, the figurines had become Sachi's inheritance, and she would treasure them all the days of her life, especially the broken fishing girl.

Billy walked into the house with tools from the barn.

Yoshida asked, "Where did you get those? I thought we sold all the tools?"

Billy smiled and said, "Not these. I hid these this morning. I wanted to keep them."

He opened his suitcase and in the middle of his clothes inserted the hammer and some nails then locked it closed again.

Yoshida asked, "Billy, what are you doing with those?"

"Packing them."

Sachi said, "The evacuation instructions clearly state we cannot bring anything that might in any way be used as a weapon of any kind including tools."

"I don't care," Billy said as he continued packing. "We don't know where we are going or what we'll find when we get there. Each one of us is taking some tools: a hammer, some nails, a rope, a small shovel, those kinds of things. There's no knife or gun or anything like that."

"We are not taking those things," Sachi insisted. "They are considered contraband. We could get into more trouble. They might even arrest us."

Billy said, "Mom, what do you think they are doing to us? We're being arrested. Besides, from what I hear, they are not searching most of the luggage. They can't. There are too many people and too many bags. We might need these things and we are taking them."

He continued to open bags and pack the tools and said, "Grandmother, get needles and thread. We will need them. I am certain."

Sachi stood over him, "No. We are not…"

Billy stood up. He was more than a foot taller and towered over her.

He said, "I am the man of this family for now, at least until Father returns. I have made this decision and this is what we are going to do. I love you, Mother, but you are not hearing the things I hear and you do not know what conditions may be like wherever we go. We will need tools. Trust me."

Jack's voice rang in her ears as she heard her son repeat the same words: "trust me."

Sachi looked up at her boy, proud of his independence, but angry at his disobedience. She was afraid for him, knowing the oldest male would be the first they would arrest if they found this contraband. She didn't trust the system to protect her family and she didn't know what to expect. She sighed deeply and decided this was one those moments she just had to do nothing and just let go.

"All right Billy," she said. "I do trust you."

John lay on the floor of the only home he'd known in his ten years and hugged Dusty. Sachi said it would be okay for Dusty to sleep inside this last night.

As Sachi bent down to kiss him good night he turned away. She sat on the floor next to him.

"I know this is hard," she said, not knowing what else to say.

He sniffled, his face turned from her, but his arm still around Dusty who lay on his other side. "Everything will be gone tomorrow. It is like a book where someone wakes up and overnight their life is completely different. My friends, my house, my school, even my dog…"

At the mention of Dusty, John begin to sob. He had been so strong for a little boy. Tears began to fall from Sachi's eyes as well. Her son was mourning the loss of his dog and there was nothing she could do to comfort him.

Sachi whispered, "The Goodmans will take care of him."

John turned around quickly and faced his mother. His eyes were red and tears streaked his cheeks. "Do you think…" he asked."Do you think Dusty will like them so much that maybe he won't even miss me?"

Sachi gently brushed the dark hair from her son's forehead. She said, "I think Dusty will miss you as much as you will miss him. It is like that with best friends. But he will know you are coming back and he will wait. I know it."

John searched his mother's eyes as if wanting to believe her words. "Maybe," he said.

Sachi waited until John had fallen into a deep sleep. Dusty lay next to him, not moving, but not sleeping either, as if he knew danger lurked somewhere close. He would keep watch over John, especially tonight. Sachi was more tired than she could ever remember being in her life. She walked to the bedroom to sleep for a few hours, if she could.

The next morning Jack arrived on time and loaded the bags with Billy and Mitchell. He brought fruit and doughnuts. Ikuko and the two oldest boys got in the truck with Jack. John sat on the porch with Dusty, rubbing his neck and talking softly to him, private words between a boy and his dog.

Sachi said goodbye to her bedroom, the place she first called home in America, the place she'd become a woman lying with her husband, the place she'd birthed her three boys. She looked into the mirror and remembered her wedding day and how she felt in her mother's kimono. She looked at herself now in her lavender skirt and matching jacket with the white shirt that accented the darkness of her hair and eyes. She had more lines on her face and a slight touch of gray in her temples. Her life flashed before her and she thought of all the challenges she'd faced and would face ahead. But there was no time to think about that now. She drew in a deep breath and left her bedroom.

As she walked into the living room and was about to leave the house she heard a sound coming from the kitchen. She walked in and found Yoshida in her gray dress and matching pumps sweeping the already-clean kitchen floor.

They looked at one another. Sachi said nothing. She knew it was Yoshida's way, the Japanese way. A house, even one that would not be lived in, must be clean. It was a matter of pride. Yoshida finished the floor and put the broom away in the cabinet. She followed Sachi to the front door. They turned and looked at their home devoid of much of its best furniture, cleaned and prepared, like a body to be buried.

Yoshida prayed aloud, "Bless this house and thank you for the years of shelter and comfort and joy it has brought us."

Sachi looked at her mother-in-law, this woman who had worked hard much of her life and for the first time she saw herself in Yoshida. She was a woman, alone, scared, and unprotected, having to make such difficult decisions and losing so much. Sachi began to cry. Yoshida raised a hand to her daughter-in-law's shoulder and pulled her toward her. In all the years they'd known one another, Yoshida had never given Sachi a hug, but now she clung to her as if her very life depended upon it. They embraced for several minutes. Then just as suddenly Yoshida pulled away, handed Sachi a tissue from her pocket, and used one herself. Sachi stepped outside holding the door for Yoshida. She knew she would have to pull her youngest son from his dog and she dreaded this moment for him and for herself.

Yoshida held her head proudly, stuffed the used tissue in her pocket, and turned to Sachi, "We have survived much. We can do this, too."

Then, as if they were off to a party, she added, "Let's not arrive late."

CHAPTER THIRTY-FIVE

The train station was crowded with Japanese faces and baggage. The Watanabe family waited in a long line to receive their family number, 465686, which was tagged on each piece of their baggage to help insure its arrival to them at the assembly center. It was also pinned on each one of them, like their baggage, for presumably the same reason, to insure arrival. Ikuko received a different number as she was of a different family, but they were all going to the same facility and Sachi felt lucky, at least, about that. They would not be separated as many friends and families had been, at least for now.

There were very few white faces among the crowd except for a handful of visitors saying good-bye to Japanese friends and the armed military men standing guard with rifles to guarantee order. All who were there knew many of those white people who came to say their goodbyes could possibly pay for it afterward either by losing their jobs or losing friends. The only one, other than Jack, Sachi recognized was a schoolteacher of Mitchell's, Mrs. Price. She was there to say goodbye to several students, including Mitchell. She encouraged him to continue in his studies regardless of the conditions he might face. She gave him several paperback books.

Mrs. Price told Sachi Mitchell had much promise and not to let him give up on his studies. She promised to forward his grades, provide him with academic recommendations, and write to him when she could.

Mrs. Price quickly hugged Mitchell with tears in her eyes and said she would be praying for him every night. As she started to pull away from him, Mitchell, for a brief moment, held on to her, not quite willing to let go just yet. The feather from her hat was in his face, but he took no notice. He held on, and then the moment was over, and he released her. She stood back from him with tears in her eyes. As the time came to board the train, Jack said good-bye to everyone, last of all Sachi.

"Well, I don't know what to say," he mumbled, as her family watched.

"Goodbye, Jack and thank you for the ride today and the food and watching the place while we're gone. I can't tell you how much that means. We'll write as soon as we get wherever we are going."

Jack leaned toward her so only she could hear him over the noise of people all around them. He whispered, "You know yesterday when you said your honor and your family were all you have left. It's not true. You have me as well."

Before she could say anything he kissed her cheek, squeezed her hand quickly, and turned, disappearing into the sea of people.

They were on the train only a few hours. All shades were to be drawn so as not to frighten the American citizens who might see them from the outside and so, presumably, no one would know who was on board, a trainload of Japanese and Americans of Japanese descent headed for an unknown destination. No one on the outside would be witness to their journey.

The train was filled with aging fishermen and farmers, boys in Cub Scout uniforms, pregnant and nursing mothers, young children, old women, wives and mothers and young men. All were tagged like their baggage. This was the "subversive" group of which America was afraid.

After nine hours the train arrived at Tanforan Race Track in San Bruno, California. Sachi thought of the times when thousands of people had arrived at this very destination, excited, feeling lucky, and looking forward to spending a day at the races. There were no padded seats, daily doubles, and takeout food waiting for them today.

The horse stalls had been quickly whitewashed to serve as housing for the over 8,000 Japanese and Americans to be interned. It was a temporary facility set up by the War Time Civil Control Administration, the 118 acre track with recently-installed guard towers housing armed military police 24 hours a day and barbed wire surrounding them. It was as tightly guarded and secure as any prison filled with criminals. Of course, these people had committed no crime, except to be or look Japanese.

They entered their "room", a white-washed horse stall that still smelled of manure, with a naked light bulb hanging from the ceiling over the hay stuffed mattresses. For several minutes the family stood, unable to believe this is where they were being sent - even though it was only temporary - a horse's house. Sachi couldn't help but wonder where the horses were now living. The boys went to find their luggage, which had all been dumped in a massive pile.

Yoshida stepped out to go find where meals would be served. Sachi suspected Yoshida simply couldn't face the cramped surroundings, particularly after the crowded train trip.

An hour later the family was gathered again in their room. Their luggage was stacked by the door. The boys sat in a semi circle around Yoshida and Sachi as they pulled food from the basket they brought with them. Yoshida handed John a sandwich and said, "I went to this place they call the mess hall where we will be eating. I don't know what we are going to do. One lady who has been here a week told me the cooks are all Caucasian and they cook with no Japanese spices, just lots of salt and pepper. They said their lunchmeat is green and their bread is moldy half the time."

Sachi said, "I am sure she is exaggerating. They wouldn't give us food that is inedible."

Yoshida shook her head and said, "Well, the woman I spoke to says it is food she would not have fed to her animals…when she had animals."

Billy swallowed the last bite of his apple and tossed the core angrily into a box of trash. He said, with bitterness in his voice, "They have us eating and sleeping like animals."

Sachi and Yoshida were silent. Billy had expressed in words the pain and disrespect they all felt. As they sat finishing their meal, Sachi said, "Boys, after you're done, go to the bathroom and get ready for bed. Let's try and get some sleep tonight."

To Yoshida she said, "Come on, let's go check out the bathroom facilities here."

"No," Yoshida said. "The woman in the next stall over told me they are very dirty. I will wait."

Sachi grabbed two towels and some soap. She shook her head and said, "Wait? For what? Until you explode? Come with me now."

A voice from the stall next to theirs rose over the partition. She said, "They are horrible. Not fit for the horses that once lived here."

Sachi sighed, realizing there would be no privacy, shook her head, and grabbed Yoshida by the arm. "Let's go."

They walked from the stalls to the bathroom facility for their section. Sachi joined the line that had formed. Yoshida walked ahead and peeked into the facility. She came back to where Sachi stood, a look of horror on her face, and whispered, "I cannot go in there. There is no privacy."

Sachi held her arm and said, "You have to go. You'll get sick if you don't. There are some things about which you have no choice and this is one of them."

Yoshida hung her head, staring at the ground, and said, "We have no choice in anything."

As they entered the bathroom Sachi saw what caused Yoshida's panic. The "toilets" were holes cut in large boards covering pits for urine and feces. There were no partitions of any kind and the women were forced to use the toilet as they had perhaps used beauty parlor seats months earlier, right next to one another. The showers were simple showerheads sticking out of the walls without partitions. This was difficult for all the women, but particularly the older Japanese women whose culture had taught them extreme modesty. Sachi took Yoshida by the arm and led her to an open toilet toward the end of the bench and then stood in front of her, holding up the towels she'd brought trying to provide some protection from the eyes of others. Of course, most of the women were horribly embarrassed, eyes cast downward.

"I can't go."

Sachi sighed heavily, trying to hold up the towel, and, like when she used to deal with her toddler sons, she said, "Just try. I know you have to go. Just concentrate."

"I can't."

After five minutes of this back and forth Sachi was rewarded by the tinkling sound from behind the towels.

Sachi overheard two women in line talking. The shorter one said, "My mother-in-law is sick from waiting too long to use this dreadful place."

The taller one nodded and said, "My mother waits until late into the night when the fewest number of people are here. She gets to feeling very sick as well."

That next morning Billy took a chance. He gathered some scrap wood that lay about left over from the hastily assembled "apartments." With that and his hammer and nails, he put up several partitions in the bathroom closest to their stall. Yoshida was grateful and proud of her grandson for having the forethought to pack such necessary items.

The next day several women from another section of stalls came to their door to ask Billy to do the same in their bathroom. For three days it was the same.

Finally Sachi said, "Billy, you must be careful. Do not put up these partitions anymore. You could get caught and then get into trouble."

Yoshida said, "The women in this camp need those partitions and Billy is smart. He won't get caught."

"That's right, Grandmother," Billy said, "And I like doing it. These bosses think they can toss us in these cells, take the modesty from our women, and reduce us men to do nothing, but sitting around. They can't. And we'll show them."

"We?" Sachi asked. "Who are 'we'?"

"Just some guys I have met the last few days. Guys who think like I do."

"Kias?"

"Listen, Mother, I have to go," he said as he pulled the hammer and nails from underneath one of the mattresses.

He smiled proudly, "I told you these would come in handy. I knew they wouldn't put us anywhere nice. It was going to have to be a dump. I knew it."

Yoshida said, "He can pull the nails out before we leave this place. It's only temporary."

"It's not the nails I am worried about."

As the weeks and months went on in the temporary internment center, a daily rhythm took over. Ikuko, who had been assigned housing several housing blocks away, came to visit daily and stayed until just before dark. The long summer days were blistering and there was no insulation in the horse stalls. Internees who were teachers began working with the administration who lived on the premises in the clubhouse, a much nicer facility. These teachers began teaching school.

Medical workers worked in the medical facility and farmers, some of whom had the foresight to bring seed with them, started planting.

Yoshida surprised Sachi informing her that she too had brought seed, but said, "Unlike the rest of these thoughtless people I am not wasting good seed in temporary ground."

They began to settle in and Yoshida even began to contemplate a winter garden. They were hoping perhaps this would be the worst of it. Maybe it was taking so long because they would be going home soon, but in December, just as it was growing cold, they received word they would be moving to their permanent internment camp, Poston, Arizona.

The only good news was they were told Takeo had been cleared and would join them at Poston. The boys dragged Yoshida from her bed where she had spent more and more time and made her dance around the room, happy they would see Takeo soon, making resettlement a little less painful. Sachi was relieved. Now Takeo could take over worrying about the children and he would be able to put his foot down and make sure they did as they were told, instead of running off at all hours with unknown children doing who knows what. They would be a family again. Some kind of peace and harmony and unity would return to them.

Mitchell informed them that Poston would be much hotter and much colder than Tanforan. It was located in the desert on Indian reservation property.

378

Mitchell said, "You know The United States didn't give the Indians land worth anything so you can guess what it's going to be like when we get there."

Ikuko came over late that morning. Her face was pinched as if she were exerting a great effort not to cry. She had grown thin in the last few months, as had many of the women, although others, who were eating the heavy starch and carbohydrate meals, were growing heavier. All things were out of balance.

Ikuko sat on one of the beds and held Sachi's hand. She said, "Were you notified?"

Sachi nodded then said, "Poston."

Ikuko could no longer hold back the tears. They burst forth like water through a dam and before she lost her ability to speak she said, "Topaz. Utah."

They fell into one another's arms and cried for a long time. For the first time since she'd arrived in this country twenty years ago she was to be separated from her best friend. Thoughts flashed through her head like a visual scrapbook, Ikuko telling her about America, attending her wedding and the births of all three of her boys, taking care of her children and helping her when she needed it, being there at Duke's death and the detainment of their husbands, and their internment. Sachi didn't think she could stand parting from this woman who was as close as any sister to her. She held Ikuko and wished desperately to be on her front porch, stitching or sipping tea and listening to Ikuko talk. For Sachi it was like listening to the breeze. It was a part of the rhythm of her life and now it was being taken away. She thought how afraid her friend must be. Then she realized if she had been notified about Takeo maybe Edo was joining her at Topaz as well.

Sachi asked, "Have you heard anything about Edo?"

Ikuko shook her head, "No. I have heard they look at childless Japanese couples with more suspicion, as if we don't have children so we can attend to our spy duties free of any baggage. If they only knew how hard we'd tried to…"

Ikuko stopped. "I can't think of that. Not now," she said and changing the focus from her, she asked, "What about Takeo? Do you know where he is?"

Sachi didn't want to say for some reason. She thought it would make Ikuko feel worse and worry about her own husband more, but she could not lie to her best friend, her sister.

She nodded and said. "He is meeting us in Poston."

Ikuko began to cry again and after several minutes said, "I am very happy for you, Sachi. You know that. It's just I worry about my Edo. I worry I have not heard."

The following days were filled with what little packing they had to do and saying good-bye to the new friends they had made. The night before they were leaving the boys went around and removed most of the nails Billy had used. They didn't know what kinds of conditions they would face in Arizona. Billy left one partition in each bathroom for those who were staying. Ikuko was leaving after them and Sachi wished she were first so Ikuko would not be the one left behind.

The day they were to depart, Ikuko came over to say her goodbyes. "I cannot do it in front of the gates with everyone there," she said to Sachi.

She hugged John and Mitchell, in turn, and gave them small brown-paper wrapped packages. "It is candy," she said. "I was saving it for Christmas presents, but since I will not be with you for…"

She stopped, unable to continue, tears filling her eyes. She turned to Billy, handing him a package of candy as well, and apologized, where no apology was needed, "I'm sorry. I know you are too old for this, but it is all I had."

Billy hugged her tightly and said, "I am not too old for candy. Goodbye, Auntie Cukie."

She smiled, tears falling down her cheeks. "You have not called me that since you were a little boy."

He nodded. "But I remember."

Ikuko respectfully bowed to Yoshida in the old way and then quickly hugged her. Yoshida whispered in her ear, "*Ningen banji saiou ga uma.*"

It meant one's luck is unpredictable and constantly changing. Ikuko smiled recognizing the old words from the country she had known so long ago.

When she came to Sachi, she wiped her face with the back of her sleeve, quickly drying her tears. Sachi grabbed her hand, placing in it Duke's opal ring.

Ikuko said, "Oh no. I cannot accept this. Duke wanted you to have it."

Sachi smiled and said, "And I want you to have it. Keep it and remember friendship, our friendship with Duke, and with one another."

Ikuko's bottom lip quivered as if she would cry despite her efforts not to and said, "But it means so much to you."

"Yes it does," Sachi answered. "That's why I am giving it to you."

Ikuko, unable hold back the tears, threw her arms around Sachi's neck and put her head on Sachi's shoulder. Sachi wrapped her arms around her friend and they hugged, as sisters, saying goodbye.

Ikuko quickly dried her eyes again and said, "I have cried enough over you, my friend. I will not cry anymore. Not until the day I see you back in Orange Grove."

CHAPTER THIRTY-SIX

The train ride to Poston was a long two-day ride, but Sachi did not complain. Many people traveled much farther to Arkansas's two internment centers or the one in Wyoming. She counted her blessings, again, that she did not have small children as she saw many young mothers with babies or, even more difficult, toddlers. The mother's efforts were spent trying to quiet them, feed them, distract them, and comfort them. There were many pregnant women trying to fight morning sickness and trying to get comfortable.

Poston was much like Tanforan, but instead of previously used horse stalls their "apartments" were newly-constructed plywood structures with tarpaper roofs and no insulation. A pot-bellied stove sat as lone welcomer next to mattresses stuffed with hay. A bare light bulb hung from the ceiling, and they were afforded two rooms, reminding Sachi in some small way of her home in Japan on the coast. She'd left it only to end up in this. They had left the temporary housing naively thinking they were headed for something better. It was cold and windy when they arrived late that evening and Billy started a fire in the stove with scrap wood he managed to round up. Living in California, they were not prepared for the kind of cold that seizes the desert at night. The boys bundled up together and Yoshida and Sachi shared a bed as well. Takeo had always been so warm to sleep next to and Sachi wished he had been there to meet them.

Weeks went by before Takeo arrived. He did not write and Sachi was told her letters would not reach him, so she set her family to work on more practical matters. The

383

bathrooms at least already had some partitions put up and Billy finished the job. Mitchell and John collected wood, and all three boys helped new arrivals, fetching their bags so they could unpack. There was nothing surrounding the camp and Sachi thought to herself that Mitchell was right - this was forgotten land wanted by no one. It was a place where you could put people, Indians or Japanese, so no one had to look at them and perhaps they would be forgotten right along with the land. Like the horse stalls, barbed wire surrounded the encampment and armed guards stood in the guard towers and walked patrol.

The internees learned from the temporary housing that setting up the community as quickly as possible was important. They immediately went to work organizing school, the hospital, and helping at the mess hall. Sachi went right to work at the school teaching English and reading. There were few books to use but she would check into ordering some.

Several weeks after their arrival, Sachi received a letter from Ikuko. She'd arrived in Topaz and Seda, Yoshida's old friend from temple, was there with her family. Though she did not know them well, they were kind to her and at least they were familiar faces.

The holidays came and with hardly any notice. The most difficult time was Christmas morning when the boys awoke and there was nothing, no tree, no gifts, no smells of Christmas to awaken them and no father. Turkey was served at the mess hall and Sachi ate with the boys and Yoshida, insisting, for once, they would eat dinner in this place as a family.

When they returned there was a package at the front of their door. It had been opened and a letter was in the box, which had also been opened. It was from Jack. The box was filled with food, several books, gloves for each of them, scarves, skeins of blue yarn and a quilt he had purchased from one of the ladies in town. His letter was the first they had received and he said he finally had a chance to write back to them as things were very busy. He listed everything he'd sent, but one item was blacked out with permanent marker as were several sentences in the letter. Administration officials had censored it, but at least they had received it and on Christmas day as well. It was a gift from heaven.

Everyone's spirits were lifted a bit and Yoshida sat for several minutes before saying, "I know what item was crossed off. I bet it was knitting needles. Why would he send yarn without needles?"

Then she went to her bag and pulled out one small crochet hook. "Billy is not the only one who can sneak in contraband. I thought this might come in handy along with the needles and thread."

Yoshida went right to work on a blue afghan while the boys sat around the stove listening to Sachi read from *Treasure Island*. Billy was restless and Sachi knew he wanted to be out, roaming the sections with the group of boys he had met. They were a rough-looking bunch, who seemed to do little but complain about conditions and violation of their rights. But then, what did young men with uncertain futures do when corralled behind barbed wire, especially with no grown men to guide them?

And, as if in answer to her prayers, there was a knock on the door. Sachi stopped reading and looked up and the door burst open. She saw the shadow of a man in the doorway and her heart jumped with fear. It was Mitchell who spoke first. "Father!"

It was Takeo. The boys jumped up and wildly ran to their father, almost knocking him off his feet. Sachi and Yoshida stood to greet him. He stepped toward Sachi and she realized why she had not immediately recognized him. He looked like an old man, thinner, flabby and weak, not as hearty as he'd been. He was beginning to lose some of his hair toward the front and it was much grayer than just one year ago. She tried to hide her surprise at his appearance and smiled.

She stood, happy to see him, and said, "Welcome home, such as it is."

He smiled and hugged his sons. Watching him with the boys, Sachi felt the tension release from her body, tension she had been storing up for months.

He bowed to his wife and mother, a custom that now seemed so foreign to Sachi and, under the circumstances, so cold. But she did not press him. He sat by the stove, warming himself, and the boys recounted their year to him. He said little of his time away except he had missed them and things had been difficult. As Sachi watched her family again, even in this harsh place, she began to feel hope and strength surge through her. She felt as if a heavy burden had been lifted from her back and she was able to feel again. Takeo was home and she was not alone.

The hour grew late and John was sent to bed in the other room. Billy smiled at his father and said, "Finally, now we can get to work."

Yoshida said, "Let your poor father rest. Takeo, you look like you could sleep for a year."

And sleep he did. He slept all that night and all the next day not rising until breakfast the following morning. He still looked as tired and as aged as when he arrived and Sachi wondered how Edo would look when Ikuko saw him next.

When Sachi and Takeo finally had a few minutes alone, he did not mention his time away and she did not ask him. If he wanted to talk about it, he would. She told him how hard it was keeping three young boys, men really, from getting into trouble. Mitchell was focused on finishing high school and even doing college work, but Billy was running with a group of "trouble makers" as Yoshida called them and John was not too far behind him.

She thought Takeo would consider the situation and tell her what he was going to do and how he was going to get the boys in line. Instead he said, "Well, there's not much to be done right now."

Sachi said, "Of course, there is much to be done. I am working with the school and the children need to attend class and get their degrees. Billy is just a few classes short, but he refuses to attend and it's all I can do to force John to come. He wants to spend all day walking the blocks with his brother and friends."

"Edo is dead," Takeo announced.

Sachi felt as if he had punched her in the chest. She was talking about their boys' future and he chose this time to deliver such news without warning or prelude.

"How do you...," Sachi began.

Takeo interrupted and said, "He was in Lincoln with me. I never saw him, but I heard through some of the others. He had a heart attack while they were questioning him. Of course, they decided it's probably because he had something to hide. They did not consider it could have been the hardships he's had to endure. And he wasn't young."

"When?"

"A few weeks ago."

All Sachi could think of was that there would be no one to comfort Ikuko when she got the news. Sachi could not be where she wanted, at her friend's side. She said, "Poor Ikuko. Now she is truly alone."

Sachi began to cry for her friend and Takeo did nothing to comfort her. He sat staring at the clouds in the gray sky as if checking for rain. Through her tears she looked at Takeo and realized she was also alone in her grief. He was somewhere else. She dried her eyes and stepped outside.

As the weeks dragged on Sachi noticed a change in her family. The tension between Takeo and Billy had grown almost unbearable. He could not accept his father's defeatist attitude and Takeo was not up to taking charge of his family. Yoshida on the other hand, seemed to have more energy. She did not sit still, but catered to her son constantly even bringing him his meals in bed on the many days he did not feel like rising from it.

Mitchell kept telling Sachi, "*Gonan*" meaning everything will come in time. They were the same words Yoshida and she gave the boys throughout childhood and now, they were coming back to her.

John, who had missed his father most of all and was in a crucial stage of development from boy to young man, received no affection or acknowledgement from his father. He began staying out late with his own group of friends. Mitchell had taken to calling them the "Little Bills" because they spoke like Billy and his friends, calling for "prison breaks", mad at the world.

Mitchell met a girl named Leigh Ann. He brought her home several times and she was like Mitchell, studying hard to obtain her high school degree. She was a year behind him and they spent all their time together. Sachi worried that perhaps they spent too much time alone, but Mitchell assured her they were studying and talking of the future, nothing else. At least, nothing he told Sachi about.

CHAPTER THIRTY-SEVEN

Dewitt sat smoking the large Cuban cigar. He drew the smoke into his mouth for a moment tasting the earthy, dark tobacco and then exhaled slowly. Standing and staring out the window to his right was Assistant Secretary of War, McCloy. To his left was New York Senator Jetter and sitting behind the desk directly facing him was Texas Senator Connally.

"Smooth as silk," Dewitt said, after exhaling. He rolled the large brown cigar between his fingers and examined it admiringly.

Jetter smiled and said, "I hear these are rolled between the thighs of 18 year old virgins down there in Cuba. That accounts for the sweet taste."

"Cuba sounds pretty good right about now," said Connally. "I think that's where I'll head for a month long vacation when this war business is over."

McCloy, who had been deep in thought, turned from the window, and said, "I've been thinking. I'm going to suggest it to Stimson. He'll talk to the President and the Joint Chiefs. I think we need a unit, a Japanese unit."

Dewitt sat up in his chair and said, "A Japanese unit of what?"

"A fighting unit."

Connally snickered, "That's not going to happen. First of all, most of them have been interned or arrested at this point, haven't they, Dewitt?"

Dewitt nodded, "Yes. And no white man is going to fight with a Jap soldier. Think of all the dissention in the ranks. It won't work."

"That's why I am going to suggest a separate unit. One made up entirely of Japanese soldiers."

Jetter stood and slowly began pacing in front of Connally's desk. He said, "What's the point? It'll look like we're trying to recruit them to kill them off and they can't fight in the Pacific. It would get too confusing."

"We let them fight so we can prove we aren't prejudice just taking security precautions and they can prove they're patriotic. It will give the Japanese American boys a way to prove their loyalty and allegiance. That's what the Japanese American Citizen League has been pushing. It's just no one takes them seriously. But I do. I think it's a damn good idea for a lot of reasons. Look, if they agree to join up, fight in Europe, then maybe they're on the up and up. And, if some of those boys refuse to fight, that'll tell us something, too."

Connally shook his head and said, "You're asking these boys to fight for the country that put them behind barbed wire. I don't think it's going to work. I think it could backfire."

"We'll get thousands of volunteers. They'll join all right. If we give these boys a chance to do their patriotic duty, they'll jump at it. "

Dewitt tilted his head back and exhaled, watching a cloud of smoke rise over him. He said, "Maybe. If we position it just right, make them sign something proving their loyalty before they're allowed to fight. Might be a good idea."

Within months President Roosevelt requested Japanese American volunteers for a newly-formed fighting unit, the 442nd Regimental Combat Team. The War Relocation Authority and the Army devised an application that went to all Nisei men, American citizens born of Japanese parents, of fighting age, including Billy and Mitchell Watanabe.

CHAPTER THIRTY-EIGHT

Everyone knew the questionnaire would arrive in the next several days. Sachi and Takeo sat down to speak with Mitchell and Billy. Their answers to the questions would determine their futures and their fates.

As usual, Takeo lay in bed. Mitchell was reading on the floor and Sachi was darning Billy's socks. She looked over at Takeo, his feet pointed toward the ceiling where they had spent most of the day. One foot had a sock half on, covering the toes, but revealing a cracked heel beneath. The sock looked like a snake that had just unhinged its jaw and begun devouring its prey, the foot. His socks rarely needed darning these days Sachi thought.

John and Yoshida were sleeping or, at least, trying to. It was difficult when everyone did not go to bed at the same time, but there was quiet until Billy entered the room.

Takeo sat up, not even bothering to pull up his sock.

"Billy, we want to talk to you. We asked Mitchell to wait up with us since it seems the only time to catch you is late at night anymore. What do you do all day? Your mother says you're not in school."

"What do you do during the day, Father?"

All were silent. They knew what Takeo did during the day lately. Takeo pulled up his socks and tried to straighten his rumpled clothes as best he could.

Sachi said, "Billy, Mitchell, we want to talk to you about the questionnaire."

Billy and Mitchell were silent.

Sachi continued, "You understand if you answer yes to questions 27 and 28 you will either go into military service or at the least you may be eligible for early resettlement, which might mean going to college or working somewhere for real money. If you answer no, you will be taken away, imprisoned like this, maybe worse, and you will be separated from us."

Takeo added, "We want you both to answer yes to those questions."

Billy asked, "So I should lie?"

Mitchell interrupted, "It is not a lie to foreswear allegiance to an Emperor you were never loyal to in the first place. It is not a lie to fight for the ideals in which you believe. I will prove my loyalty in the military."

Billy turned and asked, "Prove it with your life?"

Mitchell spoke calmly, "If that's what it takes."

Billy turned to his parents, with his voice raised, and said, "It is a lie to say I will serve a country that hates me. It is a lie to say I believe in the ideals that are apparently only meant for the whites. It elevates even the Italians over the Japanese. They have politicians and the great Joe DiMaggio. They are not interned now. And where are the Germans? The Japanese are less than everyone else.

"You say, "*Gomen*". I'm sorry. Excuse me. You say "*shikataganai*". It can't be helped. Be patient. But those who are going along, patiently waiting for something to happen are weak. Old and weak and they didn't know what to do, still don't know what to do and so they did nothing. They do nothing. In fact, they did worse than nothing, they helped. They helped these round-eyed jailors to capture us and imprison us. We hopped on those trains without batting an eye because we didn't want to cause any trouble. We didn't want to be branded troublemakers."

Takeo looked tired and sighed heavily. He said, "Billy, you must be a river."

Billy laughed a hard, offensive laugh and said, "A river? That was for children. I am no longer a child, Father. Americans don't tell their children to be rivers. They tell them to be oak trees, tall, strong, and immovable. The river goes around the oak tree and keeps on moving. The oak tree makes the river move. Whites are aggressive and vulgar and rough. They only know and respect those who are equally strong and aggressive and rough. They only respect those who fight. We did not fight and we are not respected. We won't be respected until we demand it."

Mitchell looked deep into his brother's eyes and said in a quiet, yet firm voice, "You won't be respected until you stand up for what you believe."

Billy returned the intensity of his brother's gaze. "That's what I'm doing, little brother."

Mitchell shook his head and said, "Not really. You are talking about standing up for things you don't believe in. You don't believe you should have been sent here with your family. You don't believe people should treat one another the way we have been treated. You don't believe many things, but what do you believe in? If not, America, than what?"

Billy answered quickly, angrily, turning on his brother, "What do I believe in? I don't have anything to believe in anymore. I can't believe in this country or this government. Even my own family doesn't see what is happening. I have no beliefs anymore and they, the white American government, took it from me. They took my loyalty and beliefs and crushed them into the dirt and now they want me to prove myself. Why didn't they ask for proof of loyalty before they tore my life apart?"

Mitchell shook his head. "I don't know. What I do know is decisions are made by people. People are flawed and because of that the system is sometimes flawed, but still, in spite of it all, America is the greatest form of government in the world. I can tell you what I believe. Even though people are making mistakes and trying to take away my rights I still believe I have a duty to defend my country and my freedom in any way possible."

Billy sat with a smirk on his face and clapped slowly, loudly, mockingly.

"Well, little brother," he said, "I can see the Americanization classes have worked wonders on you. You are red, white and blue inside. But you are still yellow on the outside and that is the only color the white bastards see."

"Billy, do not speak such language," Sachi cautioned. "These are the kinds of things that will get you into trouble."

Billy spoke the words to his mother all the while looking at his father and said, "Mother, I'm in jail. What more can they do? Besides, there are worse things to be branded in this life than troublemaker. How about coward?"

Takeo rose and walked over to his son. Standing close to him, Takeo asked, "Is that meant for me? Do you see me as a coward?"

Billy stood over his father and said, "I see you as doing nothing like most. Lying in bed like an old woman. Not having the energy or the passion to fight. The great yellow peril. Is it a coincidence that yellow is what they call us and is also the color they chose for cowardice?"

Takeo faced his oldest son, his hands clenched as if ready to fight, as his child hurled accusations of cowardice at him. Every word was like a stone driving Takeo back to sit on his bed. Takeo stared at the ground, drained, unable to defend himself, Sachi realized, as he had been unable to do for so long it seemed.

Billy took two great strides and stood over his father, not allowing him to retreat to his bed. He continued, "Do you know what those two questions ask, Father? Question 27 wants to know if we will serve in combat for a country that has taken away our rights. They want to know if we would be willing to give up our lives for a country that keeps us like sheep behind barbed wire with watchdog guards. Question 28 wants to know if we'll forswear allegiance to the Emperor of Japan as if I had somehow been loyal to him to begin with. Who are they to ask me my beliefs while they have me behind barbed wire? Let them ask me when I am free. I will not go quietly into their battlefield as I was forced to go quietly into this prison. I am tired of going along and seeing my father go along. You may still have some patience, but I do not. I will not crawl into bed and wait. Someone in this family has to take a stand. And since my father won't…"

Before Billy could finish Sachi rose from her seat, stood before her son, and slapped him as hard as she could across the face. It was the first time she had ever struck anyone and the image of her father slapping her years ago immediately stuck in her mind. Billy did not flinch. His eyes widened and watered slightly from the sting of his mother's hand. He stood in disbelief.

Sachi's hand hurt from striking her son and her eyes stung as tears welled up, but she spoke clearly and without hesitation, "Do not ever speak to your father in that manner again. Your father has been far braver than you realize. He has displayed courage in a way you may never understand, but it is his way.

"You are old enough to see the world does not center on you. This is not about just us. Have you learned nothing of your Japanese ancestry? This country is at war and your father, we, did what we thought was best for our country and our families. We did what we were asked to do. We did not want to do it, but to fight against it would have caused more pain and grief for our families and our country. Perhaps we should have fought. Maybe we would not be here. But perhaps we would be here anyway and with greater wounds. I do not know. But I do know your father is no coward. Some day you will realize this and you will hate yourself for hurting him so. I just hope you have the chance to apologize when that happens."

Billy could not look at his mother. He looked at the ground and in the voice that reminded Sachi of her little boy he whispered, "I remember your words, Father. Even water cannot get in. And now I understand."

Billy walked quietly outside and disappeared into the night of the camp. Takeo sat on the bed, deflated and drained. Mitchell sat in the corner, staring into space. Sachi went back to darning the socks. At least that was an effort that would not be wasted. Her sons would need their socks wherever they went.

The decision came a week after the boys filled out their questionnaires. Mitchell was to undergo another physical and, if he passed, he would be sent away for military training. Billy was being sent to Tule Lake. It was another internment camp for those wishing to be repatriated back to Japan and the "less controllable" internees. The young men who had answered no to questions 27 and 28, called the 'no-no boys' were all being sent there, where they could be watched more efficiently.

On the morning Billy was to leave for Tule Lake, a dirty bus covered with the dust of the camp waited at the front gate. The family was readied to walk to the bus and say their good-byes. Billy and Sachi stepped outside and looked up. It was habit, checking the weather. The wind blew the clouds overhead. They moved quickly as if even the clouds couldn't stand to be still in this barren place for long. The wind also constantly stirred the dust in camp, so much so that Sachi and Yoshida swept daily, sometimes more.

Billy muttered, breaking the silence, "I won't miss all this wind and dust."

He turned searching his mother's face and added, "But I will miss you, Mother."

She turned toward her young man, still such a little boy in her eyes. In all of her dreams for her oldest child, she had never imagined losing him this way. In her dreams for him, there was a wife and children and working on their land, but never anything like this. Her voice cracked as she tried to control it. "And I will miss you terribly, my son."

They walked in silence to the front of the camp and the family arrived minutes later.

Yoshida cried and hugged Billy goodbye, supporting him and his decision. Takeo stood next to Yoshida. Billy stuck out his hand and they shook hands like American strangers who did not know one another, instead of father and son. Takeo said nothing and Billy whispered, "Good bye, Father."

Sachi hugged her son. He held on to her for a long time and he suddenly felt like a little boy again in her arms. She breathed him in, as she had when he was a baby. He smelled of this place and the soap used to clean his clothes and something more. She could not identify it except she knew it was him.

She whispered into his ear, "We love you. Be good. Do what you are asked and come back to us when this is all done."

Billy looked at Sachi with tears in his eyes, which he quickly wiped away. John stood next to his mother. His eyes were red and he tried not to cry, but the tears began to spill out as Billy picked him up and told him to do as his mother said. He promised to take John for ice cream when they met again at home. He tousled John's hair and said goodbye.

Most of the families had said their goodbyes and the bus was readying to depart. About fifteen young men were in the process of loading. Families, broken, disassembled, crying, waiting to catch the last glimpse of their loved one. Guards stood around the group, carefully watching in case of trouble. Their guns were raised on their shoulders, ready for, but not expecting, any violence.

Mitchell ran up to the group. He had spent the morning studying with Leigh Ann and lost track of time. He approached Billy, breathless, and said, "I was afraid I'd missed you. Take care, brother. I know we've chosen different ways..."

"You've given in," Billy interrupted. "Do you think the white man gives a damn that you are willing to risk your life to prove your loyalty?"

As Billy spoke the guards moved in closer and their weapons came off their shoulders. Billy saw them, but their actions seem to incite him further, and he continued, "They see it as another great way to get rid of Japs. Throw em' into battle. Let em' think they're hot shots proving something and let em' all get killed. Send em' right up to the front. You won't be serving with any white men, brother. You just don't see it. You don't have any passion. Just like father, you go along and ..."

Suddenly, Mitchell hauled back and hit his brother, hard in the mouth. Billy reeled back. He was bigger and stronger than Mitchell, but he was caught by surprise. Mitchell threw a left to the jaw and a right to Billy's stomach. Mitchell rammed his head into his brother's stomach causing Billy to fall to the ground, landing in a small group of young men who had yet to board the bus. Mitchell sat on top of him as if to punch him again, but didn't.

The guards moved in closer, but did nothing to stop the fight. People gathered nearer to watch, but it was over almost before it began. In spite of all of his talk of fighting back,

Billy did not fight back against his brother. He saw anger in his brother's eyes he had never seen before. Mitchell was always cool and collected, never succumbing to pressure, but not today. Billy saw the fury and recognized it. It was like his own.

Mitchell jumped off his brother and there were cries from those on the bus, "Get him Billy", "Show that Kyoin what for", "Teach him a lesson."

Billy rose and the two brothers stood facing one another, but neither moved. Billy tried to brush the hated dust from his clothes and said, "Damn it, Mitchell."

He was more irritated than angry. The guards backed away, uninterested in a squabble between brothers. Mitchell had tears in his eyes and he screamed above the others, "Billy, don't you get it? When I said I believe it is my duty to defend my country against all enemies I didn't just mean those abroad. I didn't just mean the Germans and the Italians and the Japanese. I meant them."

He pointed to the guards with guns. "I meant those white men you are always pointing out. This is the best way to fight them. They don't want me in their army. That's too damn bad. I'm going. They don't want me in their schools. To hell with them. I'm getting an education. They don't want me in America. Well, fuck them. I'm here and if I die on the battlefield in some foreign country, guess what? I'll be a war hero. They'll send a purple heart to my mother. The same Purple Heart American patriots through the years have received. That will stick in the throat of every prejudice son-of-a-bitch out there. That will be the statement I leave to this world. And it's a much stronger statement than being a "no-no" boy sitting locked up in some juvenile detention center for troublemakers. I'd rather die a man in battle than sit, whining, like a little boy who's been sent to his room."

Those seated on the bus were suddenly quiet and the only sound was the wind, that constant wind that never stopped. It howled and in the silence, sounded louder than usual. The stragglers got on board until only Billy was left. The two brothers faced one another. Sachi watched Billy and thought he looked, for a moment, regretful, as if he almost wished he had done things differently.

Mitchell shook his head and said helplessly, "Billy..."

Billy smiled slightly and said, "Well, I gotta get on the bus. Good luck, little brother."

He turned to leave and Mitchell ran up behind him, grabbed him around the middle and squeezed. Billy would not turn around to return the hug, but Sachi heard him whisper out of the side of his mouth, "Don't get yourself killed over there. I'd like to get to know you better."

Sachi turned to Takeo putting her hand on his sleeve. He stared straight ahead, looking at the two men in front of him. They could have been anyone's sons. Without a word or a look toward Yoshida or Sachi, Takeo turned and walked back to his barracks. Yoshida stood, with tears in her eyes, and said to Sachi, "Not all casualties in this war are on the battlefield."

Billy was sent to Tule Lake in the high desert on the Oregon/California border. Tule Lake was first a Relocation Camp and now a segregation camp for those who appeared disloyal, including the no-no boys. Mitchell went to Camp Shelby, Mississippi to train.

He was one out of eight hundred Japanese Americans from the continental United States

accepted into the Japanese-only military company – the 442nd.

CHAPTER THIRTY-NINE

Sachi received letters regularly from Mitchell who missed Leigh Ann and made plans to meet her after the war and internment. She knew this would be her new daughter and so she made an effort to get to know her and spend time with her. Like Sachi, Leigh Ann loved working in the school. It was more than just a distraction from daily life and boredom that could be overwhelming at the camp. Sachi felt she was accomplishing something, helping prepare these children for their eventual release.

She and Leigh Ann initially traded information about Mitchell back and forth. He told them the people in Mississippi were very receptive to them, kind and warm, emphasizing the southern hospitality. He spoke rarely of the hardships of military training, but Sachi knew her son well enough to read between the lines in his letters. He was fighting for what he believed, but she knew he was scared as well.

Sachi made a daily trip to the post office that was established in camp. She often thought to her childhood in Japan when she would walk to get the mail from Mr. Yakusho.

She wrote letters weekly to Mitchell, Billy, Ikuko, the Goodmans, and Jack. Writing filled her days even when there was not much to tell. She was always careful in her letters, especially the ones to Jack. She knew they might be censored. When a letter arrived for the Watanabes it was the highlight of her day.

It was a long time after Edo's death before Sachi received a response from Ikuko to any of her letters. Ikuko finally wrote in the summer of 1943. Sachi sat on the steps outside the school house and read her letter. Ikuko said she was happy and talked about a man, Yuji Yamomoto, she'd met at camp who had helped her the first few weeks. He was a widower who had run a fishing operation in southern California before the war. This made Sachi fearful of the fact that her best friend might not return to Orange Grove, but she felt immediately selfish for thinking it and resolved to be happy for her friend. She returned to the letter, which sounded like the old Ikuko full of funny stories about the residents and their daily doings.

At the end her friend, who knew her so well, wrote, "P.S. Yuji would come with me if it goes that far. Don't worry. I'll see you in Orange Grove when we get sprung."

Sachi smiled. Not a day passed without her missing her friend. She re-read the letter and then went to lunch by herself. Takeo was having a particularly bad day and was staying in bed. Yoshida had eaten earlier, bringing food back for Takeo and then working in her garden, a small patch of land by their building. This was often how their days were spent, solitary endeavors, their paths crossing in the mornings and evenings, sometimes at meals, but most often not.

John spent much of his time in the recreation center playing cards, especially Black-Jack, or playing baseball with the other boys. John was changing and growing tall. He was proud of his brother Mitchell and Mitchell occasionally sent things he bought for John, an airplane model, some postcards, books, and candy. Sachi began to hold out hope that John would not follow in Billy's footsteps, but he still ran around with the boys she did not like. Takeo was no help and she thought the sooner they were out, the better for John.

It amazed Sachi that, like John, the camp had grown and changed as well over several years. There were warehouses for dry goods and cold goods, an administration, schools, canteens, a library, religious services, a hospital, a livestock breeding facility, and, of course, the post office. There was even a small stage in the auditorium named the *Kabuki* Theater for student and community plays and programs. Internees worked as groups to help with the war effort and manufactured camouflage nets and ship models to be used for training naval personnel.

The time of internment passed slowly and Sachi kept busy teaching school and reading. Jack had stopped writing altogether. Occasionally they received letters from the Goodmans asking after them and telling them about their daughters or things with the war efforts. They sent money and mentioned they had seen Jack in town or at the Grange and Jack asked that they write and send whatever money might be in the envelope. Sachi took it to mean that Jack was indeed keeping the place up and was continuing to pay the mortgage and taxes for them. She trusted him. She had to.

She wrote to Mitchell and had tea with Leigh Ann almost daily. Mitchell was busy, but somehow he'd managed to keep up writing to both women. Then he was sent to Europe and the letters were less frequent and instead of two there was only one letter addressed to them both, but always sent to Leigh Ann. Initially it hurt Sachi, but she recognized it was the way of things. The way things should be. She went to church every day praying for her sons and wishing to hear from Billy, but when she did she almost wished she hadn't.

He was in the detention center and labeled one of the no-no boys. How often had she uttered those words to her son? No-no, Billy, don't do that. No-no. Sachi read his letter of despair alone at night just as she had read Takeo's letter of hope so many years ago in Tanchoichi. Her village and that time seemed worlds away. She had a candle to read by, just like then, so as not to wake anyone. She had waited until Takeo was asleep because the letter was not addressed to him and it would have hurt him to see it was addressed Dear Mother.

He started by talking about the deplorable conditions in which he found himself. It was a jail, he wrote, and she could sense the fear in his every word, almost hearing his voice.

"Mother, the worst of it is how the entire time I feel ashamed of myself and my ancestry. I have done nothing wrong and yet I am ashamed. I pray each night asking why I had to be born Japanese and I hate America for making me feel this way. I believe I now hate both sides of myself equally, Japanese and American.

"I am here now with little to do but think. I remember you asked me if I wanted my friends to say good-bye to me at the station when we left Orange Grove. I never answered you, because I didn't want to shame you. I didn't want my white friends coming to the station to say good-bye.

"You say, "Wait and be patient just a little while more." But wait for what? Wait for them to put us on boats to Japan. I say no. It is the only control I have anymore. It is the only control they gave me. And because I said no they will surely ship me to Japan, a country as foreign to me as it is to any of my white jailors.

"Because my face is different they imprisoned me and took away my family. All of my things were left behind. I wish now I had burned all of our belongings rather than let them fall into the hands of some stranger. America is not the home of the free unless you are white.

"I do not know where they will send me, but I will write to you. I hope you get this letter and they do not confiscate it, like so many things. I will write as soon as I know where I am going. Say hi to Mitchell and Grandma. I love you, Billy."

Sachi finished the letter with tears in her eyes, thinking of the little boy following his father into the fields, the older boy who had once so valued being an American, and the young man who now sat in prison for refusing allegiance to America. How much had transpired to cause such a man to give up on his own country?

411

CHAPTER FORTY

Sachi tried to spend most of her time at the school, working with the children in some way. The pay scale for professionals, doctors, and teachers was nineteen cents an hour and non-professionals like teacher's assistants and medical assistants earned sixteen cents an hour. Many of these people were use to making much more, but they did not work for the money. They worked to improve the lot of the people who were interned and they worked to escape the boredom and the insanity that would eventually come with it.

John continued in school at Sachi's insistence, but after school he was off with other boys running the blocks and going to the mess hall. Often Sachi would not see him until bedtime. Many of the mothers complained their children were out all day and didn't return until evening. They felt they were losing touch with their children and their families.

Takeo did not help to make John come home after school. He lay in bed many days staring up at the ceiling and the naked light bulb as if he were not really here, but had transported himself to another time or world. Yoshida moved much slower, but still catered to her son bringing him meals or tea without being asked. She continued to work the soil even here. With the seeds she'd brought and those she exchanged with others she grew a marvelous garden.

The soil was poor. When she first began, some neighbors and administrators scoffed at the idea of trying to grow a garden in the hard nutrient free soil that was exposed to coldness of 20 degrees or less in the winter and 120 degrees in the summer. But Yoshida

413

would not listen for gardening was a part of her very soul. If Yoshida had not been allowed to garden, she might have given up completely as Takeo seemed to have done. She started seeds in dirt dug up and fed with compost from the mess hall. She planted the seeds in egg cartons or cans from the garbage and as the seedlings grew strong she prepared the dirt by the back of their barracks with the same kind of natural nutrients and watered each day, placing mulch or compost from the mess hall, over the ground to protect it from heat or cold.

One late spring morning in 1944, one of the administrators was walking by while Yoshida and Sachi were working in the garden. Yoshida grew lettuce, beans, carrots, herbs, wild flowers, and tomatoes. She'd started strawberries and peas, whose seasons were shorter due to the extremes of heat and cold. Yoshida carefully watered the large green leaves. The green garden contrasted against the gray living quarters, the gray barbed wire, and the barrenness of the land everywhere else in the camp. It was a refreshing sight for anyone.

The administrator, a heavy set Caucasian man with too little hair on his head and too much mustache on his upper lip, stopped and looked at Yoshida's garden. He saw her on her hands and knees tending to her plants.

He said, "You have a beautiful garden, ma'am."

Yoshida nodded to him, acknowledging his presence, but did not speak. Sachi knew gardening had become difficult for her and it took all Yoshida's energy to raise these plants, the bending and stooping, fetching water to carry each day, worrying and planning. Maintaining her garden and her son took all her time and energy.

He continued to stand and look at it. He asked, "What are you growing here?"

It was a direct question and Yoshida and Sachi both knew Yoshida would have to rise and speak to the man. She started to rise and he rushed to her side to help her up. She did not accept his hand and climbed off her hands and knees without his assistance. She brushed off the dirt and proceeded to name items she grew.

"Amazing," he said. "To think you could perform such magic out here in the middle of nowhere. Nothing grows out here, but I've noticed that somehow you and several others have created quite an oasis."

Yoshida said, "It is not magic. It is a miracle and it takes a lot of hard work. As you said we are in the middle of nowhere."

Yoshida's meaning did not register with the man. He continued, as if he hadn't heard her, "You know this would be a perfect article for the camp newsletter. This is an achievement that I'm sure everyone would like to read about. I'll send one of the reporters over."

He spoke as if speaking to himself, and without asking Yoshida's opinion or permission, took his leave. An hour later a young girl of about 15 stood at the door to the Watanabe household wanting to take a picture of Yoshida by her garden.

The newsletter was put out once a month by students at the camp school and censored and authorized by the administration. As a result, nothing of any real news or opinion ended up in the newsletter. The girl took Yoshida's picture by the garden and asked several questions. She was soft-spoken with short dark hair and large, quick eyes that seemed to take in everything around her. The two sat for almost an hour talking together. They talked first about gardening and then about Yoshida's grandchildren and what she thought about as she gardened. This young girl had a manner about her, a quality that brought something out of Yoshida, and they chatted like friends until it was time for the girl to go. She promised she would return.

Several weeks later the article appeared. It was entitled "The Gardens of Poston" and Yoshida was quoted along with others stating that, though gardening was difficult here, they persevered and were rewarded for their patience. One woman was even quoted as saying she appreciated the administration's leniency because they didn't have to let them grow gardens at all and it was just like home.

Sachi read the article to Yoshida and Takeo one late afternoon when she had returned from working at the school. Yoshida listened and, when Sachi finished, she said, "Bah. That is not what I said. That girl. I thought she understood. No matter. It is done."

Takeo said, "Gardening. We are sitting in this place marveling over your little garden when we should be at home making a living by farming, growing. But they make a big deal over a garden. What does it mean, a little garden? Nothing."

Sachi did not respond to him. Instead she smiled, holding up the photo, and said, "The picture is good. We will have to save this and send a copy to Billy and Mitchell. Maybe we will send it to the Goodmans and Jack and Ikuko, too."

Yoshida shook her head, "We will not. I will not have that picture or those words floating around this country as if I were proud of them. I am not and it will not leave this room."

Sachi shrugged her shoulders and tucked the article in her small vinyl bible.

A little while later, as Yoshida and Sachi were preparing to go to dinner, there was a soft knock on the door. Sachi answered it and the young girl who had written the newsletter article stood with a folder in her hand. She looked up at Sachi and smiled slightly.

She said, "Good-afternoon. Is Mrs. Watanabe in? I'd like to speak to her for a moment, please."

Sachi offered her one of the two chairs they had and the girl sat down in one while Yoshida sat in the other. Takeo rose from the bed and sat on the edge smoothing his rumpled clothes and patting down his hair for the unexpected guest. Sachi sat on the edge of the other bed.

"Good afternoon," the girl started. "Did you see the article I worked on?"

Yoshida nodded, "Yes, I did."

"What did you think of it?"

"I did not think it was the kind of article you intended to write. It was informative enough, I suppose. It had some thought..." Yoshida said.

The girl interrupted, "But not much heart, huh?"

Yoshida nodded once as if to say yes.

417

The girl handed Yoshida a piece of typed paper. She said, "This is my article, but it would not pass the administration censors so I did two articles; one for them and one for you and myself. I thought perhaps you would like a copy of the article I would have written if I had been allowed to write as I felt."

Yoshida accepted the paper and the girl rose to her feet.

"I must go to dinner now. My family is expecting me."

The girl walked to the door and opened it. She turned and looked at Yoshida and said, "I always write two articles. The one they want and the one I will write when I leave this place, when things change and we can say and do what we want. Someday I will be allowed to be who I am."

She walked out and closed the door. Yoshida looked at the paper in her hand and handed it to Sachi who read:

Victory Gardens of Poston

While Americans on the outside raise their own vegetables in what have come to be called Victory Gardens to show support for the war effort, Poston residents are growing their own Victory Gardens.

Like the Japanese, these gardens have survived in the harshest of climates and the worst of conditions. They have not only survived, but they have flourished in this place where most people predicted nothing would ever grow.

Yoshida Watanabe (pictured above with her own Victory Garden) said, "When I first started on this, many people told me I couldn't get a good crop of crabgrass going in this climate. They told me not to waste my time as if I had so many other things to do here."

It has been difficult for residents to obtain fresh vegetables, particularly those used in traditional Japanese cooking, but some residents have overcome that and, instead of waiting on administration officials to get these things for them, they have started growing their own. But there are far more important reasons these gardens exist.

Mrs. Watanabe said, "I wanted to do it because they said I couldn't. I needed to do it because it is what I come from, who I am. I am a gardener, a farmer's wife. They can take me away from my home, but they cannot take who I am. We cannot let them take who we are. If we do, then we are nothing."

She said, "Some call it magic, but that means that somehow there is a trick, a slight of hand. This is not magical. Gardening is a miracle. If life and sustenance can spring from a small dead-looking seed in this barren place, then there is hope that life and happiness can spring from all of this, all that we have gone through, all that we will go through."

These Victory Gardens are more than a sign of hope for victory abroad. They are signs of hope for a victory at home as well. A victory against those who hate us for possessing the face of the enemy. They are also signs of hope for victory within ourselves.

Yoshida sighed and nodded. She said, "That's more like it."

To Sachi she said, "This one you can send to everyone."

Takeo said nothing, climbed into bed and rolled over, his back to them.

CHAPTER FORTY-ONE

1945

Nineteen forty-five was indeed the worst year in Sachi's life and it was one of the worst years for the country of Japan, too. On April 12, 1945 Franklin Delano Roosevelt died and the heart of the United States was heavy in mourning. For all his work, his sweat, and his energies, FDR did not live to see the end of WWII. V-E Day, the end of the war in Europe, happened less than a month after Roosevelt's death, May 7, 1945. The papers talked of the war ending and the Allies headed toward victory. Sachi's hope was high that Mitchell would return to them soon.

On May 9, 1945 Sachi, like most days, had worked at the school. It was a beautiful spring day and she felt herself feeling almost light-hearted as she walked slowly, admiring the blue of the sky. Even the constant wind seemed to have died down.

When Sachi entered her family's apartment, at first, everything seemed the same. Takeo lie on the bed as usual, and she assumed Yoshida was getting lunch. She heard a sudden deep moan from Takeo and walked over to the bed. She asked, "Takeo, what is the matter?"

He did not respond. She felt his forehead, but there was no fever.

She asked, "Have you eaten anything today?"

It was not unusual for Takeo to go all morning with nothing more than a cup of tea and a pipe full of tobacco to fortify him. Sachi assumed he was most likely weak from hunger. She stepped outside and asked one of the neighbors passing by to find Yoshida

421

and ask her to bring Takeo's lunch, but Yoshida was already coming down the walk, carrying lunch. Five minutes later Sachi was standing over Takeo, encouraging him to eat, as he continued to groan in pain.

She bent over to check him, to see where he might be hurt or ill and she noticed the paper in his fist. She tried to retrieve it, but, like a corpse where rigor mortis had set in, she could not pry it loose.

She grabbed his face between her hands and yelled at him, "Takeo what is wrong? Where are you hurting?"

Her loud voice seemed to break through for just a second long enough for him to throw the paper at her and turn on his side, still moaning. For a split second Sachi held her breath. She remembered her father, looking much the same, throwing a piece of paper at her that informed them of her mother's death. She brushed that thought quickly from her mind and concentrated on trying to get Takeo to roll over so she could see what was wrong with him.

Out of the corner of her eye she saw Yoshida retrieve the paper and look at it, but Sachi's attention was focused on Takeo and she was thinking they needed to get the doctor. Her back was to Yoshida. but she heard the trembling in her mother-in-law's voice as she asked, "Sachi. What is this?"

Sachi turned, aggravated at Yoshida for asking questions while Takeo was obviously not well.

"What is what?" asked Sachi.

422

Yoshida held it out, the paper fluttering in her shaky hand. Yoshida said, "It is a telegram and it has Mitchell's name on it…"

Sachi snatched it quickly and read, "We regret to inform you your son, Mitchell Dyuke Watanabe, was killed…"

Sachi could read no further. The piece of paper slipped from her hands and floated to the ground. Sachi fell to her knees, which were unable to support her anymore. Tears burst from her eyes and she rocked herself back and forth screaming, "Oh no. Not my Mitchell. Not my Mitchell."

Yoshida sank down into one of the chairs and began sobbing, without sound, tears flooding her face, her shirt.

Sachi had experienced the grief and sorrow of losing her mother, her home, her friends, and even lost love, but this pain was far beyond anything she had ever felt before. She could not breathe. Her senses seemed to shut down like a closed factory. She did not feel or smell or hear or see. Nothing existed but the intense pain of this loss. It was the intense labor of her child leaving this world and it was much more intense and painful than when he entered it.

The three of them sat, rolled into their own balls of pain, for a long time. Moaning and wailing was heard by the neighbors outside and there was no privacy for their grief, but at that moment they didn't care. At that moment nothing mattered until the door flew open and John ran in.

"What happened?" he asked, dropping to his knees by his mother. "One of the neighbors came and got me. She told me something terrible must have happened and I needed to get home. Are you sick?"

He looked around the room and noticed Yoshida and Takeo also in the midst of their grief and he knew, somehow.

He sat back and crossed his legs in front of him. Sachi could barely focus on him. Her tears and her pain blurred John's small image and she felt like she could barely make him out. She reached out to him trying to find the words to tell him his brother was dead, but he found them for her.

John asked, "Is it Mitchell? Is he…Is he dead?"

Sachi cried even more hearing the words spoken for the first time and from the mouth of her youngest son. She tried to say something, but could only nod her head. John saw the telegram on the floor and picked it up.

He learned his brother had died in battle at Mount Musatello, Italy on April 21, 1945, 18 days earlier. The notice also said he was to be awarded the Military Order of the Purple Heart for bravery in battle.

Several months later two military officials, a legless white man and the graying camp chaplain, who had originally delivered the telegram to Takeo, arrived at the Watanabe quarters early in the morning before school. The Watanabes were waiting for their guests. The room was swept clean, as clean as possible after the daily dust storms, and they wore their Sunday clothes.

The visitors were there to give Takeo the Purple Heart award posthumously to Mitchell for bravery above and beyond the call of duty. They had notified the Watanabes that the white legless man, Private A.W. Sneed, was the last man to see Mitchell alive. He was in a wheel chair and the two military officials lifted the chair up the five steps to the Watanabe home and in the door. Sachi had borrowed several chairs from friends so there were enough for everyone, but the quarters were tight and there was just enough room.

The two military officials and the chaplain sat as Takeo indicated they should. John and Yoshida sat on the edge of one of the beds and Sachi positioned herself next to the legless man, leaning forward to hear his every word.

He spoke with a southern accent and said, "It was Mount Musatello. We'd been fightin' hard there all around for a few days. A bunch of units got pinned in, trapped. I took a couple in the back. I went down losing lots of blood and I couldn't feel my legs. I figured this was it. I must have blacked out. I don't know for how long. When I came to, things had quieted down some. I heard machine gun fire to the left, but it seemed far away. At least, I thought it was. I saw someone coming toward me.

"You have to understand. I was dyin'. I couldn't move. I had never seen a Japanese person. I mean, I'm from Arkansas. We don't have any Japanese people. I'd seen pictures of Japanese mainly in the paper having to do with the war. I guess I hated the Japanese as much as anyone and I didn't much distinguish between people, just races. I guess I should say between the white race and then all the others. Anyway, the person coming toward me was your son. He had seen me go down earlier and he'd come back for me even though his own unit had been trapped and was escaping. He came back to get me."

Takeo interrupted, "And you shot him?"

The man looked in horror and said quickly, "Oh no, sir. No. I didn't shoot him."

Then the man stopped, hung his head and stared at the ground, "But I guess I might as well have. I saw his face and I was scared. My thinkin' was fuzzy. I was dyin' and scared and I saw this Japanese face. I thought, 'Here's the enemy.' I screamed with all I had left in me.

"Your son, he put his finger over his lips to tell me to quiet down and he pointed to his uniform. I realized he was an American and I'd heard about that group of Japanese boys that had enlisted and I did admire them for it. I felt bad for screamin', but it was too late. My scream brought your son to the attention of a Kraut nearby with a machine gun. I guess that was the firing I'd heard. He fired his machine gun and your son just fell down on top of me, the man he was trying to save."

The man was in tears as he recounted what happened, but his voice remained strong and clear. He continued, "Your son looked at me, straight into my eyes, and his last words were, 'I'm not the enemy. I'm an American." I told him, 'I know. I'm so sorry." I felt the life leave his body and he died with my arms around him. In the arms of a white man who moments before didn't particularly have any use for the Japanese.

"I grabbed your son's gun and fired to my left, emptied the whole round. I blacked out again and a little while later another unit picked me up. They'd heard the firing. Even though I was about dead I told one of em' to look. They told me the Kraut was dead. I'd got him. I closed my eyes ready to go. Next thing I know I was in an I-talian hospital hooked up to all kinds of tubes. Everybody kept askin' how I was doin' and how I was feelin'. All I could think was I'd left my legs and the man who'd come back to save me out in those damn woods.

"But there are two reasons I had to come here today. One is to tell you how sorry I am that I cost your boy his life when he was trying to save mine."

The man choked back tears and continued, his voice getting shakier, "The other is to tell you your boy's life was not in vain. I have changed my thinking. I will try and have a little of the courage your son had. He was....remarkable. I will remember him every day."

Sachi sighed, "And me."

The man said, "I cannot ask for your forgiveness, but I wanted you to know how sorry I am and how brave he was. "

Takeo stood, somber, unmoved, and said, "I have heard enough. Out. I don't need you to tell me how brave my son was. Don't sit there crying for him and tell me he did not die in vain. Go away and take your empty awards with you. We do not want them. They mean nothing."

"Mr. Watanabe…" one of the military men started.

"Enough," Takeo said and walked to the wall turning his back on the men who had come. The legless white man turned his wheelchair to leave and the military officials rose

427

to open the door and carry his chair down the steps. Tears still fell from his eyes and the chaplain patted him on the shoulder.

Sachi rose as well, interrupting their exit, and said, "*I* want the Purple Heart."

Takeo turned to her, his face contorted in anger, but said nothing. Yoshida looked at the ground. Everyone turned toward Sachi and one of the officials handed a velvet box to Sachi. She opened it and lifted it out of the box. Suspended by purple and white ribbons was the Purple Heart framed in gold plating with a bust of George Washington against the deep purple background. Above Washington was the Washington coat of arms - stars and stripes. It was heavy and shined in the light coming through their only window.

Sachi cried, but her voice did not falter. She stepped close to the man in the wheel chair and looked into his blue eyes. It was the last sight her son saw on this earth. They were a light blue, the color of the sky as the sun rises in the morning, the color of heaven and new beginnings and peace. A color she'd seen before.

She said, "Some of my son's last words in my presence were about this medal. He said something to the effect, 'They don't want me in America. Too bad. And if I die on the battlefield in some foreign country, I'll be a war hero. They'll send a purple heart to my mother. The same Purple Heart American patriots through the years have received. That will stick in the throat of every prejudice son-of-a-bitch out there. That will be the statement I leave to this world."

Sachi looked at Takeo who stood, stubborn and angry, refusing to look at her now. Yoshida continued to look at the ground, but John looked up at his mother, listening to her words, to Mitchell's words.

Sachi turned back to the legless man and said, "You did not pull the trigger killing my son. You did not start this war. This is not a matter of blame or forgiveness and you look like you have paid a very high price of your own. I will treasure and keep my son's statement to the world. I will teach it to my youngest boy. I will pass it on and I hope you will pass it on."

With that she walked to the door and held it open. The foursome left and Sachi shut the door. She placed the Purple Heart on top of her Bible and no one spoke of it again.

Since the war in the Pacific was not yet over, they would not be going home. For many months Sachi did not care anymore. In many respects, the death of her mother and her son were the same. She had been informed of their deaths by words on a page. There was nothing, but paper and ink to verify their loss, not even a body or a tombstone. She often thought during those difficult days that she would have let herself die if it had not been for John. John was the only reason to go on living anymore. The thought of him drove her from her bed each morning and to her work when she would have much preferred to stay there. For the first time she knew how Takeo felt. The overwhelming sadness could paralyze, it could numb a person to the point where they could not move or think, but barely breathe.

She whispered to herself each morning as if in prayer the traditional Japanese words, "*Kodomo no tami ni*" (for the welfare of the children) and with the little energy left in her, she rose and went about her day. It became her mantra and each time she thought she couldn't go on she whispered those words to herself, the words that so many Japanese families survived by, "*Kodomo no tame ni.*"

CHAPTER FORTY-TWO

The Office of the Secretary of War, Henry Stimson, Washington, D.C. – July 30, 1945

Assistant Secretary of War, McCloy sat perched on the edge of his chair, outlining for his superior the day's work. President Truman was in Potsdam, a suburb of Berlin in Germany. He was there with the leaders of the Allied nations. Stimson was one of a small group who knew the uranium-based bomb, "the immense project", was complete. Truman had received confirmation of the successful test bomb and Stimson was only half listening to McCloy as he rambled on with the numbers of projections, equipment, and costs as he did each day.

Several times toward the end of July, Truman had sent communiqués to Japan demanding unconditional surrender. Japan refused and vowed to keep fighting, even though they were losing and they knew it. Japan was afraid their revered emperor would be hurt or killed if they surrendered and they were ignorant of the United States' newly-acquired abilities.

There was a knock on the door and his secretary handed him a cable marked 'Eyes only'. It was from the President and it simply stated "release" (of the atomic bomb) was to be scheduled, but not before August 2 when the President would return from the Potsdam Conference.

On August 6th the shocking news came to the Watanabe family and to the world. A bomb of massive destructive power never seen before in history was dropped on

Hiroshima. On August 8th another bomb was dropped on Nagasaki.

Stimson was later to read Winston Churchill's quote that the world needed this utter

destruction to bring the war to an end, to give peace to the world "…by a manifestation of

overwhelming power at the cost of a few explosions seemed, after all our toils and perils,

a miracle of deliverance."

CHAPTER FORTY-THREE

Several weeks after Sachi heard about the bombing of Hiroshima and Nagasaki, Japan, the Watanabe family received notice they were going home. Few of the families were sure what they would find in the outside world beyond the barbed-wired barracks that had been their life for almost four years. Ikuko had written a week earlier and the letter was filled with devastation.

Charlie Shimmer had not kept his promise. She and her new husband had returned to the house of Ikuko and Edo to find strangers living in it. Ikuko discovered Charlie had taken what he wanted from the home and sold the rest for what he could get. The landowner leased to another family leaving Ikuko without the home she had known for over two decades. Charlie still lived on his place and Ikuko had not yet seen him. She said she did not know what to say to him if she did see him, particularly since there were so many people that felt the same way he did, hoping, assuming the Japanese would simply not return. Many of them did not return. Some had chosen to return to Japan. Some had died in internment. Some moved back east or to the interior believing they had nothing to which they could return.

There was no mention of their home or Jack in Ikuko's letter. Writing to inquire would be a waste of time since they would be home before a letter from Ikuko got back to them. She sounded more distressed in the letter than even at the time of Edo's death. Sachi placed this last letter in the rubber-banded stack of letters she saved, including

433

Jack's letter to her. She kept them with her Bible containing Yoshida's garden article and Mitchell's Purple Heart.

Sachi had heard nothing from Jack for some time. She couldn't help but daydream occasionally about their reunion. She wondered if he was changed and realized she was anxious to see him, almost as anxious as she was to see Ikuko again. But she was nervous too. Would she be able to resist the temptation now after so much had happened? Honor had kept her from it before, but now she felt so empty much of the time and simply wanted to feel full again. She dreamt often of Jack and knew it was as Yoshida had warned, an abunai kankei, a dangerous relationship.

Finally the notice arrived they would be leaving in two weeks. They could take their possessions and were given a "gift" of $25 and a one-way train ticket to the destination of their choosing.

Sachi thought it was just in time. Yoshida seemed to grow weaker with each passing day. Her passion for her garden was diminishing and Takeo was often left to retrieve his own meals or get things for himself. When the notice arrived, Takeo was smoking his pipe walking back and forth just outside. Yoshida and Sachi were cleaning their rooms while John did his homework on the old wooden table in the corner.

John was having difficulty concentrating. He said, "I can't believe it. We are going back home soon. I wonder if Dusty is still hanging around the place."

Sachi said, "John, I have told you not to have your hopes up about that old dog. I'm sure the Goodmans did the best they could, but these years have been hard. Maybe when we get home and settle in we can get a new puppy for you. Maybe. But you will get nothing if you don't do your school work."

Yoshida said, as if to herself, "At least in here we are protected."

John looked at her and said, "Protected from what, Grandmother?"

Yoshida shook her head. "You wouldn't understand."

John said, "Are you talking about prejudice? I understand prejudice."

Yoshida turned to look at the boy and said, sympathetically, "Yes. I guess you do.

John tried to concentrate for several more minutes then looked up and asked, "Grandma, aren't you excited? You'll get to do your big garden again and..."

Yoshida interrupted, "Yes. Yes. Excited. Excited to be out of this dust hole. Now, John, if you're not concentrating, be of some use to your grandmother. Go over to the mess hall and pick up some of the tea I like. They should be open."

Then she raised her voice so Takeo could hear and said, "Take your father with you. It'll do him some good to walk farther than his front step. About time he gets use to it."

John jumped up and before Sachi could object he was out the door dragging his reluctant father behind him with smoke from Takeo's pipe trailing in their wake.

Yoshida sat down, appearing tired from the small amount of work she had done, and breathed deeply, exhaling slowly. "Sachi, I don't know if I'll make it."

Sachi was still brushing the hated dust off the table. She said, "Just rest. I'll do the sweeping."

Yoshida looked toward the ground and said, "I don't mean sweeping. I mean I don't know if I'll make it back to Orange Grove."

Sachi went to Yoshida and felt her face, checking for fever. Yoshida did not brush her daughter-in-law away as she normally would and this concerned Sachi as much as anything.

Sachi said, "You do not feel sick. You are just tired."

Yoshida shook her head slowly and said, "No. I am afraid and it is the fear that will take me before the train to Orange Grove comes for us. I feel it in my bones."

Sachi knelt beside her, brushed a strand of graying hair from her eyes, and said, "What are you afraid of? What have you ever been afraid of?"

Yoshida smiled slightly and, in almost a whisper, said, "Everything. You know, strong women like you and me. Isn't it true? We are afraid of everything, but most of all of showing our fear."

The gray strand escaped again and Sachi stood over Yoshida to refasten her hair. She pulled all the hair from Yoshida's face and worked it into the clip. As she did so, she said, "It is almost over now. We don't have to be afraid anymore."

Yoshida said, "I am more afraid now, I think, than when we were sent here. Maybe it is age, but it is also knowing no one will welcome us back with open arms. We will struggle more going back home than we ever have. I know it."

"Bah," Sachi said, using Yoshida's word. "We are going home."

Yoshida spoke, bitterness creeping into her words, "What makes you think we still have a home? Ikuko lost hers. That Shimmer character promised to take care of it and when she got back it was overrun with bums. What makes you think Jack hasn't done the same to us? Or that he didn't get greedy and buy it himself? How do we know? We have heard nothing from him. How are we to survive in a community that doesn't want us back? We don't know what we'll find when we return home, if we even have a home to return to. Life is full of hazards more treacherous than barbed wire around our camp."

Sachi set her brow in a determined look and said, "One thing I have learned through all of this is there is nothing more treacherous than barbed wire."

Yoshida sighed, "I'm not sure I can cope with any of it anymore. I am old and set in my ways. This is not how my life was supposed to end."

"And this is not how your life will end. Jack Albright is not Charlie Shimmer. He is honorable. Jack made a promise and he will keep it. I trust him."

Yoshida shook her head. "You can't trust anyone. Nothing is as it was. Our family is gone. Takeo is in no position to work the farm like he once did. He barely gets his own meals. You think I don't see that my son has given up? Mitchell is dead and Billy is gone. Takeo is empty without his sons. He has no reason to go on now."

Sachi grew angry. She did not want to think of the possibilities that something else could go horribly wrong in their lives.

Sachi spoke firmly, willing her words to make it so, and said, "He has a reason. If not for me, than for his son. He has a son to care for and dream for. Takeo may think he can roll up into a ball on this bed and give up. I let him do it in this place. I don't understand it and I don't say anything, but I tell you this. Takeo will get out of his bed at home every day and he will go into the fields where his father worked himself to death and where our children worked with him and he will grow a living for us out of that dirt whether he wants to or not. John deserves that at the very least.

"And while I'm telling you what everyone is going to do, let me tell you this. You will not die before we get back to Orange Grove. You will keep yourself alive until we get home and you can work in your garden and cook for your friends and go to your temple and sit in your rocker on your porch."

Yoshida sighed and said, "I don't think I have the energy anymore and I am…frightened."

Sachi grabbed Yoshida's hand and, with tears in her eyes, she lifted Yoshida's chin to meet her gaze. Yoshida's eyes were dark and pained. The stubbornness and determination Sachi had always seen there was gone replaced with exhaustion, surrender, and defeat. She recognized it as she had seen it in Takeo's eyes and, like a deadly virus, she was afraid of Yoshida catching it. And fearful she might succumb as well.

Sachi whispered, "Listen to me, old woman. I will not place you in this unforgiving ground. I will not leave you here. Takeo has given up. Two of our boys are gone. John needs you. I don't think I could handle things if you give up too. We have worked too hard to raise John and to keep our place. You have to help me."

She buried her head into the old woman's bosom and said, "Don't leave me now, Mother. I need you."

CHAPTER FORTY-FOUR

Home – September 24, 1945

The bus ride into Orange Grove seemed so familiar even after the passing of years. In some ways it felt as if they had only gone on a short trip, away for days rather than years. The Kitashima's fruit stand was in a dilapidated state and was falling down. Mr. Grimshaw's market looked as prosperous as ever. They passed the bank and Sachi peeked into the bank window trying to catch a glimpse of the teller who had been so cruel to her years ago. She did not see the teller, but the bank had expanded and there were more teller windows. She knew it would be a while before she could walk into that bank again and open an account.

The diner looked like it hadn't changed and the man in the white stained apron still stood behind the counter as if he hadn't moved since the day she had been in there with Jack to get coffee. The no service to Japs sign was gone, but then it probably had not been needed. Sachi wondered if it would go back up now that a few of the Japanese had returned to reclaim their homes. It didn't matter because she knew she would never eat in that diner, even if it accepted Japanese people.

The Watanabe family departed from the bus with their two suitcases apiece and without their two oldest sons. The bus stop appeared almost deserted and for a quick second Sachi wondered if Ikuko had forgotten her. A horn honked and this thought

441

vanished from Sachi's mind as she saw Bob Goodman, their old neighbor, driving their old car. It was the one Yoshida had sold them and Sachi couldn't help but smile. It stopped in front of them.

The back door flew open and Ikuko sprang out, squealing loudly and catching Sachi in her arms, hugging her tight. Sachi noticed a strange man in the back seat of Bob's car. He was staring at them with a wide grin on his face. Then Ikuko stepped back, blocking her view. Sachi and Ikuko looked at each other. Ikuko, like Sachi, had grayed some in the last few years. Ikuko looked older, but she still had the same smile that lit up her entire face. She looked so much happier than when Sachi had seen her last.

Sachi couldn't wait. She asked, "My house. Is it..?"

Ikuko said, "It's fine, of course. Didn't Jack write to you?"

Sachi said, "No. I never heard anything. I wondered… I wondered how he was doing," she finished.

John interrupted, unable to wait any longer.

He asked, "And Dusty. Is Dusty…?"

Bob interrupted and said, "Dusty is fine. He didn't want to leave for a few days after you left, but Mrs. Goodman finally persuaded him to come stay with us. Well, she had to bribe him with some of her good brisket, but he came. He's waiting for you at home."

John cheered and Sachi felt like cheering herself. Bob put their bags in the car. As they started to get into the vehicle a car drove past and a man in the passenger's seat yelled out to Bob, "You damn Jap lover."

442

Bob ignored the words as if they had not even been said and got into the car.

Yoshida said, "It seems things have not changed at all these past few years."

Bob drove home while Ikuko introduced them to her new husband, Yuji Yamomoto. She was now Ikuko Yamomoto. He was an older man as Edo had been, but much thinner and smaller with hair more gray than black. His face was etched with the lines of worry and care. They sat close to one another like newlyweds and light shown from his dark eyes every time he looked at Ikuko, which was almost constantly.

Bob drove them to their house and Sachi began to cry. It was so well cared for. Yoshida's garden area lay fallow, but the rest of the place looked much the same as when they'd left. The fields looked fine and harvest was over. The Goodmans had prepared dinner and made beds. Sleeping in her house felt like the first time she'd slept with Takeo after he'd been away for so long. It was just as she remembered and yet, strangely unfamiliar. They needed time to become reacquainted.

The next day Yoshida, Sachi and Ikuko scrubbed the house clean and made a list of the things they would need to purchase to restock the household. The Goodmans had been kind enough to give them enough food for the week, but there was the matter of beds, new linens, cleaning supplies, farming implements and tools, tables and chairs. They found they needed to replace almost everything they had sold more than three years ago.

By the end of the first day Yoshida was exhausted and she went to bed very early. Ikuko and her husband would continue to stay with them, as they had nowhere else to go.

Sachi was happy to have her best friend back, but her husband was quite talkative and Takeo was not one for conversation even on his best days.

The weeks passed without a word from Jack. They cleaned and organized the house. Sachi sent a letter to Billy who was still in Tule Lake letting him know they were back home, but she heard no response. Takeo had taken to, at least, walking around his old fields and would do so all day. John went out with him since there were four weeks before school started back again.

Takeo had refused to even go outside the first few days they were home no matter how much coaxing or pleading or yelling Sachi did. Finally on the fourth day John took his father's hand and said, "Father, show me what you and grandpa did together."

Takeo silently put on his old worn boots, which lay waiting by the back door and walked John around their fields. He spoke little that first day, but then each day following John would walk his father outside and Takeo slowly began to get a feel for his world again. He started planning and talking to John about how they would improve what Jack had done. A few weeks after they returned home late one afternoon there was a knock at the front door. Sachi opened the door and Jack stood on the front porch. In his arms he held a large white bag.

The sight of him after all this time took her breath away and she was glad Yoshida was in her garden. Without thinking, Sachi wrapped her arms around Jack, bag and all, and hugged him tight.

She whispered, "Thank you Jack. Thank you."

Jack smiled, lighting up his face, "Sachi, you look…just beautiful. But what are you thanking me for? I haven't given it to you yet."

Jack looked exactly the same as the day she had left him at the train station. It was as if the last three years had never happened except that Sachi knew she had changed, but there was something. Something was different. A shadow across his face, something she couldn't make out.

Sachi laughed, "What am I thanking you for? I'm thanking you for my home, a place to come home to after so many miserable years. Without this home I would have lost what is left of my family. You saved my life. "

Jack handed her the bag and said, "Well, add this to the list."

"What is it?" Sachi asked as she accepted the bag.

Ikuko and Yuji came into the living room from the kitchen and said hello to Jack. Sachi unwrapped the bag and pulled out her wedding kimono. It was in perfect condition.

Sachi was wide eyed, "Where did you get this?" How did you…?"

Jack said, "About two months ago a young woman stopped by when I was here working on something. She asked if I knew the beautiful Japanese woman who used to live here and if I knew when she would return. When I told her I knew you she said she was moving back east and would probably never be back this way again. She asked me to give this to you. Said she was just holding it for you until you got home. I figured she was a friend of yours."

Sachi's eyes were wet with tears and she whispered, "I guess she was."

Ikuko went to the kitchen with Yuji to fix tea.

Sachi said, "I'm sorry we cannot offer you a more comfortable place to sit. We only have the floor for now and a few pillows."

Jack plopped down on the floor and said, "Are you kidding? I think people should sit on the floor all the time. You can stretch out. You don't have to worry about spilling things."

Sachi smiled. It was like Jack always to put on a bright face even regarding something like having no furniture. At least, she had the floor. It was more than many people had.

Jack said, "I was sorry to hear about the boys, especially Mitchell."

Sachi rose and went into the bedroom. When she returned she was holding Mitchell's Purple Heart. She handed it to Jack to examine.

"It is for bravery," Sachi said proudly. "He saved a man's life."

Jack admired the medal and handed it back to her. He said, ""I wish there were medals for you, for all you have been through."

"This is enough," Sachi said, changing the subject.

She had forgotten how wonderful it felt to have the attention of a man. Takeo paid her little mind and he seemed so preoccupied with his own thoughts and grief. Jack was so alive and filled with energy. He had not suffered the same kinds of hardships as Takeo.

"So why did you not write to us? I wondered, I mean, *we* wondered, if you were alright."

Jack smiled at Sachi, seeming to understand her meaning.

He said, "Well, between this place and my work I barely had time to do anything other than eat and sleep. I came out here on weekends and in the evenings and holidays to work and to try and keep things up. I'm afraid the barn needs some work, but the house is in pretty good shape."

Sachi said, "It will be so good to see you again. You can come for dinner and we can talk about books. Oh, books. I have not read anything good in such a long time. We have...oh, I have missed you, Jack," Sachi lowered her voice. "Sometimes, during the hardest times, I thought about you and, you know, everything and it helped get me through to the next day. I ..."

Jack interrupted, "Sachi, come with me out on to the porch."

Sachi stood and walked with him outside. The clouds rolled by in waves, not unlike the ocean waves she remembered. It had been so long since she'd seen the ocean as she thought of the world in which she'd been raised. As she stood there looking at the clouds rolling in, Sachi was reminded of looking out the windows of the little house on the cliff with her mother, a lifetime ago. The air was warm and heavy, but Sachi took no notice. It was nothing compared to Poston and she was now with Jack back in her home, just like it use to be.

She stood near him on the porch and looked up into his face. This close she could see a few fine lines starting to appear, but his tan was rich and his bright blue eyes still shone like beacons. Sachi sighed. Amazingly everything was starting to feel familiar. Maybe some things could go back to the way they were. Maybe everything hadn't changed.

She said, "Jack, I can't tell you how much you have meant to me, especially the last few years. I know we are more than friends and I know your feelings for me. I think… "

"Sachi," Jack interrupted. "I'm married."

She felt her mind and body freeze and all she could do was repeat the word. "Married?"

"Yes. Her name is Abigail. I met her in town. She moved here with her sister and brother-in-law. I thought…well, I knew waiting for something that was never going to happen was a foolish way to continue to spend my life."

She had thought Jack might marry during the years she had been gone, but it was a thought she always buried quickly. Her heart had held out hope that somehow he would always be hers. She knew it was selfish and Jack deserved a life shared with someone, a life filled with love. She had spent countless hours dreaming of him and she was not ready for that dream to end, but she knew she had no choice. She had regained her home and lost a dream, a secret part of herself.

Sachi moved away from Jack and looked out into the distance. There was no barbed wire. Nothing holding them there, but the roots they'd put down years ago.

She felt a surge of jealousy she couldn't control. It was strong and unexpected. She snapped, "I thought you said you barely had time to eat and sleep."

Jack looked at Sachi, the woman he'd spent his life loving, the woman he still loved. He looked at her helpless, as if imploring her to understand somehow. "Sachi," he whispered her name.

She knew she could never have married Takeo if she had met Jack first and she wondered how he could marry another woman after telling her he loved her. She wondered how their relationship would work and how they would be able to have dinner and visit now that everything was exposed, vulnerable and open. Takeo had not seen it, but Yoshida had and certainly Jack's new wife would as well. Sachi wondered if she would be able to hide her feelings now as well as she did years ago. But Jack's words answered her doubts.

"I don't know how to say this, Sachi. But...we can't see each other anymore."

Sachi asked, "Because you're married?"

Jack looked down and Sachi knew. The shadow she had seen over Jack was sadness.

She looked up and spoke the words slowly, testing them out, "She won't let you. Is that it, Jack?"

He said nothing and Sachi knew.

"She doesn't approve. Did you tell her about....about me?"

"No," he said still looking down and shaking his head. "Just that we were friends and, of course, she knows the time I have spent over here."

Sachi sighed and said, "Well, she couldn't have been happy about that. A young newly-wed wife would not want her husband spending his free time on someone else's home."

Jack shook his head, "She just didn't understand..." He trailed off unable to explain any further.

Sachi thought for a moment and then said, "If she is not jealous, then is it because we are Japanese? She doesn't want you associating with Japanese people."

Jack looked up at Sachi and tried to explain. He said, "She thinks it will hurt us in the community. She thinks it is a dangerous time to be friends with...." He couldn't finish.

"*This* is a dangerous time?" Sachi asked. "She is obviously new to California."

Jack faltered, "She has been here less than two years. She is frightened. There is still so much prejudice out there, Sachi."

"Don't tell me about prejudice. I live it, Jack. I know. I just didn't expect it from you. I thought we would go back to the way things were. I thought you would be a part of my life. I know it is selfish. Somehow I thought maybe you were the answer to it all for me. I thought we...Oh, I don't know what I thought. And now...Yoshida is right. You can't trust anyone."

Sachi's words hung in the air like wet laundry, heavy on a clothesline, under things exposed for all to see.

Jack said, "Sachi, don't say that to me. You have been able to trust me. But what can I do? I did not know she felt this way when we married."

"Maybe you should have gotten to know her a bit better. Maybe…"

"She's going to have a baby soon."

Ikuko opened the door behind them and said, "A baby? Who is having a baby?"

Jack and Sachi turned to look at her and she knew she had interrupted.

Ikuko said hurriedly, "Uh, the tea is ready when you are. I'll meet you in the kitchen."

She closed the door behind her and quickly left.

Jack stood, tears gathering in his eyes, and said, "Sachi, I don't know what to do."

His eyes met hers and he placed his hands on her arms, holding her tightly, drawing her closer to him. He said, "My feelings for you have not changed, even now, but we were not meant to be. I waited and waited. I could have waited forever if I thought there as a chance. But I know you. That kiss we shared was the closest I would ever get to touching you. I knew there was no chance and I was stupid for thinking there was. If you were the kind of woman who would cheat on your husband, I wouldn't love you like this. So I finally decided I had to make a life for myself."

It took all her inner strength, but Sachi pulled away. He was trapped and she had helped trap him. He had refused so many women in the past because of his love for her. And she had been glad. Deep down she had wanted to keep him for herself. She realized Jack was like America to her, large and strong and overwhelming, filled with disappointments and temptations, but good and true. Sachi laid her hand on his, looking deeply into his eyes. It was the same cool blue that had stayed with her in her dreams.

"I am being selfish. I have no claim to you and owe you so much. I will miss your friendship. I will miss…you."

She removed her hand from his and stepped away from him. She continued, "Your wife is only looking out for your best interests and she is right, you know. You and I, we should not see each other. The temptation is strong. It always has been I suppose, but I was stronger then, before all of this. I fought the temptation. I don't know if I could now. I am much weaker than when you last saw me at the train station."

Jack turned and brushed a strand of hair from her face. He said, "No. You are much stronger now, Sachi. I see it in you. You have survived much."

He kissed her forehead softly and she smelled the tobacco and earth and the feelings flooded her, but there was a new smell to him, the hint of a woman's perfume, his wife.

She stared up at him, searching his deep blue eyes, wanting to remember that color for the rest of her days. She said, "Yes. We all have. I came home and I thought…I don't know what I thought, but it doesn't matter anymore. You will have a beautiful baby and a wonderful life."

Jack bent toward her and whispered, "Not as wonderful as it might have been. If only…"

Sachi smiled slightly and gently placed the tips of fingers on his lips. She shook her head. He nodded and with tears in his eyes, he turned around, got into his truck, and drove away on a cloud of dust.

Ikuko opened the door and stood next to her friend on the porch. They stood together several minutes without speaking.

Ikuko linked arms with her friend and said, "The tea is ready. You could use some."

Sachi did not move and said, "Ikuko, we are back home and all I can do is wonder why? I thought I was coming home to…well, to something I've discovered no longer exists."

Ikuko sighed deeply and said, "Sachi, I don't have an answer. I wish I could tell you…"

John interrupted her as he came running around the house yelling, "Mother. Mother. I picked these for you."

He had a handful of lavender. His hair flapped up and down on the top of his head like the wings of a black bird in flight. Any moment it looked as if he might take off and soar up into the sky. Dusty trailed after him. His smile was brighter than she had seen it in a long time and he ran up on the porch, breathing hard from excitement and exercise, and handed the flowers to his mother. Sachi hugged her son and thanked him as he quickly ran off to find more for Aunt Cukie.

Ikuko smiled and said, "There's your answer. What you came home for does exist. *Kodomo No Tame Ni.*"

Sachi smiled and repeated, "Yes. *Kodomo No Tame Ni.*"

The two friends entered their home to sit and drink tea.

Epilogue

January, 2002 – Sacramento, California

Jamal was wide awake before he even opened his eyes. The rain pouring down outside threatened to darken the entire day, but Jamal wasn't thinking about the dark or the rain. The regional science competition began that morning and Jamal was presenting his project, the one he'd worked on for over six months, and the one that could take him to the national competition in Washington, D.C. in the summer.

Jamal was a gifted student in math and science. Other subjects were of little interest to him, though his parents and teachers all encouraged him to apply the same enthusiasm and dedication to everything else. English was a difficult language. Often one word changed the entire meaning of a sentence and nuances made the conversation tricky. The language of mathematics and science was precise and changed only when the need or ability arose to be even more precise. Numbers and theories were an easier medium in which to communicate. Words were too slippery.

Both of his parents had already left for work, and the smell of espresso and steamed milk filled his nostrils as he entered the kitchen. He watched Sponge Bob Square Pants because the only other things on were the morning news programs and Dora the Explora. He had enough of the news in the evenings when his parents were home. They were glued to it during dinner. All the talk seemed to be of war and Muslims were mentioned prominently, crimes committed by Muslims and crimes against Muslims. People spoke in fearful tones about ideologies and jihads and ancient tribal wars. Jamal knew little of those things, but he knew it was a dangerous time.

His father, though fearful, continued to wear his turban despite incidents of being pushed and threatened during the last few months. When he asked his father how he could stand there and allow people to push him or yell ugly things at him without fighting back, it seemed his father often had no words for him. Sometimes he tried to explain to Jamal that this was not just one individual acting out against him as a man, but the whole of society and religion acting out against that which frightened them most. He said, "I am not fighting with just one man."

Once he tried to explain it to Jamal by quoting Kahlil Gibran speaking to a crowd from the book *The Prophet*, "As a single leaf turns not yellow but with the silent knowledge of the whole tree, so the wrong-doer cannot do wrong without the hidden will of you all."

But Jamal, lanky and tall at 15, did not understand what a yellow leaf had to do with fighting back against someone who had pushed you, regardless of the reason. He heard things at school occasionally, but Jamal had learned to avoid most confrontation, and connection, with people by putting his energy into those mediums that didn't reflect back or talk back: his studies and books.

He ate a bowl of Cheerios and dressed for school. Brushing his teeth Jamal was not unhappy with the reflection that greeted him. His teeth were white and naturally straight, never having needed braces. His parents were proud of that fact as if their good parenting, and not simple genetics, had influenced his teeth in their growth. His mocha-colored face was beginning to show signs of approaching manhood in the stubble Jamal felt was just under the surface. It was a day he looked forward to with anticipation, the day he would first shave. The only physical characteristic that provided him with some embarrassment were the long, dark lashes fanning his black eyes. Often women commented on his lashes expressing how much they wished they had been so blessed.

After brushing his teeth, Jamal went into his room and double checked the contents of the cardboard box sitting on his desk. There was really no need as he had examined it four times the previous evening, but nerves and thoroughness drove him to the box for a final inspection. His project was electronic intelligence, its history and future applications. Among other points, he reproduced transistor switches and electronic circuits and demonstrated how society moved from the simplest circuits to microprocessors containing millions of transistors. While most people found computers and electronics far too complicated, Jamal loved it all for its basic simplicity, and tried to communicate that through his project.

He put on his jacket, grabbed the box, and walked into the living room. Twenty dollars sat on the table along with the morning note his mother always left him. Today there was one from his father as well. Both wishing him luck in the science fair and telling him how proud they were of him. He usually walked to school, but today the science fair was at a school across town and he had to take the city bus. Since Jamal took public transportation often he was not worried.

The rain began coming down in sheets when Jamal reached the covered bus stop, trying to shield his box from the water. The bus pulled up to the waiting area, brakes squealing slightly, and two older women and a young man got in ahead of him. He juggled the heavy box and started to mount the steps to the bus quickly to avoid the rain.

The bus driver was a thin, black man wearing a striped beanie and sunglasses perched, just in case, on top of his head. His teeth were crooked and yellow, stained from years of nicotine use, but he smiled wide, proud, with no trace of self-consciousness, like a teenager who had just had his braces removed.

He asked, "Hey, kid. What's in the box?"

Jamal looked at him, surprised. He'd never been questioned before, but then he'd never brought a box on board before either.

"Nothing."

The driver smirked, "Hey, right. You just carryin' around an empty box?"

Jamal had no desire to be the center of attention, holding people up from their schedules. He looked at the floor and mumbled, "No. It's nothing. Just my science project."

"Let me see what's inside."

Jamal stopped next to the driver, sat his box on the floor, and began pulling out the items to create his project: Several large batteries, some green and blue wires, a wooden board with small nails hammered into it, several resistors, connecting leads with alligator clips, and some soldering equipment. He wondered how much more he would have to pull out of the box when the driver's voice interrupted him.

He said, "Science project?"

Jamal nodded. A woman sitting in the front row who had been watching Jamal display the contents of his box said, "If I didn't know better, I'd say that looks like all the makings for some kind of bomb."

The man behind her said, "Bomb? Who's got a bomb."

Jamal was stunned. How could anyone think he had a bomb?

He spoke to the person he thought was in charge, the driver, "Hey man, it's only a stupid science experiment. Look, there's nothing explosive in here."

The driver nodded, smiling again, but not as brightly. The noise of nervous people rose from the seats as Jamal hurried to return the contents of the electronic intelligence project to the box. The driver stood and waved his hands in front of the passengers. "Calm down everyone. No one has a bomb. The kid has some stuff for a science experiment. That's all. Alright kid, pay your money and take a seat."

As Jamal slipped his four quarters into the meter, the woman in the front stood and said, "I am not riding this bus if that box is on here. It just makes me too nervous."

The driver shook his head. "Ma'am, look at him. He's just a kid."

The woman next to her said, "And I read they are using kids all over the country now to blow themselves up and innocent civilians just like us."

A swirl of words came toward him, like a verbal tornado.

"He doesn't look like a kid to me."

"Damn Hajis. I wouldn't put anything past them."

"Get that box off this bus, right now."

"This is how it starts. They want it to look innocent."

"I am not riding this bus, if he does. Better to be safe than sorry, right?"

The driver shook his head, and sat back down in his seat. He looked at Jamal as if he had no authority or control. The smile had vanished and his face was as dark as the day. He said, "Sorry. Guess you'll have to leave the box or…"

Jamal left without hearing another word. He ran off the bus, humiliated and frightened. The door shut behind him. He heard the bus pull away and smelled the faint fumes of gasoline polluting the air around him. The rain seemed to fall heavier. He thought of the cell phone in his pocket, but could think of no one to call. His parents couldn't leave work and for some reason he didn't want to call them. It was a protective feeling. He didn't want them to see and feel his humiliation because it belonged to them as well. He ran down the street, angry and unsure.

Exhausted and wet he stopped in front of a large building. Jamal realized his box was getting soaked so he ran up the front steps of the building and sat on a small bench by the entrance door, protected from the rain.

The tears came slowly at first, like a storm building. Then, as the water that seemed to pour about him, the tears flowed, mixing with the rain on his face. He put his head down and cried hard. He cried for missing the science fair after working so hard. He cried for the anger he felt at the people on the bus and having no control over what they did to him. He cried about the world he was living in and the fear and anger directed at him when he was an American first and foremost. No one seemed to realize it because he looked like the enemy. And he thought of how he'd criticized his father for not standing up for himself and then what had he done? He'd run away, afraid to speak up for himself, knowing there was nothing he could say to calm their suspicions and fears.

He was so consumed with these thoughts and his sorrow that he didn't hear the foot steps approaching him or the words of the person standing in front of him.

She repeated herself, "Young man, are you alright?"

He stopped crying, startled someone was speaking to him, embarrassed at his tears, wanting them to go away and leave him alone so he could decide what to do next.

"Yes," he said, without looking up. "I'm f-fine. I'm just resting."

"Is there anything I can do to help you?"

He looked up and saw the face of a small woman bundled up in rain gear from head to toe, looking like a large cocoon. She held a key in one hand and a cane in the other.

"Come," she said. "I work here. I will open the doors and you can get dry and warm."

She walked to the entrance and held open the door for him.

He looked for a moment and then, without thinking, entered the building. Books stood at attention everywhere and he realized they were in the library. The woman flipped on the switch and the florescent bulbs brightened the room quickly with false light. Like a caterpillar transforming into a butterfly, the woman walked behind the front

desk and removed her rain coat and the scarf from her head. Under all the dark rain

things, she wore a brightly colored skirt and yellow blouse. Her long white hair was

pinned into a bun held with a hair pin decorated like an opalescent flower. She turned and

looked at Jamal and said, "Now, what is the matter?"

She looked ancient to him, but there was intensity in her eyes and voice. "Did

someone hurt you?"

Someone had hurt him, but he would not tell this old Asian woman what had

happened. Instead he said, "I…I am trying to get to the science fair at Lemby School at

9:30. I was taking the bus, but…" He trailed off.

She waited without questioning him. His silence filled the library and oddly seemed

out of place. He felt he must say something, but he couldn't think of how to explain it to

this old woman. With all the words filling that room, he could not find any to express

how he felt.

"So," she said. "For some reason you couldn't ride the bus and you need to get to

Lemby School before the science fair starts."

He nodded.

"Where are your parents? Why don't you use my phone and call one of them to

come take you?"

He thought of the cell phone in his pocket and once again how he could not call his

parents and speak of his failure to get himself to the science fair. His parents, who prized independence and self-reliance, with a 15-years-old son who could not even get a bus ride to school.

"They…I can't call them. They are working. They can't be disturbed from their work. Everything was fine if I could just have gotten on the bus."

"Then why didn't you? Did you miss it? Were you running late?"

He could have taken this excuse she was offering. He could have nodded his head, but something about the old woman told him she would know he was lying. And something within him wanted to speak the words of what had happened and wanted someone, a stranger, to hear them.

He put his box on the table next to him and sat in one of the chairs. He drew in a deep breath and shook his head. He said, "They wouldn't let me on."

"Who?"

"The bus driver and the people on the bus. They didn't want…They thought…" He couldn't form the words. Instead, as the anger rose inside, he stood up and began to unload the contents of his wet cardboard box. In the only way he could think of to explain, he pulled out the battery and wires and contents of the box he had so protected from the pouring rain. The old woman watched him carefully without expression. When he had emptied the precious box he flung it to the floor. Angrily he said, "That's why. They didn't want to ride on the bus with a…a Haji."

She looked at him questioningly.

"You know. A Haji. A Muslim. Someone from the Middle East. They thought I was carrying a…a bomb. Stupid people. What would you know about it anyway? I don't even know why I am telling you. Since 9-11… There's no way you can understand."

And then she did the last thing he expected. She smiled, a wide bright smile and her wrinkled skin pulled back as if a shade being open and letting in the sun. She walked slowly over, leaning slightly on her cane, and gently picked up the cardboard box off the floor, setting it on the table.

The front door opened and two women walked in covered in rain gear and carrying cardboard cups of steaming drinks. They waved at the old woman. She responded, "Good morning Joanne. Maria."

In unison they said, "Good morning, Sachi."

The two women continued to the back of the library.

Sachi said, "I used to have a car and loved driving it, but my eyes are failing." She glanced around the room. "Reading too much, I suppose, or being 95."

He looked at her in amazement unable to truly comprehend how long 95 years really was. "95?" he repeated.

She winked at Jamal and continued, "I have a friend and she has a car. I will call her while you pack your science experiment and she will take you to the place you must go. You will be there in plenty of time."

Jamal hesitated, not wanting to seem frightened by an old woman. "I really shouldn't take a ride from a stranger."

She smiled again. "I will accompany you to the school. And in that short ride I will tell you a little something about my life. Something I do not share with many people. But you will know that you are not alone, we are not strangers, you and I, and this will not last forever."

As Sachi walked to the phone to call her friend, Jamal began to repack his box for the second time that morning. He drew in a deep breath and, though he didn't know what this old woman could possibly have to tell him, his heart felt lighter somehow. In the midst of the dark morning he had found one person willing to help him and that one person made all the difference in the world.

466

This is a work of historical fiction, but that is often where truth is most comfortable. Sachi exists for me, and I hope now for you, as she is truly a blend of all the gracious and remarkable women I was so honored to speak with, read about, and interview. The events and some of the conversations between politicians and decision makers were previously reported in the research I reviewed and I attempted to be true to the history of the time as well as the social and political climate of America. Well-positioned American men made decisions and the Japanese and Americans of Japanese ancestry lived with the consequences. Japanese and Japanese Americans were arrested and sent to camps. Not the kind of camps with horseback riding, swimming, crafts, and friendly counselors. These camps were layered with thick dust, barbed wire around the perimeter, and guards with guns who would shoot if someone tried to escape. They were called camps, but they were prisons. Americans of Japanese ancestry were called internees, but they were prisoners. Being forced from their homes, businesses, and possessions was called evacuation, but it was arrest. I initially started this endeavor after reading a small article in The Sacramento Bee about Bob Fletcher, a white man who saved the homes and farms of three Japanese families sent to internment. That small article and my time with Bob and his wife, Teresa, in their home left me absorbed in this time period and the dangers which still exist: when security becomes more important than freedom and fear makes prejudice appear reasonable and, even necessary.

467

ACKNOWLEDGMENTS

First in all things, I thank God and my Christian faith. Thank you to all who shared their experiences with me, especially Kiyo Sato who, with much patience and purpose, allowed me to interview her for this novel. I would also like to thank Bob and Teresa Fletcher for their hardworking, plainspoken example of how to live courageously and do what is right in the midst of fear and prejudice. Thank you to the members of the Japanese American Citizens League for providing me with numerous resources, including the Oral History Collection at the California State University, Sacramento Library. Thank you to my husband, David Velez, for listening to me read aloud night after night and always being honest. Thank you to Deborah Kemp, Leigh Strohn, and Taryn Fagerness for the rewrites and editing and believing in Sachi. Thank you my Wednesday sisters Margaret Regula, Susie Hahn, Jan Laird, Nancy McMahon, and Loretta Steichen for indulging me and being some of my first readers. Thank you to Nichole Velez for finding and creating my book cover. As we know, inspiration can be found anywhere. Thank you to my friends who are always encouraging. Thank you to my son and daughter, Dave Velez and Rachel Velez, who are my constant inspirations. Now you have to read my book.

And to all the strong, loving women out there, some who have found their voices and others who are still searching. Whisper, write, scream, yell, sing, but speak your truth and that is when you will find your voice.

Questions to Consider

1. Why is Sachi's father always referred to in the capital (Father), while her mother is referred to in both capital and lower case (mother and Mother)?

2. What did the doll, Amaya, represent? Were there other references to dolls?

3. Have you ever taken a journey where you either felt forced to leave or were running away from or to something? What feelings did you have and was it as you expected when you arrived?

4. Were you aware of immigrants coming into Angel Island? Why do you think more people are familiar with Ellis Island than Angel Island in terms of them both being immigrant entry points?

5. Tea is a running theme throughout the book. When is tea consumed in this story, how is it used, and what is its meaning?

6. What do you think of Ikuko's lessons to Sachi on the art of marital persuasion?

7. How does motherhood effect Sachi?

8. Sachi and Jack talk about loss in the kitchen and Jack turns to Sachi for support. Do you agree with them that some losses never go away? If you have experienced such loss, to whom did you turn?

9. Do you see any similarities between Sachi's feelings for her two countries and her feelings toward Takeo and Jack?

10. Were you surprised by Mitchell and Billy's choices? Why or why not?

11. What is your understanding of why the Japanese and Japanese Americans were evacuated and sent to internment camps? Do you think it was to protect them? Do you think there was legitimate fear and war hysteria? What might be some other reasons?

12. Do you think things would have been different for the Japanese and Japanese Americans had they refused to enter into the camps and evacuate? Would things have been different for America?

13. Why do you think more people didn't offer to take care of Japanese and Japanese American homes and businesses until they could return?

14. What effects did evacuation and internment have on Sachi's family? How would her family have been different had there been no evacuation?

15. Sachi states. "…there is nothing more treacherous than barbed wire." Do you agree? Must an individual or a society always sacrifice freedom for security? Must we give up some safety in order to be free?

16. It was not clear the United States and the Allies would be victorious in World War II as the country was still in The Great Depression and, after the attack on Pearl Harbor, much of the American Pacific fleet was destroyed. Many people were frightened. What do you think the United States government could have done differently, if anything? How about individual communities or citizens?

17. In reading this book, were you reminded of anything you have witnessed recently?

About the Author

Katherine Kemp Velez began writing about human rights issues as a journalism student in college and for United Press International. She earned her BA in Political Science and Journalism from the University of Nevada-Reno and a Masters in Counseling Psychology from the University of San Francisco. Katherine created the Multicultural Education & Understanding (ME&U) program in response to prejudice she witnessed in her community and taught the program in the local school system. *Sachi – Drawing Pictures on Water*, Katherine's first novel, grew from her work with ME & U. She met with community leaders and Japanese women whose internment experiences were the inspiration for the main character of Sachi. Sachi represents not only the courageous women of that time, but every woman who has struggled to keep her family strengthened and united. Katherine is a therapist living in northern California with her husband of 30 years, her daughter, and her dog Cali.

Thank you for choosing to read the story of Sachi. For more information about this book and Katherine Kemp Velez visit katherinekempvelez.com.